POSSESSED BY PASSION

Matt returned to his room. He sat at the side of the bed, putting his fingers to his throbbing temples. It's the beer, he thought, for he had drunk a huge amount that evening.

"You'll be better in no time," Katie said, entering Matt's room. She held the cloth to his forehead, smoothing his thick reddish hair.

Matt looked up. He saw Katie leaning over him. He saw the loose folds of her robe and, just beneath, the curve of her full figure. Desire swept over him. The room seemed to grow warmer and he felt engulfed, as if by flames. There was a great roaring in his ears. Lights began to dance before his swimming eyes.

"My God," he moaned. It was a plea, though in vain. "Katie!" he cried out, pulling her onto the bed. He tore the robe from her shoulders, his feverish hands pressing her soft skin.

Katie was frightened. She struggled, fighting to free herself, but when Matt pressed his mouth to her naked flesh she too cried out. She stopped struggling, and now she was murmuring against him, kissing his hair, his eyes, his seeking lips. She felt his hands moving over her body and she trembled, lost in the rapture of his touch. In that moment of first love and passion his touch was the only truth, the only reality.

"Matt . . . Oh, Matt. I love you so," Katie whispered.

But as time went on she never dreamed that love would not be enough . . .

Also by Barbara Harrison
THIS CHERISHED DREAM
and published by Bantam Books

Passion's Price

Barbara Harrison

BANTAM BOOKS
TORONTO · NEW YORK · LONDON · SYDNEY · AUCKLAND

PASSION'S PRICE
A BANTAM BOOK 0 553 17208 5

First publication in Great Britain

PRINTING HISTORY
Bantam edition published 1986

Bantam Books are published by Transworld Publishers Ltd., 61–63
Uxbridge Road, Ealing, London W5 5SA, in Australia by Transworld
Publishers (Aust.) Pty. Ltd., 15–23 Helles Avenue, Moorebank, NSW
2170 and in New Zealand by Transworld Publishers (N.Z.) Ltd., Cnr.
Moselle and Waipareira Avenues, Henderson, Auckland.

Reproduced, printed and bound in Great Britain by
Hazell Watson & Viney Limited,
Member of the BPCC Group,
Aylesbury, Bucks

For my father, Alex Harrison,
with love and admiration

Katie Gallagher lifted her head to the stormy January sky and tried to catch a snowflake on her tongue. She smiled, her long braids blowing in the wind, her pale and pretty face aglow in a moment of sudden exuberance. Katie knew many such moments, fleeting moments, for always she remembered her mother's stern voice warning that life was hard, hard and cruel and not the stuff of children's games. She had heard those words all the thirteen years of her life, and now, recalling them yet again, her smile faded. The magic of a snowy winter's day was forgotten, as was the joy. She thrust her hands into the pockets of her shabby coat and quickened her pace. At the curb she waited for a carriage to pass and then crossed the street, turning a corner toward home.

Home for the Gallaghers was an area of Manhattan known as Hell's Kitchen, a sprawling neighborhood of tenement buildings, saloons, and pawn shops. To the west were the freight yards of the New York Central Railroad, to the north, the factories and stables and slaughter houses. It was a dangerous neighborhood for the unwary, and those who walked about in the shadows of night did so at their peril, risking encounters with the packs of young hoodlums who banded into gangs and sprang upon their victims from the darkness of hidden alleys. The Hudson Dusters, the Gophers, the Gorillas, the Parlor Mob—these were the gangs feared in Hell's Kitchen in 1903, not least by Katie Gallagher, who had learned caution at a very early age.

But if the mean streets of Hell's Kitchen sometimes struck fear in Katie's heart, they were more often a source of comfort to her. Here she felt part of a vast family, for in the tenements that lined the streets lived scores of families, most of them Irish, all of them spilling over with children. Katie loved children and they were everywhere to be seen in Hell's Kitchen, crowding fire escapes and stoops and sidewalks, their high young voices rising higher as they played. The older children went to school, although only a few of them would ever finish; most would leave after sixth grade, going to work to help their families.

Indeed their families needed help. The men worked hard—as dock wallopers, as teamsters, as day laborers—and the women took in washing or sewing, but still they were desperately poor. It was a struggle to put food on the table day in and day out, to put clothes on a child's back, a struggle never entirely won. Illnesses, so common in teeming flats that were icy in winter and sweltering in summer, were treated with feeble home remedies, for there was no money to be spent on doctors. There were many

8

deaths, needless deaths, and burial in the unmarked graves of the pauper's cemetery at Potter's Field was the fate of some.

The Gallaghers were among the poorest families of Hell's Kitchen. Katie's father had been dead for a year and her mother managed as best she could, taking in three enormous loads of washing and ironing each week, begging for more from the eastside housekeepers who hired her. Katie herself had a Saturday job doing the heavy cleaning at St. Brendan's rectory, and her brother, Hugh, worked on Mr. Maggio's coal wagon after school. They all took turns caring for the youngest Gallaghers: Sean, who was three, and Francis, barely two.

Now, thinking about her little brothers, Katie's smile returned. There was still an hour of daylight left and she decided she would take Sean and Francis out to play in the snow. Hurrying, her large green eyes sparkling with anticipation, she reached Tenth Avenue and ran the half block to her building. She was at the door when she felt the cold sting of a snowball graze her ear. Another snowball crashed into her shoulder, showering her coat with powdery white flakes. "Shame on you, Tommy Muldoon," Katie called, laughing, to the oldest of the Muldoon boys. She looked at their grinning, freckled faces beneath their ragged caps and was tempted to join the fun. She bent, scooping up a handful of snow, but then, remembering her mother, she let it slip through her fingers. "Shame on you," she called again. A barrage of snowballs came her way in reply, and she ducked her head, running in to the dim vestibule leading to the stairs.

9

Katie's smile was wide as she rushed up the four flights to the Gallagher flat. Once or twice she patted her coat pocket, feeling the comforting outline of the quarters that were her day's pay. She was grateful for her wages, small as they were, for she knew they would feed her family this weekend. All the Gallaghers would have a bit of meat, and the thought of meat made her mouth water. So lost was she in her daydreams of meat and bread and hot tea, she did not notice her mother standing in the doorway.

"And it's about time you're getting home, Katie Gallagher! Where have you been? Did Father Flynn keep you late?" Maeve Gallagher was frowning, her dark blue eyes steady on Katie. "Did he?"

Katie looked at her mother. Her face became quiet and her voice, when she spoke, was hardly more than a whisper. "No, Mama," she said. "It's not so late."

"It's ten minutes late by the clock. How many times have I told you not to dawdle?" Maeve's thin shoulders rose and fell in a sigh. "Well, come in before you catch your death."

Katie followed her mother into the kitchen of the flat. She went directly to the table and took the quarters from her pocket, spreading them out on the clean, frayed cloth. From her other pocket she took a small bag of peppermints. "Father Flynn gave these to me. I only ate one," she said quickly. "Sean and Francis can share the rest."

Maeve made no comment. She walked the few steps to where Katie stood and stared at her wet coat. "Playing in the snow! At your age! How many times have I told you—"

"I wasn't playing, Mama. Some of the boys were

throwing snowballs. There was no harm in it."

"No harm?" Maeve's mouth tightened. She had been a pretty girl and a pretty young woman, but now, at the age of thirty-three, worn down by work and worry and a thousand disappointments, there was an unbecoming severity to her features. Her face was pale, her brow lined. Her thick, light brown hair, rolled atop her head in a style that ladies of fashion called a pompadour and ladies of Hell's Kitchen called a washerwoman's knot, was already sprinkled with gray. "No harm?" she repeated tiredly. "Your coat's coming apart as it is. And it has to last you the winter. I have no money for new coats, Katie. I haven't even a coat of my own to give you, only my old cape." Maeve put her hand to her throat, sighing again. "You must learn to look after your things, Katie. It's little enough you have, and that's the truth, but whatever you have you must look after."

"Yes, Mama."

"Take your coat off now. Your shoes, too. I'll dry them by the stove."

"Mama, I . . . I wanted to take Sean and Francis out to play. I promise I won't get my coat wet. I'll be good."

"No." Maeve shook her head once and firmly. "There'll be no playing today. The little ones are at Mrs. Muldoon's. I took them over to her so I could have a talk with you in peace and quiet. I've been putting it off and putting it off . . . waiting for a miracle," Maeve said thoughtfully, as if to herself. "But miracles don't happen to the likes of us."

"What miracles, Mama?" Katie asked. She was confused and she sensed that something was wrong.

She clasped her hands behind her back, trying not to fidget. "I don't understand, Mama. What miracles?"

Maeve turned, looking sharply at Katie. "Never mind that. Hang up your coat and put your shoes by the stove. And be quick about it. We've things to talk about."

"Yes, Mama."

Maeve watched her daughter for a moment, then glanced away. She placed cups and saucers on the table and poured tea from a blue china pot that had belonged to her grandmother. Once there had been a whole set of blue china—plates and bowls and dainty little pitchers with fluted rims—but all of it had been sold long ago; in a rare display of sentimentality, Maeve had insisted on keeping the teapot. "Sit down," Maeve now said to Katie. "Drink your tea while it's hot."

Katie did as she was told, for she had been raised to obey her mother in all matters, large and small. Maeve was the disciplinarian in the family and had been even when Joe Gallagher was alive. It was she who gave the slaps and the spankings and, to Hugh, the most difficult of her children, the strap across the back. Katie had never felt the strap, but when she had been slow to obey, or reluctant, she had had her share of spankings. "That's the price," Maeve always said after a spanking. "Life has prices and that's the price of doing bad."

Maeve Doyle Gallagher had spent the first seventeen years of her life on a small, rented farm in Ireland. It was a hard life, filled with unrelenting work that was hers to do because her father was a drunkard and because her mother had borne no sons.

Her days then began at dawn, when she milked the cows and mucked out the barn. She went to the village school from November to March, but when spring came she put her school books away and went to the fields. She roped the horse's reins around her neck and did the plowing and planting. She repaired fences, drove the wagon to market, pitched hay, and spread manure. All this she did without complaint, though gradually, secretly, despair began to shadow her heart.

It was the despair of poverty, for no matter how hard Maeve and her mother and sisters worked, the Doyles were always in debt—to the Feed & Grain, to the Dry Goods, to their English landlord. Their few clothes were clean but threadbare, the boots patched and passed from child to child until finally they fell apart. Their meals were made of home-baked bread, home-churned butter, and potatoes and turnips from their own meager garden. There were no treats, no little luxuries. If some stroke of good fortune left them a shilling over at month's end, Maeve's father quickly claimed it and just as quickly spent it at the local pub.

The Doyles lost their farm when Maeve was seventeen. Her sisters were sent into service on the great estates of the English aristocracy, there to work fifteen hours a day in steaming kitchens and laundry rooms. Maeve and her mother and father moved in with their neighbors, the Gallaghers, a noisy and affectionate farm family only slightly better off than the Doyles. There were three Gallagher sons, tall, laughing young men who worked the farm by day and courted Maeve at night.

Maeve had never been courted before. She had never had a suitor and never expected to have one, for when she looked at herself she saw only the coarsened hands and freckled skin of a field worker. The three Gallaghers saw other things—dark blue eyes the color of the night sky, masses of thick and shining brown hair, a fine figure, an unflagging high spirit. They saw these things and they pressed their suits. Maeve liked them all, but it was Joe, the oldest son, with whom she fell in love. She fell in love with his sweetness, with his poetry and his romantic stories and his dreams.

"What's wrong, Mama?" Katie asked, putting her cup down. "You look far away."

"I was thinking about home. About Ireland. You were just five when we left. You have no memories there."

"I remember some things."

Maeve sat back in her chair. She rubbed her hands, her knuckles red and cracked from the strong laundry soap she used. "It was your papa's notion to come to America," she said slowly. "Not that I was against it, mind you. We all heard the stories about America. Grand stories they were, too. We heard how in America the streets were paved with gold." Maeve's eyes softened. She tilted her head to one side, staring off into space. "Maybe I didn't really believe in the part about the gold . . . but I believed in Joe. I always believed in Joe. Even on the boat coming over . . . with the maggots crawling in our food and the rats scrambling everywhere, I listened to Joe telling his dreams and I believed."

Katie smiled, though uncertainly, for it was not

like her mother to speak about the past. It was not like her to reminisce or to confide her feelings, especially to her family. This sudden burst of words made Katie edgy. She lowered her gaze and hid her nervous hands in her lap, out of sight.

"The sun was shining bright the day we landed in America," Maeve went on. "An omen, your papa said. He was forever talking about omens and signs. It was his nature. Some Irish are like that." Maeve paused, rubbing her hands harder, twisting the thin gold wedding band she wore. "Aye, the sun was shining bright that day," she sighed. "And then we came here, to this very flat." She nodded, glancing around.

The Gallagher flat had four rooms, one leading into the other. The kitchen, which was also the parlor, had a coal stove recessed in one wall and, next to it, a fire-heated water boiler. Next to the boiler was a pair of soapstone washtubs with a hinged wooden cover. There was a wall of cupboards, a sink, an ice box, and a table and chairs. There were no knick-knacks, no pictures on the walls or curtains on the windows. Beyond the kitchen were three bedrooms, narrow and so cramped the children were always bumping their knees against bed or dresser. All of the furniture in the flat was second hand, purchased for a few dollars years before.

Maeve stared at the dingy tin ceiling then at the stained, peeling walls. "That was the end of the sun," she said, her voice stern again. "The dreams, too, though your papa never saw it that way. Him with his head in the clouds. A dreamer 'til the day he died."

"No, Mama," Katie cried, rushing to defend the father she had loved with all her heart. "That's not *fair*. Papa—"

"It's fair. It's true. Dear knows it's true." Maeve raised her cup to her lips, sipping the tea. Her eyes, no longer soft, settled on her daughter. "Look around you, Katie Gallagher. What do we have here? Nothing! Nothing's what we have, but your papa never saw it that way. And there's nothing in the streets but what the horses leave behind. Your papa never saw that either. Too busy dreaming dreams."

Tears stung Katie's eyes and, quickly, she brushed them away. She knew her mother's opinion of tears. "Tears are for weaklings," Maeve said whenever one of her children cried. "I'll have no weaklings in my house."

Now Maeve watched her daughter struggling not to cry. She was pleased, for she believed that children had to learn to be strong. She believed that, for the poor, life was heartbreak and disappointment in equal measure, and only the strong survived. If she could give her children nothing else, she thought, she could and would give them the strength they needed. "Don't pout, Katie. Speak up, if you've something to say."

"Papa was a good man. Everybody loved Papa."

"Aye, they did. And why not? Wasn't he the first one with a smile or a joke or a shoulder to cry on? Wasn't he the first one to give a kind word or help to a neighbor?" Maeve passed her hand across her face. She closed her eyes for a moment, remembering Joe, her sweet and innocent Joe. In the beginning she had loved his innocence; at the end she had hated it, and for that she could not forgive herself. She could not forgive herself for knowing that her husband had been a weak, dreamy man, unable to keep a job for very long because he could not keep his mind on his work. He had been consumed with plans, wild and impossible plans for some far distant future. And while he had been busy with his plans, she had been busy trying to find ways to buy food and coal and to pay the rent. She had never reproached him while he lived, but in the year since his death she reproached him often, acts of betrayal that sent her scurrying to confession. "I'm not denying your papa was a good man, Katie," Maeve said. "You'll never hear me denying it. But he wasn't . . . sensible. There's a difference, and you'd best learn that before it's too late."

"Papa used to say you were the sensible one."

"And do you suppose that's an insult?" Maeve demanded, eyes flashing. "You should be down on your knees thanking God I *am* sensible. You and your brothers, too. Without me, you'd all be starvelings on the street." Maeve left the table. She went to the sink and turned on the water, splashing her flushed face. "Oh, I know what you think of me," she said. "You think I'm hard. That I have no heart."

"*No*, Mama." Katie was near tears once more, for she realized she had hurt her mother. She had not meant to. She loved her, and although it was not the same kind of love she had felt for her father, it was as real. There was, in addition, respect. Katie's relationship with her mother had always been troubled, colored as it was by their disparate natures, but her respect for her mother had never wavered. She

17

yearned for her approval, approval seldom and no easily given: "I'm sorry if it sounded like that," she said, her large green eyes entreating Maeve. "I'm sorry, Mama. Sometimes I say the wrong things. But I know how much you do for us."

"You'd better know! It's the sensible ones who do what needs doing in this life. There are those who talk and those who do. I was always the one doing. I had to be." It was true. Joe had wanted obedient children, but the details he left to Maeve. He had wanted the comforts of home, a full larder and a warm stove, but those details too he left to Maeve. He had gone about life blithely, but the many details that filled that life he left to Maeve. "Well," she said, drying her face, "I've tried my best. Whatever you think, Katie, I've tried my best." She returned to the table and sat down. Slowly, she met her daughter's gaze. "But it's no good. It's not enough."

"Mama—"

"Be still, Katie. Hear me out. I've something to tell you, something you won't like. Just hear me out." Maeve took a breath. Her mouth was pale, her fingers laced tightly together. "The landlord was here last week," she said.

"But it's not the first of the month."

"I told you to be still! I know it's not the first of the month. He was here for another reason. He came to tell me he's raising the rent two dollars. Not just us; everybody in the building." Maeve saw the surprise in Katie's eyes. She saw the questions. "He can do it, if that's what you're wondering. He can do whatever he wants. He's the landlord, isn't he? Sure and there's a special place in Hell for landlords."

Katie dared not speak, though her mind worked rapidly. Where, she asked herself, would they get an extra two dollars every month? Two dollars a month was twenty-four dollars a year. It was a fortune.

"That's only part of the news," Maeve continued in a flat voice. "I'm losing my best laundry customer too. Mrs. Winfield is hiring a laundress to work full time. Her housekeeper offered me the job. But I couldn't take Sean and Francis with me, and I couldn't leave them alone all the day long."

"There's Mrs. Muldoon," Katie suggested hopefully. "Maybe she could watch them 'til I got home from school."

"With eight of her own to watch? Three of them still in diapers? All the neighbors have enough to do just taking care of their own. The Gallaghers won't be beholden. Not while I'm alive. Do you see how it is, Katie? That's three dollars a week in laundry wages out the window. And more rent due the landlord. Do you see how it is?"

"Yes, Mama." A feeling of dread gripped Katie, for she knew what her mother was going to say next. She sat stiffly in her chair, not moving, hardly breathing. Her eyes darkened and into them came a look of resignation. "I see," she said quietly.

"You'll have to quit your school, Katie. You'll have to get a job. There's no other way. I've thought and thought. I can't see any other way." Some of the tension left Maeve's face, though not all, for while she was relieved to have her decision out in the open, she took no pleasure in it. It was the right decision, she knew, the only decision, given the circumstances, yet she was filled with regret. She had wanted her children's lives to be better than her own. There was still hope for the little ones, but what hope was there now for Katie? "I've tried my best," she said finally. "I wish things could be different, but there's no use in wishing. And besides, a job's not the end of the world."

"I have a job, Mama. At the rectory."

"Aye." Maeve reached across the table, picking up the quarters Katie had brought home. "One day a week. Seventy-five cents, and even that's more than the poor Fathers can afford."

"It's a job."

"It's not *enough*. Katie, we're living on soup and potato pie as it is. Starting next week there won't be any laundry wages from Mrs. Winfield. What are we to do then?" Katie said nothing and Maeve threw the quarters down. "You're so good at sums," she said, angry color staining her cheeks. "Tell me what we're to do. I'll have two dollars laundry wages from Mrs. Spencer. I'll have Hugh's dollar from Mr. Maggio. I'll have your seventy-five cents. Tell me how we're to manage on three dollars and seventy-five cents the week."

"I'm sorry, Mama."

"Sorry, is it? Where does *sorry* get us? Does it put food on the table? Does it keep a roof over our heads? It's easy to be sorry. But what does it mean? Nothing, that's what."

"I know I have to help, Mama. I understand. It's just . . . it's just that I was wondering about Hugh. He'd be glad to leave school. He's always playing hooky."

"And he gets the strap for it. He'll keep getting the

strap, too. Hugh needs his schooling so he can be on the cops one day. There's nothing for an Irishman but the cops. It's a steady job and good wages.''

Maeve's answer did not surprise Katie, for she had long been aware of her mother's plans for Hugh. Such plans were common in Hell's Kitchen, though in Hugh's case Katie had reason to be wary. She was close to her brother and she knew his feelings. She knew he felt only scorn for the police, scorn he did not trouble to hide. There was no fear in Hugh, no awe. If he had any heroes at all, they were the young toughs of the Gophers and the Parlor Mob for whom, it was rumored, he cheerfully ran errands. "Maybe Hugh won't want to be a policeman when he grows up,'' Katie tried again.

"He'll be what I tell him to be!''

Katie looked into her mother's resolute blue eyes and saw that the cause was lost. Hugh would stay in school, like it or not, while she would be sent to work. "Where will I get a job?" she asked quietly. "Who'll hire me?''

Maeve was slow to reply. She brushed the front of her shirtwaist, brushed an imaginary speck of lint from the table cloth. Twice her lips parted, making no sound. "Well," she said after a while, "you're already hired. I got you work at Ada McVey's boardinghouse. It's cleaning and cooking. I told Ada you weren't much use in the kitchen, but she's willing to take the chance. It's settled, Katie. You start Monday, sharp at seven.''

Katie nodded silently, for her throat was dry and aching. *Monday*! It's so soon, she thought, so soon. She began to think about her school. It was an ordinary school, drab and overcrowded and not too clean, but in it she had spent the happiest times of her life. She had a love of books and learning, an imagination that soared whenever the teacher read a poem or unfurled a map. These traits she had inherited from her father and only at school could she give expression to them. Only at school could she giggle with her friends and share secrets and be a child. Now, staring forlornly into her teacup, Katie realized the happy times were over. "Monday," she whispered, "sharp at seven."

"You'll be earning three dollars a week. Good wages for a girl, especially a girl with no training. And you'll get your meals. You can be thankful for that. You'll be eating proper at Ada's, not like we eat here—Sit up straight, Katie! Look at me when I talk to you!" Katie obeyed instantly. "Aye, that's better." Maeve sat back, studying her daughter's face. It was a pretty face, oval and smooth and the color of ivory. She had a small nose and a soft, full mouth. Her green eyes were framed by coal-black lashes, a startling contrast to the pale gold of her hair and brows. Maeve sighed. She thought, Katie's a pretty one and she'll marry young. But whom will she marry? A man like Bud Reagan who's sickly and lets his wife lead him by the nose? Or a man like Ed Ryan who drinks and beats his wife? Maybe she'll marry a man like Con Muldoon. Con's good to his wife and he's hardworking as can be, but still they have their troubles. "Life's *cruel*," Maeve said abruptly. "Cruelest of all to women. You think it's a bad thing to leave school. Well, I hope that's the *worst* thing that ever happens to you."

22

Katie was alarmed by the grim intensity of her mother's look. She forgot her own concerns, for now they seemed unimportant. "It's all right, Mama," she said, swallowing hard. "I don't mind working. I don't mind about school. We'll manage somehow. . . . Please don't be upset, Mama. It's all right."

Katie's earnestness touched Maeve. She was not a susceptible woman and her gentler emotions were buried far in the past, yet she was touched. She reached out, patting her daughter's hand. "I know it is, Katie. I'm looking on the good side of things. You almost finished grade school and that's something to be proud of. You can read and write and do sums. You know a bit of history. A girl needs no more than that." Maeve withdrew her hand. She stood, carrying cups and saucers to the sink. "Work's not so terrible," she said. "I was doing a man's work when I was ten years old. Dear knows it didn't kill me. I'm still here to tell the tale."

"I'm glad, Mama."

"Are you?" Maeve turned, staring at Katie. "Sometimes I wonder if I'm the right mother for you. I do my best and that's the truth, but I wonder all the same." She paused, a faint and wistful smile edging the corners of her mouth. "You'll understand what I mean when you have children of your own."

"I'm going to have lots and lots of children."

"Aye, and are you going to have lots and lots of money too? Mind you don't end up like me— washerwoman, hoarding pennies." Maeve shook her head. A lock of light brown hair fell across her brow and she pushed it away. "You've stars in your eyes, Katie Gallagher. But not for long. Come Monday

23

you start work, and then you'll see life plain."

"I'm not afraid," Katie replied with more confidence than she felt. "Ada McVey's a nice woman. I remember when she brought us that big pot of stew. It was after Papa died. She was nice."

"That's another thing. There are some who look down their noses at Ada. They think it's not . . . respectable for a widow lady to run a boardinghouse. They're wrong. Ada's doing honest work and there's no shame in it. But you'll hear talk, Katie. Gossip's what it is. Pay no heed. Gossip is the devil's work."

Katie wondered what gossip she would hear about Ada McVey. It was true that there were few secrets in Hell's Kitchen, for flats were crowded and walls thin. Problems with money or drink or health or children were known to all and freely discussed from one street to the next. It was gossip, but rarely was it malicious. "Don't people like Mrs. McVey?" she asked.

"Some don't. Sure and there's no pleasing some people. But never mind that. *I* know Ada's a good woman in her heart. Father Flynn agrees. I asked him and he said it was fine for you to work at the boardinghouse. We have no worries on that account." Maeve untied her apron and folded it neatly on the counter beside the sink. She walked to the window, peering across the avenue at the big clock that hung outside the pawn shop. "It's late," she said. "I'd best hurry to the store or we'll have no supper."

"Do you want me to go, Mama?"

"No, stay here. Get things started." Maeve took her cape from a hook on the door and settled it around her shoulders. Katie watched, her eyes growing sad,

24

for she knew that her mother had never had a real winter coat. There had never been enough money to buy one, and so, year after year, Maeve went about in the old cape she had brought from Ireland. Now Maeve bent over the table and swept Katie's quarters into her purse. "Be sure to get Hugh's dollar when he comes in," she ordered. "And have him fetch the little ones from Mrs. Muldoon's. They're not to have any peppermints before supper. I mean what I say, Katie. You must learn to be firm."

"Yes, Mama."

Maeve left and Katie was alone in the kitchen. A tiny sigh escaped her lips as she pondered the changed circumstances of her life. She could feel no resentment, for she knew she had been more fortunate than many of the children in the neighborhood; she had gotten halfway through seventh grade and that, by the standards of Hell's Kitchen, was fortunate indeed. Still, she could feel no happiness. It frightened her to think that her family would be depending on her wages. It was a responsibility. Her teachers had talked often about responsibility, making it seem like a splendid thing. But to Katie, nervously tugging at her braids, it did not seem splendid at all.

Katie pushed her chair back and stood up. The black stockings she wore offered small protection against the cold floor, and she put on her shoes, leaning down to button the buttons. At the sink, she scoured the cooking pot and placed it atop the stove. She set the table then, carefully, the way she had been taught. When she had finished she went to the counter, scraping carrots, peeling and quartering the two potatoes and two onions that would go into the stew. There was a sudden noise at the door and she jumped, whirling around.

"It's just me." Hugh Gallagher smiled, stamping his snowy shoes on the floor. "Did you think it was the bogeyman?"

"You scared me."

"Where's Ma?"

"She's gone to the store. Sean and Francis are at Mrs. Muldoon's. You're to fetch them home."

"Yeah, in a minute." Hugh took off his coat, a coat that had belonged to his father and that Maeve had altered to fit him. He wore a cloth cap pulled low on his forehead and, on his hands, a pair of wool socks, for he refused to wear mittens. He removed the socks now, smiling again at Katie. "I'm coal dust all over," he said, shoving his big, grimy hands under the water faucet. "It was a busy day on the wagon. Old man Maggio"—he laughed loudly—"Maggio's covered with dust top to bottom."

"*Mr.* Maggio," Katie chided her brother fondly. She plucked the cap from his head and put it aside. "Mind your manners."

"Aw, you sound more like Ma every day."

"What's wrong with that?"

"Ma's an old biddy. Always squawking about something or other."

"Hugh!"

"Well, she is."

Hugh Gallagher was twelve years old and tall for his age. He was slender but solidly built, with broad shoulders and a broad chest. His hair, like Maeve's, was thick and light brown, falling onto his brow. His eyes were like Maeve's also, though a darker and cooler blue. Father Flynn had been heard to say that he could see trouble lurking in Hugh's eyes. He was not the only one, for there was a recklessness about Hugh, a recklessness that was at once jaunty and disturbing. The older boys had nicknamed him Swag, after the swagger in his walk. Maeve was aware of the talk; she called it foolish. Katie too was aware of the talk, and she was not so sure.

"Do you have your dollar?" Katie asked now.

"Yeah, yeah." Hugh reached into the pocket of his knickers and put the bill on the counter. "There's an hour a day after school and five hours on Saturday. There's Ma's precious dollar."

"It *is* precious, Hugh. You don't know how bad things are. The rent's going up and Ma's lost a laundry customer. Come Monday, I'm going to work at Mrs. McVey's boardinghouse."

"Going to work? You?"

"Yes. It's all settled." Katie told Hugh of her conversation with Maeve. She spoke rapidly, pausing to catch her breath and then hurrying on. "That's how bad things are," she finished. "Do you understand?"

Hugh leaned against the counter, crossing his arms over his chest. His eyes narrowed. "I'm the one to quit school and get work," he said. "I can get work easy. There's always jobs at the broom factory. Or the stables."

"I told you Mama's plans, Hugh. You're to stay in school so you can be on the cops."

"I got my own plans. The cops isn't in 'em."

Katie frowned, for she did not like the hard edge

that sometimes came into her brother's voice. He seemed different at such times, closed and older than his years. "Mama's only trying to do what's best for you. You're her favorite."

"Ma don't have favorites. *Money's* her favorite— Aw, don't get mad, Katie. It's you I'm thinking of. You, doing maid's work."

"I've been doing maid's work at the rectory. It's the same thing. Work is work."

Hugh shook his head. He stuffed his hands into his pockets and walked a few steps away, throwing himself into a chair. "That was for the priests, Katie. That wasn't no boardinghouse. You know how it is at McVey's. It's all show people. People from the vaudeville."

"I know. It'll be fun."

Hugh was quiet, staring at his sister. "You're lying," he said finally. "I can tell. You don't want to work at McVey's. You want your school and your books and all that lousy stuff."

"Don't say *lousy*. Mama doesn't like you to say that word."

"Who cares?"

"Oh!" Katie turned away, annoyed. "You're just being fresh. I can't talk to you when you're in a fresh mood."

"Now you sound like Father Flynn," Hugh said. "'Sure and it's a fresh boyo you are, Hugh Gallagher.'" He laughed, mimicking the priest's heavy brogue.

"He's right, isn't he? You're his worst altar boy."

"Being altar boy was Ma's idea."

"Even so."

28

Hugh stretched his arms above his head. He was utterly unconcerned, deep in his own thoughts. His expression did not change, though his eyes glittered darkly. "I'm no altar boy, Katie. And you're no maid. It's no work for you. I'll tell that to Ma when—"

"*No!*" Katie cried. "You mustn't. You mustn't say anything. Not a word, Hugh!" Her distress was genuine, for she knew if Hugh interfered there would be a terrible argument, a dreadful clash of wills that would end, as always, with the strap. "*Promise* me."

"I'm the man in the family. It's my place to look out for you."

Katie went to her brother, resting her hand lightly on his shoulder. "Listen to me, Hugh. I'm glad you want to look out for me. But you can't, not in this. The job's set. It was for Mama to decide and she decided. It's best for all of us. *Please* don't mix in."

"Aw"—Hugh pushed her hand away—"you give up too easy."

"The job's set. What else is there to do?"

Hugh searched his mind for an answer, any answer. He realized there was none and he shrugged. "It's lousy to be poor, Katie. That's why I got plans of my own. I won't be poor all my life. Not me."

"Oh, Hugh." Katie smiled. "I suppose you're going to be rich?"

"Yeah. And when I am, I'll look out for you proper. You and Sean and Francis."

"And Mama."

Hugh stuck his tongue out, making a rude noise. "That's for Ma. That's all she'll get from me."

Katie's brows drew together in dismay. "I don't understand why you're so mean about Mama," she said. "It's not right. Mama does everything she can for us. You know that's true." Hugh's reply was a curse, calmly and clearly uttered. Katie took a step back. She gaped at her brother and then returned to the sink, busying herself with the vegetables. "Will you fetch Sean and Francis from Mrs. Muldoon's?" she asked quietly.

"Yeah, okay." Hugh was smiling when he came up behind Katie. He held out his hand, opening it to reveal a dusty quarter. "For you." He winked. "Don't worry, I earned it honest. Take it."

"No, I can't."

"Why not?"

"I can't, Hugh. Mama said—"

"Mama said, Mama said! Are you a parrot or something? Why does it always have to be what *Mama* said? Can't you never talk for yourself? Are you ascared?"

"I'm just tired of all the fighting in this house. I don't want to fight. Not with you or Mama or anybody." Katie gripped the edge of the sink, holding on to it as if for support. "We're supposed to be a family, Hugh. I just want us to be a family."

"Here, take the quarter."

"No."

"I'm not giving it to Ma."

"Keep it then. I won't tell."

Hugh dropped the quarter into his pocket. He walked to the door. "You got some funny ideas," he said, looking over his shoulder at Katie. "You're like Pa, and that's no good."

Katie's grip tightened on the sink. Her knuckles were white, her slender body taut with the strain of this day. "Go fetch the little ones."

"I'm going." Hugh opened the door. He hesitated, turning to face his sister. "Don't be like Pa, Katie. Don't be fooling yourself. Your job won't mean nothing. You'll be slaving at the boardinghouse all right, but we'll still be hungry. We'll still be hiding from the landlord. So where's the use?"

"I don't know."

"There's no use. Poor is poor. It's lousy."

Katie heard the door close. She bent her head and wept.

2

It was not yet light when Katie left the tenement and plunged into the sharp cold of Monday morning. She was tired, for her sleep had been fitful, but the icy wind roaring along the avenue brought her quickly awake. The wind singed her face, burning through her coat, through the holes in her mittens, and she shivered. She drew her collar up about her chin, hunching her shoulders as she began the walk to Ada McVey's boardinghouse.

The boardinghouse was four blocks away. They were short blocks, though in the cold, in the terrifying darkness, they seemed endless. The surrounding tenement buildings loomed as silent, ghostly shells set against the stark black sky. Katie hurried. Holding her skirts, she stepped over patches of ice and climbed over heaps of snow banking the curb. It was too early for carriage traffic and she ran across the avenue, her breath streaming out before her in frosty mists.

The streets were quiet, but Katie was relieved to see they were not deserted. She saw young women, some as young as she, hurrying to their jobs in eastside sculleries and parlors. She saw men of all ages rushing to beat the morning whistle in nearby factories. Mr. Clark, the grocer, was sweeping the sidewalk in front of his store, and she waved to him. "It's not so bad," she murmured to herself. "I'm not alone. There's nothing to be scared of." But when a cat cried suddenly in the darkness, she jumped.

Ada McVey's boardinghouse was a neat, four-story building with draperies at the windows and polished brass trim at the door. It had the look of a private residence, and, indeed, it had been built for that purpose, twenty-five years before, by a factory owner eager to be near his work and away from society's distractions. After his death the building had become a home for seamen and then a settlement house. In 1899 it had been purchased by the McVeys, retired vaudevillians who had opened a boardinghouse for "theatricals."

Now Katie huddled in her coat and stared at the boardinghouse. All through the night, tossing and turning in her narrow bed, she had imagined this moment. She had dreaded it, fearing she would fail at the job that meant everything to her family. She thought about her mother and raised a trembling hand to the heavy brass door knocker. "I can't fail," she murmured urgently. "Please, God. I can't fail."

"You're right on time," Ada McVey said, opening the door. "That's good. Come in, come in." She looked past Katie, her eyes sweeping up and down the street. "Are you alone?" she asked, surprised. "Didn't Maeve bring you?"

Katie tried to answer but the words stuck in her throat. She smiled weakly, shaking her head.

"I thought sure Maeve would bring you. Your first day at work and all. . . . Listen to me"—Ada laughed—"babbling while it's cold as a witch's heart out there. Come inside, Katie. Tea's ready on the stove."

Katie wanted to turn and run. Instead, she forced herself to enter the boardinghouse. She hid her trembling hands behind her back and wiped her wet shoes on the mat. This last she did with great care, for Maeve had warned her not to track mud across Ada's floors. She had received many warnings from Maeve, and now, anxious to please, she tried to call them all to mind.

"Follow me," Ada said. "We'll have our tea in the kitchen, where it's warm. Poor thing, you look half frozen."

Katie took a breath and followed Ada through the hallway, stealing shy glances at the striped wallpaper, the carved and polished woodwork. A framed mirror hung between two gas lamps in frosted glass globes. Beneath the mirror was a gleaming rosewood console. A fringed carpet covered the center of the hallway, muffling her footsteps. Katie, accustomed only to bare tenement flats, was awed by such grandeur. When she followed Ada into another, shorter hallway, she marvelled at the warmth of the air.

"Here's the kitchen," Ada said proudly. "It's my favorite room in the house. I've always liked a big kitchen."

Katie nodded, her eyes wide, for Ada's kitchen seemed bigger than the whole Gallagher flat. It was painted a bright yellow and had starched white window curtains that matched the cloth on the table. It had a full wall of cupboards, a double ice box, and a six-burner coal stove. Herbs grew in pretty clay pots on the sill. A fire blazed in the hearth, casting delicate shadows on the scrubbed and immaculate wood floor.

"You're rich!" Katie exclaimed. Instantly she clapped her hand over her mouth, shocked by her boldness. She stood very still and waited for the scolding she felt she deserved.

But no scolding came. Ada was amused, laughing heartily. "Rich?" she asked, throwing her head back and laughing some more. "Is that what you think? Rich! That's a good one!" Ada pulled a chair out and sat down. She took a handkerchief from the sleeve of her shirtwaist, dabbing at her eyes. "I'm not rich, Katie. I wish I was. Tim, rest his soul, and me struggled for years. Nothing ever worked for us—until the boardinghouse. It's a nice little business. I'm not complaining, you understand. But rich? Oh, that's a good one!"

"I . . . I'm sorry," Katie stammered. "I didn't mean—"

"Don't be sorry. You gave me a laugh. I like starting the day with a laugh. There are no long faces around here. We work hard, but we have our fun too. I'm babbling again." Ada smiled, slapping the table. "Tim, rest his soul, used to say if they paid people for talking, I'd be a millionairess. He was right. He was always right, my Tim." Ada looked at the small, filigreed watch pinned to her shirtwaist. "I'll get the tea while you hang up your coat. The closet's off the pantry there. And take an apron from the middle shelf."

"Yes, ma'am."

"Call me Ada. Everybody does. I guess I'm just not the fancy type."

Katie smiled. It was her first real smile since Saturday, and for the first time since then she began to feel at ease. "I was scared when I came here," she said, meeting Ada's gaze. "I'm not now."

"Maybe now you'll stop shaking. I thought you were shaking from the cold, but it wasn't that. It was from being scared. Ah well, it's natural to be scared when you start work. I was. You'll get over it. Give me a day's work for a day's pay and we won't have any problems. Don't worry about making mistakes either. That's how you learn." Poor thing, thought Ada, studying her young charge. She saw a pretty girl hardly more than a child, a waif in a thin coat too short at the wrists and hem, in shoes and mittens full of holes. She had not wanted to hire Katie. She had wanted someone older by at least two years, but Maeve had worn her down. "Will you do that for me, Katie?" she asked. "Will you try not to worry so much?"

"Oh yes, I will. Thank you. Thank you, Ada."

Katie's step was suddenly light, her head high as she crossed the kitchen to the pantry. Ada watched her. She thought: It's your fault, Maeve Gallagher, for making this child a bundle of nerves. Show her a little kindness and she opens up like a flower. She shines. But you have no kindness for your children, and that's a shame.

Ada went to the stove, pouring tea into large white cups. She was a tall woman, big-boned and too

37

heavy, yet all of her movements were graceful, a legacy of years spent on the stage. She had a square face, a pleasant face, neither pretty nor plain. She had bright brown eyes and graying hair pinned in a knot at the back of her head. Ada had always been coy about her age, though it was assumed, correctly, that she was in her early fifties.

While Ada was coy about her age, she was coy about nothing else. She smoked cigarettes and drank beer and offered no apologies. She claimed to be able to eat or drink any man under the table and she took pride in her claim. She took pleasure in naughty stories. And when, on rare occasions, she was stirred to anger, she cursed. All these things shocked the more pious of Hell's Kitchen. Men were swifter than women to condemn her, invariably harsher in their judgments. Ada never protested such assaults on her character. She considered the source and was amused, for she knew a great deal about the men who were her neighbors, and she knew their vices to be worse than her own.

"I'm ready," Katie said, slipping a starched pinafore apron over her head. "What do you want me to do?"

"Our breakfast is warming in the oven. You can fetch it to the table. Mind you don't burn yourself, Katie. Use the potholders."

Carefully, Katie took two pans of sausages and potatoes from the wide oven. Just as carefully, she carried the pans to the table. "It's such a lot," she said, her mouth watering. "Is it for the boarders?"

"You don't know my boarders." Ada chuckled. "They'd stone me if that's all I was to give them. It's

38

for us. Sit down and eat hearty. There's no time for dawdling, not with work waiting."

"It's for us?" Katie asked in amazement. "For you and me? All this?"

Ada looked closely at Katie. She winced at the child's thin, almost fleshless wrists, at her bony shoulders pressing against the fabric of her middy blouse. She did not blame Maeve; she could not, for few of the neighborhood children ever had enough to eat. "You need fattening up," she said. "And I'm the one to do it. Now sit down and eat your breakfast. You can't do a good day's work on an empty stomach. I wouldn't expect you to." Ada heaped Katie's plate with sausages and potatoes, then heaped her own plate even higher. "Go ahead now. It's getting late."

Katie hesitated only a moment. Then she was bent over her plate, stuffing food into her mouth. She finished two sausages and half the potatoes before pausing to catch her breath. She drank a cup of tea rich with sugar and milk, and as she did so she remembered her family. Their breakfast, she knew, would be dry bread and plain, weak tea. Katie put her fork down, ashamed of herself.

Ada's intuition was keen and she guessed Katie's thoughts. "Meals are part of your wages," she said. "I gave my last hired girl two meals a day, like my boarders, but Maeve insisted you had to have three. She's a good bargainer. Don't let all that bargaining go to waste."

"I was being greedy. Mama says it's a sin to be greedy." Katie stared at the food left on her plate, enough to make a meal for all the Gallaghers. "It's not fair for me to have so much.''

"A lot of things aren't fair, Katie. You'll learn that, sooner or later. Later, I hope. . . . What would Maeve say if she saw you wasting food?"

Katie was startled by Ada's question. "Oh, I wouldn't waste it," she said earnestly. "I was thinking . . . I was thinking maybe I could save some and . . . and—"

"And take it home? You're a fine, generous girl, Katie. But the answer is no. Whatever you don't eat today goes into the leftovers' bowl for tomorrow. If you saw my food bills, you'd know I can't give food away. It's a rule of mine. A strict rule." Ada heard the note of rebuke in her voice and she was sincerely sorry, for it was not in her to be hard, especially with someone as young and vulnerable as Katie Gallagher. She knew she could not break her rule, but now she sought to soften it. "On the other hand"—she smiled—"I don't like to keep leftovers around in the warmer weather. So when the warmer weather comes, there may be a little something for you to take home each week."

"No, that's all right," Katie said, blushing. "I was wrong to think it. If Mama knew, she'd be mad. Mama says we mustn't ever take charity. Mama says—"

"We don't have to talk about it today. When the warmer weather comes, we'll see. Okay? Is that a bargain?"

"Thank you, Ada," Katie replied hastily, grateful to have the subject closed. "You're nice."

"Eat up." Ada laughed. "You're on my time now."

* * *

By seven-thirty the breakfast dishes had been cleared, washed, and put away. The big table in the dining room had been set and a fire laid in the hearth. "Breakfast is served late around here," Ada explained, "because most of my boarders keep late hours. But I like to get things ready early. That way we have time for our other chores. There's no end to chores in a boardinghouse. We have to keep ahead of them, Katie. Let one thing slip by and then it's five things, or ten. Pay close attention to me. The way I'm showing you is the way I want things done."

"I'm a good learner," Katie said in a sudden burst of confidence. "And I'll work hard; really I will. It's such a grand place to work," she added, gazing wide eyed about the dining room. "It's like a palace."

"A palace!"

"To me it is. Like out of a fairy story." Katie gazed at the polished, dark wood wainscoting, at the gleaming sideboard, at the long table ringed with a dozen chairs. Above the table was a splendid crystal chandelier, its many pendants shining in the gaslight. "I never saw the like," she said honestly.

"Don't go getting the wrong ideas, miss." Ada laughed, pulling playfully on Katie's braids. "It was a rich man that built this building, and that's why we have the fancy touches. When the sun comes in, you'll see my wallpaper's faded, and my rugs. You'll see there are cracks in some of the walls . . . and you won't be so happy about all the woodwork. Not when you're spending hours keeping it clean and bright."

Katie was undismayed by such details. Sighing, she passed her hand reverently across the smooth wood of the sideboard then said, "It's grand," and

41

sighed again.

"You like to dream, don't you, Katie? You're like your pa. I'm glad."

Katie turned enormous green eyes on Ada. "Did you know Papa?"

"Sure. He used to come here. It was respectable and all. Maeve knew about his visits. He liked to sit in the parlor with my boarders and trade stories. Kept everybody laughing; that's the truth. Joe Gallagher had friends here. Of course, he knew how to be a friend. That's a good thing to know."

A smile came to Katie's lips, a radiant smile, for she was savoring this praise for her father, delighting in this other side of his life. Often in the past she had been sad about him, thinking him alone, too different from most of his neighbors, different even from his own family. Now she thought back to the day of his funeral. Almost sixty people had crowded the grave site at Holy Name Cemetery. Some of them had been neighbors, but many more had been strangers to her. She remembered asking Maeve about them, about all the flowers and Mass cards. She remembered Maeve's silence. "Mama never told me," she said softly.

"Joe Gallagher was a fine man. I guess that's all you need to know. He wasn't one for work, and that made it tough on Maeve. But still . . . ah well, come along, Katie. I'll show you the parlor. You'll do the dining room first each morning, then the parlor. Follow me."

Ada's parlor was spacious, Victorian in its over-stuffed chairs and sofas, its fringed carpet splashed with cabbage roses, its heavy, fringed draperies.

There were several round tables, all of them laden with music boxes and flower pots and assorted gimcracks. There was an upright piano covered with a fringed silk scarf, and a tufted piano stool. "It's a lot to look after," Ada conceded cheerfully, glancing at her beloved treasures. "My nephew, Matt, is always nagging me to get rid of things. I say they're my things and I can keep them if I want to. I like a cozy parlor."

"Oh yes," Katie agreed. She pictured her father sitting in the homey, cluttered room, and a light danced in her eyes. "It's just the way it should be."

"Tell that to Matt when you see him. He doesn't understand about my things. I collected them all with Tim, rest his soul. We traveled all over the country doing our act, and we bought some little souvenir in each town we played. Here," Ada said, picking up a red china vase. "This is what we bought in Sacremento, when we were working the Orpheum circuit. I still remember the day. Later we came back east and worked the Keith circuit. We bought this swan in Harrisburg."

"Was it fun to travel? In school, I always looked at the maps and imagined all the exciting places I could go to."

"It was a good life. Not much money, but what times we had!" Ada returned the swan to the table. She rearranged a row of vividly colored clowns and then walked to the far end of the parlor, straightening a fold in the draperies. "One day we got to thinking about the future, and that's when we decided to settle down. We wanted security in our old age. There're no assurances in vaudeville. It's no life

43

when you're old. . . . But all this talk isn't getting the parlor cleaned. I'll leave you to your chores, Katie. Everything you need is in the corner there. I put it out this morning before you came. You know how to clean, don't you?"

"Yes." Katie nodded. "I cleaned for the priests at St. Brendan's."

"I like the parlor to shine. If I find a speck of dust, you'll have to start over."

"That's fair."

"When you're finished with the dusting, there's sweeping. Then take a cloth to the picture frames and the woodwork. Dig deep into the corners; no cheating. You don't have to worry about the waxing. We do that Friday. Today's laundry day and that's bad enough."

"I'll have your parlor shining like the sun. I promise."

Ada glanced at the cuckoo clock above the mantel and then went to the door. "I'd best start Matt's breakfast. He eats early because he has school. Any questions before I go, Katie? Now's the time to ask."

"No questions. I just want to say thank you. Thank you for giving me the job."

"Hah!" Ada laughed, turning to leave. "Let's see if you're still thanking me at day's end. You'll be good and tired, miss. Good and tired."

"I don't mind," Katie said with a smile, her eyes roaming once more over the happy jumble of the parlor. "I love it here."

Katie was humming as she set to work. On her hands and knees, she brushed the ashes from the hearth and scrubbed the stones until they sparkled.

She dusted the furniture, the scores of bowls and boxes and figurines. She stood on a chair to clean the moldings and the curtain rods, getting down on hands and knees again to clean every inch of woodwork. She swept the floor and the carpet, wielding her broom like a weapon in some fierce battle. She plumped the many pillows and watered all the plants, and when, an hour later, she was done, she cleaned the hall and the stair.

"Finished so soon?" Ada asked doubtfully, watching Katie struggle into the kitchen with brushes and brooms and pails. "That's quick work. Maybe too quick."

"I did a good job, Ada. Really I did."

"We'll see about that. I warned you. If it's not right, you'll have to do it over. People make fun of me for being so fussy, but that's the way I am. I'm what you might call particular."

"Mama's the same way. Mama taught me how to clean. I even rolled the carpet back and swept underneath."

"Fancy that! I suppose you're expecting a reward? A raise in your wages?"

"No, I didn't mean . . . oh." Katie glanced away, her cheeks coloring. "You're teasing me."

"Sure I am. You'll have to get used to teasing. There's a lot of it around here. It's all in fun. I told you we like our fun. Let's see a smile, Katie. Ah, that's better."

"Do you want to look at the parlor?"

"Later. Matt's fed and gone, but we'll have hungry boarders coming down to breakfast any minute. Wash up in the sink and then come help me with this. Oatmeal gets lumpy if you don't keep stirring it. I never cared for oatmeal myself. My boarders like it though. I try to give them what they like. Let me see your hands," Ada said as Katie joined her at the stove. "Good. You keep stirring while I tend to the rest of the food."

It was more food than Katie had ever seen. There were two big pans of scrambled eggs and two big pans of fried potatoes, dark and crisp at the edges. On the counter were platters of hot biscuits and pots of honey and jam and brown sugar. Her mouth began to water again and, remembering the breakfast she had eaten, she averted her eyes.

"Are you still hungry?" Ada asked. "Take a biscuit."

"I couldn't. Thank you, but I couldn't."

"There's no shame in being hungry, you know. You're a growing girl." Ada looked sidelong at Katie, smiling. "Maybe you want to save your appetite for noonday lunch. It's up to you."

Katie sensed Ada's understanding and was glad of it; she also sensed that, in Ada, she had a friend. She turned her head to the crackling fire, to the herbs growing in their pretty pots, and she felt a kind of contentment. "It must be grand to live here," she said, as much to herself as to Ada.

"Well, it's home. Turn the flame off, Katie. The oatmeal should be done. Put the biscuits and things on that tray and take it to the dining room."

Katie made several trips between kitchen and dining room, carrying covered serving dishes, pitchers of water, and two large, white teapots. "Is that all of it?" she asked after her fourth trip.

"Just the oatmeal. I'll take it in. It's too heavy for you. You can fetch the extra napkins. With the Costellos around, there are always extra spills."

Katie followed after Ada. She arranged the napkins in neat stacks on the sideboard and then opened the draperies, blinking in the sudden and dazzling sunlight. Outside she saw little children playing in what remained of the snow, digging in it with discarded spoons and cups. She saw horse-drawn wagons making their weary ways east, and the rag picker, a gnarled old man known only as Sam, shuffling across the avenue. Katie observed the Hell's Kitchen morning from the warm shelter of Ada's dining room and felt blessed.

"Here they come," Ada was saying, "all my sleeping beauties. It's almost ten," she said in mock anger, her hands on her ample hips. "I thought you were all waiting for me to bring you breakfast in bed."

The boarders greeted Ada noisily and with obvious affection. "You're welcome in my bed any day," Jack Snow called loudly. "And you don't have to bring breakfast either."

Ada would ordinarily have laughed at such a remark, but now, conscious of Katie's presence, she did not respond. "That's enough of that. I want you hooligans to be quiet a minute. I want you to meet my new hired girl, Katie Gallagher. She's Joe Gallagher's daughter. Jack, you remember Joe Gallagher, don't you?"

"Why, sure I do." Jack Snow turned his head in Katie's direction. "Hiya, kid." He grinned. "Glad to see you. Joe used to talk about you all the time."

Katie looked past the sea of boarders to short, round Jack Snow and nodded shyly. She remembered him from her father's funeral, recalling the huge cross of red roses he had brought. "Hello," she said, swallowing hard.

"Hey, Ada," Jack called, sitting down, "you finally got someone pretty. What a relief, after old horse-face."

"Look who's talking," Ada replied to much laughter. "Pay no attention to him, Katie. He's a comedian. At least *he* says he is. Some audiences don't agree." Ada glanced fondly at Jack and then glanced back at Katie. "Jack and his partner have a comedy act, Rayne and Snow. And that's Herbert and Yvonne, dancers. That's Phil Smith. He plays piano at the Circle Theatre. Those four hooligans at the end of the table are the Costellos. They do a comic ballet. And that's Cornelius O'Day, Irish tenor."

Cornelius O'Day was a headliner, the only true headliner to stay at Ada's boardinghouse. He was a handsome man with a wavy pompadour of red hair and a courtly manner well known to his female admirers. "Good morning, Miss Katie Gallagher," he said.

Katie was impressed—too impressed to speak—for everyone in Hell's Kitchen had heard of Cornelius O'Day, Singer of Sweet Songs. Ada went to Katie's rescue, draping her arm about the child's shoulder. "All the ladies swoon over Cornelius." She winked. "And him with a wife and six children in Toledo."

"Wait'll I tell Mama I *met* Cornelius O'Day." Katie blushed at the laughter that followed her comment. She tried to hide her face but Ada propelled her forward, into full view of the boarders. "Now remember what I told you about teasing," she said quietly. "It's all in fun, and you have to get used to it. Katie here," she addressed her boarders, "thinks this place is a palace. She thinks I'm rich!"

Jack Snow bounded out of his chair. He was across the room in a flash, bowing elaborately to Ada, kissing her hand. "Is that really you, Mrs. Vanderbilt?" he asked in his best stage voice. "Can I have a thousand dollars for a cup of coffee, Mrs. Vanderbilt?"

"No, it's Mrs. Astor!" Phil Smith called out.

"Mrs. Astor"—Jack fell to his knees—"can I have five thousand dollars for a cup of coffee?"

Katie was scarlet with embarrassment. She struggled but could not free herself from Ada's firm grip. "Please," she said.

"It's all in fun, Katie. All these people want to be your friends, if you'll let them."

Slowly, Katie looked around. She saw only kindness in the faces of the vaudevillians, and she began to feel better. They're waiting for me to join in their game, she thought, searching her mind for something to say. "Is . . . is it really you, Mrs. Astor?" she asked, looking at Ada.

There was a burst of applause at Katie's small joke. Jack jumped up, applauding loudest of all. "We'll make a trouper of you yet, Katie."

"Bite your tongue." Ada laughed. "The little miss can do better than that. Isn't that right, Katie? See, she agrees with me. All right, hooligans, we've had our laugh, and now we'll leave you to your meal. That's a new table cloth, so try not to ruin it the first day. Especially you, John Costello."

Outraged cries came from all the Costellos, but they were shouted down by Herbert and Yvonne and Rayne and Snow. Katie found herself enjoying the good-natured banter of the vaudevillians. It was a new world to her, one she was reluctant to leave. "Is it always like that?" she asked, following Ada into the hall.

"Like what?"

"They're such happy people. Always laughing and carrying on. It's grand."

"I'm glad you think so. I didn't want you to think I was being mean to you in there. Putting you at the center of things the way I did. Maybe it was mean, but I wanted you to learn. See, if you're going to work here, if you're going to be happy here, you can't be . . . sensitive. This is no place for shrinking violets."

"I understand, Ada."

"It's like when you're learning to swim. It's best if someone just throws you in the water. That's what I did. I threw you in the water, sink or swim."

"How did I do?" Katie smiled, a faint, mischievous light twinkling in the green of her eyes.

"You did fine. You're too young for this job, and I told that to Maeve a hundred times, but you did fine. Now let's go have a look at the parlor. Let's see how you did there."

Ada made a thorough inspection of the parlor. She trailed her finger across table tops and over window sills. She looked into corners, underneath the carpet and the sofa cushions. She spent several minutes at the hearth, poking into the grates. "Perfect," she announced finally. "It it was Maeve who taught you, she taught you well."

"Can I tell Mama what you said?"

"Of course."

"I mean, would it be bragging? Mama says we mustn't brag. She says it's a sin."

"Is that all Maeve ever talks about? Sin? It's no wonder you're so nervous and shy." Again, Ada was disturbed by the tone of her voice. She looked quickly at Katie, smiling and tweaking the child's golden braids. "I won't tell you to go against Maeve's rules, but I can't see any harm in saying you did a good job. That's the truth, not bragging. And while I'm being truthful, I can't see why a young girl like you should be worrying about sin." To herself Ada thought, I'm as Catholic as Maeve. I say my prayers. I go to confession. I go to six o'clock Mass every Sunday, come rain or shine. But I'll never see the point in scaring children with constant talk of sin. "Maybe God wants us to worry," she said, "but not *all* the time. There's more to life than worry. That's how I see it, anyway."

Katie said nothing, pondering Ada's words and the ideas behind them. She was about to agree when she remembered her mother to whom life was indeed all worry, worry and work and little else. Frowning, she remained silent.

Ada gave the parlor one last look. "A good job"—she chuckled—"and only the beginning. There's the whole upstairs still to do. Come with me, Katie. I'll show you." There were three upper floors, each with four rooms, a hall closet, and a hall bathroom. At certain times of morning and night, the halls seemed

51

to be filled with crowds of people, but now they were empty and pleasantly quiet, with sunlight dappling the flower-sprigged wallpaper. "That's my room," Ada said, pointing it out. "And that room is Matt's. I take care of those. You'll be taking care of all the others. The beds are changed every Monday. The towels, too," she added, opening the door of the linen closet. "Are you listening to me, Katie? What are you looking at?"

"Oh, I'm sorry, Ada. I was looking at the telephone. You have your *own* telephone."

"For my boarders. It's an expense, and Matt's always after me about expenses, but show people need a telephone in the house. Booking agents call sometimes."

"Can I touch it? I'll be careful."

"What a funny girl you are. Haven't you ever seen a telephone before?"

"Not close up. Not close enough to touch."

"Well, now's your chance. It's easy; no trick to it. Look." Ada smiled. "You just pick up this receiver part. An operator comes on the line and asks what number you want. The pad there is for messages. If you have to answer the telephone, be sure you write the message down. The name and the number."

"Oh, I will. It's grand," Katie said, reaching her hand to the magical invention. "Imagine being able to talk to people far, far, *far* away."

"Imagine." Ada waited a moment and then tapped Katie on the shoulder. "How about imagining work?" She chuckled, one eyebrow raised. "There's a lot to do, you know. We can't lollygag around. You'll find everything you need in the closet. Change the

52

beds first. I want to start on the laundry."

"Beds first." Katie nodded.

Ada went to the landing, lifting her skirts as she descended the stairs. "Lunch is at noon," she called. "Keep an eye on the clock."

The rest of the morning passed in a blur as Katie went from room to room, making beds and putting out fresh towels and cloths. Her arms had begun to ache, but she hardly noticed, so intent was she on her chores. Each bedspread was carefully smoothed, each towel carefully folded on the rod. When she was satisfied, she heaped all the dirty laundry in an enormous basket and carried it down to the kitchen.

"Are you all right?" Ada asked when Katie stumbled. "Here"—she sighed, taking the basket from her—"that's too heavy for you to carry all at once. It's best to make two trips, or three— Are you all right, Katie?"

"Yes. I'm . . . fine." Katie leaned against the doorframe and caught her breath. The ache in her arms was sharper now, running from shoulder to elbow. "Next time, I'll make two trips."

"Sit down," Ada said, placing a cup of tea in front of Katie, "Rest a while. You look about to faint."

"Oh, I'm stronger than I look. Mama says—"

"Never mind that. Just drink your tea and rest." Ada returned to the stove, though she glanced often at Katie, concern dimming her bright, brown eyes. Her last hired girl, she recalled, had not been popular with the boarders, but she had been older and bigger than Katie, accustomed to working twelve hard hours a day. Damn you, Maeve Gallagher, she thought, for sending that child here, and damn me, for letting you. "I think you're hurrying too much, Katie, wearing yourself out. There's no need. It's not a race. I know it's your first day and all. You have to get the hang of things. Just don't try to do everything at once. There's the whole afternoon left. There's plenty of time."

"But you said you wanted to start the laundry."

"Start it, yes. I'll be doing laundry all day long. And ironing tomorrow. I didn't mean you had to have every bit of laundry down here by noon. Do I look like a slave driver?"

"No." Katie smiled. "Not you." She sat back in her chair, rubbing her sore arms. "I was showing off," she admitted quietly. "I wanted you to think I was the best hired girl ever, because I need this job. My family's depending on me, Ada. Mama lost a laundry customer and the rent's going up and they're depending on me." Katie stared at the floor, her long black lashes shadowing her pale cheeks. "It's only right. Mama's had the burden from the beginning. Papa did what he could, but Mama had the burden. Me and Hugh and the little ones . . . it's hard."

"I know." Ada's big heart went out to Katie, to all the children like Katie who learned too early the harshness of life. She herself had been one of those children, apprenticed at the age of twelve to an ill-tempered cook who had worked her fifteen hours a day, seven days a week. She had endured it for two years before running away. The following year she met Tim McVey, her salvation. Now Ada looked at young Katie Gallagher and wondered who, or what, would save her. "I know it's hard."

"There's . . . there's something else. Maybe it

sounds silly, but I love it here. It's the kind of place I always dreamed of having for my own. All warm and cozy. If I got fired . . ."

"Don't worry your head about that. You're not getting fired. Why would I fire a nice girl like you?" Ada turned back to the stove. She spooned warmed-over scrambled eggs between thick slices of dark bread and piled the sandwiches on a tray next to a bowl of sweet pickles. "Here." She smiled, putting the tray on the table. "Eat hearty. There's raisin pie for dessert."

Katie resumed her chores after lunch, sweeping and dusting all the upstairs rooms, scouring the baths. She worked undisturbed—the boarders had gone off to their early shows—though she worked at a much slower pace. Now the pain in her neck and arms could not be ignored. It was a torture to bend, to reach, and she had to stop every few minutes, wiping her wet forehead as she strained to catch her breath. When the last room was finished, she fell exhausted into a chair. She meant only to rest, but soon her head dropped to her shoulder and her eyes closed in sleep.

Matt McVey came upon the sleeping Katie an hour later. He strode across the room, a robust and smiling young man of sixteen, and bent over her, shaking her arm. "Rise and shine, little girl," he said.

Katie awoke with a start. Her heart was thumping, her eyes darting wildly about in the gathering twilight. A minute passed before she remembered that she was at Ada's, and yet another minute before she realized that she had fallen asleep. She leaped to her feet then leaned back, alarmed by the shadowy form blocking her way.

"Easy now," Matt said. "Don't be scared. Are you Katie Gallagher? I guess you are. Who else would you be? I'm Matt McVey, Ada's nephew. She sent me to see if you were all right. Are you?"

"Yes, I'm—What time is it?" Katie asked, confused. "It must be late. Is it late?"

Matt turned the gaslight up and glanced at his watch. "Four-thirty, exactly. Ada's starting supper. That's why she sent me—"

"Four-thirty! It can't be!"

"It is. What are you getting so excited about?"

Katie shook her head, angry with herself. "My first day working here and I fall asleep. What'll Ada think of me?"

"She'll think you were tired. There's no law against being tired. None that I know of. *Hey!*" Matt laughed, catching Katie as she bolted toward the door. "Slow down, little girl. Do you want to break your neck?"

"It's late," Katie protested. "Let me go." She looked up at Matt, seeing him clearly for the first time, and her gaze softened. It lingered on him, moving from his mane of reddish brown hair to his direct and uncomplicated blue eyes and finally to his smile, a wonderful smile that brought a sudden flutter to her heart. Katie, unlike her best friend, Meg Muldoon, had never shown any interest in boys. She had considered them bullies, unruly scamps who pulled her braids and tramped on her feet and pelted her with snowballs in winter and water bags in summer. But now, lost in the radiance of Matt's smile, all those indignities were forgotten. She smiled back at him, the tiniest sigh falling from her lips. "You're . . . you're Ada's nephew?" she asked when she was able to speak.

"That's right." Matt laughed again. He had a loud laugh, as loud as Ada's though deeper, and Katie thought it manly. "I'm the nephew," he said. "The one and only." He released his grip on Katie's wrists and gently turned her toward the door. "Off with you now. Ada's waiting. I'll put your rags and things away. You go on."

Katie took several steps, but at the threshold she stopped, looking once more at Matt. "Are you coming down to supper?" she asked timidly.

"I have a night job. I take my supper with me."

"Oh."

Matt saw the disappointment in Katie's expression and he was amused. "Go on, little girl," he said lightly, smiling into her innocent green eyes. "*Scoot.*"

"Yes," Katie said, but still she did not move.

"Well? Do you want me to carry you downstairs?"

Katie felt a blush come to her cheeks. She ducked her head quickly and scurried into the hall, tripping on the carpet but righting herself before she fell.

"Are you all right?" Matt called after her.

"Yes," Katie called in reply. "I'm fine . . . fine and clumsy," she muttered, hurrying down the stairs.

Ada's face was anxious as Katie entered the kitchen. "I was beginning to worry about you," she said. She wiped her hands on her apron and then came forward, peering at Katie. "You were up there a long time."

"I know. I'm sorry, Ada. I finished the cleaning and I sat down to rest a minute. I . . . I fell asleep. I'm sorry. I won't do it again."

"You fell asleep?" Ada's surprised silence was followed by a great explosion of laughter that shook her shoulders and filled her eyes with merry tears. "Ah, Katie," she said, plucking a handkerchief from her sleeve, "if you don't take the cake!"

"You're not mad?"

"There's no harm done."

"You . . . won't tell Mama?"

"It'll be our secret. Just between us."

"And Matt. He's the one who woke me up."

"I'm glad I sent him after you then. Otherwise you'd still be sleeping, and I'd have to charge you rent."

"I'm sorry, Ada."

"Forget about it. We have supper to make now, and it's getting late. Supper's always on the table at six o'clock. My boarders are back by then. They can eat in peace and leave for their evening shows in plenty of time. Come along, miss. Maeve says you're not much of a cook, but you'll learn, watching me. Meanwhile, start peeling those onions. We're having corned beef hash tonight. We always have corned beef hash on Monday nights because we always have corned beef and cabbage on Sundays. Waste not, want not."

Katie rinsed her hands in the sink and then turned to the counter, staring down at a small mountain of onions. She worked as quickly as her aching arms would allow, though her thoughts returned often to Matt. "Your nephew—" she murmured, "he's nice."

"That he is," Ada agreed proudly, for she was devoted to Matt. "He's smart, too. And he has ambition. He won't be stuck in Hell's Kitchen all his life." Ada bustled about the stove, moving pans around, adding pinches of salt and pepper and dill. She took a slab of corned beef from the ice box and began hacking it into pieces. "Not that I have anything against Hell's Kitchen," she said, knives flashing. "I like it here. It suits me. It's home now and I'm not complaining . . ."

Ada prattled on, hardly pausing for breath, and Katie smiled. Her young and pretty face was serene as she counted the blessings of her new life.

3

Katie was sorry when, at seven-thirty, the day's work done, Ada gave her her coat and pointed her firmly to the door. She was tired, her arms and neck and back throbbing with pain, but still she was reluctant to leave. Thoughts of home did not cheer her, nor did thoughts of the walk home, for it was cold and dark outside, the streets empty. She looked up at the starless sky, the tiny sliver of moon, and her gloom deepened. After a last mournful glance at the boardinghouse, she turned away.

A hand grasped Katie's shoulder as she neared the corner. She cried out, turning to see Hugh's sly grin. "You scared me to death, Hugh Gallagher," she said, her hand over her heart. "It's not funny either."

"Aw, you scare too easy."

"What are you doing here? I bet Mama doesn't know you're here."

"I snuck out when she was in the toilet. I came to take you home. It's for your own good," he added quickly, "so don't start acting high and mighty. I want the fellas to know we're together."

"What fellas? Those bad boys you go with?"

"You'll be walking this way every night. You don't want no trouble, do you? It's for your good the fellas know we're together. They won't bother you then. And who says they're bad?"

"Everybody."

"Everybody can go to hell." Hugh laughed, tossing a quarter in the air. "You want a soda? Smitty's is open another hour yet."

"No, and you shouldn't be wasting money on sodas."

Hugh stopped walking. He put the quarter in his pocket and stared at Katie. "What's the matter with you?" he asked, an edge to his voice. "You're getting sour, just like the old lady. You want to be like her? Mean and all the time nagging people?" Hugh took his cap off. He ran his hand through his light brown hair and then put the cap back on. "Don't go telling me she has it hard," he snorted. "That's how it is in this lousy neighborhood. What's the use in nagging? And when she's not nagging, she's preaching about sin. Like *she* has the say on what's a sin. Like *she* was God."

"Hugh!"

"It's the truth, isn't it? You're getting just like her. You used to be nice. You used to be okay. Now you're a damn nag."

Katie flinched as if from a blow. She gazed helplessly at Hugh, and in the dim glow of the streetlamp his eyes were terrible, a grim and icy blue. "Please don't be mad," she said. "I hate it when you're mad."

"Why?"

Katie could not have put it into words, but she

sensed the menace that lay at the core of Hugh's quiet, cold anger. The very air about him seemed to change, to become suddenly still, suddenly heavy, and she was reminded of the air before a violent storm. "I'm sorry for nagging, Hugh. I won't do it again. I promise. But don't be mad at me."

Hugh was silent. He stuffed his hands deep into his pockets and started walking, glancing once or twice at Katie. "How was Ada's?" he asked when they were across the avenue.

"Oh, I had the best time. I'll tell you a secret. I didn't want to go home. Isn't that awful? I'm ashamed of myself."

"What's awful about it? There's nothing at home."

"There's Mama and you and the little ones. There's all my family; but I was having such a good time I didn't want to go." Katie described the warm and cozy boardinghouse. She described the meals and the boarders and, lastly, Ada McVey, for whom she saved her most lyrical praise. "When you meet her," Katie concluded, "you'll see what I mean. She's always smiling and laughing. It's all fun with her."

Hugh had been listening closely, and he was surprised. He had been ready to dislike Ada, to feel the same contempt for her he felt for all employers, but now he changed his mind. "She treated you fair?" he asked. "She treated you decent?"

"Yes." Katie nodded vigorously. "She's real nice."

"And you don't care about your lousy school?"

Katie hesitated, looking again toward the dark sky. "Not so much any more," she replied after a while. "I guess I'd like to be in school . . . but if I have to have a job, this is the best job in the whole world."

"It's still slaving, morning 'til night."

"I wouldn't call it slaving, Hugh."

"*I* would."

Brother and sister were quiet as they walked the next block, for neither of them wanted another argument to flare. In the doorway of the tenement, Katie turned and, smiling, took Hugh's hand. "I'm glad you came to get me," she admitted. "I didn't fancy the walk, all by myself. It was on my mind."

Hugh pulled his hand away. "There's no worries about that now," he said. "The fellas know what's what."

"I didn't see any fellas."

"They seen you. That's what counts." Hugh grinned, opening the door to the hall. "It's my job to look after you, and that's what I done. You can rest easy."

"Hugh? You'll be in trouble with Mama. I'm sorry."

"It's nothing new."

Katie was not comforted by Hugh's flippant remark. She tried, as she had tried frequently in the past, to understand his attitude, but understanding eluded her. She looked at his calm, clear profile and was bewildered. As well as she knew her brother, she had to concede that there were some things about him she would never know. And maybe it's for the best, she thought, racing up the stairs two at a time.

The halls were noisy on this Monday night. Babies cried, mothers scolded, and fathers yelled. There was singing in the Muldoon flat and, in the Ryan flat, the Ryan's big, lop-eared dog barked furiously. Katie was familiar with the sounds of the tenement and the smells, pungent mixtures of cabbage and grease and coal smoke and diapers. "Look at that," she said, pointing to a wagon made from old wooden crates. "Billy Ryan finally finished his wagon. Maybe he'll let me take Sean and Francis for a ride in it."

"When?" Hugh scoffed. "At midnight? That's all the time you'll have to yourself from here on."

"I'll have Sundays. There's no work on Sundays."

"Are you forgetting about your chores, Katie Gallagher?" The voice, stern and chiding, was Maeve's. She stood at the top of the stairs, impatiently tapping her foot as she stared at her children. "Come inside," she said. "Be quick about it. You both have a lot of explaining to do."

Katie and Hugh followed her into the flat. Hugh removed his coat and then his cap, tossing both on a hook behind the door. Katie stood still and tried to judge her mother's mood. It was bad, she decided, glancing worriedly at Hugh. She moved closer to him, but he walked away. He pulled a chair out and sprawled in it, crossing his arms over his broad chest. "I went to fetch Katie home," he announced flatly.

"Who told you to do that?"

"Nobody."

"Didn't I tell you to stay here? Didn't I tell you over and over again?"

"Yeah, you did."

There was silence as Maeve and Hugh regarded each other. It was an uncomfortable silence, filled with tension, with the resentment of thwarted wills. "I'm waiting for an apology," Maeve said at last.

"From who? Me? All I done was fetch Katie home."

"After I told you not to."

Hugh shrugged. "That's life, Ma." He smiled amiably, repeating an expression popular with the Parlor Mob. He was still smiling when Maeve's hand shot out and slapped his face. He neither moved nor spoke, and Maeve slapped him again. Two fiery red handprints marked Hugh's cheeks, but if he felt them he gave no sign. "Are you through?" he asked.

"Go to your room!" Maeve screamed, incensed. "Go before I get the strap! And stay there!"

Hugh rose slowly from his chair. "G'night, Katie." He winked, going to his room and closing the door.

Maeve banged the chair back into place. "Stubborn as the devil he is," she said, pacing angrily about. "The devil himself!"

"Hugh didn't mean any harm. He was just looking out for me. It was dark and all."

"Dark, was it? And are you afraid of the dark now? You'd best get used to it. You'd best get used to looking out for yourself, too. You're not a baby, Katie Gallagher. You can't live your life being afraid. There'll be no mollycoddling. I won't have it. Don't stand there like a goose. Take your coat off before you catch your death."

"Yes, Mama."

"Did you ask Hugh to fetch you, or was it his idea? *His* idea." Maeve nodded when Katie failed to reply. "Well, that's the first and last time. You'll take yourself to work in the morning and you'll take yourself home at night. Do you understand?"

"Yes, Mama."

"Sit down. I want to talk to you.'

Katie eased her aching body into a chair and clasped her hands atop the table. "My pencil box," she said in surprise, for she had thought it lost. "What's my pencil box doing here?"

"You left it at school Friday. Being careless again. Meg brought it back. I'm giving it to Hugh. Maybe he won't be so careless."

"But it was a present from Papa. Look how he wrote my name on—"

"You've no need of it now. Stop fussing and be sensible for once." Maeve sat opposite her daughter. She drew a breath, twisting her wedding band around and around. "Did you do a good job today? The truth, Katie."

"Ada said I did. I tried my best."

"And what's your best? Tell me the chores you did."

Obediently, Katie recounted the details of her day. She made no mention of falling asleep, but she told Maeve everything else, answering all her questions. "Doing the supper dishes was the last chore," she explained. "Then Ada sent me home."

"Ada was pleased with your work?"

"She said she was. She said you taught me real good."

"That's a load off my mind." Maeve sighed. "There's never any knowing how these things will go, especially with a girl like you who's not used to work. Keep it up, Katie, and you'll make me proud."

Coming from Maeve, those were kind words, far kinder than Katie had expected. "Thank you, Mama." She smiled. "It's nice working there. The boarders are so funny. And there are warm fires and

67

plenty of food. Ada's always laughing, having a good time."

"Aye, I'd be laughing too if my husband left me a boardinghouse. I'd have warm fires and plenty of food, don't think I wouldn't. I could afford it. I could afford to laugh." Bitterness had come into Maeve's voice, into the dark blue of her eyes. She gazed around the dingy flat and shook her head. "But what did Joe leave me? Worries and troubles and children. That's my inheritance. And it was the same for my mother—worries, debts, everybody wanting and needing what they couldn't have." Maeve leaned forward, looking intently at Katie. "There are some in this neighborhood, in this building, who think I'm hard on you. Well, I am. Because I want better for you. I want you to get something out of life. Just living, that's not enough. The priests say it is. They say it's a gift. What gift is it to be hungry and cold all the time? Tell me that. You have to be *strong*, Katie. If you're strong, maybe you won't make my mistakes."

Katie frowned, for she could not imagine that her mother, her sure and determined mother, had ever made mistakes. "Things won't always be . . . bad," she offered in a small voice. "They'll get better. They're bound to."

"And would you like to tell me how?"

"We're in America, Mama. It's different here."

"America! That was Joe's answer to everything. America. Aye, it's a grand country if you're rich. If you're poor . . ." Maeve stood up, turning her back to Katie. "You've had a long day," she said. "Go on to bed."

"Are you all right, Mama?"

"I have to be, don't I? Go on to bed now. It's late and morning will be here before you know it."

"I'll stay with you a while, if you want."

Katie's thoughtfulness was not lost on Maeve. Her eyes softened and a rare smile played about her mouth. "No," she said. "You need your sleep. And I have things to do."

"Good night, Mama." Katie kissed Maeve and then started toward her bedroom. She stopped suddenly, tilting her head to one side. "Do you know Ada's nephew?" she asked. "Did you ever meet him?"

"Matt? To hear Ada tell it, he's a young prince. The sun rises and sets on him. But I never met him myself. Why?"

"I just wondered. He seemed awful nice."

"Maybe he is. And maybe he isn't. It's nothing to you, either way. Work's all you have to worry about. Don't be mixing in other people's business. You have enough on your plate as it is."

"Good night, Mama."

"Good night . . . sleep safe," Maeve added quietly. Alone in the bare, chilly kitchen, she extinguished the gaslight and sat in the dark, staring into space.

Katie's room was the smallest of the three bedrooms. It contained a bed, a dresser, and a cracked mirror which she had found in the street. There was a window, nailed shut, for it faced on a dark and evil-smelling airshaft. The room was freezing, and Katie undressed quickly, climbing into a thin flannel nightgown. She loosened her braids and was asleep almost before her head touched the pillow. In her dreams she saw the smiling face of Matt McVey.

Katie hardly stirred during the night. Curled beneath a blanket and an old patchwork quilt, her long golden hair spilling over her shoulders, she was a picture of sweet innocence. It was this picture Maeve saw when, a few minutes before six o'clock, she marched to Katie's bedside. She pulled the covers back and briskly shook her daughter's arm. "It's time to wake up . . . wake up, Katie . . . do you want to sleep the day away?"

Katie opened her eyes. "Is it morning?" she asked with a yawn. "I was having the nicest dream."

"There's no time for dreams now. Tea's ready, and you'd best hurry, or you'll have to go without."

Katie yawned again. She raised herself on one elbow but then collapsed against the pillow, shrieking in pain. "Mama, it *hurts*."

"What hurts? What are you talking about?"

"My back and my arms. It's like there was fire in them." Katie tried to turn. The movement, cautious though it was, brought a searing pain, and again she cried out. "It *hurts*, Mama. It hurts all over." Tears sprang to her eyes as she stared at her mother. "Do . . . do you think it's the influenza?"

Influenza was a dreaded word in Hell's Kitchen and Maeve pushed it from her mind. "Don't talk foolish," she snapped, feeling Katie's forehead. "You've no fever. Thank God for that. Does your stomach feel sick?"

"No. But I can't move. The pain, Mama. It's so bad."

"Aye, I know. And I'm remembering when the same thing happened to me. It was after I did the plowing for the first time." Maeve turned the gaslight up. She sat at the edge of the bed and brushed the hair from Katie's pale, anxious face. "I know it hurts," she said, "but it's nothing to be worrying about. You're hurting because of the work you did yesterday. You're not used to work. Your body's not used to it. Don't be a baby, Katie. I'll help you up, then we'll see what we can do to make it better."

"I can't get up."

"You can't lay abed all the day, if that's what you're thinking. You need to move around."

"I can't."

"Such talk! You can do whatever you set your mind to, Katie Gallagher. Now stop fussing and let me help you. Dear knows I've been in your place. It didn't kill me and it won't kill you." Maeve slipped her hands under Katie's back. "We'll do this quick," she said. "Quick is best."

Katie closed her eyes. She grimaced at the hot, sharp stabs of pain and held her breath, silently praying for the ordeal to end.

"There." Maeve nodded, pleased. "If you can sit up, you can stand up." She pushed the covers out of the way and swung Katie's legs to the floor. "The worst's almost over. Hold on to me and try to stand."

"Please, Mama."

"You must try, Katie. Rich people can pamper their aches and pains, but not the likes of us. Don't you think there are days I want to stay abed? Wanting's one thing; doing's another. Stand up, Katie. *Try.*"

Groaning, Katie obeyed. "It still hurts," she said, holding fast to Maeve. "All through my back

71

and arms."

"Heat's what you need. We'll go into the kitchen, and I'll heat some towels in the stove."

"My back's already on fire."

"I've no time to argue, Katie. You'll do as I say and no sass. You've a job waiting. Maybe you forgot about your job. Maybe you think pain's an excuse. It's not. I was back working the day after you were born, and that's the truth."

"I'm sorry, Mama."

"Aye, you're always sorry. For all the good it does." Maeve draped the quilt over Katie's stooped shoulders and helped her into the hall. "Hugh," she said, frowning at her sleepy-eyed son. "What are you doing up?"

"I heard yelling."

"There was no yelling. You dreamed it. Go back to bed."

Hugh ran a hand through his tousled hair. He yawned. "I know what I heard, Ma. What's the matter with you, Katie? You look sick."

"Your sister's not sick. She's a little sore from her first day of work. It's nothing. Mind your business and go back to bed. This isn't a party here. We've things to do."

"What things? What's going on?" Hugh saw Katie's halting footsteps, her arms held stiffly at her sides. "What's going on?" he asked again. "Are you sending her to work today? She can't even walk. How's she supposed to work?"

"It's all right, Hugh." Katie sighed. "Don't start trouble."

"This is crazy. You're crazy, the both of you. She

can't *walk*, Ma. Look at her."

Maeve ignored Hugh's protests. She pushed past him and took Katie into the kitchen. "Don't sit down," she warned. "Keep moving around. The more you move around, the better you'll feel. Time's the cure. A few hours from now there'll be no pain. Meanwhile you have to make the best." Maeve poured a cup of tea, thrusting it into Katie's icy hands. "Nothing like tea to set things right. And I'll heat the towels."

Hugh watched his mother rushing from cupboard to stove, his sister hobbling about as she tried to drink the tea. Suddenly, angrily, he turned and punched the wall. It was an act of frustration, for he felt helpless and indeed he was. All around him were signs of the poverty he despised yet could not change, of the grim life he yearned to escape. He glared at his mother and his hands clenched into fists.

Katie looked away, shaken by Hugh's fierce, scowling expression. Her thoughts on this Tuesday morning were not very different from his, but they were more sad than angry, and in them was the glimmer of hope she refused to deny. "Have hope in the future," Joe Gallagher had exhorted her again and again. "Have trust." Katie had not questioned her father's words then, and she did not question them now. She drank her tea and thought about the future, a magical time of magical possibilities.

"Katie? I'm talking to you, Katie Gallagher. Pay attention."

"Yes, Mama."

"Put your cup down and stand still. The towels are all ready, nice and warm." Maeve took the quilt from

Katie's shoulders and threw it on a chair. "Hugh," she said, "go back to bed. We're busy here."

"I'll go. And I'll go with Katie when she leaves. You can't stop me."

"Is that so?"

"Yeah, it is."

"Fine." Maeve nodded. "But you'll go barefoot, because I hid your shoes last night; your socks, too. You won't get them back 'til it's time for school. If you want to go barefoot in this cold, fine. Sure and it's nothing to me."

Hugh's lips parted slightly. He did not speak, though his look was eloquent, quietly and darkly murderous. He stared at Maeve for a long moment then left the kitchen.

"That's the way to handle him," Maeve said, triumph in her voice. "Don't tell me it isn't."

It's the wrong way, thought Katie, knowing Hugh would never forget his defeat. Prudently, she remained silent. She was mute even when Maeve stripped the nightgown from her shoulders and pressed hot towels to her bare skin.

"A little of this and you'll feel better," Maeve said. "This is what my mother did for me and my sisters when we had pain."

Katie uttered not a word during the next fifteen minutes. Clutching the edge of the table, she suffered Maeve's hot towels, her pummeling massage. She would not allow herself to cry. Tears came to her eyes but she blinked them back, making no sound.

Maeve, fingers flying, braided Katie's hair. She snatched a soapy washcloth from the counter and scrubbed her face and neck and ears. "That wasn't so terrible, was it?'' she asked when she had finished. She draped Katie in the quilt once more and sat her down. "Stay there while I fetch your clothes. We must hurry. The little ones will be up and wanting breakfast. I only have two hands."

"Yes, Mama."

"Don't pout, Katie. How many times have I told you not to pout?"

"I'm not."

"Aye, you are. Don't lie and make it worse." Maeve looked at her daughter. She sighed, shaking her head. "I know it was hard for you this morning, Katie. It was hard for me, too. Do you think I like sending you out? Do you think I'm glad? We do what we have to, like it or not."

"I understand."

"No. You're blaming me. Hugh's blaming me. But what choice do I have? Tell me that. If you lose your job, we'll be in the street, all of us."

"Ada wouldn't fire me."

"Ada's a good woman. Dear knows she wouldn't want to fire you. But she needs help in that big boardinghouse. She needs someone she can depend on. I had to fight to get you the job, Katie. If you're not up to it, she'll have to get someone else."

"I'm up to it. I worked real hard."

"Aye, and today you're bent over like an old lady. Do you think I'm glad about that? I know what pain is. But your job is all that's between us and the street. Do you see, Katie? Do you?"

"Yes, Mama."

"It was your bad luck to pick the wrong parents," Maeve said with a bitter smile. "You should have

75

picked rich people."

Katie did not take Maeve's comment seriously, though later, walking to Ada's, she would ponder the mystery of luck. It would occur to her that luck was but another word for money, and that money mattered above all.

"I'm fine," Katie said for the fourth time, turning Ada's objections aside. "I want to work." She moved closer to the warm hearth and stood as straight as she could. Her gaze was steady, earnest. "It's settled." She smiled.

"You're in no condition. I'd never forgive myself. You should be home, where Maeve can take care of you."

"I don't need taking care of. I *want* to work."

"Ah, you Gallaghers are a stubborn lot. There's more of Maeve in you than I thought." Ada was beginning to realize just how true that was. She had told Katie repeatedly to go home, but Katie had set her jaw and refused to leave; in similar circumstances, Maeve would have done the same thing. "I suppose there's no use arguing. Though I don't know what work you'll be able to do in your condition." Ada went to the stove, moving the kettle back and forth while she collected her thoughts. "All right," she said finally. "But we'll trade chores for today. I'll make the beds and do the cleaning and serving. You'll do the ironing. Can you iron?"

"I do it for Mama." Katie nodded.

"There's a mountain of ironing in the pantry.

You'll be at it all day. Still, it'll be easier than cleaning."

"I can do my own chores, Ada."

"You'll do as I say, miss. Let's not forget who's paying whom. Am I making myself clear?"

"Yes." Katie nodded again, coloring.

Ada's loud and explosive laugh filled the kitchen. "It's the first argument I ever won with a Gallagher," she said, her brown eyes twinkling. "I hope it's not the last. Sit down, Katie. Eat your breakfast and then I'll get the iron. It's no favor I'm doing you. Ironing's thankless work. I hate it and so will you."

But Katie did not. She enjoyed working in the warm, quiet kitchen, and she enjoyed the fresh scent that rose from the laundered sheets and pillowslips. She hummed as she worked, guiding the heavy iron across every wrinkle, every crease. She stopped working only to reheat the iron, and, while it was heating, she treated herself to a cup of mint tea.

The day passed pleasantly. If Katie's pain was no less, it was at least familiar, and she gave it little thought. She ate a lunch of corned beef hash and then returned to the ironing board. She was still there at four o'clock when Matt strode into the kitchen. "Hello," she said shyly, looking up at him through long, black lashes. "I was just thinking about you."

"You were? What were you thinking, little girl?"

Katie felt foolish. She turned away and, in her haste, knocked the iron to the floor. She tried to retrieve it, but she could not bend. Now she felt clumsy, impossibly awkward, and her face burned with embarrassment.

Matt saw Katie's distress. "I'll get it," he said, rushing forward. He replaced the iron on the board and smiled at her. "Aches and pains at your age?" he asked. "You must be older than you look."

"I am. I'm thirteen."

"Thirteen! That old!"

"You're teasing me."

Matt put his finger under Katie's chin and raised her face to him. She's a pretty little girl, he thought, startled by the perfect green of her eyes. "Do you mind teasing?"

"I'm getting used to it." Katie swallowed, for Matt was very near and his touch made her skin tingle. "I . . . I guess I don't mind. Ada says its all in fun."

"She should know." Matt walked off. He poured tea for himself and cut a slice of raisin pie. "Sit with me while I eat, Katie. I'm always eating alone. I'd like the company."

Katie hesitated. She glanced at the ironing board then glanced toward the pantry, where two huge baskets of laundry remained. "I have my work to do."

"Okay." Matt shrugged. He took a book from his bag and propped it open on the table. He ate quickly, stuffing great chunks of pie into his mouth, but his eyes never left the book. Katie watched intently, as if memorizing every line of his profile. "I thought you had work to do," he said, looking up suddenly.

"Maybe I could sit with you. Just for a minute."

"Okay." Matt closed his book. He sat back, clasping his hands behind his head and smiling. "What's the matter with your back? Is Ada working you too hard?"

"She wouldn't do that. She's too nice. It's all my own fault. It'll be better in no time. Mama said."

"You should be in school, little girl. I bet you were a good student. I bet you got good grades."

"That's in the past. My family's depending on me now."

"Depending on your wages, you mean. I know how that is." The light fled from Matt's blue eyes. His handsome mouth was unsmiling, almost harsh. "My family threw me out when I refused to work in the mines," he explained quietly. "I was twelve."

"Oh, that's awful. What did you do?"

"I hopped the first freight out of Wilkes-Barre and came to New York."

"Weren't you scared?"

"Yes, I was scared." In truth, twelve-year-old Matt McVey had been terrified, for his family had thrown him out with only the clothes on his back. He had had no money, no food, and no idea of what to do to make his way. His father, a big, red-faced Irishman, had expected him to return, cap in hand, and go meekly into the mines. But Matt had seen what the mines did to his brothers, stealing their youth and their hope and, in the end, their health, and he resolved to have no part of that mean life. He had gone to the rail yards and hidden himself in a freight car, sharing the fetid space with two hobos. "I got to the city okay," he said, remembering. "And then I wandered around for a week, trying to find Uncle Tim. He was a stranger to me, but he was blood. I hoped he would take me in. He did. He and Ada. They'd just opened the boardinghouse. They took

79

me in and made me feel like family—Don't look so sad." He laughed. "Everything worked out fine. I'm happy here. I was never happy at home. Not a day of my life."

"Don't you miss them? Your family?"

"My father's life was work and drink. My mother's life was work and crying. When they weren't doing those things, they were thrashing their kids. No, I don't miss them. I don't curse them anymore. Maybe they didn't know any better. But I don't miss them. Why would I?"

"They're your family."

"They had their chance. Besides, I'm too busy to look back. I have school and studying and work. That's enough for me now. It fits in with my plans."

"What plans?"

"To make my fortune. I'm going to be a rich man someday."

Katie always laughed when Hugh expressed similar ambitions, but she did not laugh at Matt. She believed him and in her mind's eye she could picture him years hence, dressed in fine broadcloth and immaculate white linen, a pearl stickpin nestling in the dark silk of his tie. She could picture him alighting from a sleek carriage and tipping his hat to admiring passersby. "How will you get rich?" she asked. "Men from the Tammany Hall are rich. And landlords. You wouldn't be a landlord, Matt? Mama says there's a special place in Hell for landlords."

"Are those the only ways you can think of, little girl? There are lots of ways, if a man's smart and willing to work. I'm going to be a lawyer. The law's a good starting place."

"A lawyer!"

"I'll start by being a lawyer. Then I'll have investments. That's how a man gets rich—investments. My children will be proud of the name McVey before I'm through. An Irish name and they'll be proud to have it."

"It's a grand name."

Matt shook his head. "That's not what I mean," he said. "You don't know how it is for the Irish. In some places there are still signs up: 'No Irish wanted.' You go for a job or a flat and that's what you see. Even when there aren't signs up, that's what some people feel in their hearts. To them the Irish are lower than dirt. . . . Well, I'm one Irishman who won't be turned away. It's a promise I made myself. I have plans. Not dreams, *plans*." Matt finished the last of the pie. He drained his cup and then carried his dishes to the sink. "I'm getting like Ada," he said, laughing abruptly. "Talk, talk, talk. Why didn't you stop me?"

"Oh, I wouldn't. I like listening to you." Katie went back to the ironing board, but her eyes followed Matt. She watched him sling his book bag over his shoulder. She watched him stride to the door, a young man radiating purpose and strength. "Maybe I'll see you tomorrow."

"Maybe. Don't work too hard, little girl."

"There's no getting around it."

Indeed, as the days wore on, there was no getting around it for Katie. She returned to her own chores, sweeping, dusting, washing piles of dishes reaching almost to the ceiling. She made beds and served at

81

table. She scrubbed bushels of vegetables, or so it seemed. With Ada, she washed windows and waxed floors and polished woodwork and hauled leaden trashcans out to the street.

"Aw, look at your hands," Hugh complained one day toward the end of the week. Katie looked, seeing calloused palms, red and swollen knuckles.

"I don't care," she replied truthfully. "I'm happy at Ada's and that's what counts." Her reply silenced Hugh, though it was a petulant silence, pleasing neither of them.

Saturday came, pale and cold, with snowflakes dancing in the wind. Children were out early, as were peddlers pushing their carts from street to street, calling the prices of their wares. The junkman parked his cart on Eighth Avenue and set up his scale, ready to haggle. Saturday was payday for most in Hell's Kitchen, and by afternoon the stores were thronged with women doing their weekly shopping. They took their time, surrendering precious dimes and quarters only after lengthy consideration. Meat was sniffed before it was purchased; vegetables were squeezed and tins shaken. The merchants, long accustomed to these Saturday rituals, said nothing.

Katie and Ada were amongst the shoppers. Baskets dangling from their arms, they left the boarding-house after lunch and walked to Paddy's, a vast pushcart market beneath the tracks of the Ninth Avenue Elevated. Its carts covered four wide blocks, offering foodstuffs and dry goods and any manner of notions. A few peddlers would bargain over prices, but most would not, for their prices were known to be the lowest in the neighborhood.

Ada did not try to bargain. She surveyed the contents of the carts, surveyed her shopping list, and made her selections, chattering merrily all the while. For ten cents she bought a package of needles, six spools of thread, and a darning egg. For five cents she bought a dozen bars of yellow laundry soap. She bought handkerchiefs and aprons and three pairs of sturdy cotton stockings.

Katie watched, amazed, as the parcels collected in her basket. Maeve, she knew, bought one thing at a time and argued over every penny. "It's so much," she said laughing when Ada put six large tins of tea into the basket. "We'll need a cart of our own!"

"I always spend too much money," Ada agreed. "I come here to save, and I do. But then I buy more than I planned, so I don't. Ah, there's Mr. Finelli. Mr. Finelli has the best soup greens in all New York. And he grates his horseradish fresh. Come meet him, Katie."

They spent hours at Paddy's, shopping, talking with the peddlers and with the neighbors they met along the way. "Just one more," Ada said, stopping at another cart. "This is the last." The cart contained bolts of cloth, and Ada examined each in turn. She bought two dress-lengths of navy blue wool and two of soft green cotton. "It's for you." She smiled. "You're growing out of your middies."

"For me?"

"That's right. You can't go around the boarding-house like a ragamuffin. I'll pay Maeve to do the sewing, and you'll have something nice to wear. Don't worry, it's not charity. It's for your job."

"But Mama says—"

"*I* say you're to have something nice to wear. No arguments, Katie. Do you want my boarders to think I'm keeping you in rags? Those hooligans would never let me hear the end of it."

"Thank you, Ada." There was more, much more, that Katie wished to say, but her throat was suddenly tight. She cradled the package in her arm and stared straight ahead, misty eyed at Ada's kind and generous act.

It was four o'clock when Katie arrived home. A blanket was spread on the floor near the stove, and there her little brothers sat, playing with wooden blocks. Maeve sat at the table, a mending basket open before her. "Mama," Katie cried, "Sean, Francis, I have wonderful surprises!"

Sean grinned and clapped his hands together. "Do you got peppermints?" he asked in his piping voice.

"Better than that! Chocolates!"

Sean and Francis scrambled to their feet and ran to Katie. "Chocolate," Francis squealed, tugging at her skirts. "Chocolate."

Katie plucked two bags from atop her packages. "First I want hugs. Great big hugs." She bent and drew her brothers close. She kissed their silky cheeks, their golden heads. "You're the best boys in the whole world." She laughed, giving them the chocolates. "Off with you now."

"Sure and it's a fine tizzy you're in, Katie Gallagher," Maeve said. "What are all those packages? And where did you get the sweets? If you've spent your wages on sweets—"

"I didn't, Mama. Ada sent them for the little ones.

84

We went shopping at Paddy's, and she bought lots of things. All kinds of things. I never saw the like.''

"What's in the packages?"

"Surprises, Mama." Katie tore the wrapping away and showed the cloth to her mother. "Ada said I'm to have something nice to wear at the boardinghouse. She bought all this for me.''

"Is she taking the money from your wages?" Maeve asked warily.

"No. But it's not charity. She said to tell you that. It's for my job. Please, Mama. I need something to wear. I'm growing out of my middies." Katie reached into her pocket and put a dollar on the table. "That's for you, to do the sewing. Will you, Mama? Is it all right?"

Maeve was quiet for a moment, considering. She looked at the cloth, then looked at Katie's flushed, eager face. "Aye, I suppose it's all right. If it's for your job.''

"Thank you, Mama." Katie beamed, flinging her arms about Maeve's neck. "And here are buttons and trimmings and two spools of thread. Do you think the dresses will be pretty, Mama? I never had a pretty dress, a new dress all my own.''

"Be thankful you've had food to eat," Maeve snapped. "Be thankful for the roof over your head. What good are pretty dresses if you're out in the street?''

"I didn't tell you the best surprise. It's about my wages. Ada's going to pay me an extra fifty cents every week. Because I help with her chores too. Isn't it grand?''

Surprise came into Maeve's dark blue eyes. She seemed almost to smile. "You're sure? Fifty cents more?"

"Yes, Mama." Katie reached into her pocket again. Happily, she put three dollar bills and two quarters into her mother's hand. "I couldn't believe it when Ada told me."

Maeve stared at the money. "Glory be!" she said, shaking her head in wonder. "It's good news you've given me, Katie. It's a good day for the Gallaghers. Keep it up and you'll make me proud."

"I'll try. I'll work real hard."

"Fetch my purse." Katie brought the purse and Maeve opened it, turning the contents—a dime, two nickels, and two pennies—onto the table. "I made up my mind to give you some money for your own," she said slowly. "That's only right. And you'll soon learn what money means if it's your own you're spending." Maeve hesitated. She ignored the pennies, trying to choose between a dime and a quarter. "You'll have twenty-five cents each week." She nodded. "It'll be yours to spend or save."

Katie's mouth fell open, for she had not expected anything from her wages. Her face was luminous as she took the quarter that was, to her, dearer than gold. "Thank you, Mama," she said, sniffling.

"I won't tell you what to do with your money. That's up to you. Just remember it's hard earned."

"Oh yes, I'll remember. I have to tell Meg. She's downstairs. She's going to Smitty's to buy licorice. I think I'll go with her. Can I, Mama? Please?"

"Aye, but don't be too long. I've shopping to do, and you'll have to mind the little ones."

"My own money! Wait 'till Meg hears." Katie kissed Maeve's cheek. She rushed across the room and kissed her brothers, then flew to the door. "Goodbye, Mama."

"Don't be in such a hurry," Maeve called, but the door had already closed. Her gaze moved to the table and Katie's wages. She looked thoughtfully at the money, money which should have pleased her, and she sighed. "Katie's growing up," she said to herself. "My Katie's growing up."

4

Winter did not go gently from the city. A brief February thaw was followed by more snow, by high winds, and cold, soaking rains that pounded rooftops and flooded the unswept gutters of Hell's Kitchen. The sun disappeared, sulking behind implacable black clouds. It was said that winter would never end, but in April the skies cleared at last and the air became sweet. Mittens and mufflers and woolen caps were packed away for another year. Windows were thrown open and clothes lines sprouted everywhere, as if welcoming the new season.

"Stickball, that's all the boys around here can think of," Meg Muldoon complained to Katie one bright day in June. It was Sunday, and the two girls were walking home from church, their arms linked, their long braids lifting in the breeze. "Do you know what Jimmy did?" she asked. "Jimmy cut off the handle of Ma's broom to use for a bat. There was a terrible row."

"I heard." Katie smiled. She glanced at her freckled, red-haired friend who, like all the

Muldoons, was quick to argue, quick to forgive. "It's still better than snowballs. I was getting awful tired of snowballs coming at my head. Boys are silly."

"Matt McVey is a boy."

"He's a man. It's different."

"Oh, just because he graduated from high school . . . ." Meg shrugged, unimpressed. "He won't really be a man 'til he's married." She giggled suddenly, poking Katie's ribs. "First comes love, then comes marriage, then comes Katie with a baby carriage."

"How you talk, Meg Muldoon! You should be ashamed of yourself!"

"You're sweet on him."

"I am not."

"You talk about him all the time. There's Cornelius O'Day coming and going at the boarding-house, but all you talk about is Matt. 'Matt's so handsome. Matt's so smart.'"

"Well, he is."

"You're sweet on him. Don't tell me you're not. Remember when all I could talk about was Jimmy Ryan? It's what Ma calls a crush."

"You're always having crushes. Even in third grade. Then it was Sean Clark. You wrote his name all over your desk and Teacher banged your knuckles."

"Yeah." Meg laughed. "He was the first boy I liked. He didn't like me. He punched me in the stomach."

"You punched him back."

"Sure I did." There was not a trace of regret in Meg's voice. Raised with five brothers, she had learned early to defend herself, sometimes with words, sometimes with fists. In the next moment she would be smiling, her anger forgotten. "He treated me nice after that."

Katie stopped, bending to reach a leaf lying in the street. "This is the color of the hair ribbon I bought. Isn't it a pretty green?"

"It matches your eyes. I wish I had green eyes. Green eyes and no freckles. Is your ma letting you put your hair up for Matt's party?"

"She said I was too young. I'll wear it loose. I'll wash it and rinse it in lemon and wear it loose, with just a ribbon."

"You're lucky to be going to a party. I wish I could go. Will Cornelius O'Day be there?"

Katie nodded, turning her face toward the warm sun. "He's back again. There are no shows on Sunday so he'll be there. All the boarders will be there, doing their acts in the parlor."

"Oh, I wish I could go. Promise you'll tell me all about it."

"I promise. I only hope Matt likes my present." Katie had taken money from her savings to buy a graduation present for Matt. She had browsed amongst the carts at Paddy's, finally selecting a box of six linen handkerchiefs. They were Irish linen, soft and pure white, and on them she had embroidered Matt's initials. Maeve had not been consulted. She had held her tongue, though she considered Katie's gesture extravagant, a sinful waste of money. "I was going to get him a book," Katie said now. "But I couldn't decide which one. Did I show you the handkerchiefs?"

"Three times. And you showed me the wrapping

paper and the bow. Don't worry, Katie. He'll like your present. He should. It cost dear."

"I know."

Katie and Meg crossed the avenue. Outside their tenement, young girls skipped rope and played jacks. A few stood apart, watching the boys play stickball. "There's Lizzie Pierce," Meg groaned. "She's getting so stuck up. She's had her nose in the air ever since her da was made foreman."

"I guess they'll be moving soon."

"Yeah . . . hello, Lizzie."

"Hello, Meg." Eleven-year-old Lizzie Pierce turned, tossing her black curls. "I can't talk to you, Katie. Da says you work for a bad lady. That makes you bad, too. You're a bad girl, and you're going to Hell when you die."

Katie raised one eyebrow, much as Ada would have. "Am I?" She smiled. "I didn't know it was all settled."

But if Katie was amused, Meg was not. She advanced on Lizzie, shaking her fist. "Take it back," she demanded. "Take it back and say you're sorry."

"I won't!"

"I'm warning you. This is your last chance."

"Go easy, Meg," Katie said, pulling her irate friend away. "It's not important. I've heard that talk before. Do you want to put on a show for the whole neighborhood?"

Meg looked over her shoulder to see a dozen girls crowding around. Some were merely curious, but others were eager, choosing sides even before the fight had begun. "Mind your business," she yelled. "Who asked you to stick your noses in? Get going, the lot of you!" One by one the girls turned and wandered back to their games. Meg watched them, then whirled on Lizzie Pierce. "And you! Don't you know it's a sin to carry tales? You're the bad girl. You're the one who's going to Hell—That's right, run," she shouted as the child darted off. "Have a care I don't catch you!"

"You didn't have to be so mean to her."

"She was mean to you."

"It's not important." Katie sighed, shaking her head, though she smiled fondly at Meg. "Lizzie's just a little girl."

"With a big mouth. I'm glad she's moving. All the Pierces are high hats now."

Katie leaned against the door and pushed it open. "Come on, Meg. Come inside before you get into trouble."

"Why do you let people talk about you that way?"

"There's no stopping gossip."

"Doesn't it hurt your feelings?"

"In the beginning; not any more. Ada told me gossip comes from small minds. It's the truth. You don't hear your mother gossiping, do you? She's better than that."

"When would she have time to gossip?" Meg laughed, her good humor restored. "We keep her awful busy. I don't think I want to have so many kids when I grow up."

"I do. I want a big family."

Together, Katie and Meg climbed the stairs of the tenement. They stopped outside the Wilson flat, listening as Gerry Wilson practiced a hymn for evening choir service, then went on their way.

"Gerry's going to be a priest. Did you hear?" Meg asked.

"Yes. And it's funny . . . I remember when Father Flynn was calling him a terror. That shows you how people can change, if they want to. If they try."

Meg looked sharply at Katie. "You're thinking about Hugh," she said. "He's not so bad."

"He got all D's on his report card. And then he sassed Mr. Maggio and almost lost his job. Imagine! Now that school's out there are a hundred boys chasing after every job, but Hugh almost threw his away. Mama had to apologize for him. She promised Mr. Maggio it wouldn't happen again. I hope it doesn't. Mama's counting on Hugh's wages to buy a new bed for the little ones. Their old bed's falling apart."

"Maybe Hugh wanted to spend his summer a different way."

"Oh, you're always taking his side. Even when you were young."

"I think he's nice."

"I think he's nice, too. It's just that sometimes he does . . . wrong things. He won't listen. It's like he's in his own world." They reached the top floor and Katie took her latchkey from her pocket. "Will you come in, Meg? You can help me get ready for the party."

"I have to help Ma with Sunday supper. All the cousins are coming from Brooklyn. It'll be an army sitting down to eat. But don't worry; you'll be the prettiest girl there. Everybody knows you're the prettiest girl in Hell's Kitchen. I get mad 'cause I'd like to be the prettiest, but it's you the boys gawk at."

"What are you talking about?" Katie asked, surprised. "What boys?"

"All of them. When they're not busy with their dumb stickball."

"You're making that up."

"If I was making it up, I'd make it up about myself." Meg passed her hand back and forth across the stair rail and grinned. "I bet Matt thinks you're pretty. I bet Matt—"

"Matt pays no attention to me. I'm only the hired girl."

"And who is he? The king of New York?"

"Not yet," Katie replied, her eyes twinkling merrily. "But give him time. He'll be king of the world."

"Your world, anyhow."

"I'm going inside now, Meg. See you next Sunday."

"See you . . . Have a good time."

Katie opened the door, blinking as she went from the dim hallway into the sun-splashed kitchen. A smile came to her face, for Sean was hopping about the room, playfully evading Francis's outstretched hands. She bent, gathering the boys to her, and then let them go. "It's such a fine day," she said, looking up at Maeve. "I thought you'd have the little ones outside."

"I was waiting for you. Sure and you took your time getting home from church. Jabbering with Meg again." Maeve left the table. She untied her apron and flung it onto the counter. "Aye, I heard all the dither in the hall. I'm not deaf, am I? What's this about Matt?"

"Nothing, Mama. It was nothing."

Maeve's dark blue eyes flashed. She pressed her lips tightly together, staring at Katie. "Lying's a sin, and it's twice a sin on Sunday. I want an answer. The truth this time."

"Really, Mama, it was nothing. Meg was having a joke. You know Meg."

"Aye, I know Meg. And I know you, too, Katie Gallagher. I think you're getting notions about Matt. I should have seen it before. All the money you spent on his present. All the time you spent doing fancy stitching."

"He's been nice to me. I just wanted—"

"Nice to you? How's he been nice to you?"

Maeve's hard, unwavering stare disconcerted Katie. There was truth, she knew, in what her mother said, but she dared not admit it. She shifted nervously from foot to foot and hid her hands behind her back, groping for words. "He . . . he talks to me, Mama. He tells me his plans."

"Plans! Another one with plans!" Maeve turned away. She took a deep breath and then turned again to Katie. "I won't have any more foolishness in this house," she said firmly. "I'm telling you plain. I won't have it. You're too young to be thinking about boys. Especially the McVey boy. You'll put him out of your mind and right now. Do you hear me, Katie?"

"Yes, Mama. But we're just friends. He's nice to me, that's all."

"He can stop being nice to you. And you can be friends with Meg and the other girls in the neighborhood. There's plenty of time for boys later on, when you're older and have some sense. At your age, *any* boy can turn your head. Sure and it's bound to be the wrong boy." Maeve paused. She sat down, absently twisting her wedding band. "The women in my family have been choosing wrong for generations." She sighed. "My grandda had a bit of money when my grandma married him. He gambled it away and his farm along with it. My mother married a drunkard. My sister, Peg, was only fourteen when she married. She was fifteen when her husband ran off. And I . . . I married a man who couldn't keep a job. Do you think I'll let you make our mistakes?"

"Matt's going to be a lawyer."

"A lawyer, is it? Then he'll have no need of you. He'll be out of Hell's Kitchen and doing his courting on the East Side. A lady maybe. Look at your hands, Katie. Are they the hands of a lady?" Maeve knew she had spoken cruelly. She thought, It's a sin and I'll pay for it. Aye, I'm paying for it already, seeing the pain in Katie's face. "The truth hurts sometimes," she said. "Dear knows I don't like hurting you. I don't like hurting any of my children. But sometimes it's the only way. You'll understand, when you have children of your own."

Katie's head was high, though tears hung on her long lashes and her mouth trembled. "I'll never tell my children they're not good enough," she replied.

Maeve glanced up, startled by Katie's voice, for quite suddenly it seemed the voice of a woman, an angry woman, and proud. "Well," she said slowly, "you'll be leading them to heartbreak if you don't. Children have to know their places in life. It's how I was raised."

"This isn't Ireland, Mama."

"Mind your tone," Maeve warned. "I've heard too much sass from you and that's the truth. Where are you going?"

"I have to wash my hair. The party's only two hours off."

"There'll be no party, Katie. I should have put my foot down from the beginning. I'm putting it down now. Parties, at your age!" Maeve rose. She smoothed her skirts and looked at her daughter. "You'll spend the day with your family, where you belong. We'll take the little ones to the park."

"Mama, *please*." Katie stood very still, as if rooted to the floor. Her eyes were wide and staring. "You said I could go. It was all settled."

"No."

"They're expecting me. Ada and . . . and everybody."

"And *Matt*? Do you think I'm a fool, Katie Gallagher?" Maeve walked to the sink. She wet a cloth, taking it first to Francis's face, then to Sean's. "Go fetch your sweaters," she said. "It'll be cool later on." They ran off without a word, and there was silence in the kitchen. The silence deepened, continuing until Maeve, sighing, turned and looked at Katie. "I know how it is to fancy a boy," she granted. "I'm not so old I can't remember. But one way or another boys always bring trouble, and we have trouble enough as it is. I can't keep you from seeing Matt on workdays. Parties though, that's different. There'll be no parties."

"We're only *friends*, Mama."

"Aye, that's the way it starts. You're too young, Katie. I won't have it. I'm putting an end to your

98

notions here and now."

"I don't understand. What's the harm in a party? Lots of people will be there. Ada and the boarders, and even some people from the neighborhood. I won't stay late, Mama. I promise. I'll just go for a little while and come right back. I'll be back in time to help with supper."

"Are you deaf? Have I been talking to the walls? I said you're not going and that's what I mean. Now that's all I want to hear about parties." Maeve watched Sean and Francis skip into the room. They were grinning, waving their sweaters around, and, as the sunlight struck their golden heads, she found herself wishing they could remain children forever. How long will it be, she wondered, lifting Francis to her arms, before we're arguing too? "Katie, hold Sean's hand walking down the stairs. Let's enjoy the day while we can."

"I'm staying here."

"What's that? Speak up if you've something to say."

"I'm staying here, Mama."

"A walk in the fresh air will do you good. There's no use to feeling sorry for yourself. You've had a disappointment, but you'll get over it soon enough. You're not a baby, are you?"

"*You* say I am. You're always saying I'm too young. Except when you want me to work. Then I'm a woman grown." Katie drew back, astonished by her daring, for never in her life had she spoken so impudently. She knew she should apologize, and at once, yet no apology came. She set her jaw and stared at Maeve. "It's not right," she declared.

Only with a great effort of will did Maeve manage to control her temper. She quelled the many angry impulses she felt, returning her daughter's cool, accusing stare. "And who are you to tell me what's right?" she asked. "Are you head of the house now? It's news to me if you are. I suppose it's the money that's giving you fancy notions. Do you think you can do as you please just because you're earning a bit of money?"

"No."

"It's good you don't. I'm the one who's kept this family together from the beginning. But do you care? Are you grateful? All I've done for you, working morning 'til night, worrying myself sick . . . and you throw it in my face. It's a fine example you're setting for the little ones."

"I'm sorry, Mama," Katie said, her rebellion ended. She sat down, too weary to argue any more. "I didn't mean to be fresh. I'm sorry."

Maeve looked at Katie's sagging shoulders, her wan face. She nodded. "Aye, you're sorry 'til the next time. Well, there'd best be no next time, if you know what's good for you. Think about that while we're out."

"Yes, Mama. I will."

"Be sure you do."

Katie said nothing as her mother and brothers left the flat. She heard the door close and she put her head in her hands, staring blindly into space. She sat that way for some time, held by a deep lethargy, a heaviness of body and of spirit. Laughter drifted up from the street below, and children's happy shouts, but she was not cheered. She rose and slammed the window shut, then went to her room.

Katie's other dress lay on the bed, neatly washed and ironed. Her new green satin hair ribbon lay on the bureau, next to Matt's present. She touched the shiny wrapping paper, the shiny silver bow, and her expression was transformed. She smiled, a grim smile edged with defiance. "I'm going to the party," she said. "I'm going and that's that!"

"I think this is the best day of my life." Ada beamed, glancing around the crowded parlor. Her big, square face was flushed, her eyes bright. Garnets twinkled at her ears, matching the color of her new dress, and scalloped combs adorned her upswept hair. "Well," she said, laughing, "maybe it's the second best day. The first was when I married Tim, rest his soul. But this is almost as good. To see my Matt a high school graduate, starting college soon. It's a dream come true." She raised her glass, taking a hearty sip of beer. "Look at him, Jack. Isn't he a handsome young fella?"

"Handsome young fellas make me feel old," Jack Snow answered with a grin.

"Ah, you'll never be old. Look at him, Jack. He wasn't keen about having a party, but he's enjoying himself now."

Matt stood toward the rear of the parlor, smiling and shaking hands as guests milled around, offering congratulations. At his side was the great stack of presents they had brought. He, who was surprised by any unearned kindness, was dumfounded by the kindness of these people he knew only in passing.

"My vaudevillians are family," Ada had often said. He had not disagreed but, privately, he had thought his aunt's comments wishful, even sentimental. Now he was forced to reconsider, for he felt waves of affection coming his way, and pride, as if in one of their own.

"Did I say congratulations?" Katie asked. She gazed up at Matt, her eyes huge and filled with light. "There's been such a crowd around you, I can't remember."

"You did, thanks. You're right about the crowd. I never expected so many people. It's hard to understand." Matt laughed suddenly, shrugging his broad shoulders. "I hardly know most of them."

"Oh, they're a grand bunch. Once they like you, they like you forever."

"That's a wise observation, little girl." Matt turned his head to Katie. He thought she looked lovely, her beribboned hair loose and cascading down her back, her green eyes shining. "I didn't recognize you when you came in," he said. "You look different without your pigtails. Older."

"It's a special occasion today."

"Yes, I guess it is. Are you having a good time?"

"A wonderful time. It's my first party . . . my first party that's not for children," she confessed shyly. "Ada was awful nice to invite me."

"Awfully. The word is awful*ly*."

"What?"

"The word, the way you used it, is awful*ly*." Matt was quiet, staring at Katie. He seemed to be deliberating, and Katie too was quiet, waiting. "Come with me," he said after a moment. "I have something for you." He took her arm, guiding her past clusters of guests and across the room. There, on a small table near the door, were two books covered in rough brown paper. He picked them up, giving them to Katie. "I sold my other school books," he explained, "but I held these aside. They're for you."

"For me?" Katie gasped. She looked from Matt to the books and then back to Matt again. "For *me*?"

"I know you had to leave school, but that doesn't mean you can't continue learning. Education is important, little girl. Take my word, it's the only thing that'll get you out of Hell's Kitchen." Matt smiled, nodding at the books. "They may be hard for you at first," he said. "Don't give up. You're smart and you'll get the idea in no time."

"Are they really for me? A present?"

"Haven't you ever had a present before?"

"Well, at Christmas we get oranges and winter . . ." Katie stopped, blushing, unable to speak the word "underwear" to Matt. "We get oranges and winter clothes," she said, staring down at the floor. "And when Papa was alive we got brand new pennies. But I've never had a present for no reason."

"There's a reason. You'll learn from those books, and that's a very good reason. One's a grammar text. The other is a book of essays by Emerson. He's my favorite."

"He'll be my favorite, too."

Matt laughed, delighted by Katie's sweet earnestness. "How do you know?" he asked, tilting her face up. "You haven't read the book yet."

"I'll read it tonight. I won't even go to sleep." Katie hugged the books to her chest. She smiled and so radiantly that she appeared to be wreathed with light. "Thank you, Matt," she said. "It's a present I'll always remember. Always, if I live to be a hundred."

Ada came up behind Katie. "What's this about living to be a hundred?" she asked. "Oh, I see you got the books. I'm glad. Though I don't know where you'll find time for reading."

"I'll find time."

"You probably will." Ada smiled, glancing at Matt. "Katie here doesn't look it, but she can be pretty determined. She can be as stubborn as Paddy's pig. Isn't that right, miss? Well, come along, both of you. There's going to be a nice show now. It's in your honor, Matt, so you get a front seat."

"Sit with me," he said to Ada. "You too, Katie. You helped move the furniture. It's only fair you have a good seat."

Katie, clutching her books, followed Matt and Ada to the sofa. Feeling privileged, feeling blessed, she sat down next to Matt and tried to be still. It was not easy, for her heart was pounding with excitement, with the sheer joy of this day. She thought, I was wrong to disobey Mama, but I'd do it again. I'd do anything to be here.

"Lemonade for you," Matt said, handing a glass to Katie. "Beer for me. Or is it the other way around? I was *joking*." He laughed when Ada frowned at him. "Lemonade for you, little girl."

"Thank you."

Phil Smith, Ada's one and only permanent boarder, took his place at the piano and the show began. There were jugglers and dancers and a family of tumblers who rolled crazily about the parlor, ending their performance with a giant human pyramid. Rayne and Snow did their comedy act, and then Cornelius O'Day came forward to close the show. The room was utterly silent as his beautiful voice soared, caressing the words of an old Irish ballad. "Oh," Katie murmured with a sigh, "he sings like the angels."

"Are you crying?" Matt asked. "You are." He pulled a handkerchief from the pocket of his new blue suit and dropped it in Katie's lap. "You'll need that," he whispered. "*Danny Boy* is next."

It was half an hour later when Ada slipped out of the parlor and went to answer the door. "Why, Maeve," she exclaimed, smiling, "I'm glad you decided to join us. I was hoping you would. Come in, come in. You missed the show, but there's lots of food left, and my special lemonade."

"Is Katie here?"

"Sure she is. Jack Snow's teaching her a dance step. Come in, Maeve. See for yourself."

Maeve picked up her skirts and entered the hall. Her face was grim, tired. She seemed not to notice the din of music and voices in the parlor beyond. "I've come to fetch Katie home," she said.

"Ah, let her have a good time. It's still early."

"Katie's here without my permission. Or didn't you know that, Ada? We argued over your fool party all the morning. I thought it was settled. I thought I could trust her. Now I see I was wrong."

Ada's smile faded. "I didn't know." She sighed. "I'm sorry. But what's done is done. You can't—"

"It's not done, not yet. It'll be done when I get her home."

"Come with me, Maeve. I want to talk to you."

"Talk, is it? I've no time for talk. Hugh's out somewhere and Mrs. Muldoon is minding the little ones. And her with a houseful of relatives too. I've no time for *talk*."

"It won't take long. Don't be so stubborn, Maeve. It won't cost you anything to listen to me. Come, we'll go into the kitchen. You could do with a glass of lemonade. You're pale as a ghost."

"Aye, thanks to my children. I haven't a minute's peace and that's the truth. Always something to worry about. Always! It used to be only Hugh giving me trouble; now it's Katie as well. Children are supposed to be a blessing. That's what the priests say. They wouldn't be so quick to say it if they had children of their own. Don't laugh, Ada. It's not funny."

"I know it's not. It's just the way you put things. Here, sit down." Ada smiled, pulling a chair out. She took a pitcher of lemonade from the ice box and filled two large glasses. "Drink up, Maeve. It's nice and cold."

"You won't get me to change my mind. Katie went against my word and she'll be punished."

"Why didn't you want her to come to the party?"

"I had my reasons."

"What reasons?"

"I don't have to explain to you, Ada."

"No, but I'm asking you to, as a friend."

Maeve glanced away, drumming her fingers on the table. "Well," she said quietly, "if you really want to know, it's Matt. Katie's getting notions about him."

"Is that all? For heaven's sake, Maeve, it's just a crush. I know she has a crush on Matt. I've known for months. It's natural for her to start thinking about boys. There's no harm in it. There's nothing to worry about. At her age—"

"She'll be fourteen, come September. My own sister was fourteen when she ran off to marry. And the boy she married! All charm and easy smiles, that was him. A year later he took his smiles and walked out the door. My sister never saw him again."

"Katie's not running off to marry anyone. Certainly not Matt. That's the last thing on his mind now."

"Oh, I can believe that."

Ada heard something sharp and disapproving in Maeve's voice. She leaned forward, frowning. "What do you mean? What do you mean you can believe that?"

"I was agreeing with you." Again, Maeve glanced away. She took a sip of lemonade and then another. "It's good," she said. "Not too tart."

"Don't change the subject. Tell me what you meant. You're not one to mince words, Maeve. Out with it, whatever it is."

"You'll be mad."

"When did that ever stop you?"

Maeve folded her hands atop the table. She was tired and upset but she forced herself to meet Ada's insistent gaze. "Aye, maybe it's best to have this in the open." She nodded. "Matt's the wrong boy for Katie to be thinking about. He doesn't go to church, and I don't like where he does go."

"Where?"

"He goes to visit Maisie Craig. There's been talk in the neighborhood, Ada. I don't listen to that kind of talk, but I saw the two of them together with my own eyes. I was walking home from the store with Mrs. Muldoon. We both saw them going into Maisie's building. It was Saturday. I've seen them a couple of times since."

"Just because Matt and Maisie are friends—"

"Maisie Craig doesn't have friends. She has . . . visitors."

Ada smiled slightly. She plucked a Sweet Caporal from a box on the table, twirling it between her fingers. "What makes you so sure?" she asked.

"It's no secret."

Ada could not quarrel with that statement, for everyone in Hell's Kitchen knew about Maisie Craig. A young and childless widow, she spent her days working at the Acme Laundry Company, her nights entertaining young men. She was a scandal and, worse, unrepentant. "Is it any of your business, Maeve?"

"Katie's my business. Sure and I mean nothing against Matt, but he's the wrong boy for her."

"He thinks she's a nice little girl, that's *all*."

"Little girls grow up. Katie's growing up. She's beginning to get a shape, and I'll wager Matt's noticed." Maeve paused, drawing a breath. "Dear knows I don't like talking so blunt, Ada. What choice do I have? Tell me that. There's no man in the family to look out for Katie. There's only me. I do the best I can, but it's not enough. It's never enough."

"You're too hard on yourself."

"No. I'm hard on my children."

Ada struck a match and lit her cigarette. She sat back, staring at Maeve through a haze of pale gray smoke. "Well," she said, "you're both mother and father to them, and that's a rocky road. Maybe I'd do things different, if I was in your place. Then again, maybe I wouldn't. Matt was almost grown when he came to live with us. We didn't have many problems."

"Boys aren't the problems girls are."

"Katie's no problem. You should be proud of her. She's like you, Maeve. She has your stubbornness."

"Aye, and Joe's dreamy ways. I won't have her ruining her life with dreams."

"Why in the world are you worrying about that now? She's so young. Her life's hardly begun."

"Now's the time to worry. She's too pretty for her own good, and too trusting. Any boy could turn her head. You can count on them trying. That's what I have to look out for."

"You're not talking about *any* boy. You're talking about Matt."

"He's on my mind. A boy who'll go with Maisie Craig . . ."

"I'm glad you have sense enough not to finish that sentence," Ada snapped. She crushed her cigarette in an ashtray and focused her brown eyes on Maeve. The two women had been friends for several years and in those years they had disagreed often, though never seriously. This, thought Ada, considering the insult to her nephew, was serious. Anger rose in her, and it was all she could do to keep from ordering Maeve out of her house. But if her anger was great, so was her pity. She looked at her friend's gaunt and intense face, her hollow eyes, and she sighed. "You owe Matt an apology," she said.

"I told you I meant nothing against Matt. It's Katie I'm thinking about; Katie I'm worrying about."

"Worry all you want, but not at Matt's expense. He's a man now, and he has a man's feelings. If he goes with Maisie, like you say, it's his business. He's not hurting anyone. Not you or Katie or anyone. That's the way I see it."

"Aye, that's your right."

"Maybe it's for the best. He's not ready to get married. I wouldn't want him marrying just for the bed. That's a reason, but not the only one."

"Ada, such talk on Sunday!"

"Is it less true on Sunday?"

"It's a sin."

"Well, we're all sinners, Maeve. There are no saints in Hell's Kitchen or anywhere else. People are people. We make mistakes. We even sin. That's why there's confession. If we were all saints, there'd be no need of confession."

"I won't listen to such talk, Ada McVey. I'm closing my ears."

"I don't hear you saying I'm wrong. Just that I'm wrong to talk about it. You're being a hypocrite."

Maeve passed her hand across her face. "Some things," she said, sighing loudly, "aren't supposed to be talked about."

"Do you ever wonder who makes those rules?"

"Ada, I'll agree with you that what Matt does is his business. Will you agree that Katie is my business? Will you do that? Katie's here six days a week. Sure and she can't help running into Matt. I just don't want them getting too friendly. I don't want them . . . socializing. And I'd be grateful if you'd have a word with him on the subject."

"That's putting it plain."

"It's nothing against him."

"Sure it is." Ada stood up. She walked off, her skirts rustling with each step she took. "But there's a chance," she said finally, "a *chance* I'd ask the same thing, if I was in your place. All right, Maeve. I'll have a word with him. I'm not happy about it, but I'll do it."

"And I'm thanking you. I'll rest easier now."

Ada returned to the table. She sat down heavily, shaking her head. "I've yet to win an argument with you, Maeve. You look like a strong wind could blow you away, but your will is made of iron."

"Aye, it has to be. A woman alone in the world, with four children to raise—what choice do I have?"

"Finish the lemonade. I'll get you a sandwich."

"I didn't come here to eat your food."

"No? What's wrong with my food? Don't insult me twice in one day, Maeve." Ada looked up suddenly and the smile went from her lips, for she saw Katie frozen in the doorway. "Come in, Katie. We're just having a nice talk."

But Katie was unable to move. She was very pale, her heart beating as if it would explode. She had known, of course, that she would have to face her mother sooner or later, but she had not expected it would happen here. She tried to speak; the words stuck in her throat.

"Don't stand there like a goose, Katie Gallagher,"

Maeve said. "Come in, or are you posing for a picture?"

"Hello, Mama . . . I'm sorry about—"

"Aye, I've heard that before. I wish I had a nickel for every time I heard it. We'd be rich. I could throw my washboard out and lay abed all the day, eating chocolates."

"Did you want something, Katie?" Ada asked.

"The sandwiches are running low."

"There are plenty more on the counter. Be a good girl and take them into the parlor."

"Say your good-byes while you're at it. We're going home, where we belong. Do you hear me, Katie?"

"Yes, Mama."

Katie picked up two large oval trays and hurried from the kitchen. Maeve watched her go then looked at Ada. "She's not sorry. Not a bit. It'll be a different story when I get her home. I'll make her sorry."

"Ah, Maeve, that's foolish. I don't like giving advice and you don't like taking it, but listen to me just this once. It's a confusing time for Katie. Her first job, her first money, her first crush on a boy. Try to understand, Maeve. Think back to when you were her age."

"When I was her age I'd been working in the fields for three years. Dear knows I had no time for crushes."

"All right, but that was the old country. This is America. It's not the same here."

"I'm tired of hearing about America," Maeve declared, rising. "Oh, it's a fine place if you have money in your pockets. But if you're poor, it's the

112

same as the old country—a mean life. Don't tell me otherwise." Maeve turned her head and looked at Katie. "You took your time coming back. What are those books?"

"I found them."

"Where?"

"In the trash can near Smitty's. I was passing there on my way to the party and I saw them." Katie had never lied to her mother, but this lie came easily, for she was determined to keep the books Matt had given her. "Sometimes there are good things in the trash," she added, compounding her lie, and her guilt.

"That's America for you," Maeve said to Ada. "Children digging in trash cans."

"*Some* children, anyway."

"Mama, are we going now?" Katie asked quickly.

"Aye, we're going."

Ada walked Maeve and Katie into the hall. Her face was unsmiling, and several times she glanced at Katie, who stared resolutely ahead. "Safe home," she said, opening the door.

"Aye, thank you, Ada. I'm sorry I had to take you away from your party. It couldn't be helped."

"I always enjoy seeing you. You're welcome any time."

"It's kind of you to say. Come along, Katie. The little ones are waiting." Maeve grabbed Katie's arm, pushing her into the sunny street. "There's no time for dawdling. We have to hurry."

"Yes, Mama."

"Don't 'yes, Mama' me, my girl."

"I don't know what you mean."

"You can stop acting so innocent, Katie Gal-

113

lagher. You went against my word. Sneaking out like a thief in the night! And after all I said! Are you proud of yourself? I'd be hanging my head in shame if I was you. But I suppose you're proud. Going against your mother is the *American* way of doing things."

"I'm sorry I disobeyed you."

"Don't waste your breath on apologies. You'll be punished for this, Katie. You'll learn what sorry is when I'm done. Sure and it's about time."

"I wish I could explain. I wish—"

"Be quiet! I'm tired of hearing foolishness. First your brother, and now you. If they cart me off to the crazy house, it'll be thanks to the both of you." Maeve's voice was loud, her hands slashing at the air, and people stared as she passed by. She noticed the stares, but they only seemed to fuel her anger. "Busybodies!" she cried. "I never saw such a neighborhood for busybodies!"

Katie nodded, embarrassed. "They'll be talking about us, Mama."

"Let them talk. Do you think I care?" Maeve slowed her furious pace, glaring at Katie. "It's your fault," she said. "You're the one making me chase after you. You're the one making me yell in the street. Was the party worth all that?"

Yes, thought Katie, all that and more. She felt guilty and she knew a punishment was yet to come, but still she could not deny the joy of this day with Matt. They had had three hours together, and those hours were worth everything she had risked. She did not expect her mother to understand such an attitude, for in truth she did not really understand it herself.

"Inside," Maeve ordered, pushing the door of the tenement open. "And be quick about it."

"Yes, Mama." Katie took the stairs two at a time. When she reached the top floor she stopped abruptly, her hand flying to her mouth. "Mama, look."

Maeve looked up to see a policeman standing outside their door. Hugh, his face bruised and swollen, his lip cut, stood a short distance away. She stared at her son, then grasped the rail, holding it tightly. "What happened?" she demanded. "Tell me what happened."

"I'm Officer Garrity, ma'am," the policeman said. He was young and clearly uncomfortable, for, in his two months on the force, he had had no experience with distraught mothers. "You'd be Mrs. Gallagher?"

"Aye. Tell me what happened."

"Well, ma'am, there was a fight in the alley behind the Emerald Isle Pub. It seems the lads was shooting dice, and there was a question raised about the stakes—"

"*Gambling?*"

"Aye, ma'am. It seems so. It was some lads from the Parlor Mob, and your lad was mixed in it. There's no charges being brought, ma'am, and your lad's had his lesson. But seeing as it was the Parlor Mob, I thought I'd best have a word with you."

"Hugh? You were with those devils?"

"What if I was?"

"Mind your tongue, lad," Officer Garrity warned. "In your shoes, I'd be apologizing."

Slowly, Maeve crossed the hall. "It's true?" she

115

asked. "You were with them? You were gambling?"

"Yeah, it's true."

Maeve was white with fury. She jumped at Hugh, shaking him violently. She slapped him and her blow spun him around. He staggered backward, crashing into the wall.

"Hugh!" Katie screamed. She ran to her brother, wrapping her arms protectively about his shoulders. "Are you all right, Hugh?"

"Yeah. Fine."

Doors had begun opening all along the hallway, curious neighbors wondering at the sudden commotion. Officer Garrity shooed everyone back into the flats and then led Maeve away. "Now, ma'am," he said quietly, "Your lad's had a fair beating already. I wouldn't be telling you what to do but—"

"Thank you, Officer Garrity. I'll see to my son in my own way."

"Aye, ma'am, as you say. It's sorry I am for the bad news I brought."

"I've had bad news before." Maeve turned, staring at Hugh and Katie. "Take your brother inside." She sighed. "Right now."

"Lean on me," Katie offered. Hugh shook his head, walking unaided toward the door. "Not so fast, Hugh. There's no rush."

"Ma'am, there's lots of young lads tagging after the Parlor Mob. It's exciting to them, if you see what I mean. And there's the thought of an easy dollar. But they soon learn their lesson. Your lad will, too. Well, I'll be saying goodbye to you, ma'am."

"Goodbye." Maeve went into the flat. She closed

the door, leaning against it for a moment. "Sure and it's been another fine day for the Gallaghers," she said, looking from Katie to Hugh. "One of my children is sneaking around; the other is out gambling and fighting. What did I do to deserve the both of you? Can you tell me that?" She reached her hand to the wide leather strap hanging on a hook. "You'll take your punishment now, Hugh Gallagher."

"Mama, don't," Katie pleaded. She stepped in front of Hugh, trying to shield him. *"Don't."*

"Aw, let her be. Let her get it over with. Who cares?"

"I care. Mama, please. He's *hurt."*

"And who's fault is that?" Is it my fault? Was I out gambling and fighting?"

"Hugh's sorry, Mama."

"In a pig's eye I am. I'll talk for myself. I'm not sorry, and I'm telling you to let her get it over with. She will anyhow. Don't go crawling to her. I'd sooner have the whipping."

"Are you satisfied, Katie? Do you hear him? He's asking for it."

Katie's head was aching. Pain throbbed at her temples, behind her eyes, and she wished she were anywhere but here, caught in the war between mother and son. She knew it was useless to argue, for this was an old war, and bitter. She could not bear to watch as Maeve took the strap to Hugh. Tears streaking her face, she picked up her books and ran from the kitchen.

It was a long time before Katie stopped crying.

When finally she did, she felt no better. She was sad and confused, a forlorn figure staring at the bleak walls of her room. She told herself to think of something happy, and in the same moment she thought of Matt. "Matt," she whispered with a sigh. "My wonderful Matt."

5

"I can't imagine where you get your ideas." Matt smiled. It was night, and he was sprawled on his bed, his tie loosened, his sleeves rolled to the elbow. Ada sat in a chair at the side of the bed, sipping tea. "I like Katie," he said. "I'm not interested in her though, not in any special way. She's a kid."

"Kids grow up. That's what Maeve's worried about. She doesn't want Katie growing up too fast. She may be right. We've had our differences, but she may be right about this. She's certainly right to try to protect her daughter."

"From me?"

"You know what I mean."

"Not really." Matt stretched. He sat up, brushing a lock of reddish hair from his brow. "It's kind of hard to avoid Katie. She's here all the time."

"That's just my point. If she was still in school, she'd be seeing girls and boys her own age. But she's here instead. You're the only boy she sees. She has a crush on you, Matt, in case you haven't noticed. A bad crush."

Many girls had had crushes on Matt McVey. He

119

had been the object of their admiring glances, their giggles, their blushes. He was vain enough to notice these attentions and to enjoy them, but he was not vain enough to take them seriously. "She'll get over it. They always do."

"*They*?" Ada laughed. "Are you such a prize?" Her comment was in jest, for she understood Matt's appeal. She had come across dozens of young men more truly handsome than her nephew but none who had more charm. It was as compelling as his smile, a smile which would have served him well on the stage. "Don't judge Katie by other girls," she cautioned. "Katie's sensitive, like Joe was. She's not one for trifling. . . . She's not a Maisie Craig."

"So you know about that."

"Try keeping a secret in Hell's Kitchen. It'd be a bigger miracle than the loaves and the fishes."

"Aren't you going to lecture me?" Matt asked, laughing.

"When did I ever lecture you? Besides, you're a man now. What you do is your business. Except when it comes to Katie. She's working for me and I feel responsible. I know you wouldn't hurt her, not on purpose. I'm just asking you to be careful. Mind what you say to her. Don't be too friendly."

"Do you want me to ignore her, Ada? I won't do that."

"Just don't be too friendly."

"*Too* friendly? What does that mean?" Matt rose. He walked to the window, parting the curtains and staring outside. "I don't understand why we're talking about this," he said. "She's a *kid*."

"There are three years between you and Katie.

120

There were five years between me and Tim, rest his soul. I wasn't even sixteen when I married him."

"It'll be a long time yet before *I* marry. I have things to do first. I have college, then law school. I can't do all that with a wife and family to look after."

Ada frowned, for Matt seemed restless, and his voice was uncharacteristically harsh. "Why are you getting upset? What is it?"

"I'm not upset."

"Of course you are."

"This conversation is upsetting."

"Why?"

"I don't know." Matt turned around. He perched on the sill, looking at Ada. "Maybe I feel as if I'm being accused of something. Maybe I drank too much beer. I don't know."

"That's a poor answer."

"It's the only one I have."

Ada put her cup down. She clasped her hands on her knee and leaned forward. "I'm not accusing you of anything, Matt," she said slowly. "But I don't like what's going on. Katie came to your party even after Maeve told her not to. Then she lied about the books you gave her. She told Maeve she found them in the trash. Right or wrong, Maeve's her mother. When Katie starts lying to her mother, I take it serious."

"I can't help what Katie does."

"No, you can't. And you don't have to bite my head off. You're awful touchy all of a sudden."

"I'm sorry, Ada." Matt was indeed sorry. He was ashamed too, for Ada had shown him more kindness, more love, than his own parents. She had given him this room and furnished it to his tastes. She had encouraged him in his plans, cooked his favorite meals, and nursed him through influenza, remaining day and night at is bedside. He had worked at one job or another ever since arriving in New York, but she had refused to take a penny of his wages. "Save it for college," she had said, thus beginning his college fund.

"I don't know what's the matter with me. It must be the beer."

"You've had beer before."

Matt left the window and walked to his desk. It was piled high with the presents he had received, and atop the pile was the box of handkerchiefs from Katie. He touched his finger to the initials she had so carefully embroidered, shaking his head. "Did you see what Katie gave me?" he asked.

"She's a sweet girl."

"She is. She really is."

"Matt, were you telling me the truth? Do you have any . . . feelings for Katie?"

"I like her, that's all." But was it all, he wondered. He knew very well that Katie found excuses to be in the kitchen each day when he returned from school, and that he looked forward to her being there. He knew he enjoyed talking to her, watching her pretty face tilted upward in perfect trust. And he knew he thought about her often, sometimes for no reason. "Okay," he conceded. "I'm fond of her."

"I see."

"Please don't worry. Katie's still a kid, and I still have more important things on my mind. That's the truth. We're friends. We'll stay friends. But maybe it's best if we spend less time together. I wouldn't want her to get the wrong idea."

"You always had good sense. I'm glad you're using it now."

Matt went to Ada, kissing her plump cheek. "You look relieved." He laughed.

"Sure I am. The time to stop trouble is before it starts. There could have been a lot of trouble in this. I hate to think how much. I'm relieved my nephew is a sensible fella."

"If that's a compliment, thank you."

Ada smiled back at Matt. "You make me proud," she said. "It was a happy day when you came to live here. We had our doubts, me and Tim, rest his soul. We didn't know anything about kids. But it worked out fine. I'd be a lonely old lady without you."

"A lonely old lady? There's no chance of that. Everybody loves you, Ada . . . I love you." Matt had spoken those words only twice in his life, first to his uncle Tim and now to Ada. Sentiment was difficult for Matt to express, and the words did not come easily but they were heartfelt. "You and Tim saved my life."

"Ah, you'll have me blubbering in a minute." Ada stood up. She brushed at her eyes and then started toward the door. "Would you like a cup of cocoa?" she asked. "It's no trouble to fix."

"I've had enough food and drink to see me through summer. You really outdid yourself today. I bet it cost a pretty penny."

"Well, how many times do you graduate from high school? It's worth celebrating, Matt. Nobody on my side of the family ever got past fifth grade. Nobody on your side either, the way I heard it. School was something for rich people. But thank God the world's changing. It's certainly changing for the McVeys. Four years from now we'll have our first college graduate." Ada paused, smiling. "Maybe you'll be President one day."

"An Irishman? The world hates the Irish almost as much as it hates the Jews and the Negroes."

"That's changing too."

"Is it?" Matt's face darkened. His handsome mouth tensed. "The day I left home," he said, "I walked all around the town. There was a new restaurant opening up, and it had a sign in the window: No Irish or Dogs. I won't be President, Ada. I'm two generations from the bogs and one from the mines. But I'll have sons. I'll have grandsons. And I'll have the money to make them whatever they want to be. *No* door will be closed to them, not even the door of the White House."

"You were an angry little boy when you came to live with us," Ada replied quietly. "For good reason, I always thought. Now you're a man, and anger can ruin a man's life. I've seen it happen."

"Anger can also spur a man on. Anger kept me out of the mines."

"It was more than that. You wanted something better. You had dreams. A lot of men have dreams, but you're making them come true. I don't notice any doors closed to you now. That's in the past. If you're smart, and you are, you'll keep it in the past. You have to look ahead. In the old country, people are forever looking back. Here it's different. You're going to college, and that's proof of how it's different. Don't you see?"

"Yes, I see." Matt's blue eyes twinkled, for he was amused. He crossed his arms over his chest and smiled at Ada. "You should be the lawyer," he said. "You're very convincing."

"I hope I am. These years are so important. If you start thinking wrong or acting wrong, you'll regret it later. Too many people have nothing but regret to show for their lives. I don't want that happening to you . . . and that's why I talked to you about Katie. It wasn't just for her sake. It was for yours, as well. You're like a son to me, Matt."

"I know. I'll always be grateful you feel that way."

"Well,"—Ada nodded—"I've talked long enough. I've made all my speeches and I'll say good night."

"Promise me you won't worry any more."

Ada turned in the doorway, looking hard at Matt. "Is there any reason to worry?" she asked.

"No. You have my word."

Matt had little trouble keeping his word during the days and weeks that followed. Each morning he left the boardinghouse before seven, riding the subway to his summer job at a Brooklyn lumber yard. He worked outside in the hot sun, cutting and stacking wood, loading wagons, and it was after six when he returned to the boardinghouse each night. He took most of his meals in his room, reading while he ate. He took long walks. There were evenings with Maisie Craig and evenings drinking beer with his friend, Ben Rossi. In such ways did the summer pass.

September came and Matt entered City College. It was a new world, often confusing, but he was seventeen and filled with the confidence of youth. He dared to question his professors, to challenge them, for challenge was what he sought. If his spirited verbal jousts were not appreciated by everyone, they were greatly appreciated by his classmates, who began to see him as their leader.

Matt was seldom at the boardinghouse now. He had classes all day, and at night he went to his job at Porter's Stables. He did his simple chores—mucking out stalls, cleaning carriages, feeding and watering the horses—and then he studied. A bale of hay was his desk, and on it he arranged his books and writing tablets. He studied far into the night, managing only a few hours of sleep before walking back to the boardinghouse to bathe and change his clothes.

"You'll ruin your health," Ada warned time and time again, alarmed by her nephew's rigorous schedule. Her warnings were in vain, for Matt would not be deterred. "School *and* work," he always replied. "That's my plan, and I'm sticking to it. I'm happy just the way things are."

Indeed Matt had every reason to be happy. His college career had begun, and his savings were growing, achievements that had once seemed impossible. He had friends and admirers and the grudging respect of his professors. It was, by any standard, a full life, yet he felt something lacking. There was an emptiness within him, a sadness he was reluctant to admit. He kept himself busy, too busy to think, but still his sadness deepened. It's Katie, he admitted to himself finally. Damn it all, I miss her.

It was the last day of September, and Matt strode purposefully into the kitchen, a small, oblong box in

126

his hand. "Happy birthday, little girl," he said, tossing the box on the table.

Katie jumped. She had been peeling apples, and now she dropped the knife. She looked at the box, then looked at Matt. "How did you know it was my birthday?" she asked. "I didn't tell anyone."

"There are no secrets in Hell's Kitchen. There's a law against secrets. Go ahead, open the box. I've been in and out of stores all week, trying to find the right thing. I wanted it to be right. I wanted you to be . . . pleased."

Katie wiped her hands on her apron and picked up the box. After a moment, she put it down. "I don't understand, Matt. Why are you giving me a present?"

"It's your birthday, isn't it?"

"But I thought you were mad at me."

"Katie, I could never be mad at you. Never."

"Then I don't understand." Katie turned away, gazing into space. She was remembering the summer, a terrible summer, for she had seen almost nothing of Matt. He had come and gone without a word to her, without a smile. He had seemed distant and on edge, not himself at all. "I thought I did something to make you mad," she said softly. "The way you were acting, I was sure of it."

"I'm sorry if I hurt your feelings."

"You're not mad at me?"

"No. Maybe I'm mad at myself but not you. Never you."

A vast smile spread across Katie's face. "Oh, I'm so glad." She sighed, relieved. "So glad. You don't know how worried I was . . . I even wrote you a note. But then I threw it in the fire."

"Why?"

"I was afraid you'd think it was silly."

"Silly? I doubt that." Matt reached out, lightly touching Katie's cheek. Open your present now. I'm anxious to know if you like it."

Katie untied the ribbon. She lifted the cover of the box and looked inside. Resting on a bed of velvet were two ivory hair clips, polished and elegantly carved in a pattern of roses. "They're beautiful!" she cried. "I've never had anything so beautiful!"

"Do you really like them?"

"I love them. I *love* them, Matt. Thank you." Katie leaped up, taking the hair clips to the sunny window. "Look at them in the light," she said excitedly. "They're beautiful."

"Let's see how they look in your hair." Matt joined Katie at the window, turning her around. "Yes." He smiled. "They're just right for you. Where did you get such pretty hair, little girl? It's spun gold."

"Papa had the same color hair," Katie replied, for she was not used to compliments and could think of nothing else to say. "It's his hair."

Matt laughed. "Well, there's no vanity in you," he said, laughing again. "No coyness, either. . . . Come sit down. I need to talk to you."

Katie returned to the big oak table. She sank into a chair, glancing warily at Matt. "What's wrong? You have a queer look."

"I want to explain a few things. It's best to come straight to the point, so that's what I'll do. Your mother doesn't want us to . . . be friends. She had a talk with Ada, and Ada had a talk with me. She was concerned. I suppose I was too, in a way."

"Why shouldn't we be friends? I don't see the harm."

Matt sat back, considering his answer. There were several answers, he knew, but none that would satisfy everyone. "It depends on what you mean by harm," he said finally. "You know my plans, Katie. I've told you about them often enough. They're plans I made long ago, and I intend to stick to them. I can't have any . . . distractions. Not now. School and work come first."

"I understand."

"Do you? I'm not sure." Matt sighed, staring into Katie's wide and lovely eyes. "I want us to be friends, but I don't want you to get any . . . wrong ideas. I'm older than you. My life is very different from yours. And I have my plans to think about. We can be friends. But if you make more of it than that, you'll be hurt. I couldn't stand to hurt you."

"You're not that much older."

Matt was taken aback by the directness of Katie's statement, for he had expected blushes and shy, girlish evasions. "Is that all you have to say?" he asked.

"It's true." Katie smiled slightly, her gaze meeting Matt's. "But I'll be happy to be your friend. If it can be the way it was, I'll be happy. I won't make more of it. I know you're going up in the world, and I'm just . . . I'm just me."

Matt felt a lump in his throat. He was deeply touched, and he had to look away. "Don't underestimate yourself, little girl," he said when he found his voice. "You're . . . wonderful."

"Who's wonderful?" Ada walked into the kitchen.

129

She strode to the table and put her hand on Matt's shoulder. "Who's wonderful?"

"Katie is. It's her birthday today," Matt added hastily.

"I know. I'm the one who told you, remember? What are you doing here, Matt? Shouldn't you be getting ready for work?"

"There's time. I stopped to give Katie a present."

Katie slipped the clips from her long hair. "Look, Ada." She smiled. "Aren't they grand?"

"They certainly are. My nephew here has good taste. It runs in the family. Tim, rest his soul, was the same. Quick to give presents too . . . Katie, I'll need another sack of apples from the cellar. Would you be a good girl and fetch it?"

"Right away."

"And there should be a sack of cinnamon sticks on one of the shelves. See if you can find it."

"Yes, I will."

Katie hurried out of the kitchen. Matt sat back in his chair, smiling at Ada. "Well, she's gone," he said. "Let's have it. I'm ready."

"This is no game, Matt. What are you doing giving Katie such an expensive present? Have you lost your senses?"

"I don't mind spending money if—"

"Ah, it's not the money I care about. It's the ideas you're putting in her head. The very ideas we talked about months ago. You said I had your word. I could always trust your word before, but now I'm wondering. What's got into you, Matt? If you were *trying* to lead her on, you couldn't do a better job of it."

"I'm sorry."

"Sorry's not enough." A frown creased Ada's brow. She sat down, leaning toward Matt. "It was a damn fool thing to do," she said, her voice unusually stern. "We both know that. I want to know *why* you did it. What in the world were you thinking of?"

"Katie."

"Katie! Not three months ago you told me you had no special feelings for her. I remember your exact words."

"I don't have any special feelings, not the way you mean."

"You'd best tell me the way *you* mean. That's what's important now. You keep a tight purse, Matt. When you open it that far, I know something's going on. I want to know what it is."

"Now it comes out." Matt laughed, shaking his finger at Ada. "You think I'm cheap."

"You work hard for your money, and you don't throw it away. That's being smart. But what you did today isn't smart. Never mind what I think. What's Katie to think? An expensive present like that? She's bound to get ideas."

"No, Ada. We had a talk and she understands."

"Understands? Didn't you see the starry look in her eyes? Didn't you see her floating ten feet off the ground?"

Matt recounted his conversation with Katie. Ada listened, though she was not impressed. "It sounds fine," she said when he had finished. "It sounds nice and sensible. The trouble is Katie's thinking with her heart, not her head. If you ask me, so are you."

"What?"

"You heard me."

"Yes, I did. I thought you knew me better than that."

"Ah, I know you're not one for moonlight and roses. I know you're not one for fancy sentiments. But you *do* have a heart, Matt. And if you ask me, Katie's in it."

"I just wanted her to have something for her birthday. The poor kid probably won't get anything at all from that mother of hers."

"She's getting a new coat from me."

"Thank God! Her old coat's a disgrace!"

"You're trying to change the subject."

"I'm trying to explain. I wanted Katie to have something more. Something extravagant and . . . frivolous."

"Why?"

"Oh, Ada, her life is so *hard.*"

"I can't argue with that. But you're lying to yourself if you think that's all there is to it."

"I never lie to myself."

"You're human, aren't you? We all lie to ourselves from time to time, Matt. There are things we don't want to admit and so we make up excuses, stories. That's what you're doing now. If I was you, I'd take a close look at my feelings. I'd do it soon."

"Because I bought a birthday present for Katie?"

"It's her fourteenth birthday. A box of candy would have been fine. Or a pair of warm gloves. But those hair clips are a present a man gives a woman. And you better hope Maeve doesn't see them. If she does, she'll come after you with a club. I can't say I'd blame her."

"You mean I'm on my own?" Matt laughed.

"Go ahead and joke. It won't be funny when somebody gets hurt. Katie or you; maybe both. It's bound to happen. The signs are clear."

"What signs? Ada, you're worrying over nothing."

"I'll be the judge of my worrying. I've lived a lot longer than you, and I know what to take serious. I know from experience." Ada was silent for a moment, smiling slightly. She held her hand out to Matt. "Will you at least think about what I said? Will you do that much?"

Matt left his chair. He bent and kissed the top of Ada's head. "Of course I will." He smiled, wrapping his arms about her shoulders. "Anything to ease your mind. I'm a lucky fellow to have you, Mrs. McVey. I won't go far wrong with you around."

"I'd like to believe that. But I know how young people are. . . . Look at Adam and Eve. They were the first young people. Look what happened to them. Thousands of years later it's still the same. Young people do as they please."

"Didn't you?"

"Well, that was different."

"Oh."

"Don't be fresh," Ada said with a chuckle. She looked up at Matt, fondness lighting her eyes. "There's such a thing as winning the battle but losing the war. Just remember I told you. Now go on. You have work and I have pies to bake."

"Save me some."

"I always do."

Ada watched Matt stride away. Alone in her large and homey kitchen, she thought about Tim. She missed him every moment of her life, though never

133

more than at this moment, for she needed him to soothe her worries, to assure her, as he often had, that everything would be all right. "Help me, Tim," she whispered. "Bad days are coming. I'm sure of it."

"Are you talking to me?" Katie asked, glancing around. She shifted a ten pound sack of apples from one arm to the other and walked to the table. "Ada?"

"What?" Ada turned. "Ah, you're back. I guess you caught me talking to myself. I must be getting old." She rose, taking the sack from Katie. "We'll be eating pie all week." She smiled.

"I couldn't find the cinnamon sticks."

"It doesn't matter. Hurry with the peeling, Katie. It's late."

"Did Matt leave already?"

"It's a work day, even if it is your birthday."

"I wasn't too excited about my birthday before, but now I'm in the clouds. I'm so happy, Ada. Did you hear what Matt said? He said I was wonderful."

"Yes, I heard."

"Wonderful," Katie repeated, her face aglow. "Imagine!" She sat at the table, picked up the paring knife, and tried to concentrate on work. The more she tried to concentrate, the more she thought of Matt. She saw his smile and her heart fluttered wildly. Several times the knife fell from her trembling fingers. "I'm so clumsy today." She laughed.

"Mind you don't cut yourself."

"I wouldn't care if I did." Katie shook her head, her long, golden hair rippling in waves over her shoulders. "It's funny how things change," she said to Ada. "All summer I thought Matt was mad at me. It was an awful feeling. I couldn't sleep at night, wondering what I'd done to make him mad. I must have asked you a thousand questions, but still I couldn't figure it out."

"Yes. I remember." Ada was not likely to forget. Katie had been hurt and confused. She had seemed dazed, doing some of her chores twice because she had no memory of doing them the first time. That had been in July. Weeks passed and she had become less preoccupied, though infinitely sadder, as if resigning herself to yet another bitter disappointment. "I told you again and again he wasn't mad," Ada said. "He was busy. He'll *always* be busy."

"No, it was Mama. I see that now. Mama doesn't want me to have any friends."

"Katie!"

"I don't mean anything bad. That's just the way Mama is." Katie took the clips from her hair. Gently, she brushed her fingers across the polished and carved ivory. "I'm going to keep these here." She nodded toward the clips. "If Mama doesn't know about them, she won't be upset. It's for the best."

"Is it?" Ada looked sharply at Katie. She realized that the shy, frightened young girl who had come to the boardinghouse eight months ago was gone, replaced by a determined young woman. "Do what you want." She sighed. "You will no matter what I say. But don't tell me about it. I won't help you lie to Maeve. Right or wrong, she's your mother."

"I'm not lying."

"Ah, Katie, what else do you call it? Keeping the truth from her is the same as lying."

"There'd be trouble if Mama knew."

"Sure there'd be trouble. That's no excuse."

"Ada, you don't understand. I'm fourteen today, old enough to work at the Acme laundry. If Mama knew about Matt's present, she'd make me leave here and work at the Acme. She would, Ada." Katie lowered her eyes and stared at the table, pressing her hands together. "I don't want to leave here. Not ever. It's home."

"You have a home with Maeve and your brothers."

"It's terrible there. Mama and Hugh are always at each other now, going on and on and on. I *hate* it. Sometimes I feel like screaming. It's even starting to bother the little ones. They're having nightmares."

"I'm sorry."

"Oh, I shouldn't be putting my worries on you. You have your own. It's just that I have nobody to talk to. There's my friend Meg, but I only see her for a few minutes after Sunday Mass. Mama doesn't let me go anywhere else by myself. And if I'm late getting back, there's an argument. The worst is that she's always *watching* me. I can be reading or washing dishes or playing with the little ones, and she'll be watching me out of the corner of her eye."

"It's not easy raising a daughter, you're getting older—"

"Older? If it were up to Mama, I'd still be in braids and middy blouses. I *am* older, but Mama treats me like a baby."

"It can't be as bad as all that."

"It is."

"Don't be in such a rush to grow up, Katie."

"But I *am* growing up. Even Matt—"

"Matt! I knew we'd come back to him sooner or later. That's what we're really talking about here,

136

you and Matt." Ada closed the oven door. She walked to the table and sat down, staring intently at Katie. "Maeve doesn't want you having anything to do with Matt. She made herself very clear. It's wrong for you to go against her. I blame Matt for giving you the present, but I blame you for taking it . . . It's not just the present, Katie. It's the lies attached to it. I won't help you lie. You can talk 'til you're blue in the face and I won't help."

"There's no harm in our being friends."

"There's plenty of harm. He's a man; you're still a girl. Fourteen may seem grown up, but it isn't. You have nothing in common with Matt. And what kind of friend could he be to you anyway? With school and work, he hasn't a minute to call his own. Forget about him. The neighborhood is full of nice boys your age. You can have your pick, pretty as you are."

Katie looked away. Her gaze settled on the hair clips and she sighed. "I thought you'd understand," she said quietly.

"I understand you're being silly and stubborn. So is Matt. You're both putting me in a bad position. This is my house, Katie. I'm responsible for what goes on under my roof. Now I'm asking you to stop all this foolishness and be sensible. Matt's not for you." Ada studied Katie's profile, the hard set of her jaw. She shrugged. "Well, I've said all I'm going to say on the subject. You know how Maeve feels. You know how I feel. The rest is up to you."

"And Matt."

"Matt likes to flirt. He'd deny it, but it's the truth. Any girl who takes him serious is in for grief. Don't smile. I know what I'm talking about. I know men.

137

Some are the serious type and some aren't. It's not always easy to tell the difference. Especially when you're fourteen." Ada rose. She left the kitchen, returning moments later with a large box. "Happy birthday, Katie," she said.

"Now make a wish and blow out the candles. You get one wish; don't waste it." Maeve had surprised Katie with a birthday cake. She had baked it herself, frosting it with whipped chocolate and cream, and then, impulsively, she had hurried to the store for two cents worth of little pink candles. She had no regrets. It was a celebration, a way of bringing peace to her troubled household, if only for this night. "Go on," she urged, "make a wish."

"I did, Mama." Katie took a great breath and blew all the candles out. "Oh, I hope my wish comes true."

"What did you wish?" Hugh asked.

"It's a secret."

"Aye, that's right," Maeve agreed. "Telling the wish puts a jinx on it. Katie, you cut the cake. Don't be afraid to cut it thick. We're not scrimping tonight. We'll eat our fill for once."

Katie and Hugh exchanged puzzled glances. "Hey, Ma"—Hugh grinned—"did you finally find gold in the streets? Are we rich?"

"Rich! I've a dollar and four pennies in my purse. A dollar and four pennies to see us through the rest of the week. But I baked the cake special, and we might as well eat it before it goes stale."

"I'll keep some aside for the little ones, Mama."

"Aye, come morning they'll have a treat. It's good

138

to have a treat now and then. Something to look forward to."

Again, Katie and Hugh exchanged glances, for neither of them knew quite what to make of their mother's amiable manner. Hugh was suspicious, but Katie was plainly relieved to have one evening without arguments, without threats and grim mutterings. She served thick slices of cake to her mother and brother, and in the pale, shadowy gaslight, her face was radiant.

"Well," Maeve said when the last bit of cake was gone, "did you enjoy it? I hope you did, for what it cost to make."

"Oh yes, Mama. Thank you. It was delicious. Wasn't it delicious, Hugh?"

"Yeah, it was good. Now it's time for presents." Hugh reached under the table, producing an oddly shaped package wrapped in tissue paper. "Happy birthday, Katie." He winked.

Katie tore the paper away. "Oh, just what I wanted! Look, Mama," she said breathlessly. "Rose water and glycerine for my hands. And there's a bar of scented soap, too."

"Aye, I saw."

"Violets." Katie smiled, sniffing the soap. "It's like a whole field of violets. Thank you, Hugh. They're wonderful presents." She leaned over to kiss him, but he turned his head, making a face. "Don't act so tough"—she laughed—"not after giving me such wonderful presents as these."

"Aw, they're girl stuff. You're a girl, aren't you?"

"She is," Maeve said, rising. "And you're a boy who has school in the morning. Off to bed now.

139

It's late."

"I'm not tired."

"You'll be tired in the morning. Off to bed now, Hugh. Don't spoil Katie's birthday with your sass."

Hugh looked at his mother. He seemed about to reply then changed his mind. "G'night, Katie."

"Sleep well."

"Yeah."

Hugh sauntered off. Maeve, smiling faintly, carried the dishes to the sink. She removed a package from the cupboard and gave it to Katie. "It's nothing fancy," she said, glancing toward the door where Katie's new coat hung. She saw the richness of the dark green wool and she sighed, shaking her head. "It's nothing so fancy as what Ada gave you. But I don't have a boardinghouse earning money for me. I'm just a washerwoman and it's the best I could do . . . I hope you like it."

"I know I will, Mama." Katie opened the package, holding up a flower-sprigged challis blouse. The bodice was delicately tucked, threaded with exquisite white lace. There were tiny white buttons at the cuffs and at the soft, high collar. "Mama, it's beautiful. I . . . I don't know what to say." Tears sprang to Katie's eyes as she thought of all the work that had gone into the blouse. She thought of her mother standing at a washboard all day and then working late into the night with needle and thread. Guilt assailed her. She remembered her lies, her complaints, her harsh judgments, and her face crumpled. "Oh, Mama, I'm sorry," she sobbed, tears streaming down her cheeks.

"Sorry? And what are you sorry about?"

"All the trouble I give you . . . you're so good to me and I . . . I just give you trouble. I don't mean to."

"Well, that's in the past now."

But it's not in the past, thought Katie miserably. It's today and tomorrow and the tomorrows after that. I can't do what you want. I can't forget about Matt. God help me, I can't. "Mama . . . I love you."

"Sure and I'm glad to hear it." Maeve's frown deepened. "Is that why you're crying? What's the matter, Katie? Look at me and tell me what's the matter. Are you sick? Maybe you ate too much cake. Does your stomach hurt?"

"I'm not sick, Mama. I'm just sorry." Katie sniffled, new tears filling her eyes. "It . . . it must have taken you weeks to sew the blouse for me . . . all the perfect little stitches. All the lace threaded in . . . And the money. You should have spent the money on yourself. Gloves or something. Winter's coming . . ."

"You're not making a bit of sense, Katie Gallagher. You're raving and that's the truth." Maeve sat down, anxiously searching her daughter's blotched, tear-stained face. "You haven't been this upset since your papa died. What is it, Katie? What's wrong?"

"I'm not worth spending money on. I'm . . . no good."

"No good? What kind of talk is that?" Maeve pressed her hand to Katie's forehead. It was cool, but that did not lessen her alarm. She rose and poured a glass of water, placing it on the table. "Drink that," she ordered.

Katie raised the glass to her lips. She coughed,

choking on the water, on her own tears, and the glass dropped to the floor, shattering. "I'm . . . sorry, Mama."

"Stop it! Stop saying you're sorry!"

"The glass—"

"Never mind the glass. I'll see to it." Maeve pushed the fragments aside. She threw a cloth over them and returned to Katie. "I can't help if you won't tell me what's wrong. Well? I'm waiting for an answer."

Katie bowed her head, rubbing her throbbing temples. "You shouldn't have spent your money."

"Money, is it? Dear knows I didn't spend much. The challis was a remnant from Paddy's Market. The lace was from my wedding dress."

"Your wedding dress?"

"Aye. I still have it. It's in the big box underneath my bed. Many a time I was tempted to sell it. Irish lace fetches a good price. But it was my mother's, and it'll be yours one day. I took a bit of lace from the sash."

"Your wedding dress," Katie murmured, almost numb with guilt. "You shouldn't have, Mama."

"It's my dress. I can make dust rags out of it if I want. It's nothing to you; not yet." Maeve sighed. She began to pace. "I wanted you to have a birthday present, Katie. Sure and I thought you'd be glad."

"I am."

"You've a queer way of showing it."

Katie found her handkerchief and dried her eyes. "It's the excitement, Mama. All the presents. The cake and the candles. I wasn't expecting . . . a party."

Maeve stopped pacing. She turned, looking thoughtfully at Katie. "Maybe. More likely it's

142

growing pains. Comes a certain age and girls go daft. It passes. You're not the first."

"Did you have growing pains?"

"I had work morning to night." Maeve snorted. "And no days off. Growing pains or any other kind of pains, I was in the fields. You have things easy. You don't think so, but you do."

"Yes, Mama."

"You'd best wash your face and go to bed. It's a wonder you can keep your eyes open, after all that crying. Do you want a headache powder? I have some left."

"Yes, thank you," Katie said, for she felt as if her head were about to split in two. "I'll get it."

"I'll get it. You wash your face."

Katie stood up. Her legs were unsteady and she clutched the back of the chair. "I'm okay, Mama," she said quickly, seeing Maeve's questioning look.

"Aye, you better be. I'll have no more tears from you."

Katie walked the few steps to the sink. She turned the faucet on, splashing cold water over her face and neck. "Thank you." She smiled slightly, taking the glass Maeve gave her. Grimacing, she drank the bitter mixture. "Oh, what an awful taste."

"It's medicine, isn't it? Medicine's supposed to taste awful. Mrs. Muldoon puts a little sugar in, but that's mollycoddling. And a waste of sugar besides. I won't do it. Well? What are you waiting for, Katie? Go on to bed. Morning comes early."

"Good night, Mama."

"Good night. Sleep safe."

Katie gathered her presents together, resting them

in the crook of her arm. "Mama . . . the blouse and the party . . . it was the nicest birthday I ever had."

Katie went to her room. She put the soap and hand lotion atop her dresser and then looked again at the blouse Maeve had so carefully sewn. With a cry, she flung herself on the bed. She could not stop her tears nor did she try, for she felt guilty and ashamed, torn between her mother's wishes and the desires of her own heart. "Oh, Matt," she sobbed, "what am I going to do?"

6

"My God!" Ada exclaimed, staring at Katie's red
and swollen eyes. "What happened to you? You look
like you spent the whole night crying."

"I did."

"What happened? Is there sickness at home?"

"No, everybody's fine."

"What was it then? An argument? Did you argue
with Maeve?"

"No. Mama made a cake for my birthday. With
candles. And she made me a beautiful blouse. I was so
surprised." Katie slipped an apron over her head. She
went to the stove, removing two trays of muffins and
setting them on the counter. "Do you want me to
start the eggs?" she asked.

"I want to know what happened. What's all this
about? You're putting on a good act, but it's not good
enough. What were you crying for? Don't turn away,
Katie. Tell me the truth. Was there an argument?"

"It was the nicest birthday I ever had. Mama
worked hard to make it nice and I . . . I felt . . . I was
ashamed, after the mean things I said."

"I see."

"Sometimes I forget how much Mama cares. She does her best for all of us. Sometimes I forget that. I'm too busy thinking about myself, I guess." Katie took a basket of eggs from the ice box. "Scrambled or fried?" She smiled.

"Fried."

"Okay."

Ada sat down. She sipped her tea, watching Katie bustle around the stove. "So you're feeling guilty." She nodded. "I don't wonder. But what happens next? You're still here and Matt's still here. As far as I can see, nothing's changed. There'll be more lies."

"I've changed, Ada. I've decided to give the hair clips back to Matt. I'm going to stop being . . . foolish."

That morning Katie wrote a brief note to Matt. She left the note and the hair clips in his room, returning immediately to her chores. It's done, she thought, a vast and quiet sorrow clutching at her heart.

It was hours later when Matt came upon Katie's note. He read her words over and over again, then strode from his room. His face was calm as he rushed down the stairs, but his eyes were ablaze. "Katie?" he called, storming into the kitchen. "Where's Katie?"

"I sent her to the store," Ada replied.

"Of course you did. I can imagine why. It's a conspiracy!"

"Ah, Matt, it's nothing of the kind. Katie's getting some sense, and I wish you would, too. You're the one who's older, but you're the one acting like a child. And what for? There are a hundred girls in the neighborhood who'd be in the clouds just to catch your eye."

"That's beside the point." Matt looked at his aunt. He shook his head. "Katie didn't have to return my present," he said. "It was a silly thing to do."

"I disagree. Would you have her lying to Maeve? Sneaking behind Maeve's back?"

"*Maeve*. What business is it of *Maeve's* anyway?"

"When you have a daughter of your own, you'll understand."

"I'm surprised at you, Ada. Taking that woman's side. Everyone knows she's impossible. But you're different. You always listened to reason. Or you did, until this started."

Ada closed her account book. She lighted a cigarette, waving it in the air at Matt. "It's not the starting I'm worried about," she said. "It's the finishing. This flirting with Katie is going to finish in the bedroom. If you want the truth, there it is. Did you think I was fooled by all the talk of being *friends*? A fella your age meets a pretty girl like Katie, and the last thing on his mind is being friends. I wasn't born yesterday, or even the day before."

Indignation swept over Matt. His face colored dark red and his eyes flashed. "I don't need Katie for that," he roared.

"Not yet. But soon. Mark my words. And then what?"

"I won't listen to any more of—"

"I don't blame you. The truth hurts sometimes."

"Whose truth? You're wrong, Ada. I see what's in your mind now, but you're *wrong*."

"I wish I was."

"What do I have to do to convince you?"

"Leave Katie alone." Ada drew on her cigarette.

147

She sat back, watching Matt. "It's simple enough. Just leave her alone."

"Maybe I will."

"And maybe you won't. I could fire her, you know. I could fire her and put an end to this nonsense for good and all."

"You could, but you won't. Your friend, Maeve, would have her working in a factory. She'd have her working in the Acme Laundry, meeting girls like . . ."

"Like Maisie Craig?" Ada sighed. "I didn't want to hire her in the first place," she said wearily. "Such a young girl, and too damned pretty. I was afraid I'd have to keep an eye on the boarders all the time. Well, I was wrong about that. It's you I'm keeping my eye on. I'm not happy about it, Matt. Any of it. I'm in the middle, and that's a bad place."

"I'm sorry."

"I know you are, but it doesn't help. It doesn't change things. I wish you'd stop lying to yourself. You feel something for Katie. Admit it before it's too late. Before there's harm done."

"No harm will come to Katie. I promise you that."

Ada stubbed out her cigarette. She shrugged. "If it does, it'll be on your head. You've been warned. I can't see what else to do. I should fire her. But you're right; I won't. And for the reasons you said."

"I'm glad."

"I hope you stay glad, Matt. Because I'm washing my hands of the whole situation. You're responsible from here on. If you take Katie into your bed, you'll be taking her down the aisle next. That's my last warning. I hope you remember it."

Matt smiled suddenly. He leaned over and kissed Ada's cheek. "Not a very subtle warning." He laughed. "I'm not likely to forget it."

"Time will tell."

"Don't be angry with me, Ada."

"Ah, I'm not angry. I'm a little sad. But years ago I learned that what will be, will be."

Matt and Katie avoided each other during the rest of the week and throughout the week that followed. It was hard for Matt but harder for Katie, for she had no diversions to occupy her mind. She buried herself in chores, dismissing Ada's protests with a wan smile. At night she tossed fitfully in her bed, staring at the ceiling and praying for morning. She had moments of lethargy and moments when she could not sit still. One Sunday, walking home from church with Meg Muldoon, she burst into tears. "Growing pains," she explained to a startled Meg.

"It's growing pains," Katie said to Jack Snow one crisp day late in October. "Just growing pains."

Jack was not persuaded, for he had walked into the parlor to find Katie slumped in a chair, crying as if her heart would break. He had hurried to her, his round face unsmiling and etched with concern. "It looks more serious than that," he said now. "I was telling Ada the other day you looked worn out. You're getting thin again, kid. You're getting circles under your eyes. What's the matter? Can I help?"

"It's kind of you to ask, Jack. But I'm all right. Really."

Jack pulled a chair over and sat down. "You need

149

cheering up." He winked. "How's this? A funny thing happened to me on the way to the boarding-house. I heard a bow-legged man telling a cross-eyed woman to go straight home."

Katie laughed, blinking back her tears. "That's a good one. I never heard that one before."

"I hope they like it in Philadelphia. We open there tomorrow." Jack glanced at his watch. "We're catching the six o'clock train out tonight."

"I'm sorry you're leaving. It's so soon."

"That's vaudeville for you. Here today, gone tomorrow. Some life, eh? Take my advice and don't marry a traveling man."

"I'm not going to marry anybody."

"Oh, so it's love trouble. Tell me the scoundrel's name and I'll have his head on a plate."

"There's no scoundrel." Katie smiled, taking the handkerchief Jack offered. "There's . . . no one."

"No one? Are all the boys in this town blind? My boys would be slugging it out to see who'd court you first. But then they're Boston born and bred. We grow 'em tough in Boston."

"I didn't know you had a family, Jack."

"Four boys. The oldest is married, with a boy of his own. The twins are about your age. And there's Timmy, the apple of my eye. He's short and fat like me." Jack laughed. "A devil like me, too."

"You must miss them."

"That I do. I picked a hell of a way to earn my living. It's hard all the way around. That's why I say don't marry a traveling man."

"Are you getting married, Katie?" Matt was across the parlor in three long strides. He stopped at Katie's

150

chair, staring down at her. "Did I hear right?" he asked. "What's this about marriage?"

"I was giving the kid my best advice." Jack smiled. "She says she's not marrying anybody, but I'm betting some nice young fella will change her mind. What do you think, Matt?"

"I think it's a safe bet."

"The only kind I make." Jack got to his feet. "Let's see a smile before I go, Katie. Is that the best you can do? The next time I'm in New York, I want to see a smile from ear to ear. Promise?"

"Promise."

"I'll hold you to it. Now I'm off. Take care of Ada, Matt. And take care of the kid. She's special."

"I will."

"Jack? You're a good friend. Thank you."

"Anytime, kid. Anytime at all."

"Cheerful, isn't he?" Matt said when Jack had gone.

"Yes."

"How did he get on the subject of marriage?"

"I don't know. . . . I have to go back to work now. Ada's at the bank and I have chores waiting."

"Let them wait. There are some things I want to say. I want you to listen." Matt reached out to touch Katie's silken hair, then abruptly drew his hand away. He walked up and down the room, his head bent in thought. After several moments he stopped and lowered himself into a chair. "I haven't been very happy these past weeks, little girl. Neither have you, judging by the way you look." Katie only shrugged, and he went on. "The fact is I missed you. Just as I missed you during the summer. I don't understand

151

how it happened, but you've become part of my life."

"Don't say any more, Matt. Please."

Why not?"

"It's wrong."

"Well"—Matt smiled—"that's what Ada thinks. That's surely what your mother thinks. I'm interested in what you think. I . . . care about you. Is that wrong?"

Katie twisted her fingers together. She was dizzy, her heart racing, and it was an effort to catch her breath. "I made a promise to myself," she said softly. "I won't hurt Mama."

"What she doesn't know won't hurt her."

"That's lying."

"Maybe it is. But maybe she's being unfair. It's your life, Katie. You can't spend your life tied to her apron strings. She shouldn't expect you to. If you're old enough to earn your keep, you're old enough to choose your friends."

"Mama's trying to protect me."

"Do you need protecting? Are you an infant in the cradle? Are you an imbecile?"

"You're the one being unfair," Katie said, roused by the sharpness of Matt's words. "You can do as you please and no questions asked. It's easy for you. It's not so easy for me. There's always somebody looking over my shoulder, telling me what to do. There's always somebody who knows what's best for me. Mama, Hugh, Ada. Even Meg Muldoon. And now you're in on it, too."

Matt laughed, slapping the arm of his chair. "That's the real Katie Gallagher!" he cried. "Where have you been hiding her all these weeks?"

Katie took a breath. She sat back and stared at Matt. "You were trying to make me mad. *Why?*"

"You have spirit, little girl. You can hide away and wring your hands, or you can put your spirit to use. You can fight. With the right spirit, you can conquer the world."

"I don't want to conquer the world."

"What do you want?"

"A family," Katie replied. "A happy family."

"Is that all? That's not hard."

"It's harder than you think. But it's not all." Katie looked up, returning Matt's steady gaze. "I want money. Enough money to see I won't live and die scrubbing other people's floors." Katie rubbed her calloused palms, her cracked, reddened knuckles. "I want my own floors in my own house. A nice house, filled with children and laughter. Curtains at the windows. A fire in the hearth. Flowers in every room—that's what I want, Matt."

Matt felt his throat tighten. He did not speak, lest he speak rashly. He rose, walking aimless circles about the parlor.

"It's a lot to want, isn't it?" Katie asked.

"No."

"It's a lot for a girl from Hell's Kitchen. But Papa used to tell me to set my sights high."

"Do you ever get out of Hell's Kitchen? Do you ever get out of this godforsaken neighborhood?"

"When would I?" Katie laughed.

"You don't work on Sunday. You have the whole day to yourself."

"Not the whole day. Mama lets me stay out 'til four o'clock. Then I have to be home for supper. I spend

153

Sundays with Meg, but we don't go very far. We'd get lost!"

"That's exactly what you're going to do this Sunday. You're going to get lost in an exciting city. And with me. I'm taking you out." Matt's announcement came as a surprise, even to him, and he fell silent, blinking his clear blue eyes. In the next instant he was smiling. "It's settled," he said. "A day away from here will do you good. We'll have fun."

"Matt, nothing's settled. I can't go anywhere with you. If Mama hears—"

"She won't. Leave it to me."

"I can't."

"Of course you can—if you want to."

"You know I do."

"It's settled, little girl. Under the circumstances, I won't be able to call for you at your flat. We'll have to choose a place to meet. Let's see . . . We'll meet outside the Opera House. No nosy neighbors around there. Eleven o'clock sharp. We'll have the afternoon together. How does that sound?"

It sounded wonderful to Katie, an impossible dream come true. She imagined herself walking at Matt's side, his proud companion, and a thrill ran along her spine. "I want to say yes." She sighed, her long black lashes fluttering. "But . . . what about Mama?"

Matt went to Katie. Gently, he stroked her hair. He pressed his hand to her cheek. "I'll be outside the Opera House at eleven." He smiled. "I'll wait for you."

*　　*　　*

"I'm sorry to get you mixed up in this, Meg," Katie said. It was a cool Sunday morning, with an amber sun peeking between puffy white clouds. Katie had seen the sunrise, for she had awakened before dawn, fretting over the day ahead. A dozen times she had changed her mind, deciding to meet Matt, then deciding to remain at home. In the end, she had confided her plan to Meg, and the two girls had set off toward the Opera House. "You'll be in terrible trouble if Mama finds out."

"No, I won't." Meg shook her head. "My ma won't care, and your ma can't do anything to me. I'm glad to be doing something different on a Sunday. It's an adventure. And I'll finally meet your famous Matt McVey. I waited long enough."

"You'll see I was telling the truth about him."

"Maybe. You don't look very happy, considering."

"It just doesn't seem right." Katie paused as the wind caught her mane of golden hair, blowing it about her face. "Going to church one minute; going behind Mama's back the next."

"It's her own fault. She's too strict."

Katie shrugged, straightening her hair ribbon. "That's what Matt says. But I don't know. It's not easy raising children. Especially with no man in the house."

"She's too strict. Ask Hugh, if you don't believe me."

"Hugh brings it on himself—most of the time, anyway. He plays hooky to be around the boys in the Parlor Mob. Bad boys. Mama never stops worrying, and I shouldn't be adding to her worries."

"It's your day today." Meg grinned, poking Katie.

"Enjoy it. You work all week. You deserve one day for your own. A man works all week and he takes himself off to the pub come Saturday. It's his reward. This is your reward."

"My wages are my reward."

"Listen to you. They ought to make you a saint. Saint Katie of Hell's Kitchen. I think I'll write a letter to the Pope and suggest it."

"Meg!"

"Oh, you have to learn to enjoy life. The way you worry, you'll be gray before you're sixteen. I'll see an old hag in the street, all gray and wrinkled and stooped over, and it'll be you."

Katie laughed, looking into Meg's freckled face. "Will you still be my friend?" she asked.

"Yeah, we're friends for life. Remember in third grade? We swore an oath."

"I remember." Katie linked her arm in Meg's, and the two girls turned the corner onto Broadway. "Look, there it is. It's so big." The Metropolitan Opera House was huge, a yellow brick structure occupying the full block between Thirty-ninth and Fortieth Streets. During the season, scores of bejeweled Vanderbilts and Morgans and Astors swept through its doors, ascending the grand staircase to the private boxes and *baignoires* that comprised the Golden Horseshoe. Now Katie shaded her eyes and imagined the splendor of an evening at the opera. "I wonder what it's like inside." She sighed.

"It's a high-hat place. I know some kids from the neighborhood who come around at night to beg pennies—for all the good it does them. The high hat coachmen drive them off with their whips."

"I wish I could go inside. Just once."

"We'll all go when we're rich," Meg said amidst great gales of laughter. "We'll wear our diamonds and our furs."

"You have no curiosity, Meg Muldoon. That's what's wrong with—Oh, there's Matt! Hurry!" Katie waved. She began to run, dragging Meg along. "Matt!" she called. "Over here!"

Matt closed his newspaper and looked up. I'll always remember this moment, he thought, struck by Katie's beauty as she ran toward him. He could not take his eyes from her, from her hair shimmering with sunlight and her lovely face rosy in the wind. "Katie," he whispered, holding out his hands.

"This is my friend, Meg Muldoon." Katie smiled. "And this is Matt."

"Hello."

"Hello, Meg. I'm glad to meet you. Are you joining us today?"

"If you don't mind."

"How could I? A blond and a redhead. I'm a lucky fellow."

Meg looked at Katie. She shrugged. "Okay, you were telling the truth. He's handsome. Not as handsome as Cornelius O'Day, but—"

"*Meg.*"

"I'm sorry. I'm sorry, Matt. Talking about you like you weren't here. I do that sometimes. I say the first thing that comes into my head. My whole family's the same way. All the Muldoons. I didn't mean anything bad."

"I know you didn't. Besides, you happen to be right. I'm no match for Cornelius O'Day." Matt offered his arm to Meg. With a wink, he offered his other arm to Katie. "Come along," he said. "I'm going to show you a different side of the city. I'm going to show you palaces."

"Palaces?" Katie asked. "In New York?"

"Certainly in New York. There's so much money in this city you can almost smell it in the air. There are fortunes being made every day. And the people making the fortunes build palaces for themselves. Wouldn't you, if you had millions?"

"Maybe." Meg shrugged.

"Wouldn't you, Katie?"

"I don't know. It's nice to dream."

It's a day for dreaming, thought Katie as she strolled up Fifth Avenue with her friends. There were many strollers about on this fine autumn morning, and she stared wide eyed at their elegant dress, at their poised and haughty faces. There were many carriages also, sleek carriages driven by liveried coachmen who deigned to look neither left nor right. We're not far from Hell's Kitchen, she thought, but we might as well be in another country.

Matt watched Katie and was amused. "Look there," he said. "St. Patrick's Cathedral."

Both Katie and Meg stared in wonder at such magnificence. "Golly," Meg exclaimed, pointing out towers and spires and endless ornate carvings. "It makes old St. Brendan's look like a hut. Let's go inside."

"Oh no, Meg." Katie shook her head. "I couldn't. I'm not dressed right."

"It's a church, isn't it? Anybody can go inside."

"It's a *cathedral*."

"Come along." Matt laughed. "I'll show you a cathedral even larger than this."

"You're teasing. He's teasing, Meg."

"Am I? We'll see."

They continued their walk up Fifth Avenue, though they stopped often, Katie and Meg gaping at the mansions that came into view. They were proud dwellings, fortresses of granite and marble and polished stone. Katie imagined the great wealth within. She imagined that inside everyone spoke very softly, as they would in a cathedral. "Do families live there?" she asked.

"Families and servants," Matt replied. "Lots of servants. Imagine the scandal if the lady of the house had to lift a finger in work. She'd be disgraced."

"Yeah." Meg grinned. "I know the kind of lady you mean. My cousin Fanny works for one of 'em. She doesn't even brush her own hair. She has a maid to do it for her. I wouldn't want to be that rich."

They reached the corner of Fifty-seventh Street and Matt shepherded the girls across the avenue. He raised his head, his gaze sweeping from one end of the block to the other. "Well, there it is," he said. "The cathedral of Vanderbilt."

"A church?" Katie asked, frowning.

"In a way, little girl. It's certainly a place of worship. Only they worship money here—Don't laugh. It's true. This is the Vanderbilt mansion. One hundred and thirty-seven rooms. The largest private residence in America, according to the newspapers."

"A private residence? But it's a whole block long. And so deep. It's . . . it's a palace. A palace in the middle of New York!" Katie and Meg ran to the iron fence, pressing their noses in the spaces between the spikes. "Look, Meg," Katie gasped, staring at a dizzying array of peaks and gables and dormer windows. "Matt was right. It's a palace.!"

Meg turned her head, looking up. "It's just for the Vanderbilts, Matt? All this just for one family?"

"And their servants. More than thirty servants, according to the newspapers. That's in New York. They have another palace in Newport."

"How did they get so rich?"

"Railroads. Stocks."

"Hah!" Meg snorted. "I bet there was stealing, too."

"If you're rich enough it's not called stealing. It's called business."

"Funny business, if you ask me."

Matt laughed, bowing. "You're very astute, Miss Muldoon. You should go far in life."

"We'd all better go far," Katie said. "There's a policeman coming our way. Hello, Officer." She smiled brightly. "We weren't doing anything. Really we weren't."

"Is that a fact? Well, this is private property. You can't be loitering on private property." The policeman's voice was stern, as was his gaze. He looked at Katie for a moment, then looked at Matt. "Take the lasses and be off with you. It's private property here."

"Is the sidewalk private property too?"

"*This* sidewalk is."

"It's not posted."

"I'm a police officer telling you to be off. That's all the posting you need. Or would the fine young boyo like to see the postings at the station house? I'll be glad to take you there myself. All of you. It's no trouble."

"Don't argue, Matt," Katie said. "It doesn't matter. We've had our look. Let's go. Please, Matt. Let's go now."

Matt put his arm around Katie's shoulder, holding out his hand to Meg. "All right." He nodded. "We'll go. Good day to you, Officer. The next time I have tea with Mrs. Vanderbilt, I'll be sure to mention your diligence."

"You have a sharp tongue, boyo. Mind you don't cut yourself on it. I'm the law, and I'll have no sass. Off with you now. It's the last warning I'm giving."

"It's kind of you to give any warning at all," Matt replied with an insolent smile. "Good day, Officer. It's been a pleasure talking to you. A great pleasure." He turned, leading Katie and Meg away. "The bastard," he muttered under his breath.

"You wanted an argument, Matt." Katie sighed. "*Why?*"

"Why! Because we're all supposed to be equal in the eyes of the law. But we're not. Not by a long shot. If my name were Vanderbilt or Rockefeller, that cop would be groveling at my feet. My name is McVey, so he chases me off the sidewalk. A public sidewalk, for God's sake."

"It doesn't matter."

"The principle matters, little girl. This is America. Where all men are created equal. Except that some are more equal than others. If you're rich—if you're not an Irishman or a Jew or a Negro—then the world and all the laws in it belong to you. The rest of us get chased off sidewalks."

"You should be in the Tammany Hall," Meg said, impressed. "You have the gift. You have nerve, too. I never heard anybody backtalk a cop before."

"He had it coming. But I didn't mean to upset you, Katie. I'm sorry. Please don't look so grim. It's over now."

"You could have gotten into trouble."

"I didn't though. No bruises, no scrapes. No broken bones. What's more important, my pride is intact. A small victory, but my own."

"I was worried."

"About me?"

"Yes. Who else?"

"I'm sorry. Will you forgive me?"

Katie looked up at Matt. She waited for his smile, and when it came her heart soared. "Oh!" She laughed. "I can't be mad at you. It's impossible."

How radiant Katie is, thought Matt, gazing into her eyes. He was utterly engrossed, and Meg, observing this, felt uncomfortable, like an intruder, and she walked a few steps away, giving Matt and Katie a moment to themselves. Many moments passed. She glanced at their rapt faces and decided it was love.

"Come in," Katie called. She closed her library book and sat up in bed, pulling the blanket to her chin. "Hugh? What's wrong? Why aren't you asleep?"

"I want to talk to you."

"Now?"

"Yeah, now." Hugh sat at the edge of the bed. He

tucked his legs beneath him and turned to Katie. "I talked to Meg this afternoon," he said. "Now I want to talk to you. I know about Matt McVey."

"There's nothing to know."

"Stop lying. You don't have to. I think it's good you have a fella. If he's the right fella. Meg says he is. She says he's okay. So it's fine with me."

"Lower your voice, Hugh. Mama will hear."

"Aw, don't worry. I just looked in her room. The little ones are sleeping, and she's snoring to beat the band. Probably dreaming about money, her favorite subject. But I'm not here to talk about the old lady. Meg says you're going to see Matt again next Sunday. Is that right?"

"Stay out of it. You have your own worries."

Hugh grinned. "What worries?" He shrugged. "I don't have no worries. Just the old lady. I can handle her."

"Can you handle Officer Garrity? He's here so often, he should be paying rent."

"Yeah, him too. All the cops is jerks." Hugh picked up Katie's book. He glanced at it then threw it down. "You reading that for your college boy? I hear he's smart."

"I'm reading because I like to read. It wouldn't hurt you to do a little reading once in a while. Education's important, Hugh."

"Not to me. I got other plans. You'll see."

"That's what I'm afraid of."

"I can take care of myself," Hugh declared, his cool blue eyes steady on Katie. "Now about Matt . . . we'll be doing things different starting next Sunday. You'll go to church with Meg, like usual. But I'm

163

taking you to meet Matt."

Katie's lips parted. She stared at her brother, astonished. "You're enjoying this, Hugh Gallagher. And I know why. Because it's behind Mama's back. If it were out in the open—"

"Out in the open, you wouldn't need my help. You think Meg's going to go around with the both of you every Sunday? She's not. First off, she's scared she'll make a slip and say something, something Ma could hear. Second, she feels funny. Like she's spying."

"Spying!"

"Yeah. She can tell when people want to be alone. When people are making cow eyes, they don't need nobody else around. She's not blind, is she? She can see what's going on."

"*Nothing's* going on."

"C'mon, Katie. So you're sweet on him. So what?" Hugh flopped back on the bed. He folded his hands behind his head and stared at the cracks in the ceiling. "I'm glad you are. Maybe he'll get you out of this hellhole. Somebody better. It's no life for you here. Slaving at the boardinghouse all day. Coming home to Ma's nagging all night. What life is it? You'll end up a sour old lady."

"Let me worry about that."

"Matt's your chance, Katie. There's lots of boys around here who like you, but none of 'em have ten cents in their pockets. They never will. They'll be slaving in some factory, and you'll still be living in a lousy tenement. Maybe Matt's different. He's no mealy-mouth, like the rest of 'em."

Katie threw up her hands. "Now I understand," she said. "Meg told you he sassed a policeman. That's why you're being so helpful. That's all you had to hear."

"Yeah, it was. It means he's a man, not a mouse. He's got a mouth and he's not scared to use it. That's fine with me." Hugh rolled over, looking at Katie. "It must be fine with you, too. If you're sweet on him."

"I didn't say I was."

"You wouldn't be going against Ma if you wasn't. Not you. You're all the time trying to please the old biddy. You wouldn't go against her for nothing."

"Oh, you think you're so smart."

"I'm smart about you." Hugh turned and stared again at the ceiling. "You never went against Ma in your life. Not until Matt McVey. That's the truth, isn't it? I'm trying to help you. Where's the harm?"

"I don't want you getting mixed up in this, Hugh. It's bad enough what I'm doing, but to drag you into it . . ."

"You're not dragging nobody. I'm offering. It's my place to look out for you, to see you get your chance. I can make my own chances. I will, too, in a couple of years. But you're a girl. A husband's your only way out of the tenements."

"If that's what you're thinking, you'll be disappointed. Matt's not going to marry anyone for a long, long time. And when he does, it won't be me."

"Who will it be?"

"I don't know. Someone fancy. A lady maybe."

Hugh, though innocent in matters of romance and marriage, disagreed. "You're not making sense," he said. "You must be *lady* enough for him, or why else would he be going around with you? I hear he's a busy fella. Work and school and all. But he's spending his Sundays with you. How come?"

"We're friends."

"Aw, I don't believe that. Boys are friends with boys, not girls. I don't know no boys who're friends with girls. That's sissy stuff. Is he a sissy?"

"No." Katie smiled. "He's not a hoodlum either. The boys you know are hoodlums. Officer Garrity says so. Everybody says so."

"Who cares? Everybody can go to hell. Garrity can be the first one in the flames." Hugh stretched. He sat up, brushing his hair from his forehead. "I'm trying to do you a favor, Katie. You could be glad."

"I'm glad you want to. You're a good brother."

"Yeah, I'm swell. What about Sunday?"

"Let me worry about Sunday. Please, Hugh. Meg was wrong to tell you. It was supposed to be a secret."

"She wasn't wrong. She had a smart idea. I'll take you to meet Matt, then I'll go my way and you'll go yours. We'll meet again later and I'll fetch you home. The old lady won't be none the wiser. She'll be jumping with joy if she thinks we're spending Sundays together. I can't get into trouble if I'm with you. That's how she'll see it."

"I don't know."

"Matt's your chance, Katie. There's other girls around, lots of 'em, and they're probably setting their caps for him. Who're you going to worry about? Ma, or them other girls?"

It was a compelling argument. Katie did not doubt that there were other girls in Matt's life, and perhaps quite a few. She had tried to put such thoughts from her mind, for they were painful. "Are you sure you want to do this, Hugh?" she asked now, sighing.

"I said so, didn't I?"

Katie leaned back against the pillows. She imagined herself alone with Matt, the two of them strolling hand in hand, and the temptation was too great to resist. "All right." She smiled. "Maybe I'll be sorry . . . but all right."

7

"I like having you all to myself, little girl," Matt said on their second Sunday together. "Come, I'll show you Paris."

"Paris!"

"*Oui, mademoiselle.*"

They rode the streetcar to Washington Square, then walked for hours through the winding, cobbled streets of Greenwich Village. Katie was enchanted by the graceful old mews houses, by the quaint galleries and bookshops they visited. She peered over the shoulders of sidewalk artists, and later, in a candle-lit café, she drank *demitasse*. "I never want to go home," she said to Matt. "Can't we stay here forever?"

"And miss the rest of the tour? Next week I'll show you Rome. We'll go around the world together." Matt smiled, covering Katie's hand with his own.

The next Sunday they visited Little Italy, and in the Sundays that followed they visited Chinatown and Yorkville and the pushcart markets of the Lower East Side. They roamed the vast canyons of Wall Street and the waterfront of the Battery. On a gray day in December they boarded the Staten Island Ferry, holding hands as fog swirled around them and gulls cried overhead.

"I'm so happy," Katie murmured again and again. She gazed into Matt's eyes and felt such love she thought her heart would burst.

If Maeve wondered at Katie's singular radiance, Ada did not. She understood, and though she said nothing, she was dismayed. Now her face was subdued as she entered the parlor. "I see Mr. Fergus delivered the Christmas tree." She sighed. "Christmas already. Where does the time go?"

"Isn't it a wonderful tree?" Katie turned, clapping her hands in delight. "It must be eight feet tall!"

"I buy a big tree every year. My boarders have to be away from home during the holidays. It's hard for them. I try to make it nice." Ada sat down. She folded her arms and studied Katie's shining profile. "It's almost a year since you came here," she said quietly. "You've changed so much in a year. I wouldn't recognize you. You used to be so serious. Now you never stop smiling."

"It's Christmas!"

"I guess it's a busy time for Maeve. She gets a lot of extra work this time of year."

"Yes, Mama's very busy."

Too busy to notice the changes in you, thought Ada, shaking her head. "Well, I'm sure you help when you can. I'm sure you're a comfort."

Katie looked away. She was uncomfortable, for any mention of Maeve stirred dark and guilty feelings in her. She knew there would be a day of reckoning and on that day she would pay for her lies, her betrayal. "Why are you always talking about Mama?"

170

she asked.

"Am I?"

"It's your way of chiding me. I can't help what I'm doing, Ada. I can't help myself. I wish things were different. I pray every night for things to be different. But Mama's made up her mind against Matt. And once she makes up her mind . . ."

"She's no worse than you," Ada replied with a small smile. "Or Matt. Nobody's giving an inch. Three stubborn Irishers. Four, if you count Hugh. He's in on it. They say drink is the curse of the Irish. *I* say it's stubbornness."

"I wish Pa were alive. He'd understand."

"He would at that. Joe had a romantic nature, poor man. . . . Ah, Katie, I understand. I don't approve, but I understand. I was your age once, believe it or not."

Katie loosened the cord around the Christmas tree, sniffing its fragrant branches. "I bought a coat for Mama," she said. "A nice, warm coat. Mrs. Muldoon is keeping it in her flat 'til Christmas morning. And I bought long pants for Hugh. His first. He hates knickers. We bought toy trains for the little ones."

"It sounds like you spent all your savings."

"This Christmas is special, Ada. I want to share my happiness with everyone. With the whole world. Maybe it's silly, but that's how I feel."

"That's the good part of being your age."

"What's the bad part? No, don't tell me. I don't want to know." Katie smiled. "Matt said we could trim the tree together, just the two of us. Is it all right?"

"I suppose. No candles though. We almost had a

fire here last year. We were singing Christmas carols when I saw smoke coming from the tree. Jack pulled the tree down and started stomping on it while the rest of us ran for water. The parlor was a shambles when we were done. I can laugh about it now, but I wasn't laughing then." Ada rose. She crossed the room and inspected the tree. "There's a box of decorations in the cellar. It should be enough. I'll make the popcorn. You can start stringing it tomorrow."

"Can I get the decorations now?" Katie asked excitedly.

"What's your hurry?"

"I can't wait to see them. We had a tree once, three years ago. But we didn't have decorations. Just some candy canes."

"That reminds me. I have to buy candy canes . . . If you're going to the cellar, fetch the other washtub. We'd best get this tree in water." Ada stared at the tree. She shook it, watching for falling needles. "It's fresh now, but it won't stay fresh if we don't put it in water. There's nothing sadder than a wilting Christmas tree."

"I'll get the tub. . . . Thank you, Ada."

"What for?"

"For everything." Katie rushed off, her skirts flying up about her ankles. She paused in the doorway, smiling. "This is the best Christmas of my life!"

"Wait 'til you see all the chores we have, miss."

"I don't care. I'll work 'round the clock. And gladly!"

Katie's enthusiasm did not wane as the days drew

closer to Christmas. She cleaned the boardinghouse from top to bottom and did so with great zest. She washed windows and beat rugs and polished furniture. In the afternoons, she joined Ada in the kitchen, and there they baked fruitcakes and mince pies and gingerbread men with long, sugary beards. They made cider and gallons of eggnog. They wrapped presents by the dozens, placing them on a bright red cloth near the tree. It was for Katie a magical time, indeed the best time of her life.

"Merry Christmas, little girl," Matt said early on Christmas Eve. He gave Katie a cup of eggnog and then stepped back, looking around the parlor. Holly was strung across the mantel and holly wreaths bedecked the windows. There was a fire in the hearth, the sweet scent of the wood blending with the scents of cinammon and cloves. "So many presents." He smiled. "I bet some of them are for you."

Katie's green eyes twinkled. She tilted her head and gazed at Matt. "I don't want to be any happier than I am now. One more bit of happiness and I'll explode. I'll be in pieces all over the parlor."

"Oh, we can't have that. What would the boarders think?"

Katie raised her cup, touching it to Matt's. "Merry Christmas," she said. "I hope all the Christmases to come are just like this one."

"They'll be better. Wait and see." Matt sipped his eggnog. He drained the cup and put it down, striding then to the tree. "Are you going to help me?" he asked, opening a box of decorations. "Do you have any strength left?"

"All the strength in the world."

Katie and Matt looked into each other's eyes. Their hands touched for a moment, a tender moment filled with longing. "The tree," Matt said huskily.

"Yes . . . the tree."

Katie bent, taking the carved and painted ornaments from the box. She gave them to Matt one by one, watching as he tied them to the branches. Together, they wrapped garlands of popcorn and cranberries about the splendid tree. "Now the angel." Matt smiled, lifting Katie up. "That's it. It's perfect."

"Is it straight?"

"It's perfect."

Katie felt her feet touch the floor. She smoothed her skirts, blushing, for Matt was very close. Again, they looked into each other's eyes. "Matt," Katie whispered, sighing. "It's . . . it's such a beautiful tree."

"You're beautiful. My God, you're beautiful." Matt drew closer still. His lips brushed Katie's forehead and then, almost instantly, he drew back. "I'm sorry. I shouldn't have . . . I'm sorry, Katie. Forgive me."

"I'm not sorry."

Matt walked uncertainly to the far side of the room. He sat down and with shaking hand took a handkerchief from his pocket, pressing it to his face. He thought, I must be crazy. It's deep water here, and I'm going deeper and deeper. Like a blind man. Like a man who's lost his senses.

"Well," Ada said, crossing the threshold into the parlor. "I see you've finished the tree. A fine job it is, too. You can both be proud of yourselves." She turned, looking at Katie. "It's getting late, miss. And it's Christmas Eve. You should be home with your family."

"It's not so late."

"My watch says it is." Ada went to the tree. She leaned over and picked up several packages. "These are for you. Of course they're not *all* for you." She smiled. "There are gloves for Maeve and boxes of gingerbread for the boys. Merry Christmas, Katie."

"Thank you, Ada. It's kind of you, but you didn't have to. You've done so much for us already."

"Ah, it's just a remembrance. I like to remember all my friends at Christmas. Come, we'll get your coat and off you go."

"I left your present under the tree. And Matt's. Do you want to open them now? Before I go home?"

"We don't open presents 'til Christmas morning. That's a rule. Tim, rest his soul, made the rule years ago, and we never broke it. Not once. We were tempted, but we never broke the rule. Isn't that right, Matt?"

"Yes, that's right."

"I wish I could be here Christmas morning."

"You'll have a wonderful time at home, Katie. It's a time for children, after all, and you have Sean and little Francis. Be glad you do. They're darling boys."

"Oh, I know," Katie agreed, picturing her brothers' sweet, untroubled faces. "It's just that I . . . I feel as if I have family here, too."

"Sure. We're all family here. But your real family comes first."

"I know, Ada. I'll go now."

"Wait." Matt stood. He reached into his jacket pocket and removed a small box wrapped in gold paper. "I hope you like it," he said.

Katie took a step forward. She took another step, then stopped, shaking her head. "I'll open it after Christmas." When we're alone, she thought; just the two of us. "I'll save the best 'til last. Will you keep it for me, Matt?"

"I'll keep it for you. I'll keep it safe."

Ada saw the look that passed between Katie and Matt. "Come along," she said firmly, steering Katie toward the door. "Maeve will be worried."

"Yes, I'm coming. Merry Christmas, Matt."

"Merry Christmas, little girl."

It was a merry Christmas for all the Gallaghers. It was blessedly peaceful, and Katie believed that was an omen. "The worst is behind us," she said to Hugh on the first day of the new year. "Better things are coming."

The pattern of Katie's days did not change as 1904 began, but now those days seemed to hurry by. It was winter and then suddenly it was spring. Matt and Katie went to the Easter Parade, strolling arm in arm along Fifth Avenue. They went to baseball games and to picnics in the park. Summer arrived and with it a blazing yellow sun. On the hottest summer Sundays, Matt and Katie rode the train to Coney Island. They strolled the boardwalk and ate cotton candy and played in the bubbling surf at water's edge. In later years, when Katie was to look back over her life, she would remember such times, times of innocence, of love.

"And who told you you could put up your hair?"

Maeve asked shortly after Katie's fifteenth birthday. "I didn't give you permission."

"I'm not a child anymore, Mama. I can put up my hair if I want to. There's no harm in it."

"I suppose you're a woman of the world. Is that what you think, Katie Gallagher?"

"Maybe I'm not a woman of the world, but I'm not a child." Katie wore a new dress, a "store" dress of deep green wool with a lacy collar. Its skirt was stylishly flared, flowing from a tiny waist, the bodice snug against her full young breasts. Now she twirled around, smiling. "Do you like my dress, Mama? Isn't it pretty?"

"It's a dress for a woman, not a girl. Showing off your shape like that. You should be ashamed."

"The clerk in the store said this dress was the latest fashion."

"And who are you to care about fashion? You're getting above yourself, Katie Gallagher. You're the hired girl in a boardinghouse, and don't forget it. The latest fashion! I never heard such foolishness. A lot of good *fashion* will do you, scrubbing floors and washing windows. Do you think you're Mrs. Astor?"

"No, Mama," Katie replied quietly. "I just wanted something pretty. My other dress doesn't fit. You let the seams out three times. It doesn't fit."

"I offered to make you a new dress, didn't I? Didn't I tell you to buy fabric at Paddy's and fetch it home to me? For what that cost you, you could have had three dresses. But I suppose home sewing's not good enough for you now. It's not the latest fashion."

"It's nothing to be upset about, Mama."

"Throwing away hard-earned money on that

177

dress. Sure and I'll never understand why you're in such a rush to grow up. You're only young once, Katie. When your youth is gone, it's gone forever. Don't wish it away. You'll be sorry you did. When you're my age, you'll be wondering where the time went. And you'll be sorry." Maeve sat down, folding her hands atop the table. She sighed. "Hugh's the same as you," she said wearily. "He thinks he's grown because he's wearing long pants. I see him strutting in the street, cock o' the walk. Well, he'll be sorry and so will you."

"It's getting late, Mama. I'd best get to work."

"That's a fine dress for work."

"I wear an apron all day."

"Then what do you need a fancy dress for? Tell me that. It's a waste of hard-earned money. All covered up in an apron, you might as well be wearing a flour sack. What difference does it make?"

"It makes a difference to me. *I'll* know I'm wearing something pretty. It's a good feeling, Mama."

"It's foolishness, that's what it is. It's money out the window. I never thought I'd live to see the day when a child of mine threw money out the window. Didn't I teach you better? Dear knows I tried."

"I won't do it again, Mama," Katie said, anxious to end the discussion. "I'll be more careful."

"Aye, you say that now. But what about next time? Sure and I wouldn't be surprised to see you buying silks and satins. And maybe furs to go with them."

"Oh, Mama!" Katie laughed. She bent, putting her arms around Maeve's thin shoulders. "The only way I'll get a fur coat is by stealing. If you ever see me in furs, you'd best hurry for Officer Garrity."

"I won't have to hurry far, will I? He's here all the time. At least it seems like that lately." Maeve sighed again. "I don't understand my children," she said, as if to herself. "Hugh's a mystery to me. He always was . . . and you, Katie. You've changed. Aye, you have. Maybe it's work that's done it. Maybe it's just life. But you're a mystery to me, too. I suppose it'll be the same with the little ones, when they get older. I hope God gives me strength."

"You're the strongest person I know."

"I have to be. There's no one else." Maeve rubbed her hands together, staring into space. "No one else."

"Mama, it's late."

"Aye, go on to work, Katie. You won't earn any wages here. Watch out for puddles. There was rain overnight."

"I will." Katie hugged her mother. She took her coat from the hook and opened the door. "Good-bye, Mama."

"Good-bye."

Katie ran down the stairs. It was cool outside, still damp, and she raised her hand to the knot of golden hair sitting prettily atop her head. Her new hair style was meant to be a surprise for Matt, as was her new dress. Skipping over puddles on the way to the boardinghouse, she prayed that he would be pleased.

Katie's prayers were answered that afternoon, for Matt was lavish in his compliments, staring until she blushed and turned away. He turned away also, fighting an ardent desire to sweep Katie into his arms, to hold her close. He had known such desires before and had resisted them, but resistance, he worriedly admitted, was becoming more difficult with every passing week. He thought to himself, Katie's a woman now, and so beautiful it hurts to look at her.

If Matt was bedazzled, he was hardly alone. Heads snapped up as Katie walked through the streets of Hell's Kitchen, wistful glances cast by boys and men alike. Neighborhood shopkeepers were suddenly attentive when she entered their establishments, and the boarders, returning from weeks and months on the road, exclaimed their wonder.

Katie seemed blithely unaware of her many admirers. She went to work each morning thinking only of Matt, and it was Matt who came into her dreams at night. "Don't be stubborn," Ada chided. "Don't settle on one fella 'til you've given the others a chance. A girl like you can have your pick."

That sentiment was shared by Matt's friend, Ben Rossi. He had heard a great deal about Katie, but still his breath caught when he saw her for the first time. "You better marry her before someone else does," he said to Matt. "Me, for instance."

It was the day after Thanksgiving, and Matt and Ben sat in the kitchen of the boardinghouse, drinking beer. They were old friends, classmates now at City College, and they were at ease with each other. "You'll marry her over my dead body," Matt said with a smile. "Remember the warning. She deserves the best."

"Who's to say I'm not the best?"

"Are you kidding?"

"What's wrong with me?"

"For one thing, you're fickle. Every time I turn around, there's a new girl on your arm. There's a

180

string of broken hearts from here to Yorkville. And they all have your name on them."

"Not all. Half of them are yours, my friend." Ben sipped his beer, grinning. He was an attractive young man of eighteen, with a shock of jet black hair and thoughtful, dark brown eyes. Like Matt, he was the son of immigrants, and, like Matt, he had been scorned as a dirty papist. He had been exposed to years of taunts, enduring them with the patience that was part of his nature. "Oh, you've been a good little boy lately." He laughed now. "I'll give you that. But you broke quite a few hearts yourself before you reformed. Maisie Craig could tell a few tales. And she's not the only one. There's Beth Strong and Ida—"

"Okay, okay, I get the point. I have a checkered past."

"That's a polite way of putting it. More than once I expected you to be chased to the altar, a shotgun at your back."

"There'll be no altars for me. Not in the near future."

Ben shook his dark head. "I wouldn't be too sure of that," he said. "I saw the way Katie looked at you. The way *you* looked at her. It's love, Matthew. It's love or I'm Teddy Roosevelt."

"To you, Mr. President." Matt smiled, raising his glass.

"You know I'm right. Anyway, how could you not be in love with her?"

"She's fifteen, Ben."

"Old enough to be married. Mama was fourteen when she married Papa."

"That was in the old country, for God's sake. It's different here."

"Love is love, old country or new."

Matt leaned back, clasping his hands behind his head. "Maybe you should embroider that on a sampler. It's silly enough."

"Tell me I'm wrong and I won't say another word."

"I have two and a half years of college left. Law school after that. Then it will take at least a year to get our law office off to the start we planned. How can I think about love, Ben? How can I think about marriage? It would mean giving up everything."

"You have savings."

"My savings wouldn't last six months, if I had a wife to support. I'd have all the expenses of a flat. In time, I'd have the expenses of a family. And that would be the end of college. I'd need a real job. The job in the stable is fine for me now. But with a family . . ." Matt finished his beer. Quickly, he lifted the pitcher and refilled his glass. "I'd be stuck in some damn factory for the rest of my life."

"There's always night school."

"Yes, and it takes forever. I'd be an old man by the time I got my degree." Matt saw Ben's skeptical look. "Okay." He shrugged. "I wouldn't be an old man. But I'd have wasted a lot of years."

"It seems to me you're asking Katie to waste a lot of years. It's not very fair of you, Matt."

"I haven't asked Katie to do anything."

"Maybe not in so many words."

"In *no* words at all."

Ben was quiet, frowning at Matt. "You two

obviously have an understanding," he said finally. "Spoken or unspoken, it's still an understanding. You two are courting. How else would you describe your Sundays together? What about the locket you gave her on her last birthday? That's a courtship present if ever there was one."

"Because you say so?"

"I know the rules. When a fellow walks out with a girl every Sunday, he's courting. When a fellow gives a girl presents, he's courting."

"To hell with rules!"

"Rules are important." Ben smiled, stroking his chin. "In business you can bend the rules your own way. That's how people get rich. It's all right in business but not in life."

Matt considered Ben's statement, knowing it was an accurate reflection of his beliefs. Patient and pragmatic Ben Rossi believed that anything short of murder or absolute thievery was permissible in business. In life, he believed there was no worse sin than the betrayal of a friend. "Rossi's gospel," Matt said. "It never varies."

"We've talked about these things before. I never heard you disagree."

"If you're suggesting I'm bending the rules with Katie, I certainly do disagree. I've been honest. She knows what school means to me. She knows my plans."

"Is she supposed to wait around for years and years while you concentrate on your plans? Not fair, Matthew. Not fair."

"There's been no talk of waiting around. We're not engaged, after all. We're not . . . anything."

183

"I see."

"What do you see?"

"Well, if you're not anything, then Katie's free to see others. I could ask her out. She'd probably turn me down flat, but I could ask. Couldn't I?"

Irritation showed in Matt's blue eyes. He scowled at Ben. "You wouldn't ask her out and you know it. So what's the point of this conversation? Why are you goading me?"

"Professor Drake says a good lawyer should be able to argue both sides of a case equally well."

"Is that what this is? A classroom exercise? I don't like it, Ben. Not one bit. I'm not on trial here." Matt's fingers tightened around his glass. He took a swallow of beer and slammed the glass down. "We're supposed to be enjoying our holiday," he said. "Let's enjoy it. I'm in no mood for an argument. Or for preaching. If I wanted a sermon, I'd go to church."

"I'm trying to help."

"Help? You're sticking your nose in where it doesn't belong. I don't call that help."

Ben's expression was unchanged as he regarded Matt. "Would you rather talk about the weather?" he asked with an easy grin. "It feels like snow to me. Does it feel like snow to you?"

"All I feel is the urge to punch your nose."

"Why? Matt, if there weren't some truth to what I said, you wouldn't be so upset. Don't deny it. You know I'm right. *I* know I'm right. I know you. You have a way of ignoring unpleasant subjects. That's fine. But ignoring them won't make them go away."

"How about I make you go away?"

"You could try." Ben chuckled. "But I'd be back.

Sooner or later you'd have to listen to me. You're my friend, and I don't give up on my friends."

"Okay. Be my friend. Just don't be my conscience. I've been on my own a long time, Ben. I haven't done badly, everything considered. I got out of Wilkes-Barre. I'm in college. I have a future, for God's sake."

"What about Katie's future?"

Matt rose abruptly. He began to pace, his head bent, his hands clenched. "Katie is none of your business," he snapped. "You spent five minutes with her, maybe ten. And now, all of a sudden, you're her great protector. Her knight in shining armor. Well, she doesn't need your protection. I'll see to Katie. In my own way, in my own time."

"How?"

Matt turned. He glared at Ben. "This conversation has gone far enough. I'm not saying another word about Katie. Neither are you, unless you want a bloody nose—I mean it. Sometimes you're like a dog with a damn bone. It takes a rap on the snout to make you drop it."

"That's a good quality in a lawyer."

"You're not a lawyer; not yet. This isn't a courtroom, Ben. We're here to drink beer and enjoy the day. Can we do that?"

"Sure."

"I'm sorry I ever introduced you to Katie."

"I was beginning to wonder if you ever would," Ben said lightly. "She's been here more than a year. There were times I thought she was a figment of your imagination."

Matt did not reply immediately, for no reply came to mind. It was true that he had kept Ben away from

185

the boardinghouse during Katie's working hours. It had been deliberate on his part, though he was at a loss to explain his reasons.

"Maybe I knew we'd end up having this stupid conversation." He shrugged. "You have a very orderly view of life. But life isn't always orderly. There are turns in the road, unexpected turns." Matt sat down. He stretched his legs out, thrusting his hands into his pockets. "Katie's an unexpected turn." He sighed. "I'm trying to deal with it the best way I can. It's complicated. There's a lot at stake."

"For her, too."

"Don't you think I know that? I'm not a fool, Ben. Yes, I ignore unpleasant subjects. I try to, anyway. But this is one subject I haven't ignored. Katie's in my thoughts day and night. It's not so bad when I'm in class or lecture hall. Other times it's terrible. I keep looking for an answer. There is none. I go along from day to day, hoping for the best. What else can I do?"

"What do you want to do?"

"What I want and what I can have are two different things. I *want* to make the grand gesture. I want to say the hell with everything and run off with Katie. I want us to have a life together as husband and wife. That's what my heart tells me to do. But my head. . . ." Matt looked at Ben. He smiled slightly. "My head tells me I'd regret it. Romance doesn't last forever."

"Oh, I don't know," Ben said, his dark eyes twinkling. "Mama and Papa are more in love today than they were the day they were married. Mama's fat and Papa's bald, but their life is filled with romance. They're always touching and hugging, as if they

186

were newlyweds. You've seen them."

"They're . . . unusual. Your whole family's unusual. Ten children, and all looking out for each other. They're crammed into that small flat with hardly enough room to breathe, yet there's never a mean word. That's unusual. Hell, it's a miracle!"

"Maybe the same miracle will happen to you."

"I'd go crazy if I had to live that way. No offense, Ben, but that's what I escaped from. Seven children, parents, and grandparents crammed into a shack the size of this kitchen. We had nothing but mean words. We weren't family; we were enemies. That's what poverty does to some people. You start hating yourself because you can't put food on the table, and then you start hating the world."

"There was an article in the *World* the other day. It went on and on, but the point was that money can't buy happiness."

"Of course." Matt chuckled. "That's what rich people want poor people to believe. I'll tell you if it's true or not after I've made my fortune."

"A toast to your fortune."

"More toasting?" Ada asked. She walked into the kitchen, her glance falling on the almost empty pitcher of beer. "You've done some toasting already, if I'm any judge. What's the occasion?"

"We're still celebrating Thanksgiving."

"Keep drinking like that and you'll be celebrating a headache. You too, Ben. You should know better, the both of you." Ada opened the ice box door and peered inside. "Well, there's plenty of turkey left," she said. "I'll fix sandwiches. At least you won't be drinking on an empty stomach."

"Don't bother." Matt stood up, smiling at his aunt. "We're going out for a while. We'll get something to eat later."

"You have work later."

"We'll get something to eat and then I'll go to work. It'll be a slow night at the stable. It's always slow the night after a holiday. I guess people stay home."

"I wish you'd stay home."

"Oh, you can't argue with him, Ada," Ben said. He stood also, carrying glasses and pitcher to the counter. "Your nephew is as stubborn as they come."

"I've noticed."

"Where's Katie? I was hoping to say goodbye to her. There's no telling when Matt will let me see her again."

"Never mind Katie. It's Friday and she's waxing the woodwork. Leave her alone. I don't need *two* lovesick fellas around here. One's enough. More than enough."

"Nobody's lovesick. Certainly not Ben. He was born with that sappy expression. It's part of his charm." Matt kissed Ada's cheek. "I won't be back tonight," he said. "I'll see you in the morning."

"Be careful."

"I'm always careful."

"Hah! Ben, you keep an eye on him."

"I will. Good-bye, Ada."

"Good-bye."

Ada watched as the two smiling young men went from the kitchen. "Youth," she muttered. "It's a blessing and a curse."

*   *   *

Katie was on her knees buffing the woodwork when she heard Ada enter the parlor. "I'm almost finished." She smiled. "This is the last of it."

"Ah, there's no hurry. We'll just heat up yesterday's supper for tonight." Ada sat down, folding her hands in her lap. "You made a big impression on Ben," she said thoughtfully. "I think he's smitten with you."

"Ben?"

"Ben Rossi. Matt's friend."

"Oh, yes, Ben Rossi. He seemed nice."

"He's very nice. He'll make some girl a fine husband."

Katie dropped her cloth into the cleaning basket. She rose and smoothed her wrinkled skirts. "Are you matchmaking, Ada?"

"A girl could do a lot worse than Ben Rossi. He's smart and hard working. There's nothing he wouldn't do for friends or family. He has nine brothers and sisters, and they all look up to him. It shows you what a nice fella he is."

"Yes," Katie replied, hiding a smile behind her hand. "Yes, it does."

"A girl could do worse."

"I'll remember that."

"Ah, you won't remember." Ada sighed. "In one ear and out the other. Young people are all—" Ada was interrupted by the sharp ring of the telephone. "I'll answer it," she said. "You finish in here."

Katie turned, surveying the gleaming woodwork. She pushed the sofa against the wall and then straightened the cushions and antimacassars. "Finished!" she exclaimed happily, carrying her cleaning basket through the hall to the kitchen.

It was late afternoon, Katie's favorite time of day, and she poured a cup of tea, adding sugar and fresh mint. The cup was halfway to her lips when she froze, staring at the door. "Ada, what's wrong?" she cried, alarmed, for Ada's rosy face was suddenly pale, her mouth tense. "What's happened?" Katie put the cup down and rushed to Ada. She helped her into a chair. "What's happened?" she asked again. "Tell me."

"That was Lou Rayne calling. Jack collapsed on stage. Just collapsed in a heap, Lou said. They've taken him to the hospital."

"Collapsed!"

"He wasn't feeling well this morning. He didn't eat a thing. And his color was high. We were teasing him. We thought he'd had too much to drink the night before."

"But what's the matter with him? Do they know?"

"Not yet. Lou was calling from the hospital." Ada fumbled for her handkerchief. She touched it to her eyes, sighing. "Poor Jack. Poor Jack."

"How can we help, Ada? What can we do?"

"I don't know. Let me think. . . . Lou telephoned Jack's wife. But she's up in Boston. Poor Jack. I'll have to go to the hospital. You'll have to stay here and see to things, Katie. Will you do that?"

"Yes, don't worry."

"You'll have to do the cooking and serving by yourself. You'll have to stay 'til I get back. Matt's gone out for the night, and somebody has to be here."

"Yes, I'll see to everything. Don't worry. Jack's going to be fine. He has to be. He's so lively, so—"

"We'll see. We'll see how lively he is now." Ada

190

stood, removing her apron and throwing it on the table. "I'll stop at Maeve's on the way," she said. "I'll tell her you're staying. I may be late. If it gets to be too late, you can sleep in my room. We'll see what happens. I'll call you from the hospital."

"Yes, all right. I'll pray for him, Ada."

"At times like this I wonder if there's any use in praying. I wonder if God cares. I mean it. Life's unfair, Katie. Don't let anybody tell you different."

faced, as moving his head and throwing it off his
shoulder. The reproach of the chief tongue, I'll
tell her tongue is, as you wish it. And it is to me
that you can stop saying more. Wait, see what
we are fit for on this, the family there?

Kate folded. "I must be saying," she...

A time that the I wonder if she doesn't mean
proper. I would see the Lord. I think it I say
nothing. Hate your lot to say, why, why do this?"

8

It was a long night at the boardinghouse, a night filled with gloom. The vaudevillians returned from their afternoon shows, and to Katie fell the task of reporting Jack's collapse. She hoped the telephone would ring, but when it did not, she served supper as usual. Platters of turkey and dressing and turnips and cranberries sat upon the table untouched. There was a profound silence in the dining room. When the vaudevillians went back to their theaters, they went in silence.

Katie located Ada's mending basket and passed the time mending worn napkins and pillowslips. At ten o'clock she climbed the stairs to Ada's room. She undressed, slipping into a robe many sizes too big for her, and lay down on the bed. She drowsed, not quite asleep, not quite awake. When, sometime later, the telephone finally rang, she leaped up and ran into the hall. "Hello? Is that you, Ada?" she shouted. "I'm sorry, I didn't mean to yell in your ear. How's Jack? Yes . . . Yes . . . I see . . . when? . . . yes, I will . . . yes . . . good night, Ada."

Katie replaced the receiver. She turned around, her

eyes widening. "Matt!" she gasped.

"What in the world is going on?" Matt asked. He tightened the belt of his robe and stared at Katie. "What are you doing here so late?"

"I . . . I had to stay. Jack Snow was taken to the hospital. Ada left as soon as she heard. I had to stay."

Matt frowned, rubbing his eyes. "Jack? What's the matter with Jack?"

"It's his appendix. They weren't sure at first. But now he's had surgery. He's still very sick. Ada's staying with him. . . . I thought you'd be at work."

"Work?" Matt paused, trying to clear his mind. "No, I decided to come home early. I have an awful headache."

"Oh, I'm sorry. I'll get you a cold cloth."

"Thanks, little girl."

Matt returned to his room. He sat at the side of the bed, putting his fingers to his throbbing temples. It's the beer, he thought, for he had drunk a prodigious amount of beer. Airily he had dismissed Ben's protests, going from pub to pub until he had lost count. He had staggered off to his job, managing to feed and water the horses, but then he had come home, seeking oblivion in sleep.

"You'll be better in no time," Katie said, entering Matt's room. She held the cloth to his forehead, smoothing his thick, reddish hair. "Isn't that better?" she asked.

Matt looked up. He saw Katie leaning over him. He saw the loose folds of her robe and, just beneath, the curve of her full young breasts. Desire swept over him. The room seemed to grow warmer and he felt engulfed, as if by flames. There was a great roaring in

194

his ears. Lights began to dance before his swimming eyes. "My God," he moaned. "My God." It was a plea, though in vain. "Katie!" he cried out, pulling her onto the bed. He tore the robe from her shoulders, his feverish hands pressing her soft flesh.

Katie was frightened. She struggled, fighting to free herself, but when Matt pressed his mouth to her naked breasts she too cried out. She stopped struggling and began murmuring against him, kissing his hair, his eyes, his seeking lips. She felt his hands moving over her body and she trembled, lost in the rapture of his touch. In that moment of first love and passion, his touch was the only truth, the only reality. "Matt . . . Oh, Matt. I love you, I love you, I love you."

Matt awoke with a start. His heart was racing and perspiration stood on his brow. He glanced at Katie, sleeping peacefully beside him, and his hands began to shake. Slowly, he stood up. He reached for his robe and stumbled across the room. His hand went to the doorknob then fell away. There's no escape, he thought bitterly. This time there's no escape.

Matt had known fear in the past—as a young boy fleeing the home he despised and then wandering the streets of New York, penniless and alone. But those fears were small compared to what he felt now, for now he felt terror. He saw his future, his whole life, ruined, and he shivered violently. His throat was tight, his breath ragged. A drink, he thought; I need a drink. He opened the door and stumbled into the hallway, his eyes fixed on the stairs.

"Matt? What are you doing home?" Ada frowned. She stared at Matt from the shadows of her room and then motioned him inside. She turned up the gaslight, frowning again. "What are you doing home? Are you sick?"

"I . . . I . . . too much to drink, I guess."

Ada was very still, very pale. "Where's Katie?" she asked.

"Katie?"

"Where is she?"

Matt sank into a chair. "I'm sorry, Ada," he said, his voice catching. "I'm sorry. I didn't mean to—"

"Where is she?"

"In my room."

Ada did not trust herself to speak. She grasped the back of a chair, silently shaking her head.

"I'm sorry. I didn't mean . . . I don't know how it happened. I'm *sorry*, Ada."

"It's too late for that now."

"What am I going to do?"

"There's only one thing you can do."

Matt put his head in his hands. "I don't know how it happened," he said. "All the drinking . . . I was feeling sick. Katie brought me a cold cloth. And then . . ."

"Do you love her?"

"Yes."

"Well, that's good. That's something, anyway."

"I don't want to get married, Ada. I *can't*. Not yet."

Ada saw Matt's ravaged face, his empty eyes. Her heart went out to him, for he seemed to have aged years in this one night. She longed to put her arms around him and promise that everything would be

196

all right. She had made a similar promise when he had first come to the boardinghouse, a scared little boy, but he's a man now, she thought, and more's the pity. "There's no other way." She sighed. "Drinking's no excuse. It doesn't change what you did. Whether you meant to or not, it doesn't matter."

"Ada,.we're talking about my *life*. All my plans."

"What about Katie's life? You say you love her? Do you or don't you? Don't you care what happens to her?"

"Of course I do. I also care what happens to me. Is that so wrong? I didn't run away from the mines to spend my life working in a factory. To scratch in the dirt for pennies. I want more. I want a *future*."

"What about Katie's future?"

"She won't have much of a future if I'm stuck in some factory job. It'll be her mother's life all over again."

"There could be a child, Matt. From tonight there could be a child. Maybe you want to wait and find out for sure. Then you'd get married and have a 'seven-months'' baby. Oh, there are a couple of them born in the neighborhood each year. And there's no end to the snickering about them, the nasty gossip. Everybody looks at the mothers funny. The poor women are shamed. Is that what you want for Katie?"

"I hate this damn neighborhood!"

"It's no different in other neighborhoods. It's no different the world over. The world thinks it's fine if men have their fun. But women, decent women, are supposed to be virgins 'til they walk down the aisle. That's just the way it is. I'm not telling you anything you don't know. You wouldn't want to marry a woman who was . . . easy."

"I don't want to marry anyone. Not yet."

"I'm sorry, Matt. I really am. But you have to do what's right. You can't expect Katie to wait. Not after tonight."

"I'm at the top of my class in college. If I get married—"

"*If?*"

"I'd have to leave college."

"Is that such a tragedy?" Ada demanded, her patience exhausted. She was angry and made no effort to conceal her anger, for she felt it was warranted. "I'm ashamed of you, Matt McVey," she said, eyes flashing. "Stop thinking about yourself and start thinking about Katie. Start acting like a man."

"I am a man."

"You don't sound it. You sound like a crybaby. What's done is done. Accept it. If you ask me, you're lucky to be getting Katie. I'm sorry it happened this way, but I'm glad it's Katie. She'll be a wonderful wife to you."

"I hope she's wonderful with money. We won't have much of it. No one gets rich on factory wages."

"Well, you're determined to look on the dark side," Ada said, sitting down heavily. "But it's not that black. You can go to college at night. I know it'll take longer. It'll be hard. But if you want it enough, you shouldn't mind. You'll get your degree and go on to law school like you planned. In the meantime, you and Katie can live here."

"Here?"

"Why not? There's the big room off the parlor. I

198

use it for storage now, but when the house was first built it was the library. It has shelves and two closets and an alcove. The alcove could be a nursery. You could put a curtain there and it would be separate, kind of."

Nursery. The word shook Matt to his very soul, for the last thing he wanted was a child. He felt as if he were losing control of his life. Once again he had an urge to escape, to run fast and far and never look back. "You need that room for storage," he said in a feeble voice.

"Ah, it's full of old junk. Whatever I want to save, I'll put in the cellar. The rest I'll leave out for the trashman. It's no hardship, Matt. I'm glad to do it."

"You're glad to get me married."

"You had a choice," Ada replied, shaking her finger at Matt. "You had the choice of keeping away from Katie or not. I warned you. I warned you exactly what would happen. The signs were clear. I don't know why you're surprised."

"I wish I'd listened to you. If only I'd listened."

"Stop feeling sorry for yourself."

"My life's been turned upside down, Ada. One mistake and everything's changed."

"Is that what Katie is? A mistake?" Ada's eyes narrowed on Matt. "I don't like what I'm hearing," she said. "Sure everything's changed, but it's not the end of the world. You're young and strong. You're smart. A beautiful girl is in love with you. You should be counting your blessings. There are a lot of fellas who'd be happy to switch places with you. That's the truth, Matt. You can go on seeing the dark side if you want. Or you can count your blessings."

"You don't understand."

"I understand more than you think. I was your age once. Now I'm my age. I didn't get to be my age without learning a few things about people. Some people come undone when life doesn't go exactly their way. Other people take what life gives them and make the best. They're the ones with courage. The priests call it faith. I call it courage."

"Are you saying I don't have courage?"

"I'm saying life isn't always going to go your way. You have so much in your favor, so much to be grateful for. But all you can see is the dark side."

"I'm not *ready* to get married."

"You should have thought of that before."

"Yes. I know." Matt rose. He strode the length of the room, clenching and unclenching his fists. "How well I know."

"What's done is done. Accept it."

"I don't seem to have any choice."

"Ah, Matt, it's not as terrible as all that. If you love Katie, it's not terrible at all. You do love her, don't you? You weren't lying?"

"*Yes*, I love her. I've loved her for a long time. So what? Love doesn't last. My parents loved each other in the beginning. As years passed, they started hating each other. There was no happiness in their house. With all the tears and all the yelling, there was misery morning to night."

"Don't judge everybody by your parents."

"It wasn't only them, Ada. It was the same with all the families on the row. It's the same in this godforsaken neighborhood. *Love* isn't enough."

"It was for me and Tim, rest his soul."

"You had the boardinghouse. You didn't have to worry about making ends meet."

"Didn't we?" Ada laughed shortly. "That's not the way I remember it. There was a time when we didn't have two nickels to rub together. It wasn't easy getting started in vaudeville. We lived on hope and potato sandwiches. Once, when we were stranded in Kansas City, we lived the whole week on a small sack of apples. Things got better for us after a while, but they never got easy. It took thirty years of saving to buy this boardinghouse."

"Thirty years! A lifetime!"

"Good years, Matt. There was love. From first to last there was love. We had our arguments now and then. We didn't always see eye to eye. But we were happy."

"You were lucky."

"That too."

"What if Katie and I aren't so lucky?"

"Ah, I can't give you a guarantee. I can't put it in writing that everything will go your way. You have to trust."

"Trust in what?"

"Love."

Matt considered Ada's answer ridiculous, fanciful, and too simple by far. His lips parted in protest but, weary of arguments, he did not speak. He paced, staring straight ahead and seeing nothing.

"You're putting holes in my carpet." Ada sighed. "Ah, Matt, you can't walk your problems away. Face them, for heaven's sake. You'll feel better."

"It's hard thinking of myself as a married man."

"You'll have time to get used to the idea. You're

not getting married today."

"Today, next week, next month. What difference does it make? There's still an altar waiting for me."

"An altar, not a hangman's noose." Ada shrugged, smiling kindly. "Cheer up. You might like being married. You might even enjoy it. Some men do. Most men, if you ask me. It's a good feeling to know you're not alone in the world."

Matt nodded, for he found that aspect of marriage appealing. "I've felt alone all my life," he said.

"I know."

"I don't mean here. You gave me a home, Ada, and I'm grateful, I'll always be grateful."

"I did what I could. You needed mothering when you came here. It seems like only yesterday . . . but now . . ." Ada paused. She wiped her damp eyes. "Now you need a wife."

"Yes, maybe you're right."

"Praise be! I'm finally right about something tonight!"

"Okay," Matt said, managing a small smile. "You're the expert. Tell me what to do next."

"What do you think? You propose to Katie."

"Propose?"

"Of course. And be nice about it. Try to be romantic. A girl remembers a proposal her whole life."

"Propose." Matt put his hand to his head. "Oh, my God."

Katie, wrapped once again in Ada's robe, was curled upon the window seat, her long, golden hair

202

tumbling over her shoulders. She was smiling, lost in the memory of this sweet night with Matt. In memory, she felt his touch, heard his murmurings, and her heart leaped joyously. "Matt . . ." She sighed.

"Yes, I'm here, Katie."

"Matt!" Katie ran to him, throwing her arms around his neck. "I love you, Matt," she cried. "I love you so much."

"We . . . We have to talk."

"All right." Katie nodded against his shoulder. "Anything you say."

Matt stepped back. He walked a safe distance away and sat down, trying to calm his nervous hands. "How do you feel?" he asked. "Are you . . . okay?"

"I'm wonderful!"

Matt averted his eyes, for Katie's radiance was painful to behold. "I thought you'd be upset."

"Upset? But why?"

"I took advantage. I . . . I'm sorry."

"I'm not sorry, Matt. I'm not sorry at all. I've never been happier. I love you."

"I'm not good enough for you."

"Oh"—Katie laughed, kneeling beside Matt's chair—"that's silly. It's the other way around. I'm the one who's not good enough. I'm nobody. Just a scrubwoman from the tenements."

"Stop it, Katie. You mustn't say such things. You're more than what you do for a living. You're very special."

"Am I? Really?"

Matt turned his head, gazing at Katie's lovely face, her lovely body. He recalled the pleasures of her body

203

and, to his shame, new desires stirred within him. "Yes, really," he snapped. He rose, striding across the room to another chair. "Stay where you are, Katie. I can't think clearly when you're too close."

"What are you thinking about?"

"Us. We have some decisions to make."

"Are you mad at me?" Katie asked quietly. "Are you mad about . . . tonight?"

Matt took a moment to reply, for in truth he was both sorry and glad. "The word is angry—No, I'm not angry, and I'm not sorry either. Look at you, Katie." He sighed. "You're so beautiful. How could I be sorry?"

"Then what's wrong?"

"Nothing. Sometimes I'm a damn fool. That's not an asset in a husband. I'll be a trial to you."

"Husband? Did you say husband?"

"Yes." Matt smiled. His face softened and the light returned to his eyes. "I said husband. I happen to love you, Miss Kathleen Gallagher. Will you marry me?"

"Marry . . . Oh, Matt . . ." Katie flew to him, covering him with kisses. "Yes, yes, I'll marry you. I'll make you happy, Matt. You'll see. I'll be the best wife in the world. We'll have a wonderful life. You'll see. I love you so much."

Matt stroked Katie's silky hair. "I love you too," he said. "You stole my heart, little girl. Now it's yours to keep forever. You're stuck with me."

"Stuck with you! What a thing to say! I've been dreaming about you since the first day we met. You were my last thought every night and my first thought every morning. I hoped you'd love me. I prayed you would. But I never let myself believe it. I couldn't. Even now ... Am I still dreaming, Matt? Am I dreaming or is it real?"

"It's real. If you have any doubts ..." Matt pressed his lips to Katie's. He held her tightly, feeling the wild beating of her heart against his own. "I want to make love to you for the rest of my life," he said. He kissed her again and then, shaken, walked away. "I'll never get any work done with you around. I'm bewitched."

"I'm glad you are."

"We'd better hurry up and set a wedding date. I'll see your mother tomorrow. I'll wear my good suit and be properly respectful."

Katie paled, for she had given no thought to Maeve during this night. Sudden panic assailed her, and she had to strain to catch her breath. "I forgot about Mama," she gasped. "Matt, I forgot. I don't know what she'll say. It'll be a terrible shock. What if ... What if she says no?"

"It doesn't matter what she says. She can't stop us."

"But she *can*."

Matt went to Katie, taking her in his arms. "Don't worry, little girl. She won't stop us. I won't let her. With or without her permission, we'll be married. And soon."

"I'm afraid, Matt."

"You don't ever have to be afraid again. You have me. We both have Ada. She's on our side."

"Does Ada know about ... Is Ada home? Is that where you were? With Ada?"

"She came home an hour ago. Jack was better and she came home. We talked. Don't worry, she's on our side." Matt saw a question in the depths of Katie's green eyes. He saw a flicker of hurt and he felt badly. "I wanted to tell Ada about my plans," he said. "I wanted to discuss them. Marriage is a big step, Katie. I wanted to discuss it with Ada. She's been like a mother to me, after all."

"It was your idea to marry me? Ada didn't force you?"

"Force me? Who's being silly now? No one has to force me to marry you. I love you. I have for a long time."

"You really want to marry me? You're sure?"

"I'm sure," Matt replied, and if his reply was not completely true, neither was it entirely false.

"What do you want here?" Maeve asked, opening the door.

"I'm Matt McVey, Mrs. Gallagher."

"Aye, I know who you are. What do you want? Has something happened to Katie? I haven't seen her since yesterday. Ada said she was staying overnight at the boardinghouse. Is she all right?"

"She's fine. I'd like to talk to you, Mrs. Gallagher. May I come in?"

"Katie's all right?"

"Yes, fine."

"I'm busy. I've my work to do. But if it's important . . . aye, come in."

"Thank you." It was just past noon on Saturday. Matt had spent the morning reassuring Katie and trying to reassure himself. His courage had wavered, but now, dressed in his good blue suit, his shoes shined, his hair neatly parted and brushed, he was the

206

picture of a confident young man. "May I sit down?"

"Aye." Maeve gestured to a chair. "But keep your coat. It'll be a short visit. I can't offer you tea. There's nothing in the house 'til Katie brings her wages. What do you want?"

Matt smiled, staring across the table at Maeve. She was thin and haggard, yet he sensed the iron strength of her will. A formidable woman, he thought, and better a friend than an enemy. "I've heard a lot about you from Ada," he said lightly. "All nice things, of course."

"Is that so? Well, I've heard a lot about you, too. Don't waste your charm on me, Matt McVey. I've no time. I've a full washtub and then a full day's ironing. If you've something to say, say it and be done."

"You're very direct."

"Aye."

"I was hoping we could be friends, Mrs. Gallagher."

"And why would you hope that? I'm nothing to you."

"You're Katie's mother."

"Sure and did I say I wasn't? What of it? If you mean to try my patience, you're doing a grand job. I'm busy. I've work to do before the little ones come running in."

"I saw them downstairs. At least I think I did. The younger boy, Francis? He looks exactly like Katie." Maeve offered no response and Matt sighed. "I'm here to talk about Katie," he said.

"I guessed as much. What about her?"

"It's my turn to be direct, Mrs. Gallagher. I asked

Katie to marry me. She said yes. I'm here to ask your blessing."

Maeve's jaw tensed. She gripped the edge of the table, fixing her dark blue eyes on Matt. "Are you daft?" she cried. "Marry Katie? *My* Katie?"

"That's right."

"Are you playing a joke, Matt McVey? It's not funny, if you are. I never heard such foolishness. Never in all my life."

"It's not a joke." Matt smiled. "I love Katie. Katie loves me. We want to be married as soon as possible. We'd like to have your blessing."

Maeve rose. She went to the door and pulled it open. "I'll thank you to leave now. We've nothing more to talk about. You're daft if you think I'd let you marry Katie. You're crazy and they should be carting you off to the crazy house. Sure and that's where you belong, by the sound of it."

"I'll leave when we're finished, Mrs. Gallagher."

"We're finished now and you'll leave now. Do I have to get the law on you? I don't want you here. Ada's nephew or no, you're not welcome here. And that's as clear as I can be."

Matt was still. He lifted his gaze to Maeve's stern, implacable face and then looked away. He thought, The old witch is giving me an escape. I could leave and no one would blame me. I could say I tried, and it would be the truth. "Please, Mrs. Gallagher." He sighed.

"Please, is it? *Please* what? There'll be no marriage, not while there's breath in my body. I'm taking Katie out of the boardinghouse today, and that's the end of all the foolishness."

Matt sighed again, closing his eyes. He saw Katie, so young and innocent, so radiant with love. He knew he could not betray that love. "I'm staying, Mrs. Gallagher," he said. "We're going to talk. You don't frighten me. Oh, it's true you frighten a lot of people, including your daughter. You even frighten Ada sometimes. But you don't frighten me. Get the law. Get anybody you like. I'm staying."

Maeve glared at Matt. She slammed the door. "I warn you, there's no use in this. Do you think you'll change my mind? You won't. You can talk from now 'til doomsday and you won't change my mind. There'll be no marriage."

"What do you have against me?" Matt asked. "I haven't done anything to you."

"You're a heathen, aren't you? When's the last time you went to church? You're a sinner, Matt McVey. I dare you to tell me different."

"All right, I'm a sinner. We're all sinners, Mrs. Gallagher. Starting with Adam and Eve. But I'm not a heathen. I believe in God. I just don't happen to believe we can look to God for help."

"That's blasphemy!"

"Is it? Have you ever heard of a prayer being answered? Any prayer? Children die needlessly in Hell's Kitchen all the time. They go without food, without heat in winter, without medicine when they're sick . . . and they die. No prayers are answered for them. I see the good people of Hell's Kitchen going to church on Sunday—people old before their time and dressed in rags. No prayers are answered for them either. Look at the tenements. Take a long look and you'll see thousands of unanswered prayers—

What about your prayers, Mrs. Gallagher? Have any of your prayers been answered?"

Maeve was more shocked than angered by Matt's outburst. She sat down, twisting her calloused hands together. "There's faith," she said in an uncertain voice. "Sure and we must have faith."

Matt glanced around the bare kitchen. He saw the cracks in the walls, the flaking plaster, the stained floor that no amount of scrubbing would make clean again. "I have faith." He shrugged. "At the end, I believe God will consider the lives we were born to and then the lives we've led. That's fair. If God isn't fair, then it's all pointless anyway."

"I suppose if you're born poor, you're allowed extra sins."

"No." Matt laughed. "I didn't say that. But it's not fair to judge a man born to wealth the same way as a man born to poverty. The man born to poverty has much more to overcome. His struggles are greater. Would you judge Cornelius Vanderbilt and Joe Gallagher the same way?"

"Keep Joe out of it."

"But do you see what I mean?"

Maeve scowled, shaking her head. "I don't see anything. I hear fancy talk coming from you, and I'm not one for fancy talk. I'm telling you plain, you can't marry Katie. You're the wrong boy for her."

"Why? Because I'm a *heathen*?"

"Because I say so. That's all the reason you need and all you'll get."

"That's not good enough, Mrs. Gallagher."

"Well, if you really want to know, I don't like your friends. Maisie Craig and her kind."

"Maisie Craig is in the past," Matt replied, unruffled.

"Aye, now that you've had your way with her. I'll wager there were other Maisie Craigs in the past. And there'll be others in the future. A leopard doesn't change his spots. Nor a man."

"I love Katie."

"Aye, maybe you do. You're putting up a fight for her, and that's in your favor. But you're too . . . worldly. Katie's a child, a baby."

"She's a woman."

Matt had spoken only those few words, but something in his tone alerted Maeve. She looked hard at him, and it was as if she had had a revelation. Quite suddenly she understood Katie's luminous smiles, her sighs and rosy blushes. "Katie's been having a romance with you," she said, stunned. "She's been having a romance all along. And behind my back!"

"Let's talk about the future, Mrs. Gallagher, not—"

Maeve crashed her fist on the table. "I've heard enough from you," she roared. "It's the devil you are, Matt McVey. Turning Katie's head and making her lie to her own mother. How could you do it? How could you?"

"The lies were your fault. Katie wanted to be honest. She was afraid. She knew you'd force her to leave the boardinghouse and work at the laundry. That's a grim life for a girl like Katie, but you would have done it."

"Aye. There are no boys at the laundry. No boys to turn Katie's head with fancy talk. No boys to break her heart. You won't make her happy. Oh, maybe in the beginning. What about all the years after the beginning? I know your kind. Your kind—"Maeve stopped, seized by a realization more terrible than the first. "It's too late, isn't it?" she asked dully. "You and Katie . . ." She gazed at Matt, and in his eyes she saw the truth. "Well," she said, "it's settled then. What choice is there now?"

"We *want* to get married, Mrs. Gallagher."

"Aye."

"Whatever you may think, we want to get married."

"Is it me you're trying to convince, or yourself?" Maeve left her chair. She went to the sink and wet a towel, holding it to her pale face. "You'll be married in church."

"Yes, of course."

"I'll see Father Flynn this afternoon. We'll make the arrangements." Maeve turned. "How do you plan to earn your living?" she asked. "You don't get wages for going to college."

"I can go to college at night and work during the day. Ada's offered Katie and me a room in the boardinghouse. That will help. It will save paying rent. And it's only temporary."

"Only temporary? Dear knows I've heard those words before, from my own Joe. When we moved in here it was only temporary. Joe was going to be an importer. He had a notion about importing Irish crafts. Laces and wools and the like. It was his dream. It never came to anything. Dreams never do."

"I'm going to be a lawyer, Mrs. Gallagher. That's *not* a dream. That's a definite plan."

"Well, it's your life."

"It will be Katie's life, too."

"Aye." Maeve sighed. "There's no worry on that account. She's used to hard work by now."

Matt's eyes darkened. He sat very straight and stared coolly at Maeve. "If you're suggesting I won't be able to support Katie, you're wrong. I know a thing or two about hard work myself. Whatever I have I worked for, and that's fine with me. You don't hear me complaining."

"Do you want a medal?"

"I want you to understand. I'm not some fellow just out for good times. I know what my responsibilities are. Katie's my responsibility and I'll take care of her. You won't catch me dreaming the years away."

"Time will tell. What people want from life is seldom what they get. We'll see how you are about responsibility when your dreams start coming apart. Dreams or plans, it's all the same. Do you think it's easy to rise above yourself, Matt McVey? It isn't. Get a leg up and there's always something or somebody knocking you back down. You're too young to know, but that's the truth of it."

"I'll manage."

"Maybe you will and maybe you won't. Time will tell."

"I believe in myself, Mrs. Gallagher. Katie believes in me."

"She loves you. Does love put food on the table? Does love pay the bills? Ah well"—Maeve sighed again, loudly—"it's out of my hands now. There's nothing I can do. Not now."

"I hope you'll give Katie your blessing."

"She'll need more than my blessing. Sure and

you'll both need more than that."

"I'll provide whatever we need."

"Aye, I've heard those words before, too."

Matt shook his head. "Is there anything I can say to change your mind about me?" he asked.

"Talk is cheap. Even fancy talk like yours. It's actions that count."

"I promise my *actions* will please you."

"They haven't so far. . . . I'll make you a bargain, Matt McVey. I'll give Katie my blessing, but you stay away from her 'til the wedding day. I don't want her starting her marriage in a cloud of gossip. Dear knows this is a neighborhood for gossip."

"Don't worry. I'm moving in with my friend, Ben Rossi. I'll have a cot in the Rossi kitchen. It's all arranged. You have my word."

"Your word? Your word and a nickel will get me on the streetcar."

"What a hard woman you are."

"Not hard enough, by the look of things. I'm losing my daughter, my Katie. Two months past her fifteenth birthday and I'm losing her."

"I'll be a good husband, Mrs. Gallagher. Katie will be happy."

"We'll see about that, won't we? Aye, we'll see."

Matt sighed in relief as he left the tenement. He breathed deeply of the cool autumn air and he felt like a man suddenly released from prison, Maeve Gallagher's prison. The old witch is impossible, he thought as he hurried away. He was near the corner when he heard his name called. Smiling, he turned, holding out his hands to Katie. "It's all right, little girl," he said. "Everything's all right."

"Is it?" Katie asked, her eyes wide and glittering with hope. "What did Mama say? I can't wait another minute. Tell me what Mama said."

"We have her blessing."

"Really? You're not teasing?"

"She's going to see Father Flynn this afternoon."

Katie jumped a foot off the pavement. She flung her arms around Matt, laughing and crying at the same time. "Oh, I'm so happy. I love you so much, Matt."

"I love you—Katie, people are staring."

"Let them stare! Let the whole world stare! I'm going to be Mrs. Matt McVey!"

9

Katie and Matt were married during Christmas week. It was a small wedding, attended only by family, a few friends, and a few curious neighborhood children who hid, giggling, at the rear of St. Brendan's. Hugh escorted Katie down the aisle. She was an exquisite bride, sweetly demure in Maeve's lace wedding dress and veil, a bouquet of tiny pink roses clasped in her hands.

Matt watched Katie glide toward him and was almost overcome. His heart seemed to swell and he felt tears mist his eyes. A moment later he felt Ben's steadying touch on his elbow. "Thanks," he whispered.

"Good luck, my friend."

The music stopped and Father Flynn cleared his throat. "Dearly beloved," he began.

A hired carriage awaited the newlyweds as they emerged from the church. Shaking off bits of rice and confetti, they climbed into the plush back seat and rode to the boardinghouse. Their guests followed in another carriage, waving grandly at the crowds of Saturday shoppers. "It's my nephew's wedding day," Ada called out several times, enjoying the occasion. Maeve, seated next to her, was silent.

Ada had planned the wedding lunch, for Maeve had expressed little interest. Now she presided over a table set with her best linen and china and adorned with delicate paper doves. Tall white candles twinkled on the mantel and twin baskets of flowers bedecked the gleaming sideboard. The food was plentiful—cold ham in plum sauce, cold chicken, spiced squash, and raisin bread. There was champagne, the first any of them had ever tasted, and there was a wedding cake strewn with spun sugar roses.

Many wedding gifts were proudly displayed, including a teapot from the Muldoons and a bread plate from the Rossis. Jack Snow, recuperating at his Boston home, sent a lace table cloth and Cornelius O'Day gave the young couple a silver pitcher. From the other boarders came a variety of dishes and kettles and bed linens. Hugh's present was a set of stereopticon slides. Maeve's present was a handmade quilt.

"I have something for you too," Ada said, leading Katie into the hall. "I hope you'll be pleased."

"You've done so much already."

"This is special."

"I know. I know what it is. It's the room you fixed up for Matt and me. Our very own room. I can hardly wait to see it. I tried to peek a few times"—Katie smiled—"but the door was always locked."

"That's right. I had Mr. Cory put a new lock on. It'll give you privacy. Privacy's important when you're first married. The first years are never easy, take my word. You'll have your little arguments. And there'll be people ready to stick their noses in. Don't let them. Just turn the lock and work things out for yourselves."

"We won't argue, Ada. What would we argue about?"

"All married couples argue once in a while. It's not the end of the world. It's healthy, if you ask me. It clears the air. Some women like to be martyrs. They're so good, they wouldn't say boo to a goose. But that's wrong. If you're upset, make sure Matt knows you're upset. Talk it out. You'll feel better."

"Mama says it's a wife's duty to obey her husband."

"Ah, that's a funny kind of word, obey. I never thought it belonged in the marriage ceremony." Ada laughed, seeing Katie's startled expression. "I don't mean you should go against your husband," she added hastily. "I don't mean that at all. But you're entitled to your own opinions. It's not breaking the oath if you disagree with your husband. He'll disagree with you often enough, and fair is fair."

"Oh, Matt and I have the same opinions."

"Now you do." Ada nodded, chuckling. "Let's see if you still think that a year from now."

"I will."

Ada took a key from the pocket of her dress. "I can tell you something you disagree about," she said. "You like rooms to be cozy. Matt likes rooms to be simple. Well, there's only the one room for both of you . . . so I tried to make it cozy *and* simple. I hope it came out all right." She smiled, opening the door.

219

"Ada! Ada, it's wonderful!" Katie's face shone as she gazed around the room. It was a wide room, and deep, with dark wainscoting and dark hardwood floors. There was a brass bed, purchased at a secondhand shop, and a new feather mattress covered with soft blue quilts. Near the bed was a double dresser and, above it, a framed mirror. Across the room was a slender rosewood desk and a matching rosewood chair, also purchased at a secondhand shop. Two cushioned wing chairs were placed by the hearth, an oval table between them. The draperies were polished ivory cotton, their scalloped hems billowing over rows of potted plants. "I don't know what to say. How can I thank you? It's the most wonderful room I ever saw."

"Well, it'll be home to you, maybe for a long time. I want you to be happy here. Do you really like it, Katie? You can add your own touches. Don't worry about hurting my feelings."

"It's perfect just the way it is. I can't believe . . . has Matt seen it yet?"

"Ah, he insisted." Ada winked. "He didn't trust me. He was sure I'd have it filled with gimcracks and tassels. I surprised him. Of course he won't be here much. Working and going to school, he'll be away more than he's here, so I put in some things for you. The plants, the embroidered footstools. I almost bought a rocking chair. I had to drag myself out of the store."

"I love it, Ada. I can't believe it's ours."

"Are you crying? You mustn't cry on your wedding day."

"I can't help it." Katie sniffled, wiping her eyes.

"It's all so wonderful. It's all my dreams coming true. Thank you, Ada. Thank you for giving us our home."

"I'm only giving you the room. It's up to you and Matt to make it a home. You're both very young, and young people have to learn to be patient. It doesn't come natural. But if you're patient, you'll get through the bad times as well as the good. You don't think there'll be any bad times, do you? There'll be some. Not many, if you're lucky, but some."

"Are you sorry Matt married me?"

"Why, Katie, what a question! I'm not sorry. I'm delighted. You're the daughter I always wanted." Ada smiled. She reached out, smoothing Katie's upswept curls. "You were such a skinny, scared little girl when you first came here. Scared of making a mistake. Scared of your own shadow it seemed, sometimes. Look at you now. You're a beautiful young woman. There never was a more beautiful bride. Even Father Flynn took notice, and he's watched hundreds of brides walk down the aisle, maybe thousands."

"I wonder if Matt took notice."

"He's not one for flowery talk, but I saw his face. He loves you, Katie. There's no doubt about it."

"Aye, there'd better not be." Maeve's dark gaze moved from Ada to Katie. "There's no changing his mind now."

"Come in, Maeve. You probably want a word with Katie, and I should be getting back to the guests. I didn't mean to be gone so long. How's the punch holding out? It's my own recipe, but last time I made it too sweet. Did you taste it?"

221

"Sean and Francis liked it fine."

"I'm glad." Ada turned. Smiling, she put the key in Katie's hand. "It's yours," she said. "Be happy."

"I will, Ada. *We* will." Katie walked to the windows then to the hearth. She touched the chairs and the oval table, trailing her fingers over its burnished surface. "Am I dreaming, Mama? I'm afraid I'm going to wake up and find this is a dream."

"Would you be sorry if it was?"

"I'd die."

"Such talk! You're being fanciful, Katie. If dying was that easy, the streets would be full of corpses."

"I want to live forever. Right here in this room. Isn't it a grand room, Mama?"

"Aye, it is. I could never give you anything so grand. But then my husband didn't leave me a boardinghouse. Ada can afford to be generous. I have to make do day to day."

"Please Mama," Katie said quickly, "come sit down. I'll light the fire and we can have a nice talk."

"I'll sit, but only for a minute. I've laundry waiting for me at home. And Sean and Francis are getting restless. They'll be running wild in the parlor." Maeve folded her hands and stared at Katie. "Well, you're a married woman now. Do you feel any different?"

"I'm in the clouds. I'm *happy*, Mama."

"Aye, you look it. You made a lovely bride. An Irish rose, Mrs. Muldoon said, and she wasn't far wrong—Don't start crying, Katie. Can't I give you a compliment on your wedding day?"

"It's just that you . . . surprised me." Katie took Maeve's hand, pressing it to her cheek. "You don't give many compliments, you know. Not to me."

"Not to anybody. Do you expect me to sit about all the day thinking up compliments? I'm too busy thinking how to put food on the table. Maybe you won't have that worry. I hope you won't. It's no fun squeezing every penny tight."

"I know, Mama. That's what I wanted to talk to you about. I'm going to keep working here. For wages, I mean. And I'm going to give you half. Two dollars a week. It's not much, but it'll help. It's only right, Mama. It's my place to help with Sean and Francis."

Maeve was very still, gripping the arms of her chair. Several moments passed before she was able to speak. "Are my ears playing tricks?" she asked. "What did you say?"

"It's all settled. You'll have half my wages. I wanted to tell you last week, when I talked it over with Matt. But I was afraid there'd be an argument." Katie smiled, once again taking Maeve's hand. "I knew you wouldn't argue with me today. You wouldn't argue with a bride, would you?"

"Ada's going to pay you wages? Living here for free and getting paid in the bargain?"

"Yes, Mama. Ada said if I work I have to be paid. I want to work. What would I do with my days if I didn't work? We can certainly use the money. Half for you and half for savings."

"Glory be!" Maeve leaned back, shaking her head from side to side. "It's a miracle. I was laying awake nights worrying how I'd manage. Sean will be in school next year, and Francis the year after. I can get work then. Good, steady work. But 'til then there's only my laundry jobs to see us through. There's my laundry jobs and Hugh's dollar every week. Dear knows it wouldn't be enough."

"You don't have to worry. I'll be helping too."

"Did Matt say it was all right for you to work?" Maeve asked suddenly. "Sure and I heard a lot of talk about how he was going to be the provider."

"He will be, Mama. In time. But he has to finish school. I'll work until he's finished."

"And it's all right if you share your wages with us? You're a married woman now. Your husband is your family, and family comes first."

"Oh, Mama, you and the boys will always be my family. Nothing can change that. Not a husband, not ten husbands. Did you think I'd turn my back on you because I got married? I wouldn't do that. I couldn't."

"Aye, but is it all right with Matt?"

"Of course it is."

Maeve tilted Katie's face toward her. "Is it?" she persisted. "Are you keeping something from me? I want the truth, Katie."

"I'm telling the truth. Matt's agreed this is the right thing to do. He approves." Katie did not feel it necessary to add that Matt's approval had been grudging. He had hesitated, pacing around the kitchen for long moments. When finally his approval had come, it had come without enthusiasm. "Please don't argue, Mama. There's no reason to argue. We've already decided, Matt and I. It's settled."

"Why should Matt want to help us?"

"You're family. The Gallaghers and the McVeys

224

are *family*. I don't understand you, Mama. A minute ago you were saying it was a miracle. You were relieved. Now you want to argue."

"I want to be sure there's no trouble between you and Matt over this. I know how stubborn you are, Katie Gallagher."

"Katie McVey."

"You're Katie Gallagher to me." Maeve stood. She walked away, then turned and retraced her steps across the room. A frown creased her brow as she stared down at Katie. "It's true," she said. "I look at you and see my daughter, not Matt's wife. It's hard letting go. You'll know how hard when you have a daughter of your own. Daughters are different from sons. You worry more about a daughter. And maybe you care more."

"Hugh was always your favorite, Mama."

"I don't have favorites. I love all my children the same." Maeve gazed into Katie's disbelieving green eyes. "I love all my children the same," she said again, sighing, "but I'll tell you a secret . . . Hugh's the one most like me. You're like your father, but Hugh . . . it's my vanity, Katie. Vanity's a sin, and I'm paying the price for my sin. Hugh will never be on the cops. He'll be lucky just to stay out of jail. Aye, there's trouble ahead, bad trouble. As long as I live, I'll know I had a hand in it. Because of vanity."

"Hugh will be all right, Mama."

"No. He won't. But you have a chance, and I'm thankful for that. I wish you happiness, Katie McVey. All the happiness in the world."

• • •

225

"It's getting late, Matt," Ada said, propping her tired feet on a kitchen chair. "Don't keep your bride waiting."

"I thought Katie should have some time to herself. It's been a crazy day."

"All wedding days are crazy. They're supposed to be. That's part of the fun. You'll look back years from now and laugh."

"Will I?"

"Sure. You'll remember the rushing around, the butterflies in your stomach, and you'll laugh about it. You'll have stories to tell your grandchildren on *their* wedding days."

"Grandchildren." Matt winced. "You're making me feel like an old man. I'm harldy old enough to have a wife. A wife! My God, it still seems so strange."

"It always does, in the beginning." Ada studied her nephew's drawn face, his dark restless eyes. "You're not the first groom to be nervous." She smiled. "Walk a man down the aisle—any man—and suddenly he's having trouble breathing."

"Women don't seem to have that trouble."

"Marriage comes natural to women. Men have to get used to the idea. Men think they're giving up their freedom."

"Aren't they? Aren't *I*?"

"Well, it depends. If you'd planned to spend your life chasing every pretty girl in the city, then the answer is yes. Is that what you'd planned?"

"I don't know. Everything's happened very fast."

"Ah, you're just nervous. By this time next week you'll be wondering what you were nervous about. I promise you won't be hiding here in the kitchen with me."

"Hiding? I'm not hiding."

"What do you call it? You know more words than I do. Is there a better word for this? Why are you sitting here? If it was a girlfriend waiting, you'd be long gone. But it's your bride, and so you're nervous." Ada chuckled, ruffling Matt's hair. "There's no cause," she said. "You'll like marriage, believe me."

"I wish I could—Where are you going?"

"I've been up since five. I'm tired and I'm going to bed."

"You're leaving me alone?"

"I'm leaving you to your wife. Good night, Matt."

"Good night."

Matt stared at Ada's retreating back and indeed he felt alone. He reached for a cigarette then flung it away, rising abruptly. He damped the fire and turned out the lights. "My wedding night," he muttered, angry with himself, angry with Katie, though he knew she was blameless. "My God, I'm married!"

That thought weighed heavily on Matt's mind as he strode through the hallway. It was not a new thought. He had spent weeks trying to accept the fact of his impending marriage, trying to allay his many doubts. He had tried and, to his dismay, he had failed. "Katie?" he called now, entering their darkened room. "Where are you?"

"I'm here, Matt." Katie stepped out of the shadows. She was smiling, her hair a golden mantle in the flickering firelight, her face tender with love. "I'm here."

Matt gazed at his radiant young bride. He could see

the curves of her body beneath her nightgown and a wild rapture came upon him. His breath quickened. He heard again a roaring in his ears, the roaring he heard whenever she was near. "Katie," he cried, tearing her gown away. He gasped at her nakedness, pressing his hungry mouth to her breasts. Murmuring incoherently then moaning, he threw off his robe and seized her in his arms.

Matt and Katie lay on the bed, desire raging within them. Their bodies touched and their hands sought each other passionately. Katie trembled, consumed by an ecstasy that was as sweet as it was savage. "I love you," she said again and again until Matt could not remember when her words became cries of rapture and their love was one with the blaze of the fire and the passing of the moon.

Sunday brought winter's first snowstorm, but the newlyweds hardly noticed. They remained in their room, the curtains drawn, the door locked. Left to themselves, they slept and made love and ate the meals Ada placed on trays in the hall. Few words were spoken, for the yearnings they felt spoke more than words.

Matt awoke Monday morning at dawn. He stretched, smiling from the depths of a great contentment. He opened his eyes to see Katie leaning over him, her face smooth and rosy, love lighting her eyes. "Good morning," he said, lifting his hand to her cheek.

"Good morning, husband."

"What?" Matt blinked. His gaze darted quickly

about the unfamiliar room, and it was a moment or two before he realized where he was. "Oh, yes." He sighed, falling back against the pillows. "Yes, I'm a husband now."

"Did you forget?"

"Almost . . . you're dressed. Why are you dressed?"

"It's time for work. If I'm late there'll be funny looks and teasing." Katie laughed, shaking her head. "You know how the boarders are. I want this to be just another day, even though it isn't. I love you, Matt McVey."

"I love you. Come to bed."

"Later." Katie stroked Matt's face. She bent and kissed his lips. "I'll be here when you come home from work. I'll be waiting. Tonight and every night after that for the rest of our lives. I promise."

"The rest of our lives. That's a long time."

"I hope it's a hundred years. Two hundred. It still won't be long enough." Katie rose. She seemed to dance around the room, touching furniture and walls, glancing lovingly over her shoulder at Matt. "I hope it's forever."

"You're a romantic."

"I'm happy. I'm so happy I could burst. It's the most wonderful feeling, Matt. Right here, in my heart. Does that sound silly? I don't care if it does. I don't care about anything but you." Katie held out her hand. She touched her slim gold wedding ring. "Mrs. Matt McVey." She beamed. "Imagine!"

Matt was entranced by Katie's youthful gaiety. He watched her, mesmerized, and thought that she had never looked lovelier. He recalled her passion and his pulse began to race. "Come to bed," he said huskily.

"I have to work. You have school."

"School!" Matt groaned, striking his forehead. "I forgot about school. My God, I really am bewitched. See what you've done to me?"

"I love you."

"Come over here and say that. No, don't. Stay where you are. I have a paper to write before school. I've been putting it off, but it's due today. It won't get written if you come any closer."

"All your books are on the desk." Katie smiled. "I'll let you get started . . . Matt? When I was straightening the room I found an envelope with five dollars in it. Is it yours?"

"It's ours. It's a wedding present from Ben."

"But Ben already gave us a present. The bread plate with the pretty roses in the center. You saw it. I showed it to you."

"That's from Ben's family. The money is from Ben."

Katie frowned. "You're going to give it back, aren't you?" she asked. "Ben can't afford five dollars. It's a lot of money to him."

"It's a lot of money to me, too, little girl. Maybe Ben can't afford it, but I can't afford to give it back. I need every dollar I can get my hands on, especially now. There were wedding expenses. Your ring and your flowers and the carriages didn't come free. There'll be other expenses as we go along."

"Ben is poor."

"*Ben* is poor. What do you think I am?" Matt sat up. He grabbed his robe and put it on, looking intently at Katie. "I can finish my second year of college *if* I'm careful with my savings. Next fall I'll have to enroll in night school. I'll be working days in the lumber yard and going to school at night. God only knows when I'll have time to study. It's a hard road. Harder than Ben's, *poor* or not."

Katie was startled by Matt's outburst. She was distressed, and she wrung her hands together. "I'm sorry," she said earnestly. "I didn't mean anything. I didn't mean to upset you."

"Use your head, Katie. Money doesn't just fall from the sky. It doesn't grow on trees for the picking."

"I know. I know all about money worries. There hasn't been a day in the last ten years when Mama didn't remind me. Mama—"

"*Mama's* doing fine. She's getting half your wages."

"That's not fair, Matt. We talked it over. We agreed. I knew you weren't happy, but I thought you understood."

"I do. What I don't understand is your attitude. Wanting me to give Ben's money back. Whose side are you on?"

"How can you ask such a question? I'm on your side. I love you." Katie sank into a chair, covering her face with her hands. "Oh, Matt, we're having an argument. Two days married and we're having an argument. It's my fault. I'm so sorry."

Matt gazed at his tearful young wife and his anger vanished, replaced by the sharp pang of guilt. "No, it's not your fault." He sighed and went to Katie, wrapping his arms about her and holding her close. "It's my fault, little girl. I'm an awful fool some-times. And when it comes to money . . . well, that's a sore point. The truth is I thought about refusing Ben's money. I knew it was a sacrifice for him, and I wanted to refuse it. But I couldn't. Right now every dollar is precious. I have to be Scrooge."

"I don't care if you're Scrooge." Katie sniffled, raising her eyes to Matt. She saw his smile and her heart fluttered. "You're the man I love."

"The lucky man."

"About my wages—"

"That's all settled. We'll help your family as much as we can. I was wrong to complain. I was wrong to snap at you. Forgive me?"

"Are you sure you don't mind?"

"I say stupid things when I lose my temper. Pay no attention."

"I don't want us to argue, Matt."

"We won't. Just leave money matters to me from here on."

"Oh, I promise. I *promise*."

"Money's not worth arguing about," Katie said to Ada one day in February. "Besides, I promised."

"But you're entitled to some spending money of your own. You work hard enough. You work from morning 'til night, and still there's never a penny in your pocket. Has Matt turned into a miser?"

"It's not worth arguing about."

"I'll tell you what it's not. It's not fair."

Katie had reached the same conclusion during the two months of her marriage, though she had kept her thoughts to herself. She refused to argue with Matt, refused even to question him. Each Saturday she took her wages into their room, putting half in the yellow teapot, half in an envelope for her mother. That was the first and last she saw of the money she had earned. Matt went often to the teapot, taking whatever he needed for books or carfare or Saturday night beers with Ben, and clearly he considered it his right to do so. Katie watched, saying nothing. "Matt has a lot on his mind, Ada. It's his final term at day college, and the closer it gets to the end, the more upset he is."

"I understand that. But what about you? If he can go to the pub of a Saturday night, you can have new shoes. Look at your shoes, Katie. They're a disgrace!"

"Don't blame Matt. He's too busy to notice my shoes."

"Make him notice then. Have you lost your tongue?"

"Oh, I don't want to bother him. He comes in late from his job and we . . ." Katie blushed, glancing away. "We have so little time together. I wouldn't spoil it talking about money."

"You listen to me, miss. Love is all well and good, but talking is just as important. He used to complain that Maeve let you go around in rags. Now he's doing it. You have to speak up."

"Rags!" Katie smiled. "Matt gave me a new shirtwaist for Christmas. And a box of stockings."

"When he was courting you, he gave you jewelry."

"Well, we're not courting any more. Marriage is . . . different. It changes things." Katie's voice was wistful, for she was remembering the wonderful presents of their courtship, the romantic trips about the city. Now there were no presents and no trips; indeed they seldom left their room. "Matt's schooling comes first, Ada. I wouldn't want him wasting his money on foolishness."

"What do you call going to the pub? That's wasting money on foolishness. There's beer in the ice box. All he wants. He doesn't have to go out for it."

"All the men go to the pub."

"If all the men jumped off the roof, would Matt jump too? Talk about foolishness! It's not a sacred tradition, Katie. It's a bunch of men throwing hard-earned money across a bar. In Matt's case, it's your money he's throwing. His own wages are safe in the bank."

"For his schooling. For the future. I understand that."

"*I* don't," Ada said, her eyes flashing in an unusual display of anger. "He's got you waiting on him hand and foot and paying for the privilege. That's not marriage. Marriage is sharing. It's giving up the pub to buy your wife a new pair of shoes. He needs reminding, and I'm the one to do it."

"Please, you mustn't. I know you only want to help, but you mustn't say anything."

"Matt's got my Irish up, and my one quarter German. I've kept quiet long enough. I don't like the goings on here. Tim, rest his soul, must be spinning in his grave."

"*Please*, Ada." Katie slammed the cupboard door and ran to Ada. She was pale, her chin quivering. "It's the wrong time. There'll be trouble."

"What are you talking about? Katie, you're white as a sheet. What's the matter? For heaven's sake, you're not afraid of Matt, are you?"

"No. No, it's nothing like that. It's just the wrong time."

"Why?"

"You have to believe me, Ada. It's the wrong time, that's all."

"*Why?*"

Katie turned. She stared down at the floor, a sigh falling from her lips. "Because I'm going to have a baby," she said.

"A baby! Ah, that's wonderful. That's the best news I ever heard." Ada clasped Katie to her bosom then held her away, looking into her lovely young face. "There's no mistake?" she asked. "You're sure?"

"I'm sure."

"A baby! How do you feel, Katie? Do you feel well?"

"I'm sick every morning, but I'm supposed to be. I remember how Mama was with Sean and Francis. And I remember Mrs. Muldoon with her youngest. It's natural. Once the sickness passes I feel fine. By afternoon I'm so hungry I could eat everything in sight."

"Of course. You're eating for two. We'll have to see you eat proper. Lots of meat and vegetables and fruit. Not too many sweets. Sweets only put weight on. I should know." Ada laughed, slapping her broad thighs. "Lots of milk. I'll tell the milkman to bring extra. A baby! I couldn't be happier if it was my own. Congratulations, Katie."

"Thank you."

"If I was you I'd be shouting the news. You seem

235

kind of quiet. Is it Matt? He's not unhappy about the baby, is he?"

"Matt doesn't know. I haven't told him yet." Katie walked to the table. She sat down and folded her hands in her lap. "I'm worried," she admitted. "Maybe it's the wrong time for a baby. The expenses will just be another burden on Matt."

"Ah, he doesn't have so many burdens. Compared to some in Hell's Kitchen, he has it easy. I know he wants children. He always talks about making his fortune so his children can thumb their noses at the world."

"But does he want children *now*? All his plans, Ada. Getting married set his plans back. Having a baby will set his plans back again. I'm worried how he'll take it. Maybe he won't be unhappy, but maybe he won't be glad either."

Ada's smile faded, for she sensed the truth of Katie's speculation. "Well, Matt never fancied surprises," she replied carefully. "He's the type who likes being in control of things. Give him a while to get over the surprise, and he'll be glad."

"Do you really believe that?"

"Matt planned on having a wife and family, Katie. It's happened sooner than he expected, but that's not the end of the world. He's young. He has his whole life ahead of him. It's not a tragedy if he has to struggle for a few years in the beginning."

"He may think it is."

"Never mind what he thinks. A baby is a blessing. You should be jumping with joy and instead you're worrying. You're glad about the baby, aren't you?"

"Oh yes." Katie nodded, resting her hand on her stomach. "I can hardly wait. Everything would be perfect if only Matt . . . I'm worried how he'll take it."

"Stop pampering him."

"What?"

"You treat Matt like he's lord of the manor. He's your husband, Katie. Sure it's your place to make him happy. But that doesn't mean you have to wear yourself out smoothing the way for him. He can smooth his own way."

Katie bent her head. A tear slipped down her cheek and she brushed it away. "I . . . I couldn't stand it if Matt didn't want the baby."

"That's silly talk," Ada said firmly. "I won't listen to silly talk."

"I'm *worried*."

"There's nothing to worry about. I've known Matt longer than you have. I'm not pretending he's a saint. He can be selfish at times. He can be thoughtless. That's his youth, Katie. Underneath it all he has a good heart. He wouldn't hurt you for the world."

"I know."

"Then stop worrying." Ada wet a cloth and brought it to Katie. "Wipe your eyes." She smiled. "That's better. Let me tell you something, miss. You try too hard to please the people you love. You do it with Maeve, and now you're doing it with Matt. You take their lives on your shoulders, as if you were responsible. They can manage fine for themselves. They're not made of sugar. Iron is more like it. If a building fell on Maeve, she'd get right up and go

237

about her business. So would Matt. There's no stopping those two. That's the truth."

"Yes."

"You can't earn love by doing good deeds, Katie. Ah, your kindness is one of the things Matt loves about you, and Maeve too. But they'd love you no matter what. Don't be afraid."

"I guess I am, in a way. Mama stopped loving Papa. It was after we came to America. I guess, in the back of my mind, I was always afraid she'd stop loving me. I'm afraid Matt will stop."

"Well, you have it wrong. Maeve never stopped loving Joe. She stopped understanding him. Here they were in a strange country, with no money, no friends, no prospects. She was concerned. But Joe was Joe. Tell him about the high price of potatoes and he'd tell you a new idea for getting rich. There are two ways to handle a man like that. One is to keep at him 'til he hears you. The other is to let him be. Maeve let him be. She took all the problems on her own shoulders, and her marriage suffered because of it."

"Matt isn't Papa."

"He's a man. Don't expect a man to read your mind. I'm not saying you should nag him, Katie. I'm saying you should talk to him. Marriage is hundreds of everyday problems, like needing new shoes. And it's a few special occasions, like a baby coming. Now, you talk to him or I will."

"No, Ada. I'll do it."

"When?"

"Soon."

"What about today?"

238

"Today is Saturday. Matt will rush home to change his clothes and then he'll be meeting Ben. I'll be visiting Mama. You know how Saturdays are. I promise I'll talk to him tomorrow." Katie looked up, smiling slightly. "Marriage is so complicated."

"Life is complicated. Sometimes it plays tricks."

10

"Mama?" Katie called, entering the Gallagher flat. "Mama, are you . . ." She paused as she saw five-year-old Sean huddled by the stove, his cheeks pink with cold, his hands plunged into the pockets of his knickers. "I know a little boy who forgot his sweater again." She smiled, quickly closing the door. "Where's your sweater, Sean?"

"In my room."

"Hurry and fetch it. It's freezing in here."

"I can't. Mama said."

"What did Mama say?"

"I have to stay here and be quiet. Francis is sick."

"Sick?" Katie frowned. She removed her coat and draped it about her brother. "Take my gloves, Sean. Put them on. What's the matter with Francis?"

"I don't know. Hugh's gone after the doctor."

"The doctor!" Sudden anxiety clutched at Katie's heart, for she knew doctors were summoned to the tenements of Hell's Kitchen only when all else had failed. It was a last, desperate resort. "The doctor? Are you sure?"

Sean nodded, lowering his solemn blue eyes.

"Francis is terrible sick. Mama said. Is Francis going to die, Katie? Is he going to heaven, like Papa? Heaven's far away. It's far in the sky. I don't want him to go there. Tell him not to go. Will you tell him?"

Katie stared helplessly at Sean. Her lips parted, but no comforting words came. She swallowed, fighting back her fear. "Francis will be fine. The doctor's on the way and Francis will be fine. Children get sick all the time."

"Mama was crying."

"No, it's just the cold. The cold makes her eyes tear."

"She was *crying*."

Katie gathered Sean to her. "Don't fret," she murmured, kissing his silky blond head. "Everything will be fine. You stay here and wait for the doctor while I go see Francis. When I come back I'll put the kettle on, and we'll have tea."

Sean fished in his pocket, extracting a small sack of marbles. "Give that to Francis," he said. "That's my best ones. He'll be happy."

"I'll give it to him right now." Katie turned, walking out of the kitchen. She walked the few steps to her brothers' room and then stopped, taking a deep breath. Dear God, she prayed silently, please let Francis be all right. He's only a little boy. Please let him be all right. "Mama?" she whispered, opening the door. "I'm here, Mama."

Maeve was leaning over the bed, staring down at Francis. Her eyes were sad, dark hollows in her ashen face. Her lower lip was bitten almost raw. "Is that you, Katie?"

242

"Yes, Mama. How is he?"

"He's bad off. Aye, very bad. I thought it was another cold. Sure and he's always having colds. I kept him indoors yesterday. But by night he was shaking with chills. Burning up." Maeve pressed her hand to Francis's forehead. "He's still burning up. I sent Hugh after the doctor, but it's a miracle we need."

"Don't say that, Mama."

"Why not? It's the truth. I wish it wasn't, but will wishes make Francis better? I've been here all the night, wishing and praying. All the day, too. He's no better. He's getting worse. I lost two children to fever before you were born, Katie. I know the signs. I know . . ." Maeve's voice trailed away. She looked at her daughter. "That's right." She sighed. "There were two before you, two boys. We never told you. What was the use? I wouldn't have told you now except I'm so tired I'm not thinking straight."

"Mama, I had two other brothers?"

"Aye. Babies they were when they died. That was part of the reason we left Ireland. There was so much sickness, especially with the young. There was so much dying. . . . People say I'm hard. Well, I am. But I wasn't always. It's the heartbreak that did it. Heartbreak at every turn." Maeve went to the dresser. She immersed a towel in a basin of cold water and wrung it out, taking it to Francis. "You'll understand what I mean when you have children of your own and no money to give them the things they need. You'll understand when your child is sick because you couldn't afford coal for the stove."

Katie clasped her hands protectively over her

stomach. "That won't happen, Mama. I'll give my children what they need. I'll find a way. Matt and I—"

"Hush, Katie. Keep your voice down or you'll be waking Francis. He hardly closed his eyes all the night. Let him sleep now if he can. Sometimes sleep is medicine."

Katie gazed at her brother. His face was flushed, his body hidden under several threadbare blankets and Maeve's coat. He slept, though not peacefully, for even in sleep his legs thrashed. "He's trying to kick the covers off, Mama," she said, kneeling beside him. She saw his dry and swollen lips. She touched his burning cheek. "He's on fire."

"Aye. First it was chills, then the fever."

"Isn't there anything we can do?" Katie's eyes beseeched Maeve. "There must be something. He's on *fire*."

"Sure and I don't need you to tell me that. It's the fever I've been fighting all these hours. I've done all I know to do. Poultices, hot salt, mustard. I fetched a bit of poteen from Mrs. Muldoon and rubbed his chest with it. I fed him clove tea, spoonful by spoonful . . . I did all I could and still he's getting worse."

Katie smoothed Francis's tangled hair. "Poor boy," she said. "What's keeping the doctor? Why didn't you call the doctor yesterday, Mama?"

"Look in my purse and you'll find a dime and four pennies. Tell me how I was supposed to call the doctor with fourteen cents in my purse."

"Hugh always seems to have money."

"Hugh!" Maeve snorted. "Hugh wasn't home

yesterday. He left for school in the morning and that was the last I saw of him 'til this afternoon. He comes home, cock 'o the walk, and starts blaming me because there's no coal, because Francis is sick. But where was he when Francis took sick? Where were you?"

"I'm sorry. I wasn't blaming you, Mama." Katie reached into her pocket. She held out an envelope. "There's my two dollars. I'm sorry it's not more. I'll talk to Matt and—"

"And what? The Gallaghers are no concern of Matt. Dear knows it's kind of him to let us have the two dollars each week. He's doing his part. It's enough. He has his own expenses to worry about."

"The money is mine too. I work for it. I can have a say in how it's spent."

Maeve glanced sharply at her daughter. "That sounds like Ada talking. Sometimes she has queer ideas. Tim went along, but don't think Matt will. Tim and Matt were cut from different cloth. I saw that the day he was here. He'll be making the decisions in your family, and without asking your say. It's his nature. Ada can talk all she wants about sharing, but Matt will be boss regardless. Has he asked your say in anything yet?"

"He's . . . very busy. There isn't much time to talk."

"Ada's probably telling you to find time. Well, Matt's not the type, and it's just as well. A husband should be boss, though he'll have his hands full with you. You're a stubborn one, Katie."

"So are you."

"For all the good it's done me." Maeve turned,

again dipping a towel in cold water. She brought the towel to Francis's fiery brow. "Living like animals in a cave," she said, her eyes locked on her son. "And this is the result. I don't care if you blame me. I blame myself."

"The doctor will be here soon, Mama."

"The doctor's here," Hugh announced. He stood in the doorway, pointing to the slim, mustached man at his side. "Dr. Morton. Go on, Doc. Fix Francis up."

Dr. Daniel Morton was new to Hell's Kitchen, having inherited his uncle's practice only weeks before. He was a quiet young man, blessed with what his uncle had called "noble intentions," and with keen diagnostic ability. He had never before doubted his skill, but now, confronted daily by the realities of poverty, he had reason to wonder if skill would be enough. "Mrs. Gallagher?" he asked, looking from Katie to Maeve.

"Aye, I'm Mrs. Gallagher. My son, Francis, is bad off. It's the fever."

Dr. Morton walked to the bed. "You may stay, Mrs. Gallagher. The others will have to wait outside."

"C'mon, Katie," Hugh said. "I bought bread and cheese and baloney. You can make sandwiches. C'mon, you're no use here. Sean's starving," he added, seeing her reluctance to leave.

"Yes, I forgot about Sean." Katie rose, taking the sack of marbles from her pocket. "Sean wanted Francis to have these," she explained. "A present."

"Later. C'mon and get out of the doc's way."

Katie put the marbles on the dresser. She found Sean's sweater and folded it over her arm. "I'll be

246

right outside, Mama. I'll be in the kitchen." She looked back at her stricken brother. Sighing, she followed Hugh into the hall. "I'm worried. He's awfully sick."

"Blame it on the old lady. She waited 'til today to call the doctor, didn't she? Scared it might cost her money."

"Oh, Hugh, that's so unfair. She didn't *have* any money. If you'd been here . . . why weren't you here? Mama said you stayed out all night."

"Business."

"Business! You're fourteen. What kind of business could you have? What kind of business keeps you out all night?"

"Matt's out all night, or close to."

"He's at the livery stable. That's his job, Hugh. Don't tell me you have a night job."

"I've had my fill of jobs. Breaking my back hauling coal in winter, ice in summer. All for the lousy dollar a week Maggio paid. Slave wages. I'm no slave."

"Aren't you working on Mr. Maggio's wagon any more?"

"Not since summer. I quit. Ma don't know. I give her her dollar every Saturday like usual and she's happy."

"Where does the dollar come from?"

Hugh shrugged. "Wherever it comes from, it ends up in Ma's purse. A dollar's a dollar. It don't matter where it comes from. Who cares?"

"Would Officer Garrity care?"

"The hell with Garrity. He's another dumb Mick hiding behind his badge. What's a badge but a hunk of tin? Now if it was gold, I might—"

"Oh, you're impossible!" Katie pushed past Hugh into the kitchen. Sean, looking small and lost amidst the folds of her coat, was still seated by the stove. "I brought your sweater, Sean. Here, put it on. I'll make you a nice sandwich. Are you hungry? I bet you are. It's almost six o'clock."

"Is Francis better?"

"The doctor's with him. Don't worry."

"Is he better? Did you give him my marbles? Was he happy? What did he say?"

"So many questions, Sean. First let me make your sandwich. I'll make sandwiches for all of us. And tea. It's freezing in here. Hugh, you're rich. Why don't you buy coal?"

"I did." Hugh rocked back on his heels, grinning at Katie. "There's a whole bag right beside you. I bought it when I bought the food. I have extra money sometimes." He shrugged. "I offer it to Ma but she won't take it. The devil's money, she calls it. She takes the Saturday dollar and that's all. Meanwhile, Sean and Francis eat scraps in a cold kitchen."

"Mama refuses your money?"

"The *devil's* money."

"Well, she does what she thinks best. She has her reasons."

"Yeah, she always has reasons. And you're all the time agreeing with her. Like a parrot."

"I try to see her side, Hugh."

"You try to see everybody's side. You try to be fair. It's a waste. Nothing's fair in life. You won't get nowhere being fair, being good. I'll take smart over good any day."

248

"What you're doing isn't smart."

"How do you know what I'm doing?"

"I don't, not exactly. But I hear things. I hear about *Swag* Gallagher and his hoodlum friends. There's trouble at the end of that road."

Hugh smiled. It was a chilly smile, as chilly as his dark blue eyes. "Meanwhile there's coal for the stove," he replied. "Or is it better to freeze? That's what the old lady thinks. Sure and it's better to freeze than to burn in Hell. Me, I'll take my chances."

"Mind you don't take them in jail," Katie muttered. She carried a platter of sandwiches to the table, setting it down with a thump. "Make yourself useful, Hugh. Get a fire going. The coal's no help to us sitting on the counter. Sean, come and have your supper."

"What about Francis? Where's his supper?"

"He can't eat now, Sean."

"When can he?"

Katie's face softened. She took her brother's hand and led him to the table. "Look at the delicious sandwiches," she urged. "Cheese and baloney—your favorites. Go ahead. I know you're hungry. I can hear your stomach growling. It sounds just like the Ryan's dog."

"Does not." Sean giggled, patting his stomach. "The Ryan's dog says *woof.*"

"That's what I'll say if you don't start eating. Hurry before Hugh eats them all. He won't leave a crumb. Will you, Hugh?"

"Listen to her, kid. Once I sit down there'll be nothing left. Get your share while you can."

Sean picked up a sandwich and bit into it. "Good,"

he pronounced between swallows. "You have some, Katie. Get *your* share while you can."

"Oh, don't worry about me. I'm hungry."

But Katie, hungry as she was, could not eat. She was troubled, distracted by thoughts that rushed chaotically from Hugh and his wayward life, to Maeve and the two children she had lost, and then to Francis. She remembered his little face so flushed with fever. She remembered the thrashing of his legs. Dear God, she prayed again, please let Francis be all right.

Hugh sat opposite Katie, his arms crossed, his glance roaming idly around the room. He appeared unconcerned, but his voice, when he spoke, was anxious. "The doctor's been in there a long time," he said. "I wonder how come. It must be Ma's fault. She's probably chewing his ear off."

"I doubt it. She's too scared."

"Scared? Her? That'll be the day."

Katie put her finger to her lips, nodding in Sean's direction. "Believe what you want, Hugh. I was with Mama. I know what I saw."

"Yeah, scared 'cause it's going to cost her money."

Katie had no time to reply, for Dr. Morton had entered the kitchen. She stood. "Is Francis all right?" she asked.

Dr. Morton walked to a corner of the kitchen, motioning Katie and Hugh to join him. "I'm afraid the news isn't very good," he said quietly. "Francis has scarlet fever. There are several cases in the neighborhood just now. Some more serious than others."

"How serious is it with Francis?"

"His fever is quite high. I must tell you that isn't a good sign." Dr. Morton paused, looking first at Hugh, then at Katie. "It's best to speak frankly," he said with a sigh. "Francis is in no immediate danger, but if the fever continues as it is, or rises, his chances will be poor."

"Doc can't you do nothing for the fever?"

"I've left some medicine with your mother. I can't promise it will help. There are many complications in scarlet fever. Francis's age is against him. The younger the child, the more severe the complications. I'm sorry."

"Are you saying he's . . . is Francis going to die?"

"I'm hopeful the fever will break," Dr. Morton replied, stroking his ginger mustache. "I can't promise. We're not sure how the disease works, and so there's little we can do for it. We treat the symptoms. That's all we can do."

"What use are you then?" Hugh demanded. "Save the speeches, Doc. We got you here to fix Francis up. It sounds like you done a lousy job."

"Stop it," Katie said, for she saw the pained look in Dr. Morton's eyes. "Don't you think he wants to help? Don't make things worse."

"They're already worse."

"I'm afraid your brother is right," Dr. Morton said with a small, sad smile. "Sometimes doctors are useless. There's too much we don't know." He glanced around the kitchen, seeing everywhere the stark evidence of poverty, and again he sighed. "I'll have to examine your other brother. Sean, is it? He's been exposed to the fever, and in such close quarters . . ."

"Oh, God," Katie cried. She took Hugh's hand, clinging to it. "Not Sean. Not both of them."

"Please try not to worry. It's just a precaution. Even if Sean were infected, and I say *if*, it wouldn't be half as serious. Catching the disease early makes a difference."

Katie and Hugh looked at each other. "You mean," Hugh said, "if you'd been here yesterday, Francis would be okay now?"

"I mean only that it's easier to treat disease early on. In Francis's case, a day or two probably made no difference at all."

"Probably?"

"There are no absolute answers, Hugh. Not in life, not in medicine. Will you introduce me to Sean? I wouldn't want him to be frightened."

"Sean," Katie called, holding out her hand, "come meet Dr. Morton. Come on. He won't bite . . . that's my good boy." She bent, pressing her cheek to his. "Say hello to Dr. Morton, Sean."

"Hello."

"Hello, young fellow. Perhaps you can help. Do you happen to know anybody who likes chocolate drops? I have a bag of chocolate drops, and I don't know who to give it to."

"Me! Give it to me!"

Dr. Morton smiled. He took the bag from his pocket, passing it to Sean. "I need another favor," he said. "Francis is sick, and I need to be sure you're not sick too."

"I'm not sick. I'm *strong*."

"Well, let's be sure. Come along with me and we'll have a look at you. We'll go into your mama's room.

252

All right? I promise it won't hurt."

"It's all right, Sean." Katie nodded. "Go with Dr. Morton."

"It won't hurt?"

"Not a bit." Dr. Morton lifted Sean up. "I'll give you a ride. No charge."

Hugh watched them go and then turned away, kicking the wall. "I'll kill her! I swear I'll kill her! I'll wring her lousy neck for this."

"For what? You heard the doctor. He said a day or two made no difference at all."

"He said *probably*."

"What's the point looking back, wondering what if? Francis is sick. You can't change that. Kill a hundred people and Francis will still be sick." Katie sat down. Sighing, she brought her unsteady hands together. "I know how you feel, Hugh. No matter how badly you feel, Mama feels worse."

"You think she cares?"

"I suppose you're the only one who cares," Katie snapped, sudden anger darkening her eyes. "In the whole world, you're the only one who cares. Fine. Have it your way. But be quiet about it. My God, it's like a war here. As long as I can remember, you and Mama have been fighting a war. Sometimes I want to scream. What's wrong with you two? Are you both crazy?"

Hugh went to his sister. "Don't cry," he said. "I didn't mean to make you cry."

"Oh, leave me alone. Why can't people get along?"

"There's no getting along with Ma."

"You don't *try* . . . leave me alone, Hugh. I'm tired and my head is splitting. Just be quiet."

"I'm sorry, Katie."

"Just be quiet."

"You want a cup of tea? The water's hot."

"I want *peace*." katie looked up. She dried her eyes. "I'd gladly trade my soul for a minute's peace."

Hugh said nothing more. He poured a cup of tea and silently placed it before Katie. He did not seem to know what to do next. He stared out the window. He paced. He nibbled on a piece of bread. Finally he sat down, tossing a coin in the air.

It was several moments later when Sean skipped back into the kitchen. "I'm a big strong boy." He smiled. "Doctor said."

"Yes, that's what I said," Dr. Morton agreed. "You needn't worry. Sean has no fever, no rash, no swelling. His throat is clear, and his chest. He could do with a few more pounds, but otherwise he's in good health."

"Thank God."

"There is one thing. It would be best if Sean were away from this flat for a while. Scarlet fever is contagious, and I don't believe in taking risks. Have you family he could stay with? Or perhaps neighbors? Just to be on the safe side, you understand."

Hugh looked at Katie. "The boardinghouse?" he asked.

"I had the same thought, but I don't know. I'd have to talk to Ada. And Matt . . . I don't think Matt would fancy the idea."

"Then it's the Muldoon's. Sean's always staying at the Muldoon's, Doc. Trouble is they have a bunch of kids there. They might be scared, with the fever and all. If it's catching."

"Sean isn't infected. Are they home now? The Muldoons? I could explain the situation. I could ease their minds as to the fever. It's contagious through Francis, not Sean."

"C'mon, Sean. You and me and the doc is going to visit the Muldoons. Maybe you'll stay a couple of days." Hugh took his brother's hand, leading him to the door. "You like it there, don't you? You have fun with little Brian."

Katie held the door open. "It's kind of you, Dr. Morton," she said. "To take the time, I mean. What . . . What about Francis?"

"I'll be back later tonight. Things may look brighter then. I can't promise, but there's a chance."

"Yes. Thank you, Doctor."

Wearily, Katie returned to Francis's bedside. She drew a chair next to her mother's and the two women began their sad vigil. They were silent, though occasionally they touched hands, as if seeking strength from each other. Hours passed, and still Francis tossed and turned, his body raging with fever.

It was after midnight when Matt let himself into the boardinghouse. He was not drunk, but neither was he sober, a fact confirmed by his lopsided smile, by his weaving gait. Katie, standing in the doorway of their room, watched her husband's uncertain approach and shook her head. "Are you all right?" she asked, reaching out to steady him. "I have tea waiting."

"Tea?" Matt pulled Katie close. He kissed her long and hard, then let go. "I don't want tea. You know what I want."

Katie shut the door. "I have to talk to you," she said. "There's trouble at home. Sickness. It's Francis. He's very sick, Matt. The doctor says it's scarlet fever."

Matt fell into a chair. He unlaced his shoes and kicked them off, stretching his stockinged feet to the fire. "I hate this damn neighborhood." He sighed. "The day I get my law degree is the day we move."

"What are you talking about? Didn't you hear me? I said Francis is sick."

"I heard. Scarlet fever. It's the tenements, Katie. They breed disease. Disease is in the *air* here. It's a miracle we're not all dead."

"Here, drink some tea. It'll clear your head."

"There's nothing wrong with my head. I'm sorry Francis is sick, Katie. I'm just not surprised. The way children have to live in this neighborhood is a crime. We were talking about it at the pub tonight. How's Sean? Is he okay?"

"Yes, but the doctor says he has to be out of the flat for a while. He's staying with the Muldoons." Katie twisted her hands together. She paced back and forth in front of the fireplace, her skirts rustling softly. "That's fine for a few days, Matt. After that it wouldn't be fair. It wouldn't be right. Sean belongs with family."

"I suppose."

Katie stopped pacing. She turned. "We're Sean's family. You and me."

It was a moment or two before Matt understood what Katie meant. He frowned, picking up his cup and staring into it. "I see what you're getting at. I'd like to help. I want to help. I really do. But he can't stay here. We only have this one room. We'd be tripping over each other. And there's Ada to consider. She's running a boardinghouse, not a nursery."

"Ada's willing to put a cot in the alcove. She doesn't mind."

Matt continued staring into his cup, for he could not bring himself to meet Katie's gaze. "I mind," he admitted finally. "It sounds terrible, but look at it from my side. I come home late every night and get up early every morning to study. I have little enough time as it is. I can't afford to lose that time, Katie. Final exams are coming soon."

"You have time to go to the pub."

Katie's bluntness startled Matt. He glanced at her then glanced quickly away. "I need to . . . relax. I work hard."

"You're not the only one. We all work hard."

"I don't expect you to understand," Matt replied. His reply was truthful, for he could not expect Katie to understand that the only way he was able to endure marriage was to live his life as if nothing had changed. He came and went as he pleased, just as he always had. He had the same friends he had had as a bachelor and, with them, he visited the same pubs he had enjoyed as a bachelor. In his secret heart, he thought of Katie as his mistress, never his wife. "Women are content to stay at home," he said defensively. "Men need to get out. They need to relax with their own kind."

"I'm not asking you to stay home, Matt. I'm asking you to share your home for a little while. Sean's a good boy. He won't cause any trouble."

"All children cause trouble. They can't help it. They're always asking questions, endless questions. They're always getting into things. I'd be distracted from my studies. I'm sorry, but I can't afford that now."

Katie sat down. She stared at the fire, watching the crackling reds and blues and golds. "A fire's so cozy on a cold night," she said quietly, lifting her hand to her pale throat. "If you watch long enough, you can see pictures in it."

"Please try to understand how I feel, Katie. In an emergency I'd be glad to have Sean come here. Or your whole family, for that matter. But it's not an emergency. He's safe at the Muldoon's. They're *like* family to him."

"Oh, I won't press you, Matt. We won't talk about it any more. I understand you want your privacy. Privacy's important."

"It is now. With final exams—"

"I understand. We won't talk about it any more."

Matt put his cup on the table. He sat back, pressing his handkerchief to his damp brow. "I don't like being the villain, Katie," he said. "Both you and Ada are willing to take Sean in. That makes me the villain of the piece. If this were happening on a stage, everybody would be hissing and booing and I wouldn't blame them. I'm not proud of myself. Don't think I am. But there are other things to consider and Sean is fine where he is."

"I understand."

"It must seem selfish, putting my studies first."

It has nothing to do with studies, thought Katie. It's your comfort you're putting first. "A man's entitled to privacy in his own home." She shrugged.

258

"Especially when home is only one room."

"You'd behave differently in my place. You'd make the sacrifice."

Katie was slow to disagree, for sacrifice had been part of her life from the cradle, as ordinary and unquestioned as the air she breathed. Whether this was good or bad she did not know, but she sensed that most people made sacrifices for the ones they loved. "I'm so tired, Matt. I just want to sit back and watch the fire."

"You need sleep. Come to bed."

"Oh, I couldn't sleep. I'd keep you awake all night. I'll curl up here," Katie said, tucking her legs underneath her. "Maybe I'll drowse off later."

"You're angry."

"No."

"Look at me, Katie. If you were any other woman, I'd accuse you of using wiles—of using the bed to get your way. But you're an innocent. This damn neighborhood, this damn world hasn't touched you yet. It will. It'll be a sad day."

"You've had too much to drink."

"My drinking is none of your concern. I'm not a boy in short pants. I'll drink whatever I want, when I want." As if to prove his point, Matt rose and went to the closet, searching the top shelf until he found a bottle of blackberry brandy. "This was a wedding present from one of the fellows at school," he said. "I think it's time I opened it."

"Don't, Matt. You'll be sick tomorrow. You'll have an awful headache."

"That's only fair. Fair punishment for a villain."

*　　*　　*

Katie stirred in her chair, roused from sleep by a knock at the door. She sat up, rubbing her eyes, and was surprised to see it was morning. "Matt?" she called softly, but Matt was sprawled on the bed, sound asleep, a half-empty brandy bottle by his side. "Oh, Matt."

There was another knock at the door, more insistent now. Katie scrambled to her feet. "I'm coming. Just a minute, I'm coming. Ada," she said, opening the door. "What's the matter?"

"Where's Matt?"

"He's sleeping. What's the matter?"

"Let me in, Katie. I have to talk to both of you." Ada entered the room. She walked directly to the bed and shook Matt's shoulder. "Wake up. Wake up, Matt." She pulled the pillow away and then the blanket. "Wake up, Matt."

"What the hell . . . Ada, what the hell are you doing? I need sleep. My head is—"

"Never mind your head. You can worry about your head later. Get up. I don't want you dozing off on me."

"All right," Matt groaned. "I'm up. Maybe you'll tell me *why* I'm up. I don't know what this is about, Ada, but it could have waited."

"No, it couldn't. I'm afraid it's bad news."

Katie's hand flew to her heart. "My God, it's Francis. Is it Francis, Ada?"

"I'm sorry. He passed on at five this morning. It was peaceful. He just stopped breathing . . . I'm so sorry."

Matt saw Katie sway. He put his arms around her and helped her to a chair. He stroked her ashen cheek, gently murmuring words of consolation. Katie seemed not to notice. She raised her head, staring past Matt to Ada. "Is Mama here?" she asked.

"Hugh was waiting outside when I got back from church. He told me what happened. He's gone back to the flat now, but I said you and Matt would be there as soon as you could. I'll be over after I get breakfast served. It's a time for family to be together." Ada paused, wiping her eyes. The pain in Katie's face was more than she could bear, and she had to look away. "It'll be a long day." She sighed heavily. "You'd best have some tea before you go. I'll fix it."

"There's no time," Katie said, her voice breaking. "I have to hurry. Mama will need me."

"There's time for tea. I'll fix it while you change your clothes. You'll be no good to Maeve or anybody else if you get sick. It's a terrible thing, Katie, but still you must take care of yourself."

"Ada's right." Matt nodded. Again he stroked his wife's cheek. "A few minutes won't matter."

"How is Sean? Did Hugh mention Sean?"

"Ah, they haven't told the little fella yet. I think Maeve's waiting for Father Flynn to come. Father has a way with children. He explains things nice, even things like . . ." Ada went to the door. "I'll bring your tea when it's ready," she said, closing the door behind her.

Matt, alone with his wife, felt a great cloud of guilt descend upon him. "I'm sorry, Katie," he murmured. "I didn't realize it was so serious. I guess I wasn't thinking. I behaved badly . . . I should have been comforting you, but instead I—will you forgive me?"

"What? Oh, it's not important. It's over and done."

"I *am* sorry."

"I know." Katie stood. Her legs were weak and she clung to the chair, steadying herself. "Francis was only a little boy," she cried suddenly. "Only four years old. It's wrong. It's cruel." Tears splashed her face. Matt brushed them away, surprised to see that his own hand was trembling. "He was such a good little boy."

"You ought to lie down, Katie. You've had a shock and—"

"No, I'm fine. We have to hurry. Think how it is for Mama, all by herself in that flat. Papa died there, and now Francis."

"Hugh's with her."

"Hugh! He means well, but he can't help causing trouble. Mama has enough trouble . . . We have to hurry, Matt. Do you want your blue suit? I pressed it and sewed the button back on the sleeve."

Matt hesitated. He drew his hand across his chin, sighing. "I was wondering," he said slowly, "if I could have an hour. Just *one* hour to finish writing my paper for school. It's due Monday morning. If I could have just an hour to finish it . . . then I'll meet you at the flat and all my time will be yours. I won't leave your side after that."

"You're not coming with me?"

"If I could have just one hour . . . the paper counts toward my final grade, Katie. I wouldn't ask otherwise."

"I see."

"You'll want some time alone with your mother anyway. An hour isn't so long. I promise I'll be finished in an hour. I'll rush right over."

262

Katie stared at Matt, hurt and anger mingling in her dark gaze. "Don't rush on my account," she said aloud, but to herself she thought, Poor Francis is dead, but that's nothing to you. What's death compared to your precious grades, your precious school? "Don't rush," she said again. "We'll manage by ourselves."

"If you're going to be upset—"

"I have better things to be upset about, Matt. You stay and finish your paper. You warned me from the beginning that school came first."

"And you agreed."

"Yes, I agreed. It's settled, isn't it?" Katie went to the closet, pulling a clean shirtwaist from the hanger. "Maybe you could spare the time to go see if Ada has tea ready. She won't let me out of here until I have tea."

Matt reached for his robe, throwing it atop his rumpled pajamas. "It's just an hour, Katie. Try to understand."

"Oh, I understand. Don't worry about that."

Matt heard the edge in Katie's voice. He saw the stubborn set of her jaw and he shrugged, crossing the room to the door. "I'll get your tea."

"Thank you."

There was a sullen expression on Matt's face as he walked into the hallway. He was angry with himself, but he was angry with Katie too, for he felt that she had not really tried to understand his position. It was a logical position, he thought; an hour was not a lot to ask, no matter the circumstances.

"Still in your robe!" Ada exclaimed. "And still smelling like a brewery! You'll have to hurry, Matt.

I'll take the tea in. You get bathed and dressed."

"I'm meeting Katie at the flat. First I have a paper to finish for school."

Ada turned away from the stove. She was quiet, regarding her nephew through narrowed eyes. "You're *what*? *Meeting* her?"

"That's right."

"That's wrong. Wrong as can be. There's been a death in the family. You can't stop to finish papers for school. Katie needs you now."

Matt sat down, putting his aching head in his hands. "What about my needs, Ada? Aren't I allowed any needs of my own?"

"Ah, you do okay. I haven't seen you denying yourself anything. You preach about not wasting money or time, but you waste plenty of both every Saturday night. If that paper was so important, you should have stayed home and done it. You went gallivanting instead, like always. Forget the paper. Katie needs you. It's family, Matt. You can't turn your back on family."

"It isn't my family."

"Sure it is. By marriage."

"Don't remind me."

"Stop whining," Ada said sharply. "You have a beautiful young woman waiting on you hand and foot, and warming your bed besides. What are you doing for her?"

"I'm doing my best. Believe it or not, I'm doing my best. I didn't want to get married, Ada. I had to get married because of . . . because of Jack Snow and his damned appendix. If you hadn't been visiting Jack in the hospital that night—"

"Matt!" Ada cried, for she saw Katie frozen in the doorway. "Matt didn't mean it, Katie. It's the drink talking. He had too much to drink last night and today he's in a nasty mood. *Tell* her, Matt."

Slowly, very slowly, Matt looked up. His face was white, and his mouth also. "I'm sorry, Katie. I didn't mean it the way it sounded." He struggled to his feet and went to Katie, but she pushed him away. "Please listen," he tried again. "I didn't mean it. I love you, Katie. I wouldn't hurt you for the world. I love you."

"I'm going to Mama's now."

"Let me explain. *Please.*"

Katie gazed at Matt, all youth and innocence gone from her lovely eyes. "There's nothing to explain," she said. "That's what's so sad." She lifted her hand and then let it drop, walking swiftly into the hall.

"Don't leave. Not like this. Don't . . ."

"Are you just going to stand there like a fool?" Ada demanded. "Get dressed and go after her."

"I need a drink."

"A drink! What's happening to you, Matt? Do you think you'll find answers to your problems at the bottom of a bottle? That's where you've been looking lately. It's the wrong place. All you'll find there is trouble. Mark my words."

"The hair of the dog," Matt replied with a feeble smile.

"Ah, I've heard that one before. Never mind making excuses. You'll get nothing stronger than tea from me. And you won't even get tea 'til you're bathed and dressed. I'm not running a shelter for bums."

Matt shrank back, stung by Ada's words. "How

can you speak to me that way?"

"How? Take a look at yourself. Your eyes are bloodshot, your hair hanging down. You need a shave, but your hands are too shaky to hold a razor. If that's not bad enough, you smell like a brewery. What happened to the fella who was going to conquer the world?"

"He got married."

Ada slammed the kettle on the stove. She walked to her nephew and pushed him into a chair. "Now you listen to me, Matt McVey," she said, eyes blazing. "There'll be no more whining. No more feeling sorry for yourself. So you had to change your plans a little. So what? You're not the first. Stop acting like it was a tragedy."

"It was to me."

"Then you don't know the meaning of the word. What happened to Francis was a tragedy. Go around the neighborhood and knock on a few doors. You'll see real suffering. Cold, hungry children. Sick children. That's tragedy. You—you're lucky. You have a nice warm place to live and plenty of food on the table. You have your school and you have a wonderful wife. How dare you complain?"

"I'm sorry, Ada." Matt stared morosely into space, pressing his hands to his throbbing temples. "I don't know what's wrong with me."

"You're spoiled; that's what's wrong. I could kick myself for making things too easy. Well, no more. You're going to face up to your responsibilities. You're going to go after Katie and beg her forgiveness. You're going to be a man."

"Katie won't want to see me now."

"That's not true. She's hurt, and she has reason. But if you try hard, you'll set things right. You *must* try. Do you hear me, Matt?" Ada sat down. She seemed to hesitate for a moment. "Matt, Katie's going to have a baby."

"What?"

"Katie's going to have a baby."

There was a chill through Matt's body, a terrible sickening. The room became cloudy, as if suddenly filled with pale mists coming ever closer. "A baby?" he asked, grasping Ada's hand.

"Yes. Come fall you'll be a father."

"Oh, my God."

11

"Here's Francis's insurance policy," Katie said to the undertaker, Mr. McCarthy. "Mama's signed it. She wants a simple funeral. As simple as possible."

"Could I have a word with her, do you think?"

"No, I'm sorry." Katie looked in the direction of Francis's room. There, she knew, Maeve sat rigidly, staring upon the face of her dead son. "Not now." She sighed. "Mama's left the . . . arrangements to me."

"I see." Mr. McCarthy glanced at the policy, his practiced eye picking out the amount; one hundred dollars. "Well, McCarthy's can offer a fine two-coach funeral with a nickel handle coffin for seventy-five dollars. That's my hundred dollar funeral, mind you. I'm not asking a penny's profit."

"Oh?"

"It's the truth," Mr. McCarthy declared, thrusting his right hand into the air. "The pure truth."

"Seventy-five dollars." Katie remembered Maeve putting aside the insurance money every week, five cents for each of her children, ten cents for herself. She had refused to discuss it, fearing bad luck, but those dimes and nickels had come before food and coal and all else. "I don't want to haggle at a time like this," Katie said now. "Still, seventy-five dollars is a lot of money, and we're poor people."

"That includes the Mass and a spray of carnations," Mr. McCarthy added hastily. "It's a fair price."

"Yes."

"Are we agreed then?"

"Yes, all right."

"You won't be sorry." Mr. McCarthy took up the policy, turning it over in his hand. "What I said about not making a profit . . . that wasn't exactly true. I'll make a profit. Only a fair profit, and it's my due. It's business. But you're a nice girl, Katie. I wouldn't want to fool you."

"You didn't."

"So you were on to me, were you? Well, there are some who enjoy the haggling. It's part of the ritual, if you see what I mean. You're not like that. You're the new generation. I should have known, and I apologize."

"No need."

"I'll give your Francis a first-class funeral. You have my word on it. And now you have money coming. Twenty-five dollars." Mr. McCarthy smiled, reaching into his pocket. "Has the priest been here yet?"

"Father Flynn's coming after eight o'clock Mass."

"There'll be the last rites and then the rosary. I'll be back after nine for the . . . for Francis. I understand there's to be no wake."

"Mama's had her fill of wakes."

"I understand. The poor woman; she's had her troubles." Mr. McCarthy looked at Katie and his eyes softened. "I'm sure you're a comfort to her. She can be proud of you. It's a hard job, handling the arrangements. You did it well."

"Thank you."

Mr. McCarthy buttoned his coat. He gathered his hat and gloves and went to the door. "I'll be back after nine," he said. "Good morning to you, Katie."

"Good morning, Mr. McCarthy."

Katie's face was impassive as she swept the twenty-five dollars from the table. She folded the crisp new bills, tucking them safely away in Maeve's purse. She tidied the kitchen, washed a small stack of cups and saucers, and put water on for tea. I must keep busy, she thought. If I just keep busy, I'll be all right.

It was fifteen minutes later when Matt burst through the door, pale and out of breath. "I'm here, Katie," he said.

"Yes, I see. Why are you here?"

"I . . . I wanted to be with you. I hurried. I ran the whole way, Katie. Because I wanted to talk to you. We have to talk—please stop fussing with the teapot. And please can I sit down before I fall down?"

"Go ahead."

"I'm sorry I hurt you. I didn't mean it. I want to explain, if you'll let me. If you'll listen."

"I have no time for talk. You can stay or you can go back to the boardinghouse. It's up to you. But I have no time for talk. I'm busy. There are people coming."

Indeed many people came to the Gallagher flat on this gloomy Sunday. Father Flynn was first to arrive, followed within moments by Dr. Morton. Ada ar-

271

rived next, and then Mr. McCarthy and his helper. Neighbors, singly and in groups, began arriving at noon, offering condolences to a silent Maeve. Ada put out trays of sandwiches she had brought from home. Katie served endless cups of tea. Matt, feeling very much left out, stood off to one side, smoking nervously.

The last caller departed at seven o'clock, and Maeve went immediately to her room, closing the door. "Well, it's over," Matt said with a sigh.

"Over? There's the funeral."

"It's over for tonight. I think we should go home now, Katie. You have to get some sleep. You're exhausted."

"I'm staying here. Mama may need me."

"Please leave the dishes alone and look at me. Katie, your mother doesn't want anybody around. She made that clear enough. She hardly said two words all day. Besides, Hugh will be here."

"Are you sure? I'm not. I don't know if Hugh's coming back tonight. Neither do you. He's been in and out a dozen times. I don't know what he's planning. I'd feel better if I stayed. Not only for Mama; for Sean."

"Sean's at the Muldoons."

"I want to be close by. I'd feel better."

"You mean you'd feel better away from me." Matt slumped in his chair, shaking his head. "That's it, isn't it, Katie? You don't want to be with me."

"Not tonight."

"You won't change your mind?"

"No."

"I guess there's nothing more to say."

"No."

Francis Gallagher was buried at Holy Name Cemetery, not far from where his father lay. It was a rainy morning, and the freshly turned earth had a sweet, clean scent that reminded Katie of spring. But Francis won't see another springtime, she thought, and tears started in her eyes.

Katie had not cried during the funeral service. Kneeling between Maeve and Hugh, she had stared straight ahead, her hands clenched so that the knuckles sprang out under the skin. Ada had sniffled loudly throughout the service and Sean had sobbed, as much as in confusion as in grief, but Katie had not uttered a sound. Maeve, behind her black veil, had been silent also. Hugh had shifted about in the pew, glaring at Maeve, at Father Flynn, at anyone who chanced to look his way.

Now Katie watched Father Flynn sprinkle the four corners of Francis's tiny coffin with holy water. He intoned a prayer and made the sign of the cross. "Amen," Katie murmured. Through her tears she saw the coffin lowered into a plain wooden box and then into the ground. Someone pressed a lump of damp soil into her hand. I can't, she thought. I can't. But Maeve was pushing her forward, toward the edge of the grave. Slowly, she opened her hand and the soil dropped with a thud. "Good-bye Francis," she whispered. "Good-bye."

Matt rode home with Katie and the other Gallaghers in the first coach. He tried to cheer them, making light and harmless conversation, but no one listened and no one smiled. After a while he conceded defeat, and the remainder of the journey passed in profound silence.

When the Gallaghers arrived home, they found the table laden with food, for in Hell's Kitchen neighbors traditionally brought gifts of food to the bereaved. They brought what they could afford—a cake from the Muldoons, a pot of stew from the Wilsons, a platter of sliced baloney from the Reagans, two loaves of bread from the Ryans, six hard-cooked eggs from the Kelleys. Ada had brought a ham and a jar of plum preserves. Dr. Morton had brought a large basket of fruit. Mr. Clark, the grocer, had brought a pound of tea, a pound of sugar, and three lemons.

The sight of so much food seemed to frighten Sean. "Mama," he cried again and again, clinging to Maeve's skirts.

"What's the matter, Sean? You're not sick, are you?" Maeve felt her son's forehead, and she was visibly relieved to find it cool. "It's just the day." She sighed. "The day's been a strain. I'm thinking a nap will do you good."

"I'm too *old* for naps, Mama. Naps are for *babies*."

"Aye, but this one time a nap will do you good. Are you hungry? Do you want something to eat before I tuck you in? Look at all the grand food, Sean. The neighbors left it while we were . . . out." Maeve's gaze roamed over the many bowls and platters. "There's Mrs. Muldoon's layer cake. And Mrs. Nolan's vanilla cookies."

274

"Cookies," Sean said, scooping up a handful. "I like cookies."

"That's enough now. After your nap you'll be having supper."

"I'll put him down for his nap, Mama," Katie offered. "Come along, Sean. Come along. You can take the cookies with you."

"No. I want *Mama*, not you. You lied to me, Katie. You said Francis would be all right. That was a lie. Francis was terrible sick and he had to go to Heaven. He had to go far, far away. You didn't tell me."

"I didn't know."

"You lied. You made a sin."

"Mind your tongue, Sean Gallagher," Maeve warned, lifting him into her arms. "Is that any way to talk to your sister? Sure and I'm ashamed of you. Say you're sorry."

"No."

"Say you're sorry. Be quick about it."

"*No*. No, I *won't*."

Maeve was astonished by her son's defiance, for he had always been an obedient child, docile and accepting. Hugh and Katie were obedient children too, once upon a time, she thought to herself. Then Hugh started defying me at every turn. And Katie began when she met Matt. But Sean's only five. He can't be starting yet. Please God, not yet. "It's a fine example you've set for your brother," she said, looking from Katie to Hugh. "Of all the things you could have taught him, you taught him to sass me. I hope you're happy," she added, carrying Sean from the room.

"Don't pay any attention," Katie said when Maeve

had gone. "Mama's just worn out. She didn't mean it."

"Yeah, she did. It's okay. It's the last time." Hugh went to the cupboard. He removed a bulky paper bag, setting it on the floor. "The last goddamn time, and that's a promise."

"What are you talking about?"

"You'll see."

"Take it easy, Hugh," Matt said. "We're *all* worn out. Let's try to be calm. At least let's try not to argue. Another argument won't solve anything."

"Thanks for the advice, Professor. But I don't need no advice." Hugh grinned, crossing his arms over his chest. "I guess you got a right to put your two cents in. You're family. But I do what I want. I don't like nobody telling me different. Understand?"

Matt was disconcerted by Hugh's chilly blue stare. He felt threatened, and he had to remind himself that Hugh was just a young boy. "You put on a good act," he replied. "Sorry, I'm not intimidated."

"Hey, Katie? Is he always using them big words? I'd get a headache listening to him. Only kidding, Matt." Hugh winked. "I'm real glad she married someone smart. Most of the guys around here is jerks."

"Thank you, if that was a compliment."

"It was."

"Thank you." Matt said no more, for Maeve had returned to the kitchen. She had taken off her veil, and he was shocked to see the gaunt, sunken hollows of her cheeks, the lines etched deeply about her mouth. "Wouldn't you like to sit down?" he asked, pulling out a chair. "You must be very tired."

"Can I fix you a plate, Mama?"

"I'll fix my own plate when I'm ready. But you go ahead, all of you. Don't be shy. There's two weeks' food on the table. Eat your fill. What's that bag over by the cupboard? Pick it up before somebody trips."

"It's mine," Hugh said. "It's my clothes."

"Your clothes?"

"Yeah. I'm moving out, Ma. Today. I'm not asking you for nothing, but I figure I got a right to my clothes."

"What foolishness are you talking now, Hugh Gallagher? Moving out? Moving out where? You're only a boy. Sure and you're a foolish boy if you think I'd let you leave."

"You can't stop me."

"Is that so? Maybe you'll change your tune when you feel the strap across your back."

"Not this time, Ma. I've had the last of the strap and the last of you. I'm moving out."

"Mama, he's *serious*," Katie cried.

"Serious! We'll see how serious he is. It's no fun starving in the street. That's what he'll be doing. Talk is cheap. Talk doesn't buy food or pay rent."

"I won't starve. And I got a place to live. Yeah, that's right." Hugh grinned, seeing his mother's startled expression. "I got a place with friends."

"You're lying," Maeve said, though even as she spoke she knew Hugh was telling the truth. "What friends?" she demanded. "Those hoodlums? Those *devils* you go with? They're halfway to jail, the lot of them. You'll have a place to live, all right. You'll have a place in jail. Bread and water for your supper."

Hugh's grin widened. He hooked his thumbs in his belt and stared at Maeve. "Many's the time I had bread and water for my supper here."

"Hugh!"

"I'm sorry, Katie, but she had it coming. She's always pushing me too far. Now I'm pushing back."

"Now? You've been going against me as long as I can remember, Hugh Gallagher. I tried to raise you decent. I did everything I could, and this is my thanks. Why don't you just stick a knife in my heart? Dear knows it would be kinder than this."

"Yeah, I'd have to find your heart first. Where do you keep it, Ma? In the icebox with all the other cold stuff?"

Maeve started toward Hugh, and Matt stepped quickly between them. "Stop it! Stop it, both of you! Hugh, get over there and be quiet. You've said enough."

"Stay out of my business. I told you before."

"I don't care what you told me. I'm telling you to be quiet. Sit down, Mrs. Gallagher. Let's try to be calm. Hugh isn't going anywhere."

"Who says?"

"Hugh, I understand wanting to be on your own. But you can wait a couple of years. You're fourteen, for God's sake. What's the hurry?"

"I got plans."

"They'll wait."

"I won't."

"Will you use your head? It's not easy out there. Grown men have trouble earning a living. What chance do you think you'll stand? A boy your age? Be reasonable, Hugh. At least finish school. Then you can go anywhere you want. No one will stop you."

"Nice speech, but no one's stopping me now. You don't listen good. I told you I got plans. Katie understands."

All eyes turned to Katie. She was pale and very still, watching her brother. "You've made up your mind, haven't you?" she asked.

"Yeah. I'm tired of the war."

"War?" Matt frowned. "What war? What are you talking about?"

"Katie understands."

"What's he talking about, Katie?"

"Oh, it doesn't matter. He's made up his mind. There's no use arguing." Katie walked a circle around the kitchen, pausing behind Maeve's chair. "This day's been coming for a long time," she said wearily. "Ever since Papa died. Maybe even before that. I know I should be trying to stop you, Hugh. I also know there's no use."

"Let him go, if that's what he wants. Aye, let him learn his lesson. He thinks the world is waiting for him with open arms. He'll be wishing he was home."

"Don't hold your breath, Ma."

Maeve sighed, plucking at her handkerchief. "And what am I supposed to tell Sean? Or did you forget about Sean? He's already lost one brother today."

The grin disappeared from Hugh's face. He lowered his eyes, scuffing his foot back and forth across the floor. "It's not the same thing," he replied. "Sean and Francis was close. They was like twins. It's not the same with him and me. Don't make out it is."

"You're brothers, close or not. He won't understand."

"Wait'll he's a couple years older. He'll understand okay. Meanwhile I'm doing him a favor." Hugh went to the door, pulling the strap off the hook. "I'm taking this with me," he said. "I'm throwing it in the river. Maybe I can't do nothing else for Sean, but I can see you don't use the strap on him."

"I never did."

"Too busy using it on me."

"You got only what you deserved, Hugh Gallagher."

"Yeah, well now I'm getting out. I'll leave two dollars in the mailbox every Saturday. I don't care what you do with it. Burn it, for all I care."

"Save your money. Sure and you'll need it."

"I won't need nothing." Hugh picked up his bag. His eyes glanced once about the kitchen then settled on Katie. "I'll be seeing you." He smiled. "That's a promise. So long, Matt. Look after my sister."

"You're making a mistake, Hugh. I wish you'd reconsider."

"Don't worry about me. Just look after Katie. I wouldn't want to hear she was unhappy." Hugh opened the door. "So long, Ma. Maybe I'll see you around."

Maeve offered no reply. She sat stiffly, her gaze averted, her lips compressed in a thin line. Katie's hands tightened on her shoulders and still she did not move.

"Mama, Hugh's going."

"Aye, let him go."

Katie left her mother and ran to Hugh. "Take care of yourself," she said, hugging him. "Remember I'm at the boardinghouse if you need anything. Anything at all . . . I love you, Hugh. Promise you'll take care of yourself." She brushed her tears away, staring into Hugh's dark eyes. "I don't want to say good-bye. I can't."

"I'm not going to the moon." Hugh laughed. "I'll be around. Quit worrying, Katie. This is the best thing I ever done. For Ma too. If I stayed here I'd end up wringing her neck. I already come close a few times. So now I'm getting out."

"Be careful."

"I'll take smart over careful any day," Hugh said with a wink. He was quiet for a moment and then, in the next moment, he was gone.

Maeve rose. She pushed Matt aside and walked to the window. She stood there, a silent, wraithlike figure, gazing blindly at the street below. She did not notice when Katie joined her, nor when Matt put his arm about her shoulder. She continued to stare at the street, tearing her handkerchief to shreds.

"Hugh will come back, Mama."

"He'll never come back," Maeve replied, her voice catching. "Never. It's two sons I'm mourning today. Two sons lost, God help me."

"Sit down, Mama. I'll make tea."

"You go home with your husband. You've been here since Saturday. It's time to go home."

"I can't leave you alone, Mama."

"And why not? Am I a baby who needs watching? Go home, Katie. Your place is with your husband."

"Mama—"

"Go home. Let me mourn my sons in peace."

Matt took Katie's hand, drawing her away from the

window. "She wants to be alone," he said. "Don't argue. We've had enough arguing. Let's go home."

"Mama? Will you be all right?"

"What choice do I have? Tell me that."

"Come along, Katie," Matt said. He found their hats and gloves and led his wife to the door. "We'll be back tomorrow, Mrs. Gallagher. If you should need anything—"

"Just let me be. Let me be."

Matt opened the door, tugging Katie into the hall. "Why are you rushing?" she asked. "Are you worried about your afternoon classes? I won't keep you from them. Go on to class, if that's what you want. But stop pulling my arm."

"I'm not worried about my classes. Well, I am, but right now I'm more worried about you. You must get some sleep, Katie. I doubt you've slept at all since Saturday."

"Don't be silly. Of course I've slept."

"An hour here, an hour there. You'll make yourself sick."

"What if I do? Would you care?"

"Katie!"

"I'm sorry. I shouldn't have snapped at you." Katie paused on the stairs and once more dried her eyes. She longed to feel the comfort of Matt's arms, yet she turned away from him. In her mind she heard the cruel words she had been hearing for days: *I didn't want to get married.* Hard as she had tried, she could not forget that Matt had spoken those words. "I'm sorry." She sighed. "I guess I am tired."

"We have to talk, Katie."

"Not now."

"When?"

"I don't know when. I can't think straight, Matt. With all that's happened, I can't think straight. Don't expect me to. I want to scream, but I'm afraid if I started screaming I'd never stop."

"You've had a lot of stress these past days," Matt said patiently. "I understand. Hugh was the last straw. He was wrong to leave. Very wrong. I wish I could have talked some sense into him. He won't find it easy out there."

"You never cared about Hugh before. You're just worried we'll have more responsibility for Mama now."

"How can you say that? My God, do you think so little of me?"

"My thoughts are all confused."

"We have to settle things between us, Katie, and soon." They reached the ground floor. Matt followed Katie through the foyer into the rainy street. "Will you listen to me?" he asked, catching her hand. "Listen to me. Katie, I know about the baby."

"I see. Ada wasn't supposed to tell you."

"Why not? It's my baby too."

"A baby you don't want. Oh, Matt," Katie cried, wrenching her hand away, "if you don't want a wife, you certainly don't want a baby."

As days passed, Matt and Katie retreated into their separate shells. They shared the same room, the same bed, but they did so with the wary politeness of strangers. Their conversations were brief and careful. They did not argue, for they feared the words that might be uttered recklessly. They rarely smiled. At night, Katie lay on her side of the bed and feigned sleep. Matt, on his side of the bed, made no protest.

It was an impossible situation and, toward the end of March, Matt sought a remedy. Harking back to the giddy days of courtship, he sought to woo Katie all over again. There were romantic little presents shyly offered. There were bouquets of spring flowers. There were walks about the city. Matt took Katie on carriage rides through Central Park. He took her to vaudeville shows and to the roof garden of Hammerstein's Victoria for dancing. If, inwardly, he bemoaned the cost of these excursions, outwardly he was sanguine. He seemed himself again, young and charming and quick to laugh.

Katie was not fooled by Matt's efforts, but she had little inclination to turn them away. She was unwilling to risk confrontation, and so she suppressed her doubts. She and Matt resumed their life. They were considerate with each other, immensely gentle. They were husband and wife once again, though Katie knew they were not the same people they had been before. I don't love him the same way, she thought one night as Matt took her in his arms. It was a night she would remember, for it was a night that marked the end of her youthful dreams.

Katie began buying baby clothes in June. She bought only a few things, diapers and tiny shirts, and she hid her purchases in the closet, safely out of sight. "You should be excited about the baby," Ada often chided. "If it was me, I'd be jumping with joy." But Katie felt no joy. She touched her swelling stomach and was reminded of all the things she wanted to forget—a reluctant husband; a marriage going wrong.

Summer came to Hell's Kitchen and with it came blistering heat. The sun was merciless, a blaze of yellow fire that scorched the pavements. There were days when steam actually rose from the pavements, and on those days people fled to fire escapes, to rooftops, to any place offering a breath of air. Children ran after Mr. Maggio's ice wagon, clamoring for bits of ice, while their mothers gathered on stoops and fanned themselves with newspapers. Everywhere in Hell's Kitchen people felt the fierce sun and recalled the sweet, gentle breezes of Ireland.

Katie had never been troubled by the heat before, but now, nearing her ninth month of pregnancy, she found it almost unendurable. Day and night her brow streamed with perspiration; her throat burned. She strained for breath, and every breath was painful. She slept very badly, if at all.

"Didn't I tell you to take a nap?" Ada asked as Katie struggled into the kitchen. "You look like you painted your eyes with coal dust. You're exhausted."

"It's too hot to sleep."

"It's too hot to be in here. I had the stove going. I just now turned it off."

"You're *cooking* today?"

"My boarders have to eat." Ada shrugged. "I can't throw a raw chicken on the table. Come sit down if you're staying. And there's the footstool. Now tell me what you're doing in here. Why aren't you resting? It's not too hot to rest."

"I can't stay in my room all the time. I need something to do, Ada. I need work to do. At least let me peel the vegetables. I want to be useful."

"Having a baby is useful enough."

"I'm not having it yet."

Ada patted Katie's enormous stomach. "I don't know about that." She chuckled. "It could be any day, by the look of you. I'm glad I bought the cradle when I did. You'll be filling it soon. Ah, it'll be nice, a baby around the house." Ada carried a pitcher of lemonade and two glasses to the table. "Drink up," she said. "You'll feel better."

"I'll feel better if I have something to do. Please, Ada. I can't stand doing nothing. I'm not used to it. I wasn't born to be a lady of leisure."

"Enjoy it while you have the chance. Once the baby comes—"

"I've had the chance for two months. Three, if you count the month you made me stop doing floors and woodwork. I'll go crazy. I swear I will."

"Ah, you're just cranky 'cause it's almost your time." Ada sat across from Katie. She smiled, mopping her damp face. "You're supposed to be cranky. It's natural. Once the baby comes—"

"I'm going back to work the day after."

"We'll see. Katie, did you and Matt pick names for the baby yet? You said you'd talk to him last night."

"He came home too late last night. He was tired."

"Late?" Ada frowned. "That makes three times this week he's been late. Put your foot down, Katie. He's slipping back into his careless ways. Not long ago he was sticking to you like glue. Now he's slipping back."

"I know."

"Well, what are you planning to do about it?"

"There isn't much I can do." Katie's answer was truthful, for she had given a great deal of thought to Matt, and she had begun to understand him. She understood that he would never change, that his own interests, be they school or work, would always be first in his heart. "After Francis . . . After the funeral," she said slowly, "we weren't getting along. He tried awfully hard then. I think he was courting me, sort of. But courtships don't last forever. Oh, Ada, don't scowl. Matt can only be himself. He didn't want a wife and baby. He's doing his best, considering."

"Not by my lights."

"By his."

Katie's easy acceptance disturbed Ada. "You're doing what Maeve did," she said. "You're letting your husband go his merry way."

"Mama knew she couldn't change Papa. I know I can't change Matt. I had funny ideas about marriage, in the beginning. I thought it solved all the problems. It solves some, but there are always others."

"You shouldn't have any problems yet. You're not even married a year."

"It's been a short time." Katie smiled. "But I've learned a lot. So much has happened. Especially to Matt."

"To Matt? You're the one having the baby."

"Yes, and because of the baby Matt's working full time at a lumber yard. He's working at a job he hates. Instead of starting his third year at City College, he's starting night school, something else he hates. That's a lot to happen. He planned his life one way and it

287

went another." Katie raised her glass to her parched lips. She drank thirstily, then put the glass down. "So if he's late coming home from work or school or anywhere, I guess I can't complain."

"Sure you can."

"Will you let me peel the vegetables now?"

"Veronica already peeled them."

"I hope Veronica understands her job is just until the baby."

"She's a good girl. She understands. Don't be too anxious to get your job back. Your baby will keep you busy enough." Ada pushed her chair away and stood up. She was clearing the table when a bell clanged. "Someone at the door. I'll go see. It better not be boarders. We're full. All right, all right, I'm coming," she called as the bell clanged again.

Katie drew a handkerchief from the rolled sleeve of her blouse. She pressed it to her hot, streaming forehead and to her neck. She closed her eyes and wished for rain.

"Katie, there's someone here to see you."

"Me?" Katie turned. "Officer Garrity! What's wrong?"

"It's sorry I am to be bothering you, Mrs. McVey. Please don't be alarmed. There's no cause."

"What's wrong? What's happened?"

"Well," Officer Garrity replied, switching his hat from hand to hand, "the truth is we're trying to find the whereabouts of your brother, Hugh. Please don't be alarmed, Mrs. McVey. We have a few questions for the lad; that's all."

"What kinds of questions?"

"Well, Mrs. McVey, it seems there was a robbery at

288

Thompson's Warehouse last night. The watchman took a nasty blow on the head, and the safe was broken into. It was the Parlor Mob behind it. We're sure of that, ma'am. But we're thinking maybe they had extra help, maybe Hugh's lads."

"Hugh's lads?"

"Aye, ma'am. He has his own lads. A gang, you might call them. And it's a fair-sized gang they are, too."

Katie stared in amazement at Officer Garrity. "Hugh's fourteen years old," she said. "How can he have his own gang?"

"Begging your pardon, Mrs. McVey, but he wouldn't be the first. The lads here start early. That's the truth of it, ma'am." Officer Garrity fell silent. He was an experienced policeman now, though he was still uncomfortable invading people's homes with questions or with bad news. "I'm not saying Hugh and his lads was part of the robbery. We only want to have a word with him. If you'd be willing to help, ma'am?"

"I don't know anything."

"Could you tell me the last time you saw him? And where he's living now? We've been turning the neighborhood inside out, ma'am. There's no sign of the lad."

"Hugh never gave me his address. If I want to reach him, I leave a message at Smitty's." Katie clutched her stomach, for she felt a sudden, sharp pain. The pain vanished as quickly as it had come, and she sat back, sighing. "I can't help. I don't know anything."

"I wouldn't be bothering you, Mrs. McVey, but it's important."

"Of course it's important," Ada said, going to Katie's side. "But she doesn't know anything. She can't tell you what she doesn't know. Hugh was here two weeks ago Sunday. That's the last we saw of him. You're free to look around the boardinghouse. We're not hiding him."

Officer Garrity shook his dark head. "No, ma'am," he replied. "I'll be taking your word on it. Thank you for your time. I'll be saying goodbye now. Don't trouble to show me out. I'll find my way."

"I wouldn't worry," Ada said when Officer Garrity had gone. "I'm sure there's nothing to it."

"Are you? I'm not."

"Ah, Hugh's wild and all, but that doesn't mean he's breaking into warehouses. Gambling's more in his line, from what I hear. Even if he has his own gang—What's the matter? Why are you holding your stomach like that?"

"Pain," Katie gasped, doubling over. "I think . . . I think it's the baby."

12

Katie stirred, slowly awakening from the oblivion that had engulfed her for hours. She heard the sound of rain beating at the windows, of thunder as loud as cannon, and she frowned in confusion. She tried to raise her head, but the effort took all her strength, and she fell back against the pillows.

"Doctor!" Ada cried. "Come quick! She's awake!"

Katie opened her eyes and Ada's big, happy face swam into view. "Ada . . . I don't understand. Where . . . Where am I?"

"You're in your room, in your very own bed. Don't worry. The medicine will wear off soon and you'll—"

"Medicine?"

"Katie, you have a baby boy. A wee little baby boy. He's so beautiful. There never was a baby so beautiful! You had a hard time of it, poor thing. I had to call Dr. Morton. But you're fine now, and you have a beautiful baby boy."

"A baby boy." Katie remembered Ada helping her to her room, she remembered lying down, and then she remembered the pain, the fiery claws of pain raking her body, tearing her in two. She remembered whispered conversations, people coming and going from the room. She remembered Dr. Morton shouting over her screams. At the last, she remembered the doctor pressing a foul-smelling cloth to her nose. "A baby boy, Ada?"

"He's sleeping safe in his cradle. I'll bring him to you."

No, thought Katie, I don't want him. I don't want to see him. "No," she said, turning her aching head away. "Not now."

Ada was startled by Katie's response. She looked at Dr. Morton and he stepped forward, bending to his patient. "Katie, your baby is fine," he said. "Quite small, of course, but quite healthy. You mustn't be afraid."

"I'm not afraid."

"Surely you want to see him? To hold him? The poor little fellow had a difficult time coming into the world. He needs his mother's arms."

"Not now. Let him sleep."

Dr. Morton stroked his ginger mustache. He walked a few steps from the bed, motioning to Ada to join him. "Such a difficult birth," he said quietly. "Sometimes there is depression afterward. And Katie's so young. She's scarcely more than a child herself. Children having children." He sighed. "Sometimes they're not prepared. The experience can be frightening."

"Well, you're the doctor, and you'd know about these things. Maybe you're right. The way she's acting . . . it's not like her."

"She's never been a mother before, Ada. Give her

time. I notice she didn't ask for her husband. Is there a problem?'

"Could be. You saw Matt when he was here. Roaring drunk. I gave him a piece of my mind and Maeve did too, but I'll wager he's back at the pub right now."

"That's not unusual." Dr. Morton smiled. "You'd be surprised how many new fathers head straight for the pub. When the first pain comes, they're out the door. The human race would die if childbirth were left to men."

"Men are happy enough to get babies started."

"Indeed." Dr. Morton nodded. "That's the easy part. The hard part is wisely left to women."

Ada glanced at Katie. "I can't help worrying about her," she said. "There never was a kinder girl, more loving girl. To turn away from her own baby . . . it's not like her at all."

"I don't think it's anything to worry about. The baby will need to be fed soon. Katie will hardly be able to turn away then." Dr. Morton took his watch from his pocket. "I must be on my way. I'll look in tomorrow. I don't foresee any problems. He's a sturdy fellow, despite his size."

"Thank you for coming. I'm grateful."

"I'm the one who's grateful. With all the sadness I see, babies are a pleasure. Not that I get to deliver many babies. The midwife gets all the calls."

"Well, I'm glad you delivered *this* baby. Only three hours old and he's already the apple of my eye."

"Good night, Ada. I'll see myself out."

"Good night, Doctor. Thank you." Ada returned to the bed. She stared at Katie's pale, closed face and

293

she sighed. "Would you like to sit up?" she asked. "You might feel better. Here, I'll help you. That's the girl. Now I'm going to help you into a fresh nightgown and brush your hair."

"You don't have to pamper me, Ada."

"I want to. It's a special occasion. Besides, you had a hard couple of days and you deserve pampering."

"Couple of days? Isn't this Friday?"

"It's Saturday, Katie. You were in labor all night Friday and half of today, too. The midwife came around noon. She said the baby was turned the wrong way, so I called Dr. Morton. Toward the end, he gave you medicine and you slept."

"Saturday? Today's Saturday?"

"Ah, you're still sleepy. And I know you're having pain. But it'll pass. By tomorrow you'll be yourself again." Ada put the hairbrush down and stepped back. "There." She smiled. "Isn't that better? You certainly look better."

"Where's Matt?"

"He was here. He left just a while ago. Gone to celebrate the birth of his son. Maeve was here, and your friend, Meg. Dr. Morton was here twice, the second time to be sure you woke up okay. Don't worry, you weren't alone for a minute."

"Did Matt see the baby?"

"Of course he did. He was real happy, Katie. He had a smile on his face from ear to ear."

"Drinking does that to him."

"It's true he'd been drinking," Ada conceded. "But he was smiling because of the baby. You should be smiling too. If you'd only look at the little fella, Katie."

294

"No . . . I can't."

"Why not?"

"I don't know. I can't, that's all. I can't." Katie rested her head against the pillows, and she thought to herself, It isn't supposed to be this way. Why can't I love my baby? Why can't I feel anything? What's *wrong* with me? "I'm sorry, Ada," she said, twisting her fingers together. "I'm ashamed of myself, but it's as if . . . it's as if I'm numb."

"I'm trying to understand. You're not making much sense."

"I'm sorry," Katie started as the baby began to cry. "What's the matter?" she asked. She leaned forward, her eyes fastening on the polished wood cradle. "Why is he crying?"

"He's hungry."

Katie drew back in alarm. "No, Ada." She shook her head. "I don't know how to feed him. I don't know what to do."

"Ah, he'll know what to do. It's nature. There's nothing to be scared of." Ada bent, lifting the tiny bundle from the cradle. "Sweet little boy," she cooed. "You want to meet your mama, don't you? Sure you do . . . here she is. Here's your mama."

Katie took her son in her arms. "Oh, he's so little."

"Four pounds, ten ounces." Ada chuckled. "We weighed him on the kitchen scale."

"Oh, poor thing." Katie gazed at her son's tiny face and she smiled. Warily, her fingers brushed his fluff of golden hair. She touched his hand, and, as she did so, he grabbed hold of her finger. "Look, Ada," she cried. "Look how strong he is! And how handsome!"

"I told you."

"He's a miracle!" Katie gasped, suddenly overcome by such powerful feelings of love she thought
her heart would burst. She felt alive for the first time
in months, and when tears splashed down her cheeks
she knew they were tears of joy. "I've been a fool," she
said, laughing and crying both. "But I'll make it up
to you, my darling. I promise I'll make it up to you,
my wonderful little boy."

"Feeding him would be a good start."

"What? Oh yes, he's hungry." Katie opened the
buttons of her nightgown. She put her son to her
breast and he nursed. "Look at him, Ada. Isn't he a
miracle?"

"That he is. All he needs now is a name."

"Patrick."

"Patrick? There are no Patricks in your family."

"That's just it." Katie nodded, smiling radiantly at
Ada. "I want him to have his own name, not a hand-
me-down. No hand-me-downs for him. He's too
special. He's a miracle!"

"Ah, Patrick's a fine name. But don't you want to
talk it over with Matt?"

Katie realized she had forgotten about Matt. Once
again she shook her head. "My son's name is
Patrick," she said.

"Another whiskey," Matt said, slapping a dime on
the wide bar of the Emerald Isle Pub. "What'll we
toast now, Ben? Think of something."

"I think we've done enough toasting tonight. You
should be home with your wife and baby."

"That's it! We'll toast my wife and baby. I can

296

always count on you for a good toast. Good old Ben."
Matt spun around on his stool. "Hey," he called to
the knots of men lining the bar, "we're toasting my
wife and baby. I have a son. There's a new McVey in
the world, poor devil."

"Matt, come on. You've had your limit and more.
Let me walk you home."

"I am home. Don't you know that, Ben? I'm
home." Matt's bleary gaze roamed over the pub. It
was a friendly place, with sawdust on the floor and
big brass spittoons and a tinny piano in the corner.
Like all the other neighborhood pubs, it opened at
ten in the morning and remained open until the last
customer weaved out the door at night. The
bartender, watching Matt, had little doubt who
would be the last customer this night. "The women
decided, Ben. They decided I'm . . . unfit to be
anywhere but here."

"What are you talking about?"

"Ada . . . and Maeve, the old witch. You should've
heard what they said to me before. Maeve said I was a
drunkard. She couldn't seem to make up her mind
whether I'd end up in the gutter or burning in Hell.
Maybe I'll do both." Matt laughed. "Ada called me a
bum. . . . I guess that's another vote for the gutter."

"Stop it, Matt. It's not funny."

"It's *very* funny. The trouble with you is you have
no sense of humor."

"You're feeling sorry for yourself, my friend."

"Who has a better right? I ask you—Hah! You
have no answer. Good old Ben has no answer.
Well"—Matt shrugged, staring into his empty
glass—"why should he? Good old Ben is going back

297

to City College next week. There're no flies on good old Ben. No wife; no baby. Why should he give a damn?"

"I'd trade places with you in a minute."

"Hah!"

"I would, Matt. You don't know how lucky you are."

"Sure. I was born under a lucky star. It's luck that gave me those wonderful parents, those wonderful mines. It's luck making me leave school. Any more luck and I'll jump in the river."

"You're not leaving school. Why do you keep saying you are? Whether you go days or nights, it's still school."

"No. It's different. It'll take forever. I'll be an old man. An old man, Ben, all because Jack Snow had his appendix out. Maybe I'll throw Jack Snow in the river."

"Come on, let me walk you home."

"Don't you ever listen? I *am* home."

Ben sighed. He sipped his beer and when the bartender reached for Matt's glass, he waved him away. "What good is this doing?" he asked. "You can't solve your problems here."

"I can forget 'em here. Here I don't have to look at Katie and . . . know I'm a bastard. Have I surprised good old Ben? He didn't think I knew I was a bastard. He thought it was a secret. It's no secret. Just ask Ada or Maeve, the old witch . . . or Katie."

"Katie loves you."

"She did. She stopped loving me for a while, but I made her love me again. Now . . . oh, hell. Another whiskey," Matt called, holding out his glass.

"Love isn't like that. People don't just stop—"

"Katie did. She saw me for what I am—a selfish bastard. I made her forget. Now she's remembering."

"You must love *her*, to have gone to such trouble."

"I love her . . . I don't know, Ben. I guess I don't love her enough. Women want your whole damn life. I guess I don't love her enough to give her my whole life. You see what I mean?"

"No."

"You will. Wait'll you get trapped into marriage."

"That's going too far," Ben said, his dark eyes unusually intense. "Katie didn't trap you and you know it. If there was any trapping done, you trapped yourself. You were so used to having your way, you never stopped to think of the consequences. You *refused* to think of the consequences."

"I was drunk that night. I was alone in the house with Katie."

"You were courting her long before that night. The same thing would have happened, sooner or later. You would have had different excuses, but the same thing would have happened. Don't deny it. Not to me. Katie was an innocent young girl. You were anything but innocent. You had your eye on her all along. You set the trap and then walked right in."

"Okay, okay. Maybe I did. I'm paying now."

"If that's your attitude, it's Katie who's paying."

"Thanks."

"Matt, she wants to be your wife, not your penance."

"She's both."

This conversation was not new to Ben, for he had heard Matt's tale of woe many times in the past year.

He listened because Matt was his friend and because he had a sincere desire to help. Now, pondering the situation, he began to doubt that help was possible.

"You look sad," Matt declared, clapping Ben on the back. "Don't be sad. Be happy. Have a drink. You need a drink."

"I've had enough. So have you. It's time to go home."

"You should take his advice, Matt."

"What?" Matt turned, glancing around. "Who said that? Well"—he sighed—"if it isn't my wonderful brother-in-law. What are you doing here, Hugh? Kids aren't allowed here."

"I heard Katie had the baby."

"A boy."

"Yeah, I heard." Hugh pulled an envelope from his pocket. "This is for Katie. See she gets it."

"See to it yourself."

"I can't. I can't go over there. The cops is watching the place."

"Why?" Matt frowned. He rubbed his bloodshot eyes and peered more closely at Hugh. "Why would the cops be watching the boardinghouse? Unless . . . are they after you? Is that what you're saying? What do they want with a kid like you?"

Hugh had no chance to reply, for he saw Officer Garrity pushing through the crowd. He folded his arms and waited, a resigned smile edging his mouth. "Hello, Garrity. Looking for me?"

"Aye. And it's a merry chase you led us. I'll be asking you to come along now, lad."

"What do you want with him?" Matt asked. "He's only a kid. What's he done?"

"It's police business, sir."

"I have a right to know. He's my brother-in-law."

"Aye, sir, but it's still police business. Come along, Hugh. Don't think of making a fuss. There's police outside the door, front and back. Come along quiet and let these people enjoy their Saturday night."

"What about my Saturday night, Garrity?"

"You know the answer to that, lad."

"Yeah." Hugh's cool blue eyes darted to the door. He seemed to consider for a moment, then he shrugged, apparently unconcerned. "So long, Matt."

"What the hell's going on here? Hugh? *Hugh?*" Matt jumped off the bar stool. He started to follow Hugh and Officer Garrity, but Ben restrained him. "Let go of my arm. I have to find out what's happening."

"Don't mix in. There's nothing you can do. The police want to question Hugh about the Thompson robbery. Where have you been, Matt? It's the talk of the neighborhood."

Slowly, Matt's head began to clear. He rubbed his eyes again, watching as Hugh was escorted to the door. He was not the only one watching. A hush had fallen over the pub, and in the tense silence all eyes were fixed on Officer Garrity and his swaggering charge. "You don't got too many friends in here." Hugh grinned at the officer. "Look around."

"I've more than you think, lad. And more outside. I've only to blow my whistle."

"Yeah? Let's see." Hugh whirled quickly, fists flying. "Damn Mick," he said, his fist crashing into Officer Garrity's chin.

"Fight!" someone cried, and indeed the fight was

on. Sides were chosen, half the pub's patrons rallying to the side of the beleaguered policeman, half to Hugh's side. Their choices were instinctive, accurately reflecting the sentiments of a neighborhood in which policemen were idolized by some and despised by others. The men of this latter group remembered Ireland, where the law was turned against the Irish to favor the English landlords. They were incensed by the sight of Irish arresting Irish, and, though they had little use for Hugh and his hoodlum friends, they now rallied to his side.

Hugh was too busy to notice. Quick and light on his feet, he delivered blow after vicious blow to Officer Garrity's face. He split his lip and bloodied his nose, staggering him. "Had enough?" he called over the raucous shouts of the crowd. "No? Okay." He smiled, backing his helpless opponent to the wall.

Officer Garrity was drenched in sweat. Blood poured from his nose, from his mouth, from his bruised knuckles. His knees buckled, but still he did not go down. Choking, gasping for breath, he managed to reach his nightstick. There was a sharp crack as he smashed it on Hugh's head. Now Hugh staggered. He reeled backward, then sank to the floor unconscious.

"Goddamnit, let go of me," Matt screamed, for Ben had him pinned to the bar. "Let me go, damn you."

"Not a chance. Maybe you don't care if you go to jail, but Katie will. It's not your fight. You're staying out of it."

"Goddamnit, Ben, let me *go*."

"Not a chance."

302

Matt increased his struggles as dozens of policemen burst into the pub, whistles blowing, nightsticks swinging. "They'll kill him, Ben. Let me go."

"He'll be fine. Just take it easy, my friend. It's all over now. Just take it easy."

Matt could only watch as the policemen fanned out, restoring order amidst a chorus of cheers and boos. The brawlers were swiftly handcuffed and herded into the street. A stretcher was brought and Hugh was carried out. Five minutes after the fight had begun, it was over.

The pub was a shambles. Chairs and tables were overturned, and broken glass littered the floor. The mirror above the bar had been shattered as well as two of the frosted globes enclosing the gas lamps. Ben surveyed the damage, shaking his head. "What did it accomplish," he asked, "except a big repair bill for Leary? What did it prove?"

"There was a principle involved," Matt replied. He flexed his wrists, still sore where Ben had gripped them. He frowned. "You wouldn't understand."

"You're right about that."

"The cops have to know we Irish won't lie down and play dead. We're men and we'll fight like men."

"Come on, Matt. Don't make it sound noble."

"It was, in a way. You wouldn't understand because you're not Irish. The Irish have always had to fight."

"Do you think it's any easier for Italians? Everybody calls us wops and dagos and thinks we're murderers with the Black Hand. You Irish aren't the only ones with problems."

"We have Irish cops arresting their own."

"You can't expect them to close their eyes. What kind of lawyer will you be if you have no respect for the law?"

"The law and the cops aren't necessarily the same thing, Ben. Besides, I don't have to respect the law. I just have to know how to use it. I don't want to be a hero. I want to be rich."

"You were ready to be a hero tonight, trying to leap into the middle of that crazy fight. I didn't realize you were so devoted to Hugh."

"Devotion has nothing to do with it. As far as I'm concerned, Hugh can go to jail for a hundred years. But he's Katie's brother. And he's an Irishman. Irishmen should stick together."

"Katie will have to know about this, Matt. It'll be all over the neighborhood by morning. It would be better if she heard it from you."

"Yes, of course. At least I'm sober now. While I am, I'll stop in the station house and see how Hugh is and where he is." Matt stepped back as the bartender passed with his broom. He saw all the broken glass, and he sighed. "There's never any peace for the Gallaghers. It's one damn thing after another. It's a shame."

Katie was awake when Matt returned home. She sat at the side of the bed, rocking Patrick's cradle and smiling. Her face was serene, her lovely eyes radiant with love. "He's sleeping, Matt," she whispered. "He's such a good baby. He hardly cries at all. My darling Patrick."

"Patrick? Are you calling him Patrick?"

"That's his name."

"I'm sorry I wasn't here when you decided."

"I'm sorry too. But I wouldn't expect you to miss a Saturday night at the pub. Did you have a nice time?"

"About the pub . . ." Matt hesitated, wondering how to break the news of Hugh's arrest. "I have something to tell you, Katie. Something . . . happened at the pub tonight. There's no easy way to say this. Katie, Hugh was arrested. He came to the pub, and I guess the police followed him. It has to do with the Thompson robbery. He may have been involved."

"Hugh was arrested?"

"He's being charged as an accessory. That means—"

"I know what it means."

Matt took Katie's hand. "I'd do anything to spare you more pain," he said gently. "But you'd have found out in the morning. There was a fight at the pub. Hugh started it, and then everybody joined in. It was a brawl. Hugh broke Garrity's nose. He's being charged with assault, too. Anyway, after tonight, the whole neighborhood will know."

"Is Hugh all right?"

"He got a crack on the head, but he's okay. They let me see him for a minute. He doesn't seem to have any regrets."

"No." Katie sighed. "He wouldn't. Not Hugh. I'm sure he's proud of himself."

"Well, he put up a good fight. I'll give him credit."

"Who cares if he put up a good fight? It's no consolation. It won't be to Mama."

"I'm sorry. Katie . . . Hugh wanted you to have

305

this envelope."

"What's in it?"

"I don't know. It's sealed."

Katie accepted the envelope. She tore the seal and withdrew a note and a ten-dollar bill. "Hugh says he's going away. He says to spend the money on the baby. He was certainly right about going away. The judge will see to that."

"Ten dollars! It's a lot of money."

"I can imagine where it came from."

"Wherever it came from, it's yours now."

"Oh, don't worry. I'm not a fool. I can't afford to be. Money is money, and I'm keeping it."

"I'll just put it in the bank." Matt smiled.

"No. I said *I'm* keeping it. This ten dollars isn't for school or books or the pub. It's for Patrick. I'll give some to the church, but the rest is for Patrick."

"I wasn't going to steal it, Katie."

"Once money goes into the bank, I never see it again."

"We agreed you'd leave money matters to me."

"That was before. Now I have my baby to think about." Katie gazed at Patrick's tiny face, rosy and soft in sleep. She felt great waves of love, a happiness unlike any she had ever known. "School can come first with you, Matt. It's all right. I understand. But Patrick comes first with me. He'll have the things he needs, and maybe a few things he doesn't need."

"I suppose you're going to spoil him."

You're a fine one to talk about being spoiled, thought Katie ruefully. Always wanting your own way; getting drunk when something interferes. "I wouldn't be doing him any favor by spoiling him,

Matt. No, I'm not going to make that mistake."

"Then let me put some of the money in the bank."

Katie shook her head. "I told you I'm keeping it. I can be trusted with ten dollars, can't I?"

"I just hate to see it wasted. I have to work a long time to make ten dollars."

"I work too."

Matt rose. He went to the window, parting the curtains and breathing in the fresh, rain-cooled air. After a moment he retraced his steps, pausing to look at his sleeping son. "He's not even a day old. What could he possibly need?"

"Come fall, he'll need warm clothes. I thought you wanted the best for your children, Matt. You said you did."

"It'll be years before he knows what the best is—or cares."

"*I* care."

"Oh? Are you making all the decisions in the family now? What's happened to you, Katie? I know you have reason to be angry with me. I know I've disappointed you. But to treat me like this. It's wrong. A wife has a duty to her husband."

"I have a duty to my son. He isn't going to grow up the way I did, the way my brothers did. I want better for him. Is that so hard to understand?"

"You're hard to understand. You're . . . different, Katie. You sound different. You *look* different. You look . . ." Matt could not find the word he sought. He stared at his wife and saw a new assurance in her green eyes, in the set of her beautiful mouth. It was disturbing, for he sensed she was growing away from him. "What's happened to you?" he asked again.

"Patrick happened. I guess I've stopped being afraid, Matt. I've stopped being your little girl."

Katie went back to work when Patrick was a week old. She was reluctant to leave him alone even briefly, and so she arranged blankets and pillows in an old laundry basket and carried him with her everywhere. She paused often in the midst of her chores to coo over him, to catch his tiny hand in her hers. He was a happy baby, gurgling, kicking his little legs but seldom crying, and soon he was the pride and joy of the boardinghouse, "adopted" by the vaudevillians who were far from their own families.

Patrick was less than a month old when Katie marked her sixteenth birthday. It was not a day of celebration, for on that day she went to court to be with Hugh at his sentencing. She was the only family member there. She had not expected Matt to accompany her, and Maeve had refused, just as she had refused to visit Hugh during his confinement at Juvenile Hall. Her reply to Katie's many protests was unvarying: "Sure and he broke the law. Now let him pay the price."

The day was cool, with gray clouds swallowing the autumn sun. Katie looked at the clouds and bundled Patrick in a knit sweater suit and matching knit hat. She set him in his basket and, together, they rode the horsecar downtown. Courtroom attendants gave her a front seat for the proceedings. She sat very quietly, reaching now and again to touch Hugh's shoulder, saying nothing. To her amazement, she discovered that Hugh had pleaded guilty to all charges. His sentence was considered lenient: three years in the Boys' Reformatory. "Can I have a minute?" Hugh asked his guard when court was adjourned. "This is my sister and her baby. I won't be seeing them so soon."

"Okay, Gallagher. But make it quick."

"You didn't have to come, Katie. It's no place for you." Hugh grinned, looking at Patrick. "It's no place for him, neither. The kid might get ideas."

"Are you all right, Hugh? Three years. That's such a long time. I can't bear to think about it."

"I got off easy. Three years is nothing. A snap. And it's not like it's jail. The older guys got jail. They got ten years, some of 'em. It's good I'm just turning fifteen."

"You won't have much of a birthday at the Reformatory." Katie sighed. "Maybe there's some way I can send you a cake. I'll stop in the post office and ask . . . oh, Hugh, I wish you weren't going so far. It must be a hundred miles. How can I visit you?"

"You can't. I wouldn't want you to. Quit worrying. I can take care of myself."

"Yes, I see what a fine job you've done."

Hugh laughed, startling the guard who stood nearby. "Okay, Gallagher," he said. "You had your minute. Let's go. You'd think you was going to a party," he grumbled. "All youse hoodlums make me sick. C'mon, let's go."

"It's time, Katie."

"I know."

"Don't be sad. I'm not."

Katie put the baby's basket down and threw her arms around her brother, holding him close. "I love

309

you, Hugh. I'll miss you. I'll write to you every week. Every week, I promise. Do what they tell you up there. Behave yourself. If you need anything—"

"Naw," Hugh said, wriggling out of Katie's embrace. "They'll give me anything I need—free. Quit worrying, will you? The time will go fast. I'll be back before you know it. Just look after the kid. He's okay."

"I love you, Hugh. God bless." Katie watched as Hugh was led away. When she could watch no more, she picked up Patrick's basket and walked swiftly from the courtroom. "God bless," she murmured, stepping into the gray light of afternoon.

"Katie?"

"Meg! What are you doing here?"

"I had to come. Hugh told me not to, but I was going crazy. I took the day off. I said I was sick. It's not really a lie, not the way I'm feeling. *Three years*, Katie. I thought I'd faint."

"You were in the courtroom?"

"Hiding by the door."

Katie saw Meg's reddened eyes, her tear-stained face, and she frowned. "But why?" she asked. "Why are you so upset?"

"I guess you didn't know."

"Didn't know what?"

"I love him."

Meg's simple declaration shocked Katie. She stared at her childhood friend, her eyes wide and unblinking. "You love him? You love *Hugh*? Since when? Oh, Meg, you're always having crushes."

"No, this is different. I'm not a kid in pigtails any more, Katie. I'm sixteen, same as you. I'm earning my living, same as you. I know how I feel. Those other boys didn't mean anything to me. It was all in fun. It's fun to flirt. But it didn't mean anything." Meg lifted her head, meeting Katie's gaze. "I know what you're thinking," she said. "Hugh won't even be fifteen 'til next week. Well, age isn't important. He always seemed older, looked older. He wasn't like the other boys."

Patrick began to stir and Katie soothed him. She walked down the courthouse steps with Meg following behind. "Does Hugh love you?" she asked when they reached the corner.

"We never talked about it. He tries to act so tough."

"It's no act, Meg. He wouldn't be going to the Reformatory if it were an act. He has a gang, and they do terrible things. I didn't want to believe it myself at first. I couldn't. Now the truth is obvious."

"I don't care."

"He'll break your heart a thousand times over."

"It's my heart."

"I knew you liked Hugh." Katie sighed. "You were quick enough to defend him, and the only one who did. But love? It'll come to grief, Meg. It has to. Hugh's life—"

"What do you know about grief?"

Katie considered her reply carefully. "If you love the wrong person, it comes to grief, Meg. I learned that. I think Mama tried to tell me, to warn me. Ada certainly warned me. I didn't pay any attention. Nobody ever does, I guess. When you're first in love, nothing else matters."

Now Meg frowned, tugging at a lock of bright red

hair. "Katie, aren't you happy?"

"I have a wonderful son. He makes me happy every moment."

"I'm talking about you and Matt. Your marriage."

Katie smiled slightly. She glanced at Patrick then stared off into the distance. "I have a wonderful son," she said. "I have no marriage."

13

"Didn't Ben look handsome in his cap and gown?" Katie asked. "His family was so proud. Mrs. Rossi never stopped smiling and Mr. Rossi had tears in his eyes the whole time. And all those brothers and sisters! Oh, it was lovely to see. I couldn't help crying myself."

Matt was silent. He paced the room, his head bent, his reddish brows drawn together. He had endured Ben's graduation stoically, but now anger raged within him, anger born of jealousy and regret. "It should have been me," he cried. "It should have been me getting that diploma."

"It will be. Soon."

"*Soon*? I'm taking as many courses as I can and I *still* have another two years. Two years, Katie. Ben will be almost finished with law school while I'm just starting."

"It's not a race. It doesn't matter who finishes first."

"It doesn't matter to you. It matters very much to me."

"Do we have to have this conversation again? I

know it by heart. I know exactly what you'll say and exactly what I'll say. Nothing will be solved. It never is." Katie paused. She put her hand to her pale throat, sighing. "I'm sorry. Maybe it was a mistake going to Ben's graduation. It was hard on you. I'm sorry, Matt. Let's not talk about it any more."

"You're always *so* reasonable."

"Would you like me to scream and holler? I wish you'd make up your mind. If I argue, you get angry. If I don't argue, you get angry. What is it you want? I can't seem to do anything right."

"Then we're even. *Nothing* I do pleases you. You're too good, too *reasonable* to complain. But I'm not fooled, Katie. I know damn well what you're thinking. Even a simple thing like Ben's graduation present. You didn't say a word. You didn't have to. I knew you thought I was being cheap. You expected me to open my purse wider."

"Ben's your friend, your closest friend. He's certainly been generous to us. Remember the big teddy bear he bought for Patrick's first Christmas and the rocking horse he bought this past Christmas? Maybe you should have opened your purse wider. It's not as if your purse is empty. You save most of your salary every week."

"And you know why." Matt resumed his pacing, his hands clenched tightly behind his back. "I told you my plan, Katie. The city's auctioning some properties soon, and I intend to bid. I won't get much. I don't have much to spend. Whatever I get, it'll be a start. An alleyway, a vacant lot—it'll be a start."

"Why you'd want a vacant lot is beyond me."

"The city's growing. There's prosperity here. I can smell it in the air. Property, *any* property, will be worth a fortune one day. I want my share. No, I want *more* than my share. If I have to stint on presents and other foolishness, so be it. It's my money, It's my money, my choice." Matt spun around, pointing his finger at Katie. "Don't remind me it's your money too. I get enough reminders from Ada. She does her best to make me feel guilty. Let her. I know what I'm doing is right. I'm looking to the future."

"I understand."

"The hell you do! If you had your way, I'd have no savings at all."

"That's not fair, Matt."

"Isn't it? I know what you think of me."

"I think you're unhappy and trying to make up for lost time."

"Unhappy? Why would I be unhappy? I have a wife who looks at me with pity, when she bothers to look at me at all. I have a nagging aunt. I have a son who treats me like a stranger. Why would *I* be unhappy?"

"Don't blame Patrick. If he sees you ten minutes each day, that's a lot. He sees more of the boarders than he sees of you. He's only a little boy, Matt. You come in and then go right out again. To him you are a stranger."

"I suppose I should quit my job and stay home. Better yet, maybe I should quit school. Is that what you want?"

"Of course not. But you can't blame Patrick for being confused." Katie glanced at the clock. She stood, smoothing her skirts. "It's still early. I'll fetch

Patrick from Mama's. We'll have the evening together."

"*No.* She agreed to keep him overnight. That was the plan."

"We didn't plan to be home this early. Now we can have a nice family evening together, the three of us. Patrick—"

"Patrick! He's all you talk about! The world doesn't begin and end with *Patrick.*" Matt strode across the room. He opened the desk drawer and removed a bottle of whiskey, slamming it down. "Care to join me?" he asked.

"Matt, you had so much wine at Ben's party."

"I suddenly feel the need for something stronger."

"Suddenly?"

Matt shrugged. He poured a whiskey and drank it. He poured another. "Don't worry, Katie," he said. "I won't get drunk. Not tonight. I have other things in mind. . . . An evening with my wife, for example. When's the last time we had an evening alone? I can't remember; can you? Not that you give a damn. You used to wait up for me. No matter how late I was, you'd wait up . . . but that was long ago. Now you wouldn't notice if I stayed out all night. Or all year."

"Stop it."

"Hah! The truth hurts!"

"Whose truth? Yours? You have your own version of the truth. It's easier to blame your problems on other people. You blame me and Ada and even Patrick. You never blame yourself. Poor, misunderstood Matt. Everybody's making your life miserable. It's a plot. We lie awake plotting how to ruin your life."

"I didn't say it was a plot." Matt smiled. He finished his drink and sat down, staring at Katie. "I told you I wasn't good enough for you. I warned you. You refused to listen. You swore we'd be happy. The day we had our first argument, you swore we'd never argue again."

"I was very young. And probably very stupid."

"You were in love. You're not in love now, are you?"

Katie turned away. Several moments passed, and still she did not reply. She was wary, knowing the wrong reply would cause the final break in her marriage. She thought about Patrick. She thought about her mother's struggles to raise a family alone. She felt trapped, and it occurred to her that Matt was enjoying her distress. "Why are you smiling?" she asked.

"You're putting on quite a show. It's all in your face, little girl. You want to be honest, but you want to be *reasonable*, too. You want to do the right thing, but you're not sure what the right thing is. There's Patrick to consider."

"Don't call me little girl."

"Sorry. I forgot. I guess I was remembering the good old days. Whatever happened to them?"

"We couldn't be newlyweds all our lives."

"That doesn't answer my question. You don't love me any more, do you?"

"I love you, Matt. Maybe not the same way. I'm not fourteen any more. I've changed. We've both changed. We've been through so much. The early years are always hard."

"Did you read that in a book? Or is that one of

317

Ada's homey sayings?"

"Don't make fun of me."

"I'm sorry, Katie." Matt sighed. "I really am. There's nothing funny here. I hate this room, this house, this whole damn neighborhood. I hate my life."

"Your life hasn't even begun."

"At the rate I'm going, it never will. Ah, there's that pitying look. I don't want your pity. I want . . . I want you." Matt rose. He went to the door and locked it. "I want you in bed with me." He smiled. "Why are you drawing back? You're my wife. You *love* me. . . . I have a right, Katie."

"A right you lost."

"What's that supposed to mean?"

"I can't talk about it. I can't."

"You'd better."

Matt was coming closer, and Katie took another step back. "No, don't touch me. Don't. Please don't."

"I want you. I intend to have you."

"Stop it," Katie said, pushing Matt's hand away. "I know you've been visiting Maisie Craig. Everybody knows. It's not a secret. You didn't even try to keep it a secret. You go straight from the pub to Maisie's, bold as brass."

"What of it?"

"You have Maisie. How many women do you need?"

"I *want* my wife."

"Your wife!" Katie cried, her mouth trembling. "You never wanted a wife. You wanted a . . . a mistress, a whore. I won't be your whore. Go to Maisie for that. Go with my blessing."

318

Matt felt a sharp and terrible rage. He slapped Katie, then slapped her again. "Damn you! It's because of you I go to Maisie's. You turned your back on me in bed once too often. You sent me to her. And maybe I wanted you to know about it. Maybe I hoped you'd be jealous. There's no jealousy in you; no love either. Not for me. What do you give me but pity and sad looks? Oh, you take care of me. You see that my meals are hot and my clothes are clean. You get my books from the library. You darn my socks. You're my *maid*, not my wife. It's true I never wanted a wife. But I got one anyway. You'll *be* a wife, Katie. By God, you'll be a wife."

"Don't."

"Damn you, I'll *make* you love me." Matt tore Katie's blouse and camisole away. The rest of her clothing followed and, savagely, he clutched at her naked body. He pushed her to the floor, falling on top of her. "Tell me you love me," he demanded, his face inflamed with lust and anger. "*Say* it."

"I . . . love you."

Katie paused in the doorway of the kitchen. She pulled her robe close and tried to smile. "I'm sorry, Ada. I didn't know you were here," she said. "I thought I'd have a cup of tea."

"Come sit down. Are you all right?"

"Yes. Why wouldn't I be?"

"I always used to brag about my thick walls. I found out they're not that thick."

"Oh, God." Katie sank into a chair. She covered her face with her hands, too ashamed to meet Ada's troubled gaze. "Did you hear us? I suppose everybody heard."

"Lucky it's a traveling day for most of the boarders. The house is half empty. Still, there were a lot of raised eyebrows. A lot of muttering, too. Jack was ready to break the door down and give Matt hell. Ellie Costello kept saying we should get the police. I considered it myself. But there's nothing new about a man attacking his wife. It's legal. The law belongs to men. Lock, stock, and barrel."

"Matt didn't attack me."

"What would you call it? Ah, Katie, there isn't a person in this house who didn't know what was going on. All the yelling, the hollering. And then . . . well, we won't talk about it. The question is what to do about it." Ada opened the icebox. She chipped away at a large block of ice, wrapping the pieces in a towel. "Here," she said. "For your cheek. You'll have a nasty bruise, come morning."

"I'm so sorry, Ada."

"Matt's the one to be sorry. He should be horsewhipped. I don't know him any more. It's like he's gone crazy. The drinking was bad enough. But this is something I can't forgive."

"You said we wouldn't talk about it."

Ada poured tea into plain white cups. She took a seat opposite Katie, reaching to touch her hand. "I'm worried. I was thinking maybe Matt should leave for a while. He could get a room. There are plenty of rooms to be had. I'd pay the rent."

"Matt's your *nephew*. You can't send him away."

"If he wasn't my nephew, I'd have thrown him out months ago. I run a respectable boardinghouse here.

320

No drunks, no monkey business."

"Send him away and he won't come back." The prospect alarmed Katie and, despite everything that had happened, she was not surprised. She said to herself, I don't want to end up like Mama, alone and poor and fighting battles I can't win. I don't mind for myself, but there's Patrick. "You know he won't come back, Ada. Our marriage will be over."

"How can you worry about that now? Is it stubbornness? Don't tell me it's love. Not after the goings on tonight. Listen to me, Katie. I don't give in easy. I never did. Tim, rest his soul, used to say I was kin to the bulldog. I guess all Irish have a bit of bulldog in them. We call it pride. Nothing wrong with it, except when it's stupid, or dangerous."

"You don't understand. Ben's graduation upset Matt. He had too much to drink. He was in a bad mood. I should have had enough sense to keep my mouth shut. I didn't."

"So it's your fault?"

"It's nobody's fault, Ada."

"In the first place, Matt's always having too much to drink. And he's always in bad moods lately. Ben's graduation is just an excuse. He has more excuses than a one-armed juggler. It can't go on. Matt's my nephew and I love him, but a few decisions have to be made around here."

"They're my decisions. It's my marriage."

"What's left of it."

Katie looked at Ada. She saw the strain in her face, a face no longer young. She could not recall exactly when Ada had begun to show her age, but in the bright gaslight every line and wrinkle was apparent.

Her hair was thinner, streaked with white. She seemed diminished, the merry spark gone from her eyes. Guilt assailed Katie, for she knew the tensions of the last months had aged her friend. "It's so unfair," she said quietly. "It's selfish. Matt and I are busy thinking about ourselves. We don't think what we're doing to you."

"Never mind me. I've had my life—a good life. At my age, I'm not complaining. It's different with you and Matt. You're just starting out. There are choices, decisions. Decide wrong and you'll be paying all your life." Ada sighed. She lighted a cigarette and sat back. "I believed there was a chance, Katie. Ah, I was sure Matt would settle down. Whatever problems you had, you loved each other. I put all my hope in that."

"Yes, I did too."

"Now you're sitting here all bruised and hurt. Your husband's sleeping off another drunk."

"He *is* my husband, Ada."

"Does that mean you have to suffer your whole life? You have a lot of years ahead of you. What happened tonight won't be forgotten, mark my words. You won't forget. Neither will Matt. It'll be there between you, like a sickness."

"Everything's forgotten, in time."

"Is it forgiven?"

"It has to be. There's Patrick. Matt and I may not have much of a marriage, but we have Patrick."

"I think Matt should leave for a while."

"He won't come back," Katie said, twisting her fingers together. "Then what? We won't be married. We won't be divorced either. There's no divorce in the church. We'll be in limbo, all of us." And I'll be afraid, thought Katie. I'll be afraid every day of my life, just as Mama's afraid. "It's no use, Ada. We'll have to make the best."

"Well, it's up to you. But what goes on under my roof is up to me. I run a respectable place. It'll stay respectable. And there's something else. My boarders don't mean any harm. Still, there's bound to be talk. Once it starts, Matt won't find it so comfortable around here. He's the one they're blaming. He'll get his share of nasty looks. Maybe some nasty words in the bargain."

"I know. I'll talk to him. When he's feeling better, we'll have a talk. I promise . . . Ada, nothing like this ever happened before. It won't happen again."

"You're a fool if you let it. There are women who do. Fools, the lot of them. *Martyrs*. If a man ever raised his hand to me, I'd swat him good with the first thing I could grab. A vase, a chair—it wouldn't matter. Then I'd kick his backside out the door 'til he cooled off."

"It's not that simple."

"I guess it isn't," Ada said, shaking her head. "I was lucky with my Tim, rest his soul. He was the gentlest man on God's earth. No moods, no temper to speak of. I was lucky and I knew it."

"You're tired. Why don't you go on to bed?"

Ada glanced at her watch. "There'll be boarders coming in the next hour or so. The train from Boston should be arriving right now. Then there's the train from Philadelphia. Then from Buffalo. We'll have a full house by night's end."

"I'll wait for them."

"The night I can't greet my own boarders is the

night I sell this place. It's nice of you to offer"—Ada winked—"but they're used to seeing my pretty face. I wouldn't want to disappoint anybody, would I? Besides, I want to hear all the news."

"You're sure?"

"Absolutely . . . Katie, you can sleep in my room tonight."

"No. I appreciate it, but I'll be fine. I should be with Matt. Running away won't help. We'll face our problems. We'll solve them somehow. If we try hard enough, we'll solve them."

"I hope so."

"Good night, Ada." Katie left the kitchen. She hurried through the hall, thankful that nobody was about. She did not slow her step until she reached her room. She paused then, her hand on the doorknob, and took a deep breath. "Oh, you're awake, Matt."

"Close the door. I want to talk to you. Don't worry. I'm . . . in my right mind again. I really am. I won't hurt you. Please. Just hear me out. After you have, I'll do whatever you say."

Katie saw Matt's red-rimmed eyes, his tense and ashen mouth. "Of course I'll hear you out." She nodded. "Maybe tomorrow would be a better time."

"I've been pacing back and forth, calling myself every ugly name there is. You probably thought of a few of your own. I . . . I'm sorry, Katie. I've never been sorrier for anything in my life. I don't expect you to forgive me. But I want you to know I had my last drink tonight. I'm through with the stuff. I swear it."

"Are you serious?"

"I swear. I'll swear on the Bible. Where is it?"

"You don't have to do that. I believe you, Matt." At least Katie wanted to believe him. She had her doubts, but, desperate as she was to end the arguing, the pain, she put her doubts aside. "It's a relief."

"Yes, I can imagine." Matt walked across the room. He sat down, gripping the arms of the chair. "I'm really very sorry. I'll do whatever you say, Katie. I'll go, if you want. Or I'll stay. But please let's never mention this nightmare again."

In March of 1909, precisely nine months after the "nightmare," Katie gave birth to her second child, a boy named Rory. He entered the world with a furious cry, and from that moment on he seemed to cry all the time. He kicked his legs, curled his little hands into fists, and shrieked. When he had exhausted himself, he slept. Katie watched him and could only smile, for now she had two children to love.

Rory and Patrick were unlikely brothers, as different as night and day. Patrick, everyone agreed, was a restful child, serene and amiable. Rory, so dark of hair and eye and temper, was just the opposite. But despite their differences, the brothers were close.

"*My* baby," Patrick had said, viewing the newborn Rory. Katie had corrected him, to no avail. "My baby" was the way Patrick stubbornly continued to refer to his brother. "My baby crying," he would announce. "My baby hungry." On the day of Rory's first birthday, Patrick began to refer to him as "our baby." Katie considered it a victory.

"Both my sons are stubborn, Mama," Katie said one afternoon in June. "It runs in the family. Patrick smiles and Rory screams, but they're the same underneath. The both have iron wills."

"Aye, you might be right. Stubbornness is the curse of the Gallaghers."

"And the McVeys."

"Aye." Maeve sipped her tea, glancing around Ada's big, comfortable kitchen. She was forty years old, her hair grayer, her brow more deeply lined, though otherwise she appeared to have changed very little. She had weathered her tragedies and gone on, neither more mellow nor more bitter than she had been before. "Am I keeping you from your work?" she asked. "I see that basket of potatoes over there. They won't peel themselves."

"The potatoes can wait. It's nice to visit with you, Mama. It's a good time, too. The boarders are out and Ada's taking a rest. If Sean can keep the boys quiet, we'll be able to have a nice long talk."

"Maybe it won't be so nice. I've something to tell you, Katie. About Hugh. He and Meg have run off together. They're married. Mrs. Muldoon got a wire this morning. She's been crying all the day. I don't blame her. Dear knows it's the end for Meg. Marrying a convict."

"Hugh's not a convict. He was in the Boys Reformatory, not prison. He was only a child when he went away. You can't hold him responsible—"

"Can't I?"

"He paid for what he did. Three years of his life, Mama."

"Aye, and what's he done since he's been out? Tell me that. He's got himself a new gang, worse than the other. He's started up gambling again. Running dice

326

games all over the neighborhood. And numbers games, by the talk I hear. *Swag* Gallagher, cock o' the walk. The next time it won't be the Reformatory. It'll be prison. What'll Meg do then? If she's your friend, you'd best be saying prayers. She'll need them."

Katie pulled a chair out and sat down. "Meg could be a . . . good influence on Hugh," she suggested. "It's possible."

"Aye, it's possible the sky will fall. You don't see me rushing home to take the wash from the line. Good influence! Didn't he have a good influence when he was growing up? Didn't I raise him decent and proper? He's going on nineteen. It's too late to change. He is what he is. A hoodlum."

"Meg loves him. She waited all those years while he was away."

"Love, is it? Love and a nickel will get you on the streetcar. Where did love get you, Katie McVey? Oh, you're living in a better place. And you have your children. But I've only to look in your eyes to see the truth about *love*."

"That's not fair."

"Is it true? I dare you to tell me it isn't. You've tried to keep the truth from me. Fine. A wife has no place complaining about her husband to others. But I'm still your mother. I know what you feel in your heart."

"You've been listening to gossip, Mama."

"I don't listen to gossip. Gossip is the devil's work. I can figure some things out for myself. When I see Matt going into a certain building on Ninth Avenue, I can figure it out. When I see Ben Rossi paying calls on you, I can figure it out."

327

Color flared in Katie's cheeks. She averted her gaze, staring down at the table. "Ben's not paying calls on me," she said quickly. "He's Matt's friend."

"I suppose he just happens to come by when Matt's out? I suppose it's an accident?"

"Matt's always out. He visits that certain building on Ninth Avenue, or a certain building on Forty-Fourth Street, or a certain building in Yorkville. He does as he pleases."

"Aye, a man can do as he pleases in this world. It's different for a woman. A woman's good name is all she has."

"There's nothing between Ben and me. He's fond of Patrick and Rory. Of me, too, I guess, but not the way you think. He's a gentleman, Mama. He wouldn't . . . take advantage."

"Is he a saint? All men get notions, Katie, unless they're saints. Sure and Ben has nice manners. I'm not saying he doesn't. But he's a man." And you're a beautiful woman, thought Maeve; too beautiful by far. "I've kept my nose out of your business," she reminded Katie. "I haven't been running over every day to give you advice, like some mothers I know. Now it's time to speak up. What you're doing is wrong. You're a married woman. You can't be having men callers when your husband is out."

"Ada's always here. It's innocent, Mama."

"Innocent or not, a *hundred* Adas or not, you tell Ben you can't see him without Matt. And tell him tonight. It's Saturday. He'll be coming around. There are two kinds of women in this world. Maisie Craig's kind and your kind. Do you want to be a Maisie Craig?"

"Mama!"

Maeve shrugged. She gazed implacably at Katie, folding her hands in her lap. "Tell him tonight," she said.

Katie felt as if she were back in her mother's kitchen, an errant child being chastised. A sharp retort came to her lips, but it died there, for, all these years later, she was still wary of her mother's wrath. "Is that an order, Mama?"

"And does it have to be an order? Use the sense God gave you. Think of Matt."

"*Matt*? With all his women? His drinking? He promised me he'd never take another drink. Then the night Rory was born he got so drunk he had to be carried home. He's gotten drunk every Saturday night since. Think of Matt? Think *what*?"

"He's your husband. He could throw you out in the street."

"Is that what you're worried about, Mama? Ada's wanted to throw *Matt* out. Many times. I'm the one who's stopped her."

"Aye, she's a loyal friend. But Matt's her nephew, her family. And family comes first. If there's trouble between the two of you, Ada will take his side in it."

"There's already been trouble between us, Mama. Since before Rory was born. Even before Patrick was born. I'm not pretending it's all Matt's fault. That's what makes it so hard. I know it's my fault, too." Katie's green eyes were thoughtful as she recalled her conversations with Ada. She had defended Matt, but in vain, for Ada was past listening, past believing. "I'd feel better if Ada took his side. I wouldn't feel so guilty. It's terrible, Mama. They hardly talk to each other any more. When they do, they argue."

"It must be hard on Ada. She always thought of Matt like a son. I know the pain when a son goes wrong. Sure and it's a knife twisting in your heart. . . . Ada did everything for Matt. She gave him a fine room, a room she could have rented out. He was working, but she bought his clothes—a new suit every year, a sturdy winter coat. When he was sick, she had the doctor over. When he had a toothache, she took him off to the dentist. . . . The best I could do for Hugh was oil of cloves."

"Mama, don't."

"You have sons of your own now. I hope you're luckier raising them. My way wasn't right. Ada's way wasn't right. Maybe you'll find the right way, Katie. Just don't try to do it alone. You need Matt. Whatever else he is, he's hard working. He earns steady wages and he goes to school. All the rest . . . it's a small price to pay."

"How can you say that?"

"How?" Maeve smiled. It was a thin smile, and cool. "I'm thinking you have a short memory, Katie McVey. Are you forgetting life in the tenements? All the times there was no food on the table, no coal for the stove? Stop dreaming about love and remember your blessings. You can put your children to bed at night knowing they're warm and their stomachs are full. Aye, it's a small price." Maeve turned as Sean entered the kitchen. "What's the matter?" she asked, seeing his strange expression. "Well, what is it? Have you lost your tongue?"

"Ada."

"Ada? What about her?"

"She's lying on the floor. Outside the parlor, Mama. I poked her arm, but she didn't move. I think she's dead."

Maeve and Katie bolted from their chairs. They ran into the hall. "Oh, my God," Katie cried, for Ada lay in a crumpled heap, her head slumped against her shoulder, her eyes closed. Katie knelt and touched her hand to Ada's chest. "I feel a heartbeat," she said anxiously. "It's very faint. Telephone Dr. Morton, Mama. Tell him to come right away. I'll stay with Ada."

"I don't know how to work the telephone. You do it. I'll stay with her. Sean, keep the children in their room. Wait there 'til I call you."

"Yes, Mama."

Sean ran off in one direction, Katie in another. Maeve sank to her knees, bending over Ada's stricken form. "Ada . . . Ada, it's Maeve. Can you hear me, Ada? Katie's gone to telephone the doctor. You'll be fine . . . can you hear me, Ada?" There was no response, and Maeve sighed. Dear God, she thought. Dear God, not Ada too.

Katie returned moments later to find her mother wiping away a tear. "Mama?"

"I'm sorry. She's passed on."

"*No.*"

"I'm sorry, Katie."

"All the arrangements have been made," Mr. McCarthy explained to a pale and trembling Katie. "Ada visited my office more than two years ago. She told me what she wanted, when her time came. She

331

was very definite about it. It's all in the agreement. See, there's her signature."

"Do you want me to look it over, Katie?" Ben asked.

"I wish Matt were here. Where *is* he? Oh, how I hate Saturday nights. It'll be hours before he gets back."

"It won't be that long. I left word at the pubs. Everybody's watching for him." Ben took the typewritten agreement from Mr. McCarthy. He read each page slowly, carefully, and then glanced up. "It seems to be in order."

"It is, Mr. Rossi. I can promise you it is. As I say, Ada was very definite. And she knew McCarthy's would do right by her. We did right by Tim, when it was his time. We'll do right by her. You have my word."

Ben walked the length of the parlor. His face was somber, his eyes so dark they were almost black. He too was wondering where Matt was, for it was incomprehensible to him that Matt had not yet heard of Ada's death. He looked again at the agreement, nodding. "Katie, I think you should let Mr. McCarthy . . . proceed. Ada's wishes are clear. There's no reason to wait."

"What about Matt? Shouldn't he have some part in this? He was her nephew."

"I'm sure Matt would want to honor Ada's wishes."

"Yes." Katie raised her trembling hand to her throat. "Yes, go ahead, Mr. McCarthy. But I don't know if there was insurance, and I've only a few dollars in the house. I won't be able to pay you until the bank opens on Monday."

"Ada paid me the day we drew the agreement. Taking the burden off her family, she said. Ada was a remarkable woman, remarkable."

"Yes. She was." Katie found her handkerchief and dried her eyes. "Thank you."

"Now as to the wake—"

"Oh, God," Katie cried. Ben was at her side in an instant.

"Ada requested a traditional Irish wake," Ben said gently. "I'm sure Mr. McCarthy will see to the details."

"Of course. That's in the agreement also. You mustn't worry. Flannagan's will see to the food and liquor. We'll see to everthing else. My men will be here tomorrow morning to prepare. Katie, if you'll forgive my saying so, Ada wouldn't like to be remembered with tears. It's a celebration she planned. She had a happy life, and she didn't look on death as the end. She talked about joining her Tim."

"Please. I don't want to hear any more."

"Ah, I understand. I'll be leaving now. Don't trouble to show me out. I know the way. Good evening to you, Katie. Mr. Rossi."

"Good evening."

There was a deep silence in the parlor. Ben sat down next to Katie and lighted his pipe. "What can I do to help?" he asked when several moments had passed. "Just tell me. I'm ready and willing. Why don't I start by getting you some tea? Or maybe something stronger? Ada always kept a bottle of brandy in the cupboard."

"For medicinal purposes." Katie sniffled, a slight

333

smile lifting the corners of her mouth. "I'll be all right, Ben. It was the shock. Ada was looking awfully tired, but she insisted she felt fine. I asked her to go see Dr. Morton. She laughed. I should have made her go."

"You can't blame yourself. It was a heart attack. It might have happened any time. She wasn't young, Katie."

"I know. I guess Ada knew, too. It's true she was talking more and more about Tim lately. And planning her own funeral. . . . She never said a word. She never even hinted. . . . I hope she knew how much I loved her."

"How could she not?"

"Where are you going, Ben? Don't bother with the tea."

"It's no bother. I've often thought there was something mystical about the Irish and their tea. Will you let me in on the secret? A fellow could get rich on a secret like that . . . I'm sorry Katie. I'm doing a poor job of distracting you. I only wanted to stop your tears. It hurts me to see you cry. Can't I help?"

"You already have, by being here. I needed a friend tonight."

Ben took Katie's head upon his shoulder. He put his arm around her, and, as he did, Matt strode into the room. "Matt, I'm glad you're home."

"I bet! I was told there was an emergency. Is this it? You getting cozy with my wife?"

Ben jumped up. "Now wait a minute," he said. "You have things wrong. You have a hell of a nerve. I'd suggest you be quiet and listen for once. I was trying to comfort Katie. Whatever else you're thinking, you're wrong."

"Good old Ben. So quick to offer *comfort*."

"You're drunk."

"You're a *bastard*." Matt swung at Ben, knocking him to the floor. "Bastard! I ought to kill you. No, you stay out of this, Katie. This is between me and Ben, my former best friend."

"Have you gone crazy? Oh, never mind," Katie said in disgust. "There's no talking to you when you're drunk." She brushed past Matt and went to Ben, holding out her hand. "Are you okay? Did he hurt you?"

"Only my dignity."

"If you're ready to fight like a man, I'll hurt more than that."

"Stop it, Matt! You don't understand. Ben was just trying to help."

"Yes, I saw him trying to help himself to my wife."

Katie's eyes flashed angrily. She took a deep breath, and then another. "What you saw was two friends comforting each other. Something terrible's happened, Matt. Ada had a heart attack this afternoon. She's . . . She's dead."

"Dead?" All the color drained from Matt's face. The room seemed to tilt, and he stumbled toward a chair, falling into it. "Dead?" he asked again.

"We telephoned you at the lumber yard, but you'd left for the day. I'm sorry. It was . . . very sudden."

"I wasn't with her. I should have been with her."

"Don't blame yourself," Ben said. "You had no way of knowing. Ada wouldn't want you to blame yourself."

"Where is she? I have to see her. I have to tell her—"

"Tomorrow, Matt. Tomorrow."

"*Now.*"

"You can't see her now." Ben glanced at Katie. He walked to Matt's chair, putting his hand on his friend's shoulder. "Mr. McCarthy's already been here," he explained. "There'll be a wake. It's what Ada wanted, a traditional Irish wake. Mr. McCarthy's taking care of everything. Ada gave him instructions some time back. She didn't want weeping and wailing."

"Am I supposed to be happy? An Irish wake . . ." Matt shook his head. "Singing, carrying on as if it were a party."

"Maybe the Irish have the right idea. A good life deserves to be celebrated."

Ada's simple, dark wood casket was placed at the rear of the parlor and surrounded by masses of flowers. Cornelius O'Day had sent an enormous heart of red roses, Jack Snow an enormous pillow of white carnations, and the Costello family a sheaf of lilies with a satin ribbon on which were written the words: Our Dear Friend. From the other vaudevillians had come wreaths and sprays and baskets of flowers too numerous to count. There were more roses from Katie and Matt, and daffodils from Maeve. Ben had brought a basket of summer daisies.

"There's hardly room for the guests," Katie said, viewing the astonishing display. But the guests did not seem to mind. They moved about the parlor, glasses in hand, and recalled to each other the happy times they had shared with Ada McVey. They ate Flannagan's corned beef sandwiches. They told jokes. They raised their glasses and their voices in loving toasts.

"How do you feel?" Ben asked Katie toward the end of the afternoon.

"Oh, I'm fine. I didn't expect to be, but it's a

celebration after all. So many people. I knew the vaudevillians would come, if they could. They're here and half the neighborhood, too. They're remembering Ada with love, with laughter. That's as it should be. It's the way she wanted it."

"Where are the children?"

"I brought Patrick and Rory in early this morning. They didn't really understand. Mama took them to the flat. Hugh and Meg were here before. The spray of gardenias is from them."

"Gardenias! Hugh must be doing very well."

"You know what he's doing, Ben. You don't have to be polite. Mama thinks I should close my door to Hugh. Matt agrees. I just can't do it. I won't do it . . . something else for us to argue about," Katie's eyes darkened. She turned her head, looking across the crowded room to where Matt stood, alone and apart from the guests. "Matt's been standing in that corner all day. He refuses to talk to anyone. He hasn't gone near the casket. It's as if he's in his own world."

"I tried to talk to him. He mumbled a few words then stared into space. He's taking Ada's death hard."

"We all are. But I guess it's worse for him." Katie sighed. "He feels guilty. He and Ada were arguing a lot these last months. Bad arguments. She wanted him to change his ways. Poor Matt. I remember how he was when I first met him. He had such strength, such spirit. And now . . ."

"Once Matt gets his degree, he'll be himself again. It's not far off, Katie. Another year; maybe even sooner. The worst is behind him now."

"There's still law school. He measures himself

against you, and you'll be almost finished with law school by then. I keep telling him it isn't a race, but that's small comfort to him."

"I'd gladly trade places. Matt is the lucky one. He has you. He has two fine sons. That's all the comfort a man should ever need, or want."

"It's kind of you to say, Ben."

"I've said the same things to Matt. Not out of kindness either. I'd trade places in a minute." Ben paused, afraid he had said too much. "I've always wanted a family." He smiled.

"Oh, you'll have a wonderful family."

"Will I? You're sure?"

"I'm positive." Katie glanced around the parlor, her gaze falling on Matt. "Will you excuse me?" she asked. "Matt looks ready to faint. I'd best see how he is." Ben stepped aside and Katie picked up her skirts, threading her way through the crowd. "Matt," she said, quickly feeling his forehead, "are you all right? Do you want anything? A drink?"

"I want this to be over. Can't you send everybody away? It's barbaric! Laughing and telling jokes while Ada—"

"Would you rather have crying and long faces?"

"I'd rather everybody went away. This is my house now. If you won't tell them to leave, I will."

"Wait, Matt. Cornelius is just about to sing. He made a special trip to be here today. And it was Ada's wish."

"*God.* You know what we're in for, don't you? A thousand choruses of 'Danny Boy.'"

"You're exaggerating." Katie smiled. "He'll sing a few songs, and then there'll be the rosary, and then it

339

will be over. Come, let's sit down . . . come, Matt. Those chairs near the casket are for the family. We're the family."

"I'll stay where I am."

"Please, Matt, it's no time to argue. Come sit with me. Please. The sooner we sit down, the sooner it will be over."

Matt looked warily toward the casket. He pulled his handkerchief from his pocket and mopped his brow, for the mingled scents of flowers and whiskey and corned beef were making him quite ill. "I don't think I can," he admitted. "My stomach."

"I'll fix you some baking soda."

"No. No, maybe I'll feel better if I sit down. For God's sake, let's do what we have to and be done with it."

Katie took Matt's arm. Together, they found their seats and Cornelius O'Day began. He sang the "Ave Maria." He sang, in Gaelic, two ancient Irish hymns. He was beginning "Danny Boy" when Matt leaped up and dashed out of the room, his hand clasped over his mouth.

Cornelius O'Day, seasoned performer that he was, appeared not to notice. He continued singing, his magnificent voice rising and falling until tears filled everyone's eyes. When he had finished, he spoke briefly, wittily, of his friend, Ada. Glasses were raised once again. "*Bheatha!*" came the toast, the Gaelic toast to life.

Father Malone, Father Flynn's young successor at St. Brendan's, said the rosary. He made the sign of the cross, and then Katie knelt alone before the casket. "Good-bye, Ada," she whispered. "Good-bye, my dearest friend."

Ada had requested a private funeral, and this wish, too, was honored. Katie and Matt, dressed in the somber clothes of mourning, composed the funeral party. They sat silently through the Mass at St. Brendan's; afterwards, they rode behind the hearse to Holy Name Cemetery, where Ada was buried next to her beloved Tim. Matt ran off as the casket was lowered into the ground. Katie remained. "God bless," she whispered, dropping a single rose into the dark chasm.

"I'll be seeing you to your carriage now," Father Malone said. He took Katie's arm, leading her away. "I didn't know Ada long," he remarked, "but I know she was a fine woman."

"Yes, she was." Katie studied Father Malone's keen blue eyes. "She liked you. 'No false piety about him,' that's what she said. I hope we'll be friends, Father."

"Ah, I was thinking the very same myself. . . . Here's your carriage now. I'll take the other. Safe home with you."

Katie climbed into the carriage. She settled herself beside Matt, lifting her black veil. "Well, it's over," she said.

"I'm sorry. I'm sorry I left you alone. I just couldn't stand any more, Katie. Why must it be such a ceremony? I'll never understand." Matt lighted a cigarette and sat back. "When my time comes, I don't want any ceremony at all. Remember that. I don't want a circus. *God*, when I think of these past few days."

"Don't think about them, if they upset you."

"How can you be so damn calm? It's been a *circus*."

"When Papa died," Katie replied thoughtfully, "we didn't have much money for a wake. His friends visited, and there was beer—but only one glass apiece, and then Mama pushed them out the door. When Francis died there was . . . nothing. Ada's way was better—to be remembered with laughter, with friends all around, and love."

"It must have cost a fortune! I hate to think what it cost."

"It was her money, Matt, well spent, if you want my opinion."

"She had the right. I'm not saying she didn't. Still . . ."

"Are you wondering about your inheritance?"

Matt shrugged. He drew on his cigarette, watching the gray smoke curl toward the roof of the carriage. "Why should I wonder?" he asked. "I'll have the boardinghouse. If there's also some money, I won't turn up my nose."

"No, you certainly won't."

"Ada wouldn't discuss money. I don't know what she had. She wasn't rich, but she wasn't poor, either. She couldn't have been. The boardinghouse was always full. She did a good business. Oh, she was extravagant. The boarders ate like kings. And there were little gifts on their birthdays. Christmas was a festival of presents! Still, there must be some money. I'll find out soon. Ada's lawyer should be at the boardinghouse by the time we get back."

"What about the boardinghouse, Matt?"

"What do you mean?"

"Well, there are decisions." Katie sighed, for she had been dreading this conversation. The boarding-house was more than a business to her. It was home, the only real home she had ever known, and now she sensed a threat. "You haven't said anything. Will the boardinghouse go on as usual? You're not thinking of . . . selling it?"

"I'd sell it today and with no regrets. But property in Hell's Kitchen isn't worth much. Who wants to live in Hell's Kitchen? It's probably worth more the way it is. The boarders provide weekly income. Income!' Matt cried, smiling broadly. "I can quit that damn night school. I can finish my degree at City College, exactly as I'd planned. If there's enough money, I might even be able to go to New York University. It's a step up the ladder, Katie. A far step."

"I'm glad."

"It's the chance I needed, the chance I never expected I'd have." Matt looked guiltily at Katie. "Don't misunderstand me," he said. "I loved Ada. I didn't want her to die, money or no money. It was the last thing in my mind."

"You don't have to tell me that. I know."

"But she's gone, and I can't bring her back. I can't pretend I'm sorry about the money. It makes all the difference, Katie. I see daylight again."

"I know."

"It was like being trapped in a dark tunnel, the darkness pulling me deeper and deeper inside."

"Calm down, Matt." Katie was alarmed by the look in his eyes, by his hands clawing at a darkness he

343

alone saw. "I understand perfectly. All I wanted to know was if things would be the same, or if there would be any changes. I'm glad there won't be. I'm delighted."

Matt turned his head to the window, taking a breath. 'I didn't say there wouldn't be *any* changes. You'll run the boardinghouse, of course. You're the only one who knows how. But there'll be a few changes. No more meals fit for kings. And the boarders will have to pay to use the telephone from now on. There are many ways to economize. Leave it to me. First I have to look over the accounts."

"I've been keeping the kitchen accounts, Matt. Ada gave me the job a year ago. I enjoy it. I'm good with figures."

"You'll still have the job. You'll be on a budget, that's all."

"Whose budget?"

Matt patted Katie's hand. "Don't worry." He smiled. "I'll make sure the budget is fair. We can't feed our boarders gruel."

"*Our* boarders? You never cared a fig for our boarders before. You never really liked them, any of them."

"I don't have to like them. They don't have to like me. It's a business arrangement, Katie. They need rooms and I have rooms."

"It takes more than rooms. Ada knew that. That's why her boardinghouse was always full. She made it friendly, a home away from home. Cornelius O'Day is a good example. He's a headliner. He can afford a fancy hotel but he stays at Ada's instead. Jack Snow, Herbert & Yvonne . . . half our boarders can afford

344

better. They come to Ada's because it's home."

"Maybe."

"You know I'm right. You don't want to admit it."

"Katie, the boardinghouse is mine now. It's yours, too, in a way. But *I* own it. I'll do what I think is best. You can be the boarders' friend. Meanwhile, I'll see to money matters. Women have no head for money."

"No, we're scatterbrained. We can't be trusted with important things like money. We'd spend every cent on chocolates and lace dresses."

"I didn't say that. Don't be so touchy. We have a chance to start over and you're spoiling it. I wish we could go ten minutes without an argument, without you finding fault."

"You're the one who's finding fault, Matt. First you accuse Ada of being extravagant, and then you hint I can't be trusted to handle money."

"I'm trusting you to run the boardinghouse, aren't I?"

"I'll do all the work, but you'll make all the decisions. Is that fair?"

"It's best. I don't know why you're complaining. It's a husband's place to make all the decisions in the family. It's a wife's place to obey. I had to hold my tongue while Ada was alive. No more. Things are different now, and I suggest you get used to them, if not for my sake, for Patrick and Rory. You really haven't any choice."

Katie bit her lip and stared straight ahead. Her heart began to race as she acknowledged the warning in Matt's words. It's true, she thought; Ada was my protection, my security, but she's gone. Now I'm dependent on Matt. and there's nothing I can do about it. I have the children to consider. "You're enjoying this," she said aloud.

"I'm sorry Ada is dead, but I'm damn glad I'll be able to call the tune for once."

"For once?"

"That's exactly what I mean, Katie. I'm tired of your sarcasm. All right, I haven't been a very good husband. I know it. I don't need to be reminded day in and day out."

"I'm sorry."

"The hell you are." Matt lighted another cigarette, exhaled a great puff of smoke, and turned quickly to Katie. "You feel wronged. So do I. I've hated every minute at that miserable lumber yard, at that miserable night school. A hundred times I wanted to throw it all over and run away. A thousand times! But I had *responsibilities*. A wife; two children. I had Ada nagging me morning to night. *I* was the one who didn't have any choice. That's changed now. I'm going to call the tune from here on, and I'm going to enjoy it. Do you understand?"

"Yes. I understand."

"Hello, Mr. Streeter," Matt said, shaking hands with Ada's lawyer. "I apologize if we've kept you waiting. I hope Veronica made you comfortable. She's not the most efficient girl in the world."

"I'm quite comfortable."

"Good. I don't believe you've met my wife. Katie, this is William Streeter. My wife, Katie."

"How do you do, Mrs. McVey. Ada spoke of you often. In a complimentary manner, may I add."

346

"Thank you."

"Well"—Matt smiled—"now that the introductions are made, we can get down to business. You needn't stay, Katie, unless you want to. You'll only be bored, and I know you have other—"

"If I may interrupt.... It's necessary for Mrs. McVey to be present. Ada's will concerns her also. As one of the two principal heirs, Mrs. McVey must be present." William Streeter's commanding gaze swept from Matt to Katie. "Please be seated," he said, opening his briefcase. "The will contains a number of minor bequests to friends. I'll dispense with those just now and go on to more important matters."

"Yes, fine." Matt nodded. He could not conceal his eagerness, nor did he try. He sat at the edge of his chair and fastened his eyes on the portly, white-haired lawyer. "Is it a large estate?" he asked.

"'Adequate' is perhaps a better term. Now before I begin, I must state that Ada's will is legal and binding. Any contest would surely fail. Is that understood? Very well then." William Streeter adjusted his glasses. He read, "To my beloved nephew, Matthew McVey, I leave the sum of one thousand dollars. In addition, I leave him the gold pocket watch and gold collar buttons that belonged to Tim McVey. To my beloved grandnephews, Patrick and Rory McVey, I leave the sum of five hundred dollars each, to be held in trust until their eighteenth birthdays. To my beloved niece by marriage, Kathleen Gallagher McVey, I leave the boardinghouse and all its contents. I do this—"

"*What*?" Matt jumped up, his arms waving. "The boardinghouse to Katie? That's impossible!"

347

"No, it is not. I have already explained—"

"I don't give a damn what you *explained*. The boardinghouse is *mine*. It was promised to me long ago. Ada *told* me it would be mine."

"I have already explained that Ada's will is legal and binding. I'm sorry, but the law is clear in such matters."

"When was the will drawn?"

"When? Let me see . . ." William Streeter turned to the last page of the document, peering at the date. "The first of July, 1908. Drawn, signed, and witnessed."

"I see," Matt replied in a choked voice. He did not have to think back, for he realized immediately that Ada had redrawn her will after his attack on Katie. "I see."

"Ada left a letter for you. I was to give it to you following the reading of the will."

"That won't be necessary. Ada went to your office two years ago and changed her will. I suppose you wondered why. Would you like to *know* why?"

"Matt, don't," Katie said.

"It's simple, Mr. Streeter. Ada changed her will after I raped my wife."

"Now really, young man!"

"Are you shocked?" Matt laughed bitterly. He took the letter William Streeter held out and ripped it to pieces. "The *law* doesn't recognize rape in a marriage, does it? So much for the law. Ada had her own law, her own punishment."

"Matt, where are you going?"

"Out. Congratulations, my dear wife. You won."

"Matt . . . Matt, please don't go . . ." Katie sighed

348

as the door slammed shut. "Matt didn't mean what he said. He was upset. I hope you won't pay any attention. He was just upset."

"I'm aware of the difficulties that existed between Ada and Matt. We needn't speak of them."

"Thank you."

"May I finish the reading, Mrs. McVey? There are only a few lines remaining."

"Yes." Katie nodded, sniffling.

"To my beloved niece by marriage, Kathleen Gallagher McVey, I leave the boardinghouse and all its contents. I do this in the hope that the boardinghouse will continue to welcome the vaudevillians who were my friends and my second family. I do this also in the hope that Kathleen Gallagher McVey and her children will have a home in the boardinghouse for as long as she, or they, may wish. That concludes the major bequest, Mrs. McVey. There are several pieces of jewelry which come to you. Garnet earrings and necklace. Pearl earrings and necklace." William Streeter removed his glasses. He sat back, folding his hands in his ample lap. "I don't usually interfere in family matters," he said, "but I think you should know that Ada didn't trust Matt to have the boardinghouse. She didn't trust his judgment. She was concerned about her vaudevillians, of course, but she was more concerned about you and your future."

"Matt was her nephew."

"Indeed. And she left him a tidy sum of money. Enough to complete his education. That is, as I understand it, uppermost in his mind."

"Yes."

"I believe Ada made the correct decisions. Now you

349

have decisions to make. You could sell the boarding-house. Ada's will merely expresses the hope that you do not. You could sign the boardinghouse over to Matt. You could continue to run it as it is."

"Who would buy it?"

"Any number of people. As a private house in this neighborhood, it's worth nothing. But it can be made into flats. For the latter purpose, it's worth a great deal."

"Flats? Tenements, you mean. No, I won't sell. I'll run the boardinghouse myself. It's what Ada wanted. It's what I want too."

"It's my duty to mention that women in business are not highly regarded. Ada was an exception. First of all, she inherited the business from her husband. Secondly, she was an older woman. And then, having been a vaudevillian, it seemed right that she run a boardinghouse for other vaudevillians. There was a logical connection."

"There's a logical connection here, Mr. Streeter."

"Granted. Many people, however, will think a boardinghouse an unfit business for a young woman."

"I'm a married woman and the mother of two children. I've been working here for seven years, since I was thirteen. I don't see the difference between working in a boardinghouse and owning a boarding-house."

William Streeter tugged at his white mustache, smiling. "An excellent point. One in which I concur. Very well then. It's settled. When you have the time, I'd like you to come to my office. There are accounts to be examined, papers to be signed. Formalities. A lawyer's life is all formalities. . . . Here is my card."

Katie took the card. She saw the elegant East Side address and she frowned. "Can I afford you?" she asked.

"Oh, you mustn't worry about that. Ada couldn't afford me either. Not at my usual fee. Perhaps I should explain. My brother was in vaudeville with Ada and Tim. Quite the black sheep of the family." William Streeter winked. "But my brother and I remained close, and through him I met Ada and Tim. I handled any legal work they needed, at a special fee. I will be glad to do the same for you."

"I appreciate it, but I'll pay my own way."

"Please don't think I'm offering charity, Mrs. McVey. It's friendship. Ada and Tim were most kind to my brother. He died several years ago. This is my way of remembering him. There's little work involved, and I find it a pleasant distraction. I honestly don't see how you can turn me down. If I may say so, I am one of the best lawyers in New York."

"I don't see how I can turn you down either. But I have one condition. Will you call me Katie?"

"Katie it shall be." William Streeter rose. He gathered his papers together and snapped his briefcase closed. "I'll expect to see you soon. Good day, Katie."

"I hope I'm doing the right thing."

"About the boardinghouse? It won't be easy. Any business is a responsibility. I understand you are accustomed to responsibility, had it thrust upon you, so to speak."

"It's not the responsibility I'm worried about. It's

Matt. Whenever he makes plans, something happens to upset them."

"It's unwise to plan on an inheritance. Ada's property was hers to dispose of as she wished. I believe she was fair. Fairness, like beauty, is often in the eye of the beholder. But you have no reason to feel guilt."

"I'll try to remember that, Mr. Streeter." Katie walked with him into the hall. At the door she turned and shyly extended her hand. "I'm grateful to you," she said.

"Good day, Katie."

"Good day."

It was late in the evening when Matt came home. Katie had been prepared for the worst but, to her great relief, he was calm, completely sober. "Matt, you look fine. I was afraid—"

"Afraid I'd be drunk? I thought about it. I got as far as the Emerald Isle. Then I changed my mind. I took a long walk instead. A very long walk. Where are the boys?"

"They're staying overnight with Mama."

"Good. We have to talk. Katie . . . I certainly made a fool of myself, didn't I? All my big talk about calling the tune. Please, don't try to make me feel better. Don't be kind. I couldn't bear it." Matt sat down. He rested his head wearily against the back of the chair and stared into space. "I understand why Ada did what she did. I accept her decision."

"She never meant to hurt you, Matt. You must believe that."

"Let me finish. I've made a few decisions of my own. I'm quitting my job at the lumber yard and returning to City College in September. The moment I get my degree, I'll start law school. I may take a part-time job . . . but if I do, it'll be for my own benefit. You're perfectly able to support yourself now. And the boys, too. You have what you wanted, Katie. A home, children. It's time for me to have what I want."

"Are you . . . Are you going away?"

"I'm going to rent a room from you." Matt smiled. "My old room, to be exact. I'll be there some of the time. I'll be in your bed some of the time. That's my right. I'll be away a lot of the time. I intend to live my own life, no questions asked. In other words, you'll have an occasional bedmate, but you won't have a husband. Our marriage is over."

Katie stared at Matt and saw the face of a stranger, a hard face without any trace of emotion, of regret. "Do you hate me? Has it come to that?"

"Yes, I hate you. And yes, I *love* you. You're so damned beautiful, Katie. You're so damned *good*. There isn't a mean bone in your body, despite everything you've been through. I'm the envy of every man I know, and that's the truth . . . but it doesn't change how I feel. I've wasted five years, thanks to you. Years I'll never get back. I hate you for that. I hate you for being a better person than I am."

"I didn't think you had the power to hurt me any more. I was wrong."

"You'll get over it. You always do."

"Just this morning you were talking about making a new start."

"This morning seems like a lifetime ago. I don't

know, Katie. We might have had a chance. Notice I said *might*. If things had gone as I expected, I probably would have tried. But let's be realistic. There are deep wounds on both sides. You hide yours very well. I guess that's the Maeve in you. She made you strong. She made you damn near perfect."

"Stop it, Matt."

"I'm paying you a compliment, grudging though it may be. Believe it or not, I admire your strength."

"I'm sorry about Ada's will."

"You're not sorry." Matt laughed. "You don't have to pretend on my account. Anyway, her will was only the last straw. There were all those other straws piling up day after day, week after week. Face it, Katie. We had a rotten marriage. New start or no, this moment was inevitable. It should be a relief. Neither of us has to pretend now."

"It wasn't all pretending."

"More and more each year." Matt stood. He walked to Katie's chair and stared down at her. "You're so beautiful," he said, touching her shining golden hair, her pale, smooth brow. "It was your beauty that trapped me."

Katie pushed Matt's hand away. "Is that supposed to be another compliment?" she snapped. "I've had my fill of your compliments. I've had my fill of you. You're selfish, Matt. You always were. You're the biggest child I know."

"Then you won't mind if I go my own way."

"You've been going your own way for years. This just makes it official. I'm glad, as a matter of fact. At least it's out in the open. And I'm glad not to be dependent on you anymore. It was a fight whenever the boys needed clothes or shoes. It was a fight whenever I had to spend money. You didn't care if your sons were ragamuffins. All you cared about was saving money so you could buy those stupid vacant lots."

"Those *stupid* vacant lots will be worth a fortune one day."

"What about your sons? What are they worth?"

"Don't get high and mighty with me. Patrick and Rory were *my* sons only when you wanted something. The rest of the time they were *your* sons. You made that very clear, Katie. You made the decisions in the family."

"I had to. You were never home. If you were, you were drunk. There was no talking to you, drunk or sober. You resented me from the beginning. You resented Patrick and Rory. Well, now you're free. We're both free. Ada did us a great favor. We can both go our own ways. I'll pack your things and take them up to your old room. There'll be gossip, of course, but it won't be the first time. You've given people plenty to gossip about."

"I'm not alone."

"What does that mean?"

"Your cozy evenings with Ben caused some gossip too."

Katie leapt to her feet and slapped Matt's face. "How dare you!" she cried. "There was never anything between Ben and me, and you know it!"

Matt rubbed his smarting cheek. "Oh, I know it." He smiled. "You're both so pure, so *good*. I know your evenings are innocent. But the neighborhood doesn't know. There's talk, talk I do nothing to discourage. I wonder what Patrick will think of his sainted mother when he—"

"Get out!" Katie snatched a vase from the table, holding it aloft. "Get out before I kill you!"

Matt stared at Katie. He laughed and then turned on his heel and walked to the door. "Maybe you haven't won after all."

"Get out!"

The door closed. Katie put the vase down and sank into a chair, curling her legs beneath her. She sat that way for a long time, thinking not of the present but of the past, of those joyous days when she and Matt had been in love. Those days were only memories now, and memories, she realized, would have to sustain her. There was a terrible ache in her throat. She wanted to cry, but she could not, for she had no tears left.

It was dawn when Katie rose and began packing Matt's clothes and books. "Mr. McVey is moving upstairs," she explained to a curious Veronica. "He needs someplace quiet to study." This explanation she repeated dozens of times, to boarders, to Meg and Hugh, to Maeve. She did not know whether she was believed or not, and, as months passed, she ceased to care. "Life goes on, Mama," she said, ending all discussion.

Life, for Katie, meant her children and her work. For Matt, it meant the single-minded pursuit of his goals. He received his bachelor's degree in the spring of 1912, marking the occasion with a loud and drunken party in a Yorkville rathskeller, a party to which Katie was not invited. That autumn, he began his law studies at Columbia. He rose quickly to the top of his class, and there he remained. He was his jaunty, charming self again, coming and going as he pleased, paying scant attention to his wife or his sons. Indeed, only a very few of his classmates knew he was married, for marriage was a subject he took pains to avoid. "I'm going to *own* the world," he crowed to Ben one Saturday night in 1914. "You can hang a sign on it, 'property of Matt McVey.'"

"It's not so easy to own the world."

"It is if you're smart."

"I'm smart, and I don't own anything yet. I'm barely able to afford the rent on my office. My secretary heaves a sigh of relief when I count out his salary."

"Well, what do you expect with the clients you have? You won't get rich drawing leases and measly little contracts."

"My clients are good training."

"Training!"

Ben finished his drink. He set his glass atop the bar and looked at Matt. The two young men had made peace with each other, but it was an uneasy peace, achieved only after Katie had bowed to neighborhood gossip and had asked Ben to stay away from the boardinghouse. Matt had been gleeful, choosing that moment to "forgive" his old friend. "Perhaps I used the wrong word," Ben said now. "My clients are good experience. I plan to specialize in contract law, and I have to start somewhere. If I remember correctly, you thought starting small was a fine idea."

"That was before. You don't realize how far I've come, the contacts I have at Columbia. They're pure gold, Ben. With contacts like those, I can waltz into a

357

first-rate law firm. Certainly I have the grades."

"A minor qualification, I'm afraid. Fifth on the list, after the right name, the right religion, the right schools, the right clubs. Irishmen don't waltz into first-rate law firms any more than Italians do. Everybody says things have changed. And they have. Automobiles are all over the streets. Electricity has replaced gaslight. There's steam heat instead of coal stoves. But McVeys and Rossis still don't waltz into first-rate law firms."

"I'm going to surprise you." Matt smiled. He motioned to the bartender, ordering another round of drinks. "What matters is who you know. *I* know Alfred Thorndike, the son of Jonas Thorndike. Thorndike and Kingsly? *Very* first-rate."

"Very Episcopalian."

"Until next year, when I start working there. Don't worry, I'll make them find a place for you."

"You're in for a big disappointment, my friend."

"Hah! I might have believed that once, but not now. Those miserable years of disappointment, of struggle, are far behind me now. Look at my life, Ben. It's the life I'd always planned. I'm going in only one direction, and that's up. I'm going to own the whole damn world. Wait and see if I don't."

Ben said nothing, for he knew Matt had reason to be smug. His law degree was in sight, and from prestigious Columbia University. He owned several pieces of real estate, worthless now, but potentially quite valuable. He had good looks and good health. He had friends and admirers by the score. He had women, all sorts of women, who did not know or did not care that he also had a wife. Ben's eyes hardened as he considered Katie's position in Matt's life. A dreadful position, he thought, somewhere between a servant and a concubine to be used at whim. "Have you told Katie about your plans?" he asked.

"She has no interest in my plans. Oh, she'll be an asset to me one day. She's damned beautiful, but it's more than that. If you didn't know, you'd swear she was a lady."

"She *is* a lady."

"Don't bite my head off." Matt laughed. "I mean a lady by birth. There's something . . . elegant about her. Her hands are all red and swollen from work, but still . . ."

Ben studied Matt's well-cut suit, his silk necktie, and he sighed. "Doesn't it bother you that Katie works so hard?"

"It's her boardinghouse," Matt replied with a shrug. "Of course she'll have to sell it when I join Thorndike and Kingsly. Vaudeville's dying anyway. The future is in moving pictures."

"I doubt Katie will agree to sell. It's her home."

"She'll sell. She'll do it for Patrick and Rory. Besides, Alfred Thorndike would be shocked at the very idea of a boardinghouse. I intend to see he never finds out."

"You used to despise people like Alfred Thorndike," Ben said quietly. "Remember?"

"*Used* to? I know Thorndike is a horse's ass, Thorndike and his whole bunch. But the Thorndikes of the world are going to get me what I want. I need them and they need me. There's war in Europe, Ben. America's bound to become involved. If that happens, a lot of young men will be called, from

359

factories, from farms, *and* from Thorndike and Kingsly. . . . Don't you understand?" Matt laughed, finishing his drink in one swallow. "Time is on my side. The single men will go first. I'm married, a father to boot. The hell with the Kaiser. *I'm* in the clear."

15

"Come now, Rory." Katie smiled. "You can't be late your first day of school. What will Sister Josepha think?"

"School *stinks*."

"Don't say stinks, dear. It's not nice." Katie put her hand over her mouth, stifling a laugh. She did this often while in Rory's presence, for she found him a constant source of amusement. His once fiery temper had been tamed, but he remained a spirited child, outgoing and direct. He had already decided to be a vaudevillian when he grew up. "All your friends are starting school today, Rory."

"Yes, but I know the alphabet. You taught me. And I can read some words, too."

"At school you'll learn to read lots of words. You'll learn to write, to do sums. You and Patrick can do your homework together. Won't that be fun?"

"Maybe. If he doesn't boss me. I don't like him to boss me. I'm not a baby. I'm *six*."

"Such a big boy. Can I give my big boy a hug?"

"Okay."

Katie bent, gathering Rory to her. She hugged

him and then held him away, looking into his face. It was a handsome face, narrow and fair skinned, with brilliant blue-green eyes and a crown of reddish curls. "Promise me you'll be good," she said. "If you're bad, Sister Josepha will rap your knuckles. She'll make you stand in the corner."

"Did she make you stand in the corner, Mama?"

"I didn't go to St. Brendan's school, dear. There were a few small costs, and we couldn't afford them. I went to public school. Not that there's anything wrong with public school. There isn't. It's just a bit crowded these days. You'll get more attention at St. Brendan's. You're very lucky." Katie straightened Rory's shirt collar. She brushed a speck of lint from his dark blue knickers. "That's better. Pull up your stockings and off you go."

"I can go by myself."

"No. You'll go with Patrick. There are five streets to cross. What are you supposed to do when you cross the street?"

"Hold Patrick's hand."

"What else?"

"Look both ways. We have to look out for cars."

"That's my smart boy." Katie opened the door and walked with Rory into the hall. "Your brother's all ready," she said to Patrick. "Keep a sharp eye."

"I will, Mama. I promise. Come along, our Rory."

"Are you going to *boss* me?"

"Only if you cause trouble," Patrick replied cheerfully. He threw his book bag over his shoulder, taking Rory's hand. "Come along or we'll be late. Sister makes an awful fuss when kids are late. 'Bye, Mama. See you after school."

362

"Where's my kiss?"

Patrick kissed his mother's cheek. "'Bye," he called, nudging Rory toward the door. "See you."

"Good-bye. Behave yourselves." Katie watched as they walked away. She remembered back to Patrick's first day of school. She had cried then, but she was determined not to cry now. With one last glance at her sons, she turned and hurried to the kitchen. "Well, Veronica, the boys have gone."

Veronica Jones, small and dark and quiet as a mouse, looked up from the stove. She nodded. "The oatmeal's almost ready," she said. "The biscuits, too. There's still the eggs."

"I'll finish cooking while you finish setting the table. The boarders will be down any minute, and we're a little behind schedule today. Blame it on Rory." Katie smiled. "He took his time, as usual. Go ahead, Veronica. I'll finish here."

Katie was busy with chores for the rest of the morning, cooking and serving and washing mountains of dishes which Veronica dried. When Veronica went off to begin the day's cleaning, Katie scrubbed the kitchen floor and sorted four enormous baskets of laundry. At precisely eleven-thirty, she opened the front door to admit William Streeter. "Come in, William," she said, taking his hat and gloves and cane. "I've been looking forward to your visit. I even baked your favorite seed cake."

"How thoughtful. I'm afraid you spoil me, Katie. I'm not accustomed to such royal treatment."

"Oh, it's hardly royal. Seed cake and tea in a boardinghouse. Your dinners with senators and congressmen are royal. I get dizzy just reading about them. It was years before I understood how important you are."

"Don't believe everything you read in the newspapers." William sat down and Katie poured tea. "Excellent," he said, tasting it. "A new blend?"

"I mixed it myself." Katie sat opposite her guest, tilting her head to one side. "You look very well. Did you have a nice summer?"

"Newport is always pleasant. My wife enjoys the parties. I enjoy the sailing. But I confess I was happy to return to New York. A man needs work. . . . Tell me about your summer."

"I took the boys to Coney Island every Sunday. It isn't Newport"—Katie laughed—"though it's the same ocean. I *love* the ocean. And the boys had a grand time, swimming, going on rides. It was as good as Newport. I hated to see summer end. I can't imagine where the time goes."

"Nowhere near you, apparently. We all grow old, but you grow lovelier." William sipped his tea. He took a bite of seed cake and then sat back. "You haven't mentioned Matt. Tell me about him."

"Matt graduated from law school in June. He's been working in Ben Rossi's office. It's not what he . . . expected." Katie glanced away, her mouth tightening. "He expected to join Thorndike and Kingsly," she explained in a quiet voice. "Alfred Throndike was a classmate of his, you see. Alfred Thorndike didn't exactly promise anything, not in so many words. But Matt believed there was an understanding."

"Indeed."

"It still may work out. Matt still expects to have an

364

interview with Jonas Thorndike. He considers his position with Ben only temporary."

"That's unfortunate."

Katie twisted her hands together, staring at William. "Why do you say that?" she asked.

"I've known the Thorndikes practically all my life. Jonas was an usher at my wedding, years ago. Now we are members of the same clubs, and we serve on the same boards. I tell you this to make a point: I can speak with complete authority on the subject of Jonas Thorndike."

"I don't doubt it, William. I think I know what you're going to say. I'd rather not hear it."

"Would you rather Matt continued deluding himself? That is what he's doing. Whatever young Alfred may have led him to believe, there is no possibility of his joining Thorndike and Kingsly. It's absurd."

"Because he's Irish?"

"Yes, in large part. That's not all there is to it, however. If I may speak frankly, Matt has something of a reputation, an unsavory reputation, I'm afraid. I do not deny that young men have a need to sow their wild oats. In this, Alfred is as guilty as Matt. But Matt is nearing thirty. He is expected to be more sensible. At the very least he is expected to practice discretion. He cannot parade his . . . follies. I did quite a lot of checking, Katie. I'm familiar with Matt's academic record. It's exceptional. I'm sorry to say his character falls short."

"I see."

"Thorndike and Kingsly would not have engaged him in any case. Other firms, other men, might have,

365

given different circumstances."

"Might you?"

William smiled slightly, brushing his white mustache. "That brings me to one of the reasons for my visit," he replied. "My firm held a partners' meeting last week. It was a most unusual meeting, for it was suggested that we open our doors wider than we have in the past. There are many reasons. Perhaps the best reason is the war in Europe. If America enters the fighting, as seems likely, young men of all classes will be called. This raises a question—is it right to tell men they're good enough to fight for their country, but not good enough to work for Streeter, Carlyle, and Hazlet? Is it morally right? Most of us agree it is not."

"I don't have to guess who made the suggestion."

"Be that as it may, the suggestion was made. We are prepared to act on it. There are reservations amongst the partners. And certainly we could not engage a Jew or a Negro."

"An Irishman?" Katie asked, leaning forward.

"I had in mind an Italian. I had in mind Ben Rossi."

"Ben Rossi!"

"I'd heard about him from you, of course. He came to my personal attention several months ago, when he handled a legal matter for the nephew of one of our clients. It was a small matter but complicated. I won't bore you with the details. I will say his solution was brilliant indeed. I was intrigued. I was looking into Matt's records at the time. I looked into Mr. Rossi's records as well. I'm very glad I did. It's not often I come across—Katie, what's wrong? I was

366

certain you would be pleased."

"I am. For Ben." Katie's head began to ache. She passed her hand over her eyes, taking a deep breath. "I'm thinking about Matt," she said. "I know what this will do to him. He's always measured himself against Ben. He always had to be smarter, better. He had to *win*. Now he's working for Ben, and he's miserable. Oh, Ben says they're partners, but Matt knows it isn't true. The only thing keeping him going is the prospect of Thorndike and Kingsly. Or someplace like it."

"There is no prospect. I'm far less straitlaced than Jonas, yet I would not have Matt in my firm. I'm sorry."

"Don't be. I understand. It's good news for Ben."

"Perhaps. He is my prime candidate. I intend to follow his career a while longer, and then we shall see. Meanwhile, it would be helpful to have your opinion."

"My opinion? I'm sure he's a fine lawyer, William. He went from a tiny office on Lexington Avenue to a four-room suite near Wall Street."

"Yes, I'm aware of that. I'll judge Mr. Rossi's abilities as a lawyer. I'm interested in your opinion of him as a person. I understand he is from a large family. Does he contribute to their support? Does he contribute his fair share? Please don't think I'm prying. I wish only to know what sort of person he is."

"Ben does more than his share. Since his father's death, he's supported his mother and his three youngest sisters. He paid for another sister's wedding, and he helped one of his brothers to open a

367

clothing store. He's a generous man, William, but he's not a fool. He looks after his own interests too. He has great respect for money."

"Ah, that is what I hoped to hear. Mr. Rossi is of excellent character, and neither a fool nor a saint. I'm encouraged." William asked more questions, all of them smoothly, deliberately phrased. "Thank you, Katie," he said when she had finished answering. "You have confirmed my impressions."

"I'm beginning to understand why you're such a successful lawyer. You're a crafty fellow, William."

"Cautious. I must ask you to be cautious also. It is too soon for Mr. Rossi to know of our conversation. I'm trusting you to keep the secret, although you may tell Matt the part about Thorndike and Kingsly. Cushion the blow, so to speak."

"Oh no, I'm the wrong person to tell him." Katie rose. She went to the window and stared outside. She thought to herself, if I say anything to Matt, there'll be a terrible argument. He'll find reasons to blame me for his failure, just as he always has. He'll see his plans in ruins and he'll blame me. "I can't get involved in this," she said finally, shaking her head. "Maybe it's selfish, but this time Matt is on his own."

Matt observed his thirty-first birthday on a snowy January day in 1917. It was to him a sad observance, for the passing years had brought him no closer to his goals. He still worked at Rossi and McVey, half of a partnership that was, he knew, more illusory than real. Profits were shared, and most cases, but Ben reserved the right to make all final decisions, a right

368

he exercised often. The growing staff, secretaries and clerks, had little doubt as to who was in charge, and, when given a choice, clients usually chose to consult with Ben. Matt felt demeaned, though he kept his feelings to himself. Each day he hid his bitterness behind smiles and easy laughter; each night he drank himself to sleep.

Now Matt hunched over his desk and with a shaking hand splashed whiskey into his coffee. He raised his cup to his lips, looking up as the door opened. "Ben, you startled me. I thought you were out."

"Sorry, I should have knocked."

"It's all right." Matt smiled. "Just a toddy for my cold," he explained, putting the whiskey bottle away. "I can't seem to shake it. Well, where were you off to so early this morning? Miss Foster wouldn't tell me. She may be a good secretary, but she really is a dragon."

"Miss Foster didn't know where I was."

"Oh? I was hoping you'd gone to buy my birthday present."

"I bought it last week."

"Of course. That's you, Ben, always planning ahead. . . . I see you didn't plan for snow. You'd best get out of your coat. You're dripping on the carpet."

"Sorry." Ben removed his coat and scarf, folding them neatly across the sofa. "Do you have any meetings scheduled?" he asked. "Do you have time to talk?"

"Certainly I have time. Sit down and be comfortable. My office is your office—in more ways than one . . . what's the matter with you? You look strange. Are you ill? I hope you haven't caught my cold."

"I'm fine." Ben sat in a chair near Matt's desk. He struck a match and lighted his pipe. "I had a meeting at Streeter, Carlyle, and Hazlet," he said quietly. "William Streeter telephoned me at home yesterday evening. We arranged an appointment for this morning. I was there first thing."

"What did he want?"

Ben hesitated. His dark eyes were troubled, glancing around the office, settling finally on Matt. "It seems that Streeter, Carlyle, and Hazlet have decided to ... broaden ... their hiring practices. They've decided to go beyond the accepted social circles."

"I'll be damned!" Matt cried, his pulse quickening. He sprang out of his chair, going to Ben and pounding his shoulder. "I knew it would happen sooner or later. I knew it! Old man Thorndike had his chance. He treated me like dirt. Well, his loss is my gain. William Streeter. My God, his firm is even better than Thorndike's! Streeter is a friend of Katie, you know. That probably helped. At last she's done me some good. . . . Don't keep me in suspense, Ben. What did you say? What did you tell him about me?"

"Calm down. It's not what you think, Matt. I'm very sorry. The interview wasn't about you."

"Who then? We don't have any clients in their class. Why did he want to see you? Streeter's a canny bastard. Maybe he didn't come right out and *say* it was about me, but if he's planning to hire someone from ..." Matt's face was gray, for he had begun to understand. His flesh seemed to shrink, leaving only jutting bones and blank, staring eyes. "You?" he asked in a horrified whisper. "You, Ben?"

"It was a complete surprise. I'd met Mr. Streeter only once before, at Katie's Christmas party. I'd never had any dealings with him. He told me his firm had been watching several young lawyers. They made their decision shortly after the first of the year." Ben realized that Matt was not listening. He saw his sagging body, his slack jaw, and he helped him into a chair. "I'll fix you a drink," he said, pulling open the desk drawer. "There. Take it, Matt. This is one time you need a drink."

Obediently, Matt swallowed the whiskey. It seared his dry throat and he coughed. "My head hurts," he murmured, as if to himself.

"I'll get some aspirin."

"Ben? Did you accept Streeter's offer?"

"Yes." Ben's acceptance had been swift, for he knew he had been offered the opportunity of a lifetime. Positions at Streeter, Carlyle, and Hazlet were coveted, fought over by the sons of wealthy and distinguished families. To be associated with such a firm meant many things—prestige, influence, and, in time, riches. "I couldn't turn it down, Matt."

"What? No, no, of course you couldn't. . . . There's something I must know, Ben. Did you and Katie plot this behind my back?"

"Behind your back! I have never gone behind your back, nor has Katie. I visited the boardinghouse perhaps three times in the last year. You were present each of those times. There was no plot. I swear on Papa's grave there was no plot."

"Forgive me. I was wrong to ask. You're my friend.

371

You were always my friend." The pain in Matt's head was growing worse. He heard a shrieking, a harsh and ugly sound driving deeply into his skull. "I wish you had met Katie first." He sighed. "You would have married her, and we all would have been happy.'"

"Matt, Katie doesn't love me."

"That makes two of us. She doesn't love me either. Come to think of it, I don't love her. It's just sex. I love her body. Beautiful face, beautiful body. When she takes off her clothes—"

"Matt!"

"Forgive me. I apologize. I don't know what I'm saying any more. It's this stuff." Matt nodded, holding up his drink. "It's the liquor. I don't really have a cold. I can't remember ever having a cold. Measles, chicken pox, influenza, but no colds."

"Listen to me," Ben said, staring down at his distraught friend. "You've had a shock, and things look very bleak right now. Later you'll see they're not bleak at all. Rossi and McVey will be yours, to run any way you wish. I'm giving you my share . . . where are you going?"

"I'm going to get my hat and coat. Then I'm getting out of here. I have to. The walls are beginning to close in. Or maybe it's life. Life is a tricky bastard. One trick after another. . . . But that's enough of that. Congratulations, Ben. I mean it. If it couldn't be me—and it couldn't—I'm glad it's you. You're on your way . . . and I'm on mine."

"*Where*? Where are you going?"

"To Hell."

*   *   *

372

"I told you I don't want to talk about Matt," Katie said. She sat at the table in Maeve's kitchen, a cup of tea untouched before her. She was pale, and her lovely green eyes were shadowed with worry. "Nothing's changed. What is there to talk about?"

"I hear he's spending his days in the pubs."

"For someone who doesn't listen to gossip, you manage to hear quite a lot."

"Is it true?"

"You know it is, Mama. His days and his nights. He stumbles home at all hours. Half the time he's too drunk to climb the stairs to his room. He's the neighborhood scandal. Patrick and Rory are always being teased about their father."

"Where's the money coming from?"

"Ben. Ben sold Rossi and McVey. He insisted on sharing the proceeds with Matt. I warned him Matt would only drink the money away. Thank God I have the boardinghouse. Without it, we'd all be starving. It isn't the business it used to be. Vaudeville isn't the business it used to be. But I earn enough to pay the bills."

Maeve sipped her tea, studying Katie's closed face. "And what are you doing to help your husband?" she asked.

"What *can* I do? Matt's beyond help. Surely you understand that. Your own father was a drunk."

"Aye. It's a curse. They should pour every drop of whiskey into the ocean. Good riddance to it. What did whiskey ever bring but suffering? And to the innocent ones, to the children."

Katie reached suddenly for her teacup, upsetting it in her haste. "I'm sorry," she said, mopping the spill. "I'm sorry, Mama."

"You're a bundle of nerves today. What's wrong?"

"Nothing."

"Don't lie to me, Katie McVey. I can see when something's wrong. I'm not blind, am I? What is it? Bad news?" Maeve leaned forward, her dark gaze wary. "Have you had word from Hugh? Is he in jail?"

"I haven't heard anything from Hugh or Meg since they went to Chicago. They looked fine when they left. They were driving a big car, and Meg was wearing furs."

"Aye, I don't doubt it. It's ill-gotten gains. They'll pay the price one day. They'll be punished, both of them. It's bad enough Hugh's a gangster in New York. Now he has to be a gangster in Chicago, too. And Meg, going along with him. Poor Mrs. Muldoon still cries her eyes out at the thought. . . . Well, if it isn't Hugh, what is it? Speak up, Katie. Are you keeping secrets? No good comes of secrets."

"This won't be a secret for long. I'm pregnant, Mama."

Maeve's hand flew to her throat. Unlike many women in Hell's Kitchen, she was not sentimental about children, and she realized the problems a new baby would bring to Katie's life. "The priests say babies are a blessing." She sighed. "They are to some. Sure and it's the wrong time, but—"

"The wrong time! As if there's a right time! How can there be a right time when Matt's drinking himself to death? I have all I can do just seeing to him and Patrick and Rory and the boardinghouse. Hoping there'll *be* a boardinghouse next year, the year after that. Your predictions might come true yet, Mama. We might end up in the street."

"Stop talking foolishness. You own the building, don't you? A building is something you can sell. Aye, you should have sold it years ago. Didn't I tell you? Didn't I tell you it was a mistake hanging on?"

"It's my home."

"Be grateful. This is the only home I ever had," Maeve snapped, glancing around the flat. "A tenement, and before that a pauper's farm. You have it easy, Katie McVey. You have something you can sell. Something to put money in your pockets. You'll get no sympathy from me on that account."

"I'm not asking for sympathy, Mama. I know I'm better off than most of the women around here. I also know I wouldn't get much if I sold the boarding-house. Not now. It's in terrible condition. The pipes are worn. The cellar floods during heavy rains. The roof leaks. I haven't been able to afford repairs or improvements. Electricity was the first and last."

"Would you have money in your pockets if you sold?"

"A little."

"Then you'll get no sympathy from me. Your children won't go cold and hungry. You're higher up the ladder than you have a right to be. Are you grateful? No, you're complaining. I suppose you want furs and fancy cars like Meg."

Katie smiled despite herself. "Mama, you never change," she said. "I'll be twenty-eight soon, but you're still putting me in my place."

"It's a pity I have to, isn't it? You should know your place by now. Sure and it's not such a bad place, Katie McVey. You should be on your knees giving thanks."

"I spend hours on my knees every day."

"Mind your tongue. Don't be smart with me. I'm not talking about scrubbing floors. I'm talking about giving thanks. And mind your tongue when Father Malone gets here. He'll be wondering how I raised you. I didn't raise you to talk back, did I?"

"No, Mama."

"Don't shame me."

"No, Mama. I won't . . . Father Malone and I are friends."

"Is that so? What will he think of his friend when he hears her talking back to her mother?"

"I was only joking."

"Joking about prayer is a sin. You've been around show people too long, and that's the truth. Show people will joke about anything." Maeve paused, hearing a knock at the door. "There's Father now," she said. "Mind your tongue, and your manners as well." She went to the door and pulled it open, offering a rare smile to the priest. "Come in, Father Malone. We've been expecting you. Tea's on the table. And I have crackers and sweet butter fresh from the store."

"It's kind you are, Maeve, but don't trouble. I'll be eating my lunch soon . . . hello, Katie. I'm glad you could be here."

"Mama said it was a family matter. Has Sean misbehaved?"

"Ah, Sean never misbehaves. I've known the boyo since his First Communion, and never once have I seen him misbehave. I'm wishing I could say the same for some other boyos I know." Father Malone sat down, clasping his hands atop the table. He was a trim man, in his thirties now, with keen blue eyes, a ready grin, and unruly black hair that defied all efforts of comb and brush. His parishioners had come to love him over the years, though they agreed he did not look like a priest. "Do you ever ask yourself where the time goes, Maeve? One moment Sean is making First Communion, and the next he's graduating from high school."

Maeve, impatient with small talk, merely shook her head. "What are you leading up to, Father? You can say it straight out."

"It's Sean's future I'm here to discuss. Has he told you about his plans?"

"I hardly see him any more. He rushes off to early Mass each morning, then to school. After school he has his job. He spends Sundays ushering at the church. Not that I'm complaining," Maeve added. "I'm relieved he's putting his time to good use, instead of running wild in the streets."

"Sean will be graduating in two month's time."

"Aye. I'm not leaving his future to chance, if that's what you're thinking, Father. I've had many a talk with Officer Garrity. He tells me Sean will make a fine policeman. It's the job I always wanted for my sons. It's steady wages. And Officer Garrity says they won't hold it against Sean that his brother is a gangster. There's no worry on that account."

"Have you asked Sean how he feels about it, Maeve?"

"Sure and I don't have to ask. I'm his mother, aren't I? I mean no disrespect, but I'll do what's best for my son."

Father Malone was thoughtful, remembering his

arrival at St. Brendan's, eleven years before. He remembered his predecessor's descriptions of the parishioners, Maeve Gallagher among them. "She has strong ideas," the old priest had said. "She's one of those women who survives on courage and nerve alone." Now, staring into Maeve's dark eyes, Father Malone sighed. "Ah, Maeve, you haven't changed a bit. This isn't Ireland, you know. You can't decide your son's future for him. Even in Ireland the boyos are deciding for themselves. It's a different world today."

"Aye, that's the trouble. I let Hugh decide some things for himself and look what happened. He's a gangster. And in two cities!"

"Father," Katie said, "Sean hasn't spoken of his plans to us. Obviously he has to you."

"Sean wants to be a priest."

"A priest! Did I hear you right?" Maeve cried. "A *priest*?"

"He first came to me when he was fourteen. I turned him away, of course. He came again the next year, and the next. This year he began studying scripture with Father Dowd. It's serious he is, Maeve. I'm thinking he has the calling. Only time will tell. It's a long road through the seminary. Too long for some. If he has the calling, time will tell."

Maeve and Katie looked at each other, exchanging astonished glances. "Sean never mentioned anything about the priesthood," Katie said finally. "Not a word. It's true he went to church a lot. Every day. But I never dreamed it meant . . . the priesthood."

"It doesn't, for most. Church means different things to different people, Katie. To Sean it means oneness with God. He wants to serve God. There are many ways to do that, inside the priesthood and outside. He'll have to find the way that's right for him. Youngsters often say they want to be priests, or nuns. And it's sincere they are. In time, they realize it's not the life for them. That may happen to your Sean. It may not. If he has the calling, he'll walk the whole road."

"Why didn't he tell me?" Maeve asked.

"Ah, I'm thinking his silence was by way of keeping the peace. He had his doubts as to how you'd take such news. It's an honorable calling, Maeve." Father Malone smiled. "Though I admit the wages aren't so steady."

"How can he be a priest? His own brother is a *gangster*."

Father Malone's smile widened. "Like the police, we won't hold it against Sean," he replied."

Maeve shook her head slowly from side to side. She knew that, in her place, many of her neighbors would be rejoicing, for the priesthood, along with the police department and the fire department, was a normal aspiration in Hell's Kitchen. But she felt only sorrow, a vast and chilling emptiness. "I've lost both my sons now," she said. "Hugh to the devil. Sean to God."

"You haven't lost Sean, Mama."

"And what do you know of it? I've been watching boys go off to the priesthood all my life. It's the last they need of their families. The church becomes their family."

"The church is your family too, Maeve," Father Malone said softly. "The church belongs to us all."

"You understand what I mean. When's the last time you saw your own mother? At least eleven years and probably longer. Your mother is in Ireland, and you're here. Aye, that suits you fine, because the church comes first."

"There are sacrifices in life, in any life. It's hard being apart from family, but our hearts are together. My mother accepts things as they are."

"Then she's a . . ." Maeve stopped herself. She rose quickly and went to the sink, splashing water on her face. "I'm sorry, Father. I'm talking out of turn . . . I'll give Sean my blessing. That's what you came for, isn't it? I've no money to give him. If he's going to seminary, he'll have to go without help from me."

"Don't worry about money. It's your blessing that matters. Sean loves you. You mustn't doubt it. He wouldn't hurt you."

"Wouldn't he?"

Father Malone rose also. "I have a feeling I've overstayed my welcome," he said, winking at Katie. "I'll be getting back to the rectory. We'll talk again, Maeve—Maeve?"

"Aye, we'll talk another time. Good day, Father."

Katie held the door open. "I'm afraid your news caught Mama by surprise. It would have been easier if we'd had some warning from Sean. It was his place to tell us."

"Well, it's a difficult time for the boyo. He's been so worried. He really doesn't want to hurt anyone, least of all Maeve. . . . Come see me, Katie. We'll have a nice visit."

"I will. Soon. Thank you, Father. You're a brave man." Katie smiled. "You could have sent Father

Dowd to break the news. *I* would have."

"Ah, it wasn't that bad. I'll admit I've had better reactions to such news. But then I've had worse. I'm thinking it's all in a day's work."

Katie was still smiling as she closed the door, though her smile faded when she saw Maeve's stony expression. "Mama? Mama, don't be upset. Sean can't help how he feels."

"Go home, Katie. Fetch your hat and purse and go home. I'm in no mood for talk. I'm tired. Let me be."

"I'll stay a while."

"Do you want me to pitch you out the door? I have my work to finish. You have yours. Go home . . . I'm all right, Katie." Maeve sighed. She brushed a strand of gray hair from her brow and looked up. "Just let me be."

Katie put on her hat. "You drive me crazy, Mama," she said, kissing Maeve's cheek. "I hope you know that. I'll come by tomorrow."

"Aye, tomorrow."

"Give my love to Sean."

"Aye. Why are you standing there like a goose? *Go home.*"

Katie left the flat. Muttering, she hurried down the stairs and into the street. At the corner she noticed a crowd of people. It was a boisterous crowd, clearly agitated, and she stopped. "What's happened?" she asked. "What's wrong?" Katie fought her way to the curb. "My God," she gasped, her eye falling upon a lone newsboy and the headline he held aloft. She became very pale, for the headline, black and eight inches high, read WAR.

16

"I've joined the army," Matt announced to Katie three days after America's entry into the war. "I'm to receive a commision. *Captain* McVey. I'll make a good officer, don't you think?"

Katie had been reading, and now the book slipped from her hands. "You can't be serious," she said. "The army? Matt, you didn't."

"I certainly did. I report next week."

"Have you lost your mind? War isn't a game. You could be hurt. You could be killed, God forbid."

Matt smiled. He took a seat opposite Katie, stretching his legs out in front of him. "Would you shed a tear if I were killed? Would you mourn?"

"No matter what you may believe, I don't want anything to happen to you. I don't wish you any harm."

"The way I've behaved, you should despise me."

"I don't."

"Well, I despise myself. I've ruined my career, my marriage . . . my life. I'm a scandal. Worse, I'm a joke. I remember the fellow I used to be, Katie. The memory grows dimmer each year, but there are times

383

when it's very vivid. I see myself as I was then. I wasn't such a bad fellow." Matt lighted a cigarette. He smiled again. "It seems so long ago. And I guess it was. I don't know who I am now. I have no . . . identity."

"Is that why you joined the army? You must go to them and tell them it was a mistake."

"But it wasn't. I'm searching for something, Katie. I don't know what, exactly—an identity, an achievement that's truly mine. I don't know. Whatever it is, I won't find it here."

"You can go away without joining the army."

"I need structure. The army will bring structure to my life. This isn't a whim, Katie. I've thought hard about it. It's something I have to do. I hope you'll understand."

"I understand you're putting yourself in danger. You have no right. What about your sons? Did you consider Patrick and Rory?"

"They won't miss me. I'm little more than a stranger. They treat me politely, respectfully, and they keep their distance. It's my own fault. I've lived in the same house, but apart. I made myself a stranger." Matt drew on his cigarette, watching Katie through a haze of smoke. "Patrick and Rory are your sons," he said. "You raised them. You did a damned fine job. I give you credit."

"It's not too late to get to know them."

"Of course it is. Besides, I can't really say I'm interested. Don't look pained. That fatherly feeling isn't in me. I expected it would come, with time. It never did. Why pretend otherwise? Patrick and Rory are bright boys. They wouldn't be fooled. So

384

why bother?"

"You're being selfish."

"If I am—"

"If?"

"Katie, this could be my last chance to salvage whatever shreds of decency I have left. It has nothing to do with the Kaiser, or even with America. It's a test, a stern test. I may fail. I've failed at everything else. But I may not. I may find my long-lost courage, and a few other things, like honor and purpose. I'm trying to find the fellow I once was."

"You've chosen a drastic way."

"It has to be drastic. Don't you see? I *despise* what I've become. A weakling. A drunk. This is the first night I've been sober in weeks. I've been depending on whiskey to give me courage, courage to get out of bed in the morning, to face all the empty days, the empty nights. . . . What happened to the fellow who was going to conquer the world? Ada asked me that question once. It's time to find out."

Or die trying, thought Katie, touching her hand to her stomach. She had not told Matt about the child she was carrying, and she realized she could not tell him now. "Why don't you start by going back to work?" she asked.

"Where? Who would have me? The doors are barred, Katie, properly so. Oh, I could get Ben to pull a few strings. But what for? I won't be useful to anyone until *I* know who I am. Sometimes I think I just never grew up. Well, people grow up fast in war."

"People are also killed in war."

"I'd risk my life a hundred times over to find some

part of what I've lost."

"Then it's settled."

"It was settled when I signed the papers." Matt tossed his cigarette into an ashtray. He leaned forward, his blue eyes steady on Katie. "I did love you, long ago. And you loved me. That's in the past. I don't know about the future. I only know that the present is unbearable. Can you understand?"

"Yes." Katie nodded, brushing a tear away. "I wish—"

"Don't. I always said I wasn't good enough for you. In that one thing I was right. Don't waste your time on wishes."

"You're still my husband, Matt. I care about you."

"It's your weakness for lost souls."

"It's more than that. We've shared a lot of years. We've spent half our lives together."

"Not very happily."

"No." Katie sighed. "Not very. But I care what happens to you. I can't help it."

Matt stood. He paced the length of the room then turned and walked to Katie's chair. "I care about you, too, in my way. And who knows? We may still be able to make sense of all this. If first I make sense of myself."

"When are you leaving?"

"Next week. We're being sent somewhere upstate for training. After that it's a ship to France."

"France. I remember when we went to Greenwich Village and pretended it was France. Now you won't be pretending. You'll really be there, fighting a war. . . . The boys will have to know. I'd like you to tell them. They're in their room doing their schoolwork."

"You want me to tell them tonight?"

"Tonight is as good a time as any. You've never had a real conversation with Patrick and Rory. Tonight is a good opportunity. You might even enjoy it. They're bright children, Matt. You said so yourself."

"Yes, they see right through me. Especially Patrick. He doesn't say much, but he doesn't miss much, either. There's a certain look in his eyes."

"You're imagining things. I won't let you get out of this. You're going far away, and it could be many months before you return. You owe the boys an explanation. It doesn't have to be fancy. Tell them you're going away to fight the Kaiser. I think they'll be impressed. At their ages, the world is all heroes and villains; nothing in between. If only it were that simple."

"Isn't it?"

Katie gazed up at Matt. He was smiling, but behind his smile she saw pain and regret, the regret of a wasted life. "I hope you find what you're searching for," she said quietly, reaching to take his hand.

It was two months later when Katie and her sons, dressed in their Sunday best, stood on a crowded pier and waved good-bye to Matt. "Which soldier is Papa?" Rory asked, scanning the decks of the vast troop ship. "There are so many."

"I'm not sure, dear," Katie replied. "Just keep

waving. Papa will see you. Hold your flag high. You too, Patrick."

"Is it supposed to be a party, Mama?"

"It looks that way."

Certainly the atmosphere was festive, with hundreds of flags and brightly colored banners fluttering in the June sunshine. Children jumped up and down, blowing whistles and ringing cow bells. There was a band playing martial music, and there were vendors selling cotton candy and root beer. When finally the troop ship sailed away, horns blasting, there were cheers.

Katie was not surprised, for it was a time of great patriotism. Americans who had wanted no part of Europe's war now rallied to the cause. On almost every day, in almost every town and city, there were parades and bond drives and speeches excoriating the hated Germans. It was confidently predicted that American soldiers would end the fighting overnight. If there were dissenting voices, they were but a murmur amidst the rousing oratory of politicians and the stirring rhythms of Mr. Cohan's songs. George M. Cohan told the world that the yanks were coming, and his message, as cocky and sure as America herself, was hailed.

"Where are you off to?" Katie asked Rory one day in August. "And what are you hiding behind your back?"

"I'm not hiding anything."

"Let's see it."

Eight-year-old Rory sighed, holding out a bulging burlap sack. "It's rocks," he explained. "There's lots of rocks around the railyard. We collected them.

Johnny and Billy and Tommy and me."

"Whatever do you want with rocks?"

"Johnny and Billy and Tommy and me are going to Yorkville to bash Germans. See, you take a rock and then you throw it hard as you can at a window. Stores are best. They have big windows."

"Put the sack down. Put it down! Come with me," Katie said, marching Rory into the parlor. "Was this your idea? Tell me the truth. Whose idea was it?"

"Billy's. Well, it wasn't *really* his idea His brother did it first. Only he had bricks. We couldn't get any bricks." Rory perched at the edge of a chair. He smiled at Katie, swinging his legs back and forth. "Rocks are okay too."

"Why do you want to hurt people you don't even know?"

"They're *Germans*. Germans are bad."

"The people who live in Yorkville are Americans. They're as American as you are, Rory. They lived in Germany once. Or maybe their parents lived there, or their grandparents. Now they live in America. Do you understand?"

"No."

"The people in Yorkville have nothing to do with the Kaiser or his war."

"They're on his *side*."

"How do you know that? If we were at war with Ireland, would you be on Ireland's side?"

"No, Mama."

"Let's pretend we were at war with Ireland. If we were, would it be right for people to come here and throw rocks at you?"

"They better not. I'll punch them."

"Would it be right? Think about it, Rory." Katie stood over her son, staring into his brilliant blue-green eyes. "Are you thinking?" she asked.

"Yes. . . . It wouldn't be my war, I guess. It wouldn't be my fault, 'cause I'm Irish but I'm really American. And in Yorkville they're American too?"

"Of course they are. You're a big boy now, Rory. You must learn to think things through. You could have made a terrible mistake. You could have hurt someone."

Rory began to fidget, bouncing on the chair cushion. "I didn't mean it, Mama," he said. "I didn't know. Nobody told me."

"You shouldn't have to be told the difference between right and wrong. I'd hoped we were beyond that. You were always in trouble when you were little, tying tin cans to Mrs. Grogan's cat, putting pepper in the tooth powder, putting a spider down Annie Farrel's back. It was one prank after another. We had long talks about your pranks, didn't we?" Rory nodded, chastised by this recitation of his transgressions. Katie went on, "And we decided that it's fine to have fun, but it's *not* fine to scare people or to hurt them. Now I find you on your way to Yorkville with a sack of rocks."

"All the boys were going, Mama. I couldn't be a sissy."

"If all the boys jumped off the roof, would you jump also?"

"That's silly."

"Is it? You're very impetuous, Rory. You don't stop to think. I know you don't mean any harm. Whether you mean it or not is beside the point.

390

You're old enough to be responsible for your behavior. I'm holding you responsible from here on." Katie smoothed his thick, reddish curls. She smiled. "Okay?"

"Okay."

"If you get confused about things, come to me and we'll talk."

"Yes, Mama."

"Run along now. Tell your friends you can't go with them. And tell them why. I don't expect you'll change their minds, but tell them anyway."

"That's all?"

"That's all. I won't punish you this time. Make sure there's no next time."

Rory's handsome face brightened. He bounded out of his chair, clapping his hands as he went to the door. "Hi, Jack," he said, grinning up at Jack Snow. "I was bad again. But I learned the dance you showed me. Want to see?"

"I wouldn't miss it. If your mama will give us some music."

Katie wound the arm of the Victrola, setting the needle upon a well-worn record, "The Sidewalks of New York."

"How's that?" she asked.

"That's dancing music. You start, kid. I'll join in at the end . . . remember to keep your head up. Keep your shoulders loose. . . . Hey, you're pretty good. Look at him, Katie. The kid's pretty good. He's got a future in the business."

"C'mon, Jack," Rory called. "You have to dance too. It's a double."

Jack took his place beside Rory. Together they

performed a series of intricate steps, finishing with a buck and wing, and then a deep bow. "Kid, you got what it takes. You wowed the audience."

"Aw, she's just my mother. Wait'll I have a *real* audience."

"He's another George M."—Jack laughed, winking at Katie— "full of beans and confidence."

"I'm afraid so. Run along now, Rory. Behave yourself."

"I will, Mama. 'Bye, Jack."

"See you, kid."

"Sit down and catch your breath," Katie said. "That was quite a performance."

"Yeah, and I'm getting too old," Jack replied, wiping his damp forehead. "Stage work is a young man's game. I'll be glad when we're settled in California. I hear the hours are long in moving pictures, but the work's not hard."

"Are you all packed?"

"At last. Mary and the family are already out there, you know. She says it's sunshine every day. She rented this house that has fruit trees right in the back yard, with oranges and lemons ready for the picking. I guess it'll be a whole different life. . . . Think of it." Jack chuckled. "Rayne and Snow in sunny California."

"I bet you've been waiting to use that line."

"Well, Mr. Sennett's paying us to be funny. That fellow, Mack Sennett, they say he has the golden touch with comedy. It's late in the day for Lou and me, but Mr. Sennett thinks there's life in us yet. I'm looking forward to pushing those custard pies in Lou's face. I get to do it because I'm the funny fat guy.

Lou plays straight, like always."

"I'm sorry you're going, Jack. It will be lonely around here without you. You've been such a good friend."

"That works both ways. Every time Lou and me came into New York it was like coming home. I watched you grow up, Katie. I probably saw more of you than my own kids. So you have to promise to visit. It seems far, but it's only a train ride. Your boys would love it. All the sunshine, the ocean only minutes away. Maybe I could talk Mr. Sennett into using Rory. He uses kids in his pictures sometimes. Rory has talent."

"Oh, it's much too soon to know about talent. Rory enjoys showing off. He hates the idea of being the younger brother, and he hates the idea of a new baby coming. I think this singing and dancing is his way of getting attention."

"But he's good."

"I don't encourage him, Jack. He's *not* good at schoolwork, and that's more important. I want Rory to have an education. If he choses to go into show business later, I certainly won't try to stop him. First he must have an education." Katie sat back, resting her hands on her swollen stomach. "My boys are at difficult stages." She smiled. "Patrick thinks of nothing but baseball. Rory thinks of nothing but show business, and mischief. I have to crack the whip."

"Not you. It's not in you."

"I have to be firm with them. I force myself. If I didn't, they'd be running wild."

"That's what Mary used to say about our kids.

They turned out fine. You'll meet them when you come to California . . . don't shake your head. I'm bound and determined to get you there. I know it's a bad time now, with the baby on the way, with the war. . . . What do you hear from Matt?"

"Very little. I've had one letter. Matt's in France, in the thick of the fighting." Katie glanced away, sighing, for each day she read the war news and each day she was newly horrified. "I remember the afternoon Matt left," she said. "All the flags and the music and the laughter. Patrick asked if it was a party. It *seemed* like a party. My God! How naïve we were! There were cheers when the ship sailed. What were we cheering? Young men going off to be crippled and blinded? Young men going off to die? I see no glory in war. I see death."

"America didn't start the war."

"That's small consolation. We're in it now. And some people are glad. Men, mostly. They gather in the park on Saturdays and make rousing speeches. I notice that the men making all the speeches are too old to do any of the fighting . . . or am I being cynical?"

"You're under a strain, Katie."

"Everybody's under a strain these days. We wave the flag and go to parades and try to forget. How can we? My God, how can we forget there's war?"

Summer ended and with it all the confident predictions of early victory. Hell's Kitchen began to mourn its dead. Gerry Wilson, an army chaplain, was killed when a shell exploded in the foxhole

394

where he was offering comfort to a frightened soldier. Ed Ryan's oldest son was killed in fierce fighting outside Verdun. Jimmy Muldoon was killed in a pre-dawn aerial attack. Father Duffy and the gallant men of his Fighting 69th brought pride to every Irish heart, but pride walked hand in hand with grief as, each day, more sons and husbands fell. Now there was no forgetting.

"Flowers!" Maeve snapped, closing the curtains against the bright September sunshine. "What are you doing buying flowers in the middle of a war?"

"The flowers are for you, Mama," Katie replied. "I wanted to . . . welcome you here. Do you like your room?"

"Aye, it's a fine room. I thought I'd be ending my days in the flat. And you thought so too. Oh, I'm not fooled, Katie McVey. I know you only asked me here because you need help. Your mother's some use to you after all. Well? Why are you standing there? In your condition, you should keep off your feet when you can. Sit down," Maeve said, plumping a chair cushion. "Is it a new chair? Did you buy a new chair in the middle of a war?"

"It's not new. I made a slipcover."

"In your condition, you should be resting."

"Mama, we agreed we wouldn't argue. Before you moved here, we agreed you wouldn't . . . tell me what to do."

"Is it my fault if you don't have the sense of a goose? Standing when you could be sitting?"

Katie smiled, settling her heavy body in the chair. "You never change, Mama. It's just like old times."

"Where's the good in change? They say the world's

changing. Is it for the better? Whenever the world changes, there's war."

"I wish you'd stop talking about war. I read the newspapers. That's reminder enough. Be grateful Hugh and Sean aren't in it."

"Hugh! Hugh's in the black market, getting rich while others are dying."

"People are always gossiping. You don't know if it's true."

"Don't I? Have a word with Sergeant Garrity. *He* knows. He's been keeping an eye out ever since Hugh came back to New York. Aye, Hugh and his gang are in the black market and hijacking, too. In their spare time they run the gambling games. Devils, the lot of them."

"All right, Mama." Katie sighed. "They're devils. Can't we find a different subject? *Sean* certainly isn't a devil."

"No, he's learning to be a priest. And when he's done, the army will ship him off to France, like poor Gerry Wilson." Maeve turned. She walked around the room, glancing at the sprigged wallpaper, the starched, white curtains. She ran her hand over the dresser, peeking under its latticed cloth. "Did you clean this room special for me?" she asked.

"Mama, you're impossible," Katie replied with a laugh. "All the rooms are cleaned every day. I haven't been able to do much myself lately, but Veronica is thorough."

"Is she? Does she work hard? Sure and she'll be answering to me if she doesn't."

"I want you to leave Veronica alone. Don't scare her. She's a sweet, timid girl who works *very* hard. It's a hard job, Mama."

"Well, I'm here to help, aren't I? Tell me my chores."

Katie sighed again, staring up at her mother. Maeve's hair was more gray than brown now, though her dark blue eyes were as resolute as ever. There had been no softening of mouth or jaw, no mellowing. She was, at forty-six, still the certain and stern woman of Katie's childhood. "Don't put it that way, Mama. I'm not going to give you a list of chores. Veronica does the cleaning. I try to do most of the cooking. I could use your help with the cooking, especially supper. It's a big meal."

"Aye, I'll cook supper. And I'll do the laundry. Dear knows I've had enough practice. I'll be useful."

"You have the wrong idea about this. It's true I need your help, but that's not the only reason I asked you here. With Sean gone, I didn't want you to stay in the flat. Why should you when I have room here? I admit the boardinghouse isn't what it was. At least it's comfortable. It's warm in winter. Best of all, it's where your grandchildren live. You like being around them, don't you? They're nice boys."

"I'm no judge. I thought Hugh was a nice boy. Look what happened to him. You thought Matt was a nice boy."

"He was, in the beginning. He wasn't . . . strong. That's why he went off to war. He's trying to find the strength, the courage he had once."

"Don't waste my time with foolish talk. Do you suppose courage is something you lose, like an umbrella or a glove? It's your place to defend your husband, Katie, but don't tell me tales. Men enjoy war, the idea of it, anyway. It stirs the blood. And that's why they go. When they get in the middle of it, they find it's not so stirring. By then it's too late. If it was women running countries, war would be last resort, not first."

"Mama," Katie said, her eyes twinkling, "I didn't know you were a suffragette."

"A suffragette! Are you daft? All that marching around and carrying signs. And what for? The vote? It'll be a cold day in Hell when women are allowed the vote."

"I hope you're wrong."

"Aye, you would. You were always one to hope. You're always putting a good face on things. Saying what you did about Matt is the perfect example."

"No, Mama. I meant it. I told you the truth. Matt didn't go off on a whim, not this time. His reasons may seem foolish to you. They did to me. Then I saw how serious he was, how desperate. He called it a search. He's searching for himself."

"You don't believe that?"

"Matt is many things, but he isn't a liar. He never lied about his women, his drinking. It was out in the open. The only lie he ever told was about wanting to marry me. He was trying to save my feelings. He was being . . . honorable. It was a dreadful mistake, and we've both paid the price. It cost us our dreams. People need dreams, Mama."

"Weaklings need dreams."

"Let's not argue, Mama. Now that we're living under the same roof again, let's try to get along."

Katie was to repeat those words often in the weeks that followed, though, to her surprise, Maeve adjusted well to the life of the boardinghouse. If at first she startled the vaudevillians with her blunt and acerbic comments, her feisty spirit soon won them over. They did not seem to mind being the occasional targets of her wrath, nor were they cowed. Indeed they matched her insult for insult until someone laughed and the contest ended in good humor all around. Maeve, alone so much of her life, found a home among the people she had once airily dismissed as vagabonds.

"Admit it, Mama," Katie said on a cool, rainy day in October. "You're happy here."

"Aye, I'd be happier if Veronica was soaking the laundry like I told her. I told her twice. Do I have to stand over her every minute?"

"She's just gone to answer the door. She'll be right back."

"And what are you doing peeling potatoes? You should be resting. In your condition, you should get all the rest you can."

"I may not be much use these days, but I can still peel vegetables. I'll be glad when the baby comes and I can do my work." Katie looked up, turning her head to the door. "Yes, Veronica?" She smiled. "Who was it? Not a boarder this time of day?"

"A telegram."

"I hope it's from the Costellos. They always reserve half the rooms on the second floor. We need the business." Katie struggled out of her chair. Slowly, she walked a few steps to Veronica, accepting the telegram. "It's from Washington—Oh, my God, *no*," she cried, and then a pit of blackness opened at her feet.

"Katie!" Maeve rushed to her stricken daughter. "Katie! Dear God in Heaven, she's fainted! Veronica, hurry and fetch the ammonia. Be quick about it." Maeve retrieved the telegram, her eyes blurring as she read the first two lines: "We regret to inform you that Captain Matthew McVey has been killed in action . . ." Angrily, she flung the telegram away.

"It's bad news?" Veronica asked. "Is it the mister?"

"He's dead. Sure and the army sent us fancy words about how and why. Do they think anyone cares how or why? He's dead, that's all. Where's the ammonia?"

"Here."

Maeve passed the bottle back and forth under Katie's nose. "Wake up," she said. "Wake up now."

Katie's eyes opened. They fluttered shut, then opened again. "Mama . . . what happened?"

"You fainted. Don't move too sudden, Katie. Go easy. I'll help you . . . easy, Katie. Hold on to me . . . aye, that's the way." Maeve pulled a chair out, helping Katie into it. "I'll fetch you a bit of brandy."

"Mama, the telegram . . . Matt . . . Matt was killed."

"Aye, I'm sorry, Katie. Here, take my handkerchief." Veronica brought a glass of brandy, and Maeve pressed it to her daughter's trembling mouth. "Drink, Katie. Drink it down."

Katie took a sip, choking, for the liquor burned her throat. "No more . . . I must think . . . I must . . . *Oh*," she gasped, doubling over. "Call . . . Call Dr. Morton. The baby is coming."

"You may go in now," Dr. Morton said to an

anxious Maeve. "Katie is quite well. She has another boy, a healthy boy."

Maeve rushed past the doctor to Katie's bedside. "Are you all right?" she asked, staring into her daughter's pale and tired face. "You gave us a scare. You fainted again. You fainted twice in one day!"

"I know Mama. It was the shock. There's nothing to worry about. Do you want to see your new grandson? He's sleeping in his cradle. He has my coloring, but he's the picture of Matt. I've decided to name him Matthew. Don't you want to see him? Look." Katie smiled, reaching down to draw the blanket away. "Isn't he handsome? He nursed and then went right to sleep."

Maeve gazed at the baby. She smiled slightly. "Aye, he's handsome," she agreed, bending to touch his fair cheek. "At least he's not all red and wrinkled, like some. He's not noisy. Sure and I remember how noisy Rory was."

"Where are the boys? Are they here?"

"They're downstairs with Ben. I called him up on the telephone. He came right over. He told them about Matt. I thought it was best, Katie. Dear knows you're in no condition, fainting twice in one day. I thought it was best to have it done with. I was there when he told them. Aye, he did a good job of it."

Katie fell back against the pillows, clasping and unclasping her hands. "How . . . How did they take it, Mama?"

"Patrick was very quiet. Rory was too, until he heard the part about his father being a hero. After that—"

"A hero?"

401

"Well, the telegram said something about courage under fire. I didn't read it that close. But then Ben started making telephone calls. He telephoned to Washington. He spoke to a senator first. Aye, it's true. Didn't I hear him with my own ears? After the senator it was a colonel, then a general. So many calls, I couldn't keep track. Finally Ben told us Matt died a hero. There's even a medal coming. Not to speak ill of the dead, but I didn't think Matt had it in him."

"That's what he went to find out, Mama . . . I'd like to see Ben. Alone, if you don't mind."

"Alone? In your nightgown?"

"Matthew will chaperone. Please, Mama. I want to talk to Ben."

"Aye, I'll fetch him. But I'll be just outside in the hall. And you'll put your robe on, Katie McVey. Here it is. Put it on and button the buttons. A man's a man, no matter what."

"Mama—"

"I'm going. Pull the covers up."

Sighing, Katie obeyed. She closed her eyes for a moment and saw Matt's face. It was the face of his youth, unmarked by disappointment, by failure. That's the way I'll remember him, she thought. I'll remember the beginning, not the end.

"Katie?"

"Oh, come in, Ben. Sit down."

"Thanks. How are you feeling?"

"Fine, everything considered."

"What a strange day this is. Sad, yet happy, too," Ben said, peering into the cradle. "He's a beautiful baby. The boys will be wild about him. They wanted a girl to boss around, but one look and they'll be wild about him. Does he have a name?"

"Matthew. Your godson."

"I'd be honored." Ben leaned back in his chair. He took a breath, lifting his dark gaze. "I'm terribly sorry, Katie. I can't believe Matt is . . . gone. I kept hoping there had been some error."

"How did he die? I understand you got a full report."

"Yes. Are you certain you want the details, Katie? You've been through a great deal today. Perhaps you should rest."

"I can't rest until I know how Matt died. Please tell me."

"It happened last Friday. Matt's unit was pinned down under heavy fire. Matt commenced diversionary action. He drew the German forces toward him, while sending his men in the other direction. He could have followed them to safety. Instead, he held his position." Ben's voice caught. He paused briefly, then continued. "Matt gave his men precious extra minutes, and those minutes saved their lives. . . . The citation will say that Matt acted with conspicuous bravery. He did."

"His wish was granted."

"I beg your pardon?"

"Before Matt left, he said he wanted to be tested. He wanted desperately not to fail." Katie dried her tears. She looked at Matthew, a small smile flickering about her mouth. "Thank you for telling me, Ben. I feel better now."

"Is there anything I can do? Do you need anything?"

"I'll ask another favor, if I may. The arrange-ments . . . I'm not up to facing Mr. McCarthy again."

"That won't be necessary. Matt was buried in the Argonne, next to his fallen comrades. Battle was raging on all sides, Katie. It was the best his men could do. Perhaps after the war—"

"No, Ben. It's right for him to be there. We'll have a memorial service later. Matt always hated funerals."

"I know."

Katie touched her slim gold wedding band, and once more she saw Matt's face. "Godspeed," she whispered.

17

"I'm sorry to be late," Katie said, sitting in a chair across from William Streeter. "Traffic is impossible."

"Progress has its price, I'm afraid. The automobile is a wonderful invention, but it does play havoc with traffic. I myself have begun taking the subway in the mornings."

"Oh, William, I can't imagine you on the subway."

"You would be surprised how many of my business associates I meet there. We race each other for seats. I consider it my daily exercise, more challenging than golf."

"Yes, I'm sure."

"You look very fetching today. Very stylish."

"Thank you." Katie smiled. Freed at last of her mourning clothes, she wore a long, plum-colored suit, a ruffle of white lace edging her throat. Ada's pearl earrings enhanced the outfit, as did the saucy, plum velvet hat atop her upswept hair. "I don't know what came over me, William, buying a new outfit when my finances are so uncertain. I'm ashamed of myself."

"Well, we all need a splurge now and again. As to your finances . . ." William reached out, opening a file folder. "I agree they are precarious. The boardinghouse isn't paying its way. And there is the mortgage."

"Five hundred dollars. The roof was about to fall in. I had to have it replaced. Then the pipes burst in the cellar. It scares me to think what will happen next.'

"My offer still stands, Katie. I will be pleased to lend you money."

"I appreciate it, but I can't accept. I'd only be digging a deeper hole. I've decided to sell Matt's properties. It wasn't an easy decision. I've held on as long as I could. Now it's time to sell."

"I rather thought that's what you had in mind. Sell the properties to me."

"William, what would you want with a bunch of vacant lots and broken-down stores? You're sweet to suggest it, but the answer is no. I won't take advantage of our friendship. Aren't there people who speculate in real estate?"

"Certainly. New York is growing every day. It is an excellent place for speculators. They flock here. Some go after the quick profit. Others, like Matt, are willing to wait." William glanced again at the folder. He removed his glasses, sitting back. "If you were willing to wait, Katie, just until the end of the war. . . . My sources tell me the end is in sight."

"I've heard those rumors since the war began."

"My sources are reliable."

"I don't doubt it, William. The problem is I can't

afford to wait. It may be weeks before I find a buyer, months. I have to set the wheels in motion. Besides, I have a feeling this is the right time. It's a strong feeling."

"Ah, women's intuition. I never quarrel with women's intuition. It is my duty, however, to warn you that the properties will not bring much. Their resale value is low, eliminating speculators interested in quick profit. Speculators interested in long term investment can have their pick. It's a buyer's market, you see. The war has temporarily slowed construction."

"I understand."

"Your decision is final?"

"Yes."

"Very well. Please excuse me, Katie," William said, rising. "I won't be a moment."

"You needn't hurry. I love your office." William Streeter's office was large and wood paneled, with tufted leather chairs and sofas, and handsome English sporting prints on the walls. To the left of the Hepplewhite desk was a globe set in an antique brass stand; to the right was a small table holding a crystal sherry decanter and several glasses. A Turkish carpet decorated the polished wood floor. Katie looked around, imagining the rich and important clients who visited here. She looked at her own meager folder and she laughed. "William," she said when he returned, "you really are a sweet man. I can't tell you how grateful I am. Wasting your time on my petty little problems."

"Nonsense. I'm delighted to help. Day in and day out I spend my time with dull old men, much like myself. You are a breath of fresh air. My partners are quite envious."

"If you say so."

"Indeed I do." William picked up the folder. "Katie, have you seen your properties? Have you seen them recently? I thought not. I have a car and driver waiting downstairs. Ben Rossi will escort you. He knows something about real estate. He's been studying it, anticipating a postwar boom. Ben is a bright fellow."

"I hate to take him away from his work."

"Away from his work? Ben is a member of the firm, and you are a client. I would escort you myself if I could. Unfortunately, I have a meeting. Come." William smiled, offering his arm. "I can escort you to the elevator."

They walked through a suite of paneled outer offices, past William's male private secretary, his two female legal secretaries, and the receptionist who zealously guarded the doors. Katie stopped at the elevator, pulling on her gloves. "Thank you for everything," she said.

"My pleasure. We will continue our conversation after you have seen the properties. You will have a clearer picture then. Perhaps a disappointing one."

"Oh, don't worry about that. I'm expecting the worst. I'm prepared." Katie entered the elevator, nodding at the attendant. "First floor please."

"Yes, ma'am."

Ben was waiting to greet Katie as she emerged from the building. He moved swiftly to her side and tipped his hat. "Good morning," he said with a smile. "Can I interest you in our special real estate tour? It's free."

"By all means."

"You won't be sorry."

"William thinks otherwise. He warned me I'd be disappointed. I'm prepared. My properties aren't exactly in demand, are they?"

Ben took Katie's arm, leading her to the curb. A liveried chauffeur snapped to attention. He touched his hand to his cap and then opened the door of a dark gray Pierce Arrow brougham. "Thank you," Ben said. "Katie, are you comfortable?"

"Comfortable isn't the word. I'm overwhelmed. Such luxury, Ben. I feel like a society lady. I wish Mama could see me. Or maybe I don't. She'd tell me I was getting too big for my britches, reaching above myself. And she'd be right, at least about reaching above myself. I should be satisfied with what I have. But I want more."

"Everybody wants more, Katie. That's why millions of people left their homes to come to America; why they continue to come. They're poor people seeking more from life. It's not only the poor. Every day I see rich men fighting, scheming to become richer. They scream the loudest when the government talks of an income tax. I wouldn't feel guilty if I were you. Your wants are modest, compared to some."

"Not as modest as you suppose. When I was a girl, I was content just to have a roof over my head, any roof, to have food on the table, even if it was potato pie. I've changed since then. I'm so tired of hoarding pennies."

"Are things that tight?"

"Almost. I have the children to support, and

Mama, and myself. I have to find a way to make money. I'm hoping the properties will give me . . . a stake."

"A stake?" Ben frowned. "I assumed you were going to use the proceeds to improve the boarding-house."

"Oh, that's throwing good money after bad. I love the boardinghouse. I really do. But I love my children more. I want them to have proper educations. And I want to get them out of Hell's Kitchen." Katie looked at Ben, shrugging. "It's a hard place to raise children. I'm always worried they'll fall in with the wrong crowd. Not Patrick so much. Rory. Rory will do anything on a dare.

"Boyish high spirits."

"Boys grow up fast in Hell's Kitchen. One day it's high spirits; the next it's serious trouble. I've seen it before, don't forget. Hugh wasn't born a criminal. It happened over a period of time. Those terrible gangs. All slum neighborhoods seem to have gangs. That's what I want to get my boys away from."

"I can help you, Katie. I'm not rich, but I'm not poor either, thanks to Streeter, Carlyle, and Hazlet. I know you put a word in for me with Streeter, years ago. I've wanted to repay you ever since."

"You have. You've been a wonderful friend."

"Then let a friend help."

Katie shook her head. "You know the answer to that," she said. "You've heard it often enough. I'll manage on my own somehow. Besides, it's no secret you're already helping brothers and sisters and nephews and cousins. You have your hands full."

"Italian families are close. We share. Family

includes friends." Ben gazed at Katie's lovely profile. Sighing, he reached into his briefcase and removed a typewritten list. He glanced out the car window and then turned his head. "Before we get to our first stop, there's something I must say. We've talked about friendship, Katie. . . . Surely you know that my feelings for you are deeper than friendship. No, don't stop me. I've waited a long time to speak. I would never have betrayed Matt, never by word or deed. I held my tongue during the very worst years of your marriage. I held my tongue during the year of mourning. Now . . . Now I must speak. I love you, Katie. I always have. I know you don't love me the same way, but in time . . . I'm saying this badly, but I think I could make you happy. I'm a pretty decent fellow and—"

"Please don't say any more, Ben." Katie sniffled, pressing a handkerchief to her welling eyes. "I couldn't bear it. I do love you, as a friend. My *dearest* friend."

"In time—"

"I wish I could say time would change things. It wouldn't, Ben. My marriage was a tragic mistake. It ruined Matt's life and nearly ruined mine. I don't expect to marry again, but if I do it will be for the right reasons."

"Who knows what the right reasons are?"

"I'll know. I won't make a second mistake, Ben. I couldn't live through a second mistake. I couldn't hurt you. And you would be hurt, sooner or later."

"I'm willing to risk it."

"I'm not. It would be cruel." Katie took Ben's hand. "How could I be cruel to you, of all people?

You're a *good* man. You deserve to be happy. You deserve a wife who will love you with all her heart and soul. Don't settle for less. Don't cheat yourself."

"You have a romantic nature. I should have come to you on bended knee. I should have smothered you in roses and bonbons and poetry. I've no one to blame but myself. A lawyer should know how to present his case "

"Oh, Ben." Katie smiled, once again wiping her eyes. "The answer would be the same. The right woman is waiting for you somewhere. Hurry and find her. You were meant to have a big family, a happy family."

"So my mother says."

"Listen to her. Mothers understand these things."

"We'll still be friends?"

"Always, Ben. Always."

It was night when Katie returned to the boarding-house. She went first to her sons' bedroom, straightening the blankets Patrick and Rory had kicked away, lowering a window. She found Matthew's teddy bear on the floor and gently placed it at his side. "Sleep well," she whispered, closing the door behind her.

"What a fine time to be getting home, Katie McVey! I was beginning to think you'd run off with Ben."

"I telephoned you, Mama. I said I'd be late."

"It's past nine by the clock. Where have you been all this time? The truth."

"Come into my room, Mama. We'll talk."

412

"Talk, is it? That means you're planning to tell me something. Something I won't like."

Katie removed her hat. She hung up her jacket and then fell on the bed, wriggling out of her shoes. "Ben showed me the properties," she said. "They're scattered. It took a long time. After that we stopped to have dinner."

"Dinner? Sure and you're getting fancy."

"Dinner, supper, the point is we had a lot to discuss. I've decided to open a restaurant, Mama."

"A restaurant!"

"One of the properties is an abandoned restaurant. I don't know why, but the previous owner never bothered to remove the equipment. It has stoves and ovens, almost everything I'll need. In terrible condition, of course. The stoves are coated with grease; the grills also. That's the kitchen. The dining room is a maze of cobwebs. I admit it didn't look very promising at first."

Maeve sat down. She twisted her wedding band around and around, a frown creasing her brow. "Are you daft? I can't believe what I'm hearing. What good is a dirty, filthy restaurant? Do you think people will pay to eat in such a place? It probably has bugs. And rats!"

"Ben is arranging for exterminators," Katie replied, unconcerned. "Once that problem is solved, everything else is up to me. The restaurant won't be dirty when I'm finished with it. It will be clean and pretty and . . . successful."

"Maybe you'd like to tell me who's going to make it clean and pretty and successful? The man in the moon?"

"I am, Mama. I'll hire a neighborhood girl to help you and Veronica here. Then I can spend my time preparing the restaurant. I plan to be open by Christmas."

"And what do you plan to use for money? You'll need furniture, won't you? Tables and chairs? You'll need dishes, linens."

"I have savings. Three hundred dollars."

"That's all the money you have to your name. What if you lose it? How will you pay your mortgage and support your children? Have you forgotten about your children, Katie McVey?"

"Why do you think I'm doing this? It's a *chance*, Mama. A chance to give them a decent future."

"Aye, but if you fail—"

"I won't."

Maeve saw the stubborn set of Katie's jaw, the determined line of her mouth. "Well," she said, "many's the time I prayed to God to make you strong. Now's the test. A woman alone, owing money, gambling her life savings to start a restaurant."

"It's not gambling. And I'm not alone. I have good friends. I have a family." Katie smiled suddenly. She rose and kissed Maeve's cheek. "You're strong enough for all of us."

"Aye, be grateful I am. Dear knows there's hard work ahead. You can't do it by yourself. I'll help out after my chores are done here. Patrick and Rory can help too, after school. It's better than running around the streets."

"I was expecting an argument, Mama."

Maeve shrugged her thin shoulders. "You'll go your way no matter what," she said. "I can see your mind's made. Just don't ask me to be happy about it. You're gambling, Katie. Why was the restaurant abandoned in the first place? Because it failed, that's why. You're *gambling* you won't fail."

"I have to. Nobody's going to leave a basket of money on my doorstep. The other properties are for sale now, but they aren't worth much. Several hundred dollars at most. I need a steady income. If I'm gambling, I'm gambling on myself. I know how to cook. I know how to run a kitchen and keep accounts. I learned a lot from Ada. It's time to put it to use."

"Christmas is less than three months off."

"I know. I'll be ready."

"Where is this restaurant?"

"On the East Side, Mama." Katie smiled. "The Gallaghers and the McVeys are finally making it to the East Side."

"Aye, but where?"

"Thirty-eighth Street, near Madison Avenue. It's a wonderful neighborhood, full of lovely brownstone houses. We're the only restaurant for blocks. We should have a good dinner trade, Mama. And it's near enough to the stores to have a good lunch trade as well. It's perfect!"

"It failed once."

"That was in the past. I'm looking to the future."

"Sure and there's no hope for it," Maeve declared, taking her first look at the restaurant. She clung to her opinion all through the long days and nights of renovation, though she did so with unusual good humor. "I'm the forewoman," she said, and thus the matter was settled.

Katie hired three strong teenaged boys to do the heavy work. She gave them their instructions bright and early each morning, reading from lists prepared by Maeve. While her helpers scrubbed the dining room, she scrubbed the kitchen, starting with ceiling and walls and working her way down. Black soot flew into her eyes and nose and even into her throat. At the end of the first day her knuckles were cracked and bleeding; at the end of the first week her hands were swollen to twice their size. "You're killing yourself," Maeve warned. Katie could only smile, for such warnings were invariably followed by more lists, more orders from the forewoman.

The war ended in November of 1918, and Katie declared a holiday. She and her family celebrated, as did the entire war-weary nation. In New York many thousands of people crowded the streets, shouting and cheering. Strangers embraced strangers, tears streaming down their faces. "I guess we showed the Kaiser," Rory said proudly. "Didn't we show him, Mama?" Katie agreed, though her heart remembered all the young men who had returned crippled or blinded or gassed or shell shocked, and all the young men, like Matt, who never returned.

Christmas drew near, and now Katie spent every waking moment on the details of her restaurant. She ordered furniture from a small factory on Canal Street. She ordered linens and tableware and glass. She supervised painters and paperhangers. She had fliers printed, sending Patrick and Rory to distribute them to passersby. With Father Malone's help, she

416

hired six young Irishwomen, fresh off the boat, to be waitresses. Maeve designed their uniforms—long black skirts, ruffled white shirtwaists, and ruffled caps.

"Well, Mama," Katie said the week before Christmas, "look around and tell me what you think."

"It's a miracle you've done here," Maeve replied. Her glance swept across the dining room, over spotless, pale yellow walls and gleaming light fixtures. The chairs were oak and cane, the tables dressed with crisp blue cloths, plain white china, and baskets of baby's breath. The wood floor, once so grimy, was polished and buffed to a high shine. "Aye, I can hardly believe my eyes. All your hard work. It was worth it."

"*Everybody's* hard work, Mama."

"Aye, I'll take my share of the credit. But it was your idea. You had the notion. I hope it comes to something."

"I'll stick my head in the oven if it doesn't."

"Katie!"

"I'm only joking, Mama. I have better uses for the oven."

Maeve again glanced about the dining room. "Clean and pretty." She nodded. "Just like you promised. But it's more than that. Aye, it's cozy. There's a cozy feeling here."

"Thank you, Mama."

"Sure and I'm wishing you luck, Katie. I'm wishing you a grand success when you open your doors tomorrow. Dear knows you've earned it."

The two women left the restaurant. Katie paused in front of the plate glass window, her finger tracing the simple gold letters that spelled The Country Kitchen. "Do you think it's a good name?" she asked.

"Aye. It's what I said—a cozy feeling."

The Country Kitchen was not an immediate success. Day after day the young and rosy-cheeked waitresses stood at their stations, looking hopefully toward the door. They looked in vain, for few customers crossed the threshold. Katie insisted that everything would be all right, but, as months passed, she too began to have doubts. Friends sustained her. William Streeter brought a large party to the restaurant once a week without fail. Ben brought his relatives. Dr. Morton brought his wife and twin sons. Cornelius O'Day, visiting from Hollywood, brought a rising motion picture star named Charlie Chaplin.

Katie struggled on. She cut expenses where she could, though she resisted Maeve's suggestions to change the menu. "I'm not trying to be Delmonicos," she said over and over. "I serve good, hearty American food." Indeed, the menu reflected American tastes, offering beef stew with mustard gravy, roast chicken with chestnut dressing, baked ham with sweet potatoes. There was a special dessert each day, mocha-chocolate cake or butterscotch pie or hot fudge sundaes heaped with whipped cream.

Katie's decision was vindicated in April, when The Country Kitchen showed its first profits. The next month profits soared, and, by summer, the restaurant was a runaway success. Customers filled every table at lunch and again at teatime. Reservations were necessary to accommodate the large dinner crowds.

"People are fickle," Maeve warned, suspicious of such rapid success. "They can be crowding your place today and somebody else's place tomorrow." The same thoughts occurred to Katie. Carefully she monitored the pace of her business, comparing profits week to week and month to month. At the end of 1919 she purchased the adjoining building and set about doubling the size of The Country Kitchen.

It was, Katie often joked, as if she had found a money tree. If that was an exaggeration, it was slight, for she was clearing hundreds of dollars a week, a small fortune even amidst postwar inflation. Her bank account grew fat. Her closet blossomed with new clothes. She visited a beauty parlor for the first time in her life, giggling delightedly as Miss Rose styled her long golden hair and massaged thick creams into her work-scarred hands.

"Well, here I am again," Katie said on a clear autumn day in 1920. "And once again I need your help."

William Streeter smiled, adjusting his glasses on his nose. "You flatter me. Most of our clients prefer the younger lawyers. I'm regarded as something of a figurehead now. Are you certain you wish to trust your affairs to a doddering old man?"

"Doddering old man! That will be the day. You're the wisest man I know, William. Of any age."

"May I quote you?"

"Please do."

"You have made an old man very happy. Now tell me how I can be of help."

"To begin with, there's the matter of the boarding-house. We closed for renovations several weeks ago.

The renovations are finished, and I'd like to give the boardinghouse to Father Malone. He has an idea about starting a community center, a center where the neighborhood kids could go to keep out of trouble.''

"An admirable idea. Of course you would actually be deeding the property to the church. I may be wrong, but I believe priests are prohibited from owning property.''

"To the church then. With the stipulation that it can't be sold for development. I won't have it turned into tenements. I couldn't live with myself if I thought I'd caused more tenements to be built.''

"I quite understand. Your stipulations will be included in the transfer agreement. Rest assured they will be binding. When do you propose to do this, Katie?''

"As soon as possible. We move into our new flat tomorrow. I wouldn't want the boardinghouse to be vacant too long. It needs people around . . . I suppose I'm being sentimental." Katie sighed, dabbing at her eyes. "But leaving the boardinghouse is one of the hardest things I've ever done. I believe I'd stay, if it weren't for the children. There are so many memories.''

"You're doing the right thing. The boardinghouse will be in good hands, after all.''

"Yes.''

"Is that all, Katie?" William frowned. He folded his hands atop his desk. "Surely you didn't come all the way to my office for such a simple matter? I never miss a Monday night at your restaurant. We could have discussed it then."

"Well, there *is* something else. It's so . . . fantastic, I'm afraid to tell you. I'm sure you'll laugh, or cart me off to Bellevue. Mama's convinced I belong there, with the 'loonies,' as she puts it. She may be right this time. Do you know the St. Clair Hotel?"

"Not personally. I have heard of it. I pass it every Monday. It is near your restaurant."

"The St. Clair is owned by the Jordan family. I've gotten to know the Jordans in the past year. Tom Jordan is a regular lunch customer." Katie paused, drawing a breath. "It's a lovely hotel, William. Small, comfortable. But since the war it's been going downhill. Tom wants to sell. He and his wife are tired of the problems. They want to retire."

"Oh?"

"I'm thinking about buying it."

"A hotel?"

"A hotel isn't very different from a boardinghouse. I believe I could make it successful."

"Considering your accomplishments to date, I am not likely to disagree. Still, a hotel is a tremendous undertaking. And what of your restaurant? It would be foolish to kill the golden goose. You are one person, Katie. You cannot manage two businesses."

"I can if I move the restaurant to the St. Clair. The hotel has a central lobby. It also has a second, smaller lobby. Wasted space. I can move the restaurant into that space. Relocate it."

"The cost, Katie. Have you given any thought to the cost?"

"I've been lying awake nights, thinking about it.

421

Tom Jordan wants fifty thousand dollars to sell. In addition, there are the costs of relocation, of improvements to the hotel. And there's a ten-thousand-dollar mortgage outstanding."

William smiled, stroking his chin. "You have come a long way, Katie," he said. "I remember when you talked in hundreds of dollars. Now you are talking in thousands. *Many* thousands."

"I know. It scares me to think I'm being greedy. I know what happens to greedy people. They're punished."

"On the contrary. Greedy people seem to live long lives filled with riches. You must take my word." William laughed. "I am from a family of greedy people—pious, churchgoing, greedy people. . . . Tell me, is this Tom Jordan a friend?"

"Yes." Katie shrugged. "But he's a businessman first. I don't doubt he's trying to take advantage of me. I'm a woman."

"A shrewd woman, if I may say so. You are on to Mr. Jordan, and that is to the good. Fifty thousand dollars is an absurd price, even in these inflationary times. The St. Clair is hardly the Plaza. Then there is the mortgage, which further reduces the price. Lastly, I would insist upon seeing the books."

"I've seen the books, William. The St. Clair is earning a slight profit."

"You have seen *a* set of books. I'm not questioning your judgment. I'm merely suggesting there may be *another* set. One for the buyer; another for the seller. Such things occur. Business is business. Are we agreed so far?"

422

"Oh yes. I'm here to learn."

"It sounds to me as if you have already made up your mind about the St. Clair. I won't try to dissuade you. I will, however, ask the source of your financing. No bank would offer a loan of any size to a woman. It's preposterous."

"If reasonable terms can be arranged, I will need only a small loan, small enough for the bank to trust me." Katie smiled. She sat back, absently touching her wedding ring. "Years ago, Matt told me his properties would make us rich. I thought it was talk, silly talk at that. I never believed him. Now I see how wrong I was. The McVeys may not get rich, but we're through being poor. And it's all thanks to those properties. My restaurant is the best example. It was worthless when Matt bought it, and when I took it over. Today it's worth quite a lot."

"Because of your hard work, your vision."

"I'm not talking about the restaurant itself, William. I'm talking about the property, the site. Are you familiar with Lawrence and Company? I wasn't, until one of their representatives came to see me. They want to build a big apartment house on the site of my restaurant. They offered me five thousand dollars. I have a feeling they'll go higher."

"Ah, women's intuition again."

"Lawrence and Company has already bought the properties on either side of mine. It's to be a *very* big apartment house. Twenty-two stories."

"The task before us is clear," William replied, amused. "We must convince Lawrence and Company to raise their price and the Jordan family to lower theirs. Am I safe in assuming that is your plan?"

"Yes. Do you think we have a chance?"

"I am beginning to think nothing is impossible where you are concerned. My compliments, Katie McVey."

18

Katie was optimistic as the 1920's progressed. It was an optimistic time, for prosperity had returned and the mood of the nation was jaunty. Women shortened their skirts, displaying their long-hidden legs in sheer stockings often rolled below the knee. They plucked their eyebrows and rouged their cheeks. They wore lipstick and bobbed their hair. The more daring among them danced the tango and the Charleston and the Black Bottom.

Newspaper editorials decried the changes in fashions and manners but these editorials missed the point, which was that attitudes had changed. The war had given young people their first taste of freedom and the result was a lighthearted rebellion against the stuffy conventions of the past. Americans were ready to enjoy themselves, and now they made their own rules. In this heady atmosphere, the era of speakeasies and bootleggers began.

Prohibition became law in July of 1920. The Drys, claiming God and flag on their side, rejoiced. In Virginia, the Reverend Billy Sunday gleefully eulogized the demise of John Barleycorn with these words: "Good-bye, John. You were God's worst enemy. You were Hell's best friend. The reign of tears is over." In New York, the Anti-Saloon League urged everyone to "shake hands with Uncle Sam and board the water wagon."

Fervent supporters of Prohibition believed that the new law would cure America's social ills. Slums would be eliminated and unhappy marriages would be made happy. The unemployed would find jobs, disease would vanish, and cruelty would be pushed forever from the human heart. But the law that was to bring such blessings brought instead an explosion of lawlessness. Quite suddenly the country was overrun with bootleggers, moonshiners, hijackers, racketeers, and trigger men. Protecting them was a corrupt trail of police officials, judges, and politicians, a trail that reached into every city and town.

Bootlegging was an industry unto itself, worth millions. Gangsters who had once been allies soon splintered into rival factions, fighting each other for territories and for shipments. Raids on each other's warehouses were common, as were ambushes in the dead of night. It was a never-ending cycle of attack and retaliation. It was war, and the weapon was the tommy gun.

Hugh Gallagher had narrowly escaped an ambush in 1922. "The luck of the Irish," he had said, shrugging off his brush with death. But he had a score to settle, and it was settled the following week. "Gangland Massacre," the headlines read.

Now Hugh sauntered about Katie's outer office, flipping a coin in the air. He wore a dark suit, a white shirt, and a plain, dark tie. His hat was pulled low on his forehead, gangster style. He was thirty-two years old, though his hard, icy gaze made him seem older. "What's taking so long, girlie?" he asked Katie's secretary. "I been here ten minutes already."

"I'm sorry. Mrs. McVey is a little behind schedule . . . oh, there's the buzzer. You may go inside. It's that door—"

"Yeah, I know which door it is. Thanks, girlie." Hugh entered Katie's office. He removed his hat and tossed it aside. "Look at you." He grinned. "The big shot hotel owner."

Katie rose. She went to her brother, embracing him, then drew back. "My God, did you bring a *gun* here?"

"It goes where I go," Hugh said, patting his jacket. "I got the right to defend myself."

"From me?"

"C'mon, Katie, you know what I mean. It's no secret I got enemies. I'm in what you might call a rough line of work." Hugh sat down. "I see you finally finished your office. Nice."

"Thank you." Katie had decorated her office herself, using soft blues and greens and touches of ivory. The sofas and chairs were silk, and the desk and cabinets antique rosewood. Flowers were arranged in cut-crystal vases and bowls. A single painting adorned the walls, a large, framed watercolor of the ocean at twilight. "I spent too much money."

"Who says? You're rolling in dough."

"Am I?" Katie laughed. "That's news to me."

"You're doing great. I can figure the take of every hotel and restaurant on the East Side. It's my business."

"I don't want to discuss your *business*. We agreed."

"Yeah, well, I'm breaking the agreement this one time. Some guys will be coming here, Katie. The idea is to get you to buy their booze. It's okay stuff, but my stuff is better. The McCoy, from Canada."

"I don't care if it's from the moon. I closed the bar the day Prohibition began. It will stay closed until the law is changed, not because I'm so moral, but because I don't need any trouble. I don't need government agents sniffing around, and I certainly don't need bootleggers coming and going." Katie paused. She sighed, looking into Hugh's icy blue eyes. "There are two bellhops on my staff who sneak liquor to certain guests. I know all about it. As long as they're discreet, I have no objections. That's the reality of the hotel business. But under *no* circumstances will I deal with bootleggers. The St. Clair will not deal with bootleggers."

"Geez, I guess I should be grateful you let me through the door."

"You're my brother, and I love you, Hugh. I know the good in you. I also know the bad. I try not to think about it. I'd go crazy if I did. My heart breaks whenever I read about *Swag* Gallagher and his thugs. All I can remember is the little boy who bought me violet hand lotion, the little boy who was always sticking up for his sister." Katie sighed again, dabbing her handkerchief to her eyes. "I can't bear to think what's happened to you."

"Nothing's happened. I'm the same. I was never no angel. I went after what I wanted and anybody getting in my way was sorry they did. I'm still the same. There's big money out there, Katie. I'm grabbing my share. I'm not too particular how."

"Guns and killing, that's how. . . . Please, I can't talk about it."

"Prohibition's a dumb law. People want their booze. It's dumb to pass a law against what people want. Those clowns in Washington is just making guys like me rich."

"That's beside the point."

"It's the *whole* point. Money. You think there'd be guns and killing over a few bucks? It's millions, Katie. It's *raining* money. Twenty thousand speakeasies in New York alone, and new ones opening every day. That's Prohibition for you. So I'm getting my share. So what?"

"You're not getting your share here. Nor are your friends."

"Okay. The St. Clair is your place. It's your decision. Don't worry, I'll see you're protected."

"Protected?"

"C'mon, Katie. You say you read the papers. Do I have to tell you there's guys who don't like being turned down? You want to keep your place dry? Okay, but you'll need protection. This is 1923. Nobody's kidding around no more."

"I won't allow your thugs in my hotel."

"You won't see no thugs." Hugh grinned. "You won't see nothing out of the usual. I got my ways of handling situations."

Katie stared at the bulge beneath Hugh's jacket. She left her chair, walking aimlessly about the room. "We were expecting you and Meg for dinner last week," she said after a while. "Sean was there. He

429

was sorry you stayed away."

"You mean *Father* Sean. I still can't get over it. My kid brother a priest. The last time me and Sean met up I had to listen to a lecture. I don't need no lectures. And I don't need no fish eye from Ma. I stayed away on purpose. I told Meg she could go, but she felt uncomfortable. Ma treats her funny . . . how do you stand the old biddy?"

"Oh, Mama's not so bad. She has a new hobby now," Katie said, chuckling. "The stock market. Every morning she's hunched over the dining room table, reading the financial papers and making notes. She even has her own broker!"

"Yeah? What's she paying him with? Did she finally find gold in the streets?"

"Mama has a bank account and a monthly allowance. Stop frowning, Hugh. It was the least I could do for her. She's been a great help. I couldn't go to work if I didn't have Mama taking care of things at home. Patrick and Rory are practically grown, but Matthew is only six."

"I wouldn't know. You send the kid out when I'm coming by. Like I'd hurt him or something."

"It's not that. I just don't want him getting wrong ideas. Little boys are impressionable. Your . . . business . . . seems very exciting to him. One long game of cops and robbers."

"Well, I guess I go along with you there. It's no game." Hugh's eyes narrowed on his sister. "Sit down, Katie. What are you pacing around for? You should relax, take things easy now. You got a good business, a lot of dough."

"And a lot of expenses. Don't forget I have a large payroll to meet every week, Hugh. Clerks, chamber-

maids, porters, not to mention cooks and w̶ ̶ ̶ ̶ ̶ ̶ ̶
have laundry bills and plumbing bills. I̶ ̶ ̶ ̶ ̶ ̶
three sons in private school. Come fall, Pat̶ ̶ ̶ ̶ ̶
at Yale. I assure you Yale isn't cheap."

"Is that why you're killing yourself? So your kids can go to some high hat school?"

"You sound like Mama."

"Maybe the old biddy's right, once in her life. I can see you're nervous. You're tired, Katie. You been working for twenty years. Slaving. Twelve hours a day and no vacation. Sure, your kids get their private school. Ma gets her bank account. What do you get besides worries?"

Katie was silent, though recently she had begun to ask hersef the same question. Lying in her bed at night she had begun to wonder about her life. She took pride in her business and the possessions that flowed from it—a fine apartment in Murray Hill, a shiny new car, a closet brimming with clothes—but such possessions had done little to fill the void she felt. It was loneliness, she knew, a sense of isolation that chilled her very soul. "We can't have everything." She shrugged. "My life isn't perfect, but it's a thousand times better than it was. When I think how poor we were, and not that long ago, either. You won't hear me complaining, Hugh. So many girls I went to school with are still in Hell's Kitchen. They're taking in laundry or sewing to make ends meet. Their children are going around in rags, just as we did. What do I have to complain about?"

"Are you happy?"

"Sean says to be happy is to be at peace with yourself."

"Yeah, priests is always saying things like that. I'm

431

..ng what you say."

"I don't know." Katie laughed. She sank onto the sofa, stretching her arms over her head. "I'm at peace with myself. If that's the measure, I'm happy. If you set more worldly standards, then I'm not so certain. My children make me happy. My hotel makes me happy. My brand new dress makes me happy," she said, smoothing the rich jade silk. "During the summer I grew pansies in a window box. They made me happy."

"C'mon, Katie. I'm not talking about dresses and flowers. I'm talking about *you.* Meg thinks you should find a nice guy and get married again. It wouldn't be hard, with your looks—your looks and your money."

"Thanks."

"Patrick's going away to college soon. Next it'll be Rory. Before you know it, it'll be Matthew. You want to spend the rest of your life with Ma? You'll be two sour old ladies comparing your aches and pains."

"I'm not an old lady yet."

"Time goes quick. You're no kid either. You're thirty-three."

"What a wonderful conversation this is! If you're trying to cheer me up, you're doing a rotten job."

"Maybe. But maybe I'm making sense." Hugh glanced at his heavy gold wristwatch. "Well, I got things to do. I got business," he said, rising. "You can still change your mind about the booze."

"Sorry."

"Okay. Win some, lose some. I'll see nobody bothers you."

Katie went to her brother, linking her arm in his. "You can't help sticking up for me, can you? Even after all these years. I'm touched. I really am."

"Just don't start bawling." Hugh grinned. "The least little thing and women start bawling."

"I'll try to control myself. Here's your hat."

"Here's your hat, what's your hurry. Are you giving me the bum's rush?"

"You said you had business."

"Yeah."

Katie walked Hugh through her outer office and into the lobby. The staff, clerks, and bellhops watched curiously, for they had all read about the famous gangster, Swag Gallagher. Katie felt their stares. She squared her shoulders and continued walking. "Promise you'll come to dinner soon," she said as they reached the door. "I'll telephone Meg and set a date. We'll have a quiet family evening."

"Only if you send Ma to the movies. So long, Katie. Think over what I told you. Find a nice guy before it's too late."

Katie did not reply. She waited until Hugh had gone and then turned away, retracing her steps across the lobby. It was a handsome lobby, with oak wainscotting, leather club chairs, and polished tables upon which sat bowls of fresh flowers. To the left was the reception desk; opposite was a bank of elevators leading to the St. Clair's three hundred rooms.

Katie had rejected advice to expand her hotel, for she was comfortable with its small, hospitable size, its old-fashioned atmosphere. "You're always building nests," Maeve had chided, and now Katie

433

admitted that that was true. A small, single figure in the vastness of the lobby, she thought to herself, Everyone says I've come such a long way, but I'm still a woman alone. I have my children. I have success . . . but it isn't enough. Dear God, *why* isn't it enough? What is this yearning deep within me?

"Mrs. McVey, I have quite a few messages here."

"What? Oh, I'm sorry," Katie said, glancing at her secretary. "Hold my messages for now. My calls also. I don't want to be disturbed."

"Are you all right, Mrs. McVey? You look . . . tired."

"Tired? Tired is hardly the word."

Katie attended Patrick's high school graduation in June. She cried all through his valedictory address, afterward giving him the keys to a sleek white roadster. "Well, that's your first son grown," Maeve said. But Katie needed no reminders. She watched her firstborn drive away with his friends and thought her heart would break.

Patrick went off to Yale in September and, that same month, Ben Rossi was married. His bride was William Streeter's granddaughter, Amy, a charming young woman of twenty-two. The splendid ceremony at St. James Episcopal Church was followed by an even more splendid ceremony at the Streeter estate in Hyde Park. There Katie passed amongst the elegant, bejeweled guests and knew that yet another chapter in her life had ended. "I'm crying two kinds of tears today," she said to Ben. "All the happy tears are for you. It certainly took you long enough to get married."

"I wanted to be sure."

"You can be very sure. Amy is wonderful!"

"Yes, she is," Ben agreed with a smile. "She doesn't seem to mind the difference in our ages. I confess it gave me pause. Fifteen years is not a *small* difference, but Amy told me to stop counting our years and start counting our blessings."

"She's absolutely right. Face it, Ben, you married a sensible woman. There's a lot of William in her. And speaking of William, I've never seen him so pleased. He's beaming."

"William encouraged the marriage from the beginning. He was the only one. The other Streeters were shocked, to put it mildly. They threatened Amy with the most dire consequences. She held her ground. Of course I had to make a few gestures in the family's direction. Officially I'm an Episcopalian now, and a Republican. I can imagine what Papa would say, if he were alive."

"You have your own life to live. You and Amy."

"Amy wasn't my first love." Ben smiled, taking Katie's hand. "But she'll be my last. I suppose that's what matters."

"Yes."

"Tell me about your tears, Katie. Tell me about your *unhappy* tears."

"Oh, they're because I'm feeling old and tired and . . . spent. Here I am in a mansion, surrounded by the cream of society . . . and I don't care. I don't care about anything any more. I can't explain it. Sometimes I think I need a good, swift kick."

"You need a rest. You're exhausted."

"Perhaps." Katie nodded. She sipped her champagne, staring through the French doors to the vast, terraced lawns beyond. "That's why I've decided to take a vacation. William was able to rent a house for me on Long Island. A cottage, he said. It's near the ocean." Katie's eyes seemed to brighten. She turned and looked at Ben. "I love the ocean. Maybe I'll stay in my little cottage forever."

"You are far too beautiful to become a recluse. It would be a terrible waste."

"Well, maybe I'll find a beachcomber to keep me company . . . to enchant me with tales of the sea. I'm joking, Ben." Katie laughed, seeing his quizzical expression. "Pay no attention. The champagne's gone to my head."

"Has it? Or are you really dreaming of beachcombers? I wish you'd dream of stockbrokers instead. Mark Ridgeway, for example. He's had his eye on you all day. He and a dozen other eligible men in this room."

"Are you still worrying about my future? I'm not as helpless as I look. I'm Maeve Gallagher's daughter, and Gallagher women are strong. It's our heritage, so to speak. Our fate. Like it or not, we must always be strong."

"You sound bitter."

"Do I? Forgive me. I'm tired, and I've had four glasses of champagne. I think it's time I had a walk to clear my muddled head."

"I'll walk with you."

"Certainly not! Today is your wedding day, Ben Rossi. You stay right here and enjoy yourself. Have you forgotten your lovely bride?"

"My lovely bride has six hundred guests to see to. Amy was born to these social rituals. She's very good at them. I, on the other hand, am no good at all. I just smile and try to keep out of everyone's way."

"But you're missing the party."

"In the last month alone I've attended three engagement parties, two dinners, and two dinner dances. I just smiled and tried to be unobtrusive. Oddly enough, that's all that was expected of me. Men are only window dressing at these affairs."

"Ah, the world of high society."

"I grew up thinking I would marry a poor girl from Mulberry Street. Life plays tricks."

"Ada used to say that."

"I beg your pardon?"

"Oh, it isn't important." Katie leaned close to Ben, kissing his cheek. "I'm delighted for you and Amy." She smiled. "I wish you both all the happiness there is, and all the love. You were right, Ben. First or last, love is what matters."

Love was far from Katie's mind as she set off on vacation. She wanted only to rest, to lay work and worries aside for a few weeks. "Perhaps I'm being selfish," she said to a skeptical Maeve, "but I need this time away."

"You'll miss your boys."

"Of course I will. And I hope they'll miss me. Meanwhile, they'll be in your competent hands."

"You'll miss your work."

"I doubt it, Mama. The hotel is running smoothly. If there are any problems, my assistant manager will deal with them. He too is very competent."

"Aye, he should be, for what you pay him. What will you do out there all by yourself?"

"Relax. Read. Take walks along the beach. Sleep. I plan to curl up in my little cottage and sleep and sleep and sleep."

Katie was astonished to discover that her "little cottage" was, in fact, an airy, three story house with beamed ceilings, planked wood floors, braided rugs, and stone fireplaces. There was a wine closet and a fully stocked pantry. At the front of the house was a screened sun porch; at the rear were twin glass doors opening on a path to the ocean. It was the kind of house Katie had always dreamed about, warm and sheltering. The sound of the ocean lulled her to sleep each night. Each morning she awoke to a sunrise so beautiful that tears misted her eyes.

Katie's greatest joy was the beach. She strolled the pale sands, breathing deeply of the fresh autumn air. When she tired, she sat atop a boulder, content to watch the ocean and the gulls who soared and dived just above the waves. She picnicked at the ocean's edge, collected shells and driftwood, and spent one morning building an elaborate sand castle, all turrets and balconies and tiny windows. I can be as silly as I please, she thought. There's nobody to see me. There's nobody around for miles and miles.

But that was not exactly true. Katie had been at the beach almost a week when she was surprised by a visitor, a big floppy-eared dog. He bounded along the beach, tail wagging, and planted his sandy paws on Katie's shoulders. "Well, hello there," she said with a laugh. "Where did you come from? What a cute fellow you are." She petted his silky head, laughing again. "I hope you aren't lost."

"My dog likes to go off on his own," a male voice said. "I'm sorry if he frightened you."

Katie turned quickly to see a lean, muscular man with coal-black hair and brooding green eyes the color of the winter sea. He wore a fisherman's knit sweater and twill pants frayed at the knees and cuffs. A tool box was clasped in his hands; strong, powerful hands. "No," she said. "No, I wasn't frightened. He's a sweet dog. I . . . I thought I was alone out here."

"You are. We're from the house past the other side of the point. About four miles. There isn't a soul between here and there. I'm Josh Thurston."

"Katie McVey."

"You must be renting the Winslow cottage."

"Yes, but it's hardly a cottage."

"That's the local term. Two rooms or twenty; it makes no difference. Is something wrong?"

"Wrong?" Katie blushed, for she realized she had been staring, dazzled by Josh Thurston's rugged handsomeness, his clipped and direct manner of speech. "It's . . . It's all the . . . fresh air," she stammered. "I'm not used to it. I get light-headed."

"You're a city girl."

"I wish I weren't. I'd give anything to live out here." Katie's blush darkened. She lowered her eyes, scuffing at the sand with her shoe. "It's a marvelous place."

"Lonely."

"The city is lonely too."

Josh Thurston's gaze was steady on Katie. He watched the wind catch her golden hair, blowing it about her face. He watched the color rise in her cheeks. "You're very beautiful," he said. "You shouldn't be lonely."

Katie's lips parted. Her heart began to race and she took a step backward, shaken by feelings she could not explain. I'm behaving like a fool, she thought. I'm a grown woman, but I'm behaving like a giddy, tongue-tied schoolgirl.

"I've embarrassed you." Josh Thurston smiled, his gaze roaming once more over Katie. "Sorry. I spoke without thinking. I do that often, or so I'm told. My dog doesn't mind. People are another matter."

Katie bent, absently smoothing the dog's shaggy coat. "What's his name?" she asked.

"Hobo. He's really Hobo III. My first dog was a stray I found on the road. A hobo. It was years ago. I found this fellow at the pound. He was the runt of the litter. Look at him now."

"He knows you're talking about him. His tail is wagging."

"He knows more than that. He knows it's time to eat. Are you hungry, boy?" As if in reply, Hobo jumped up, barking and tossing his head. "There." Josh Thurston laughed "I said the magic word. . . . We'll be on our way home, Mrs. McVey. I hope you enjoy your stay. I hope the weather holds."

"Please call me Katie."

"Katie then. We'll try not to trample your sand castles."

"You saw them! I can imagine what you must think. I *am* embarrassed now."

"Why?"

"Sand castles are for children."

440

"Is that a rule?"

Katie lifted her head, smiling shyly. "No, I suppose not."

With a wave, Josh Thurston started off down the beach. He was a tall man, and his stride was long. Hobo kept pace, scampering across the dunes, leaping at the wind. Katie was sorry to see them go She felt a sudden, inexplicable urge to call them back. "Don't be a fool," she murmured, but in vain, for the next moment found her running along the beach. "Mr. Thurston," she shouted over the roar of ocean and wind. "Mr. Thurston, wait." Sand flew into her eyes, into her mouth, and still she ran. "Mr. Thurston? Hobo?"

The dog heard his name. He flung himself around, galloping in Katie's direction. She gasped as two big paws struck her shoulders. Laughing, she fell to her knees. "Oh, you're so strong, Hobo," she said, falling face down on the sand.

"Hobo!" Josh Thurston called. "Hobo!" He rushed to Katie's side, pushing the exuberant dog away. "Are you all right? Did he hurt you? I'm very sorry, Katie. He thought it was a game. Are you all right? Here, let me help you."

"It's my fault. Don't worry. I'm fine. *Oh*!" Katie winced, trying to stand. "Maybe I'm not. I'm afraid I'll need your help after all. I think I've hurt my ankle."

"You cut it on those shells when you fell. I've had cuts like that myself. You'll feel some soreness tonight, but it will be gone by morning. Can you walk?"

"I can hobble home, if you'll help."

Josh Thurston lifted Katie into his arms. "I'll take you home," he said. "There's no use struggling. It's settled. I'll explain the circumstances to your husband. Is he the jealous sort?"

"My husband? I'm not married. I mean I'm a widow. The war . . ."

"You still wear your ring."

"Yes. I don't know why." And I don't know why I said that, thought Katie. She gazed at Josh Thurston. She felt the warmth of his arms and then the wild pounding of her own heart. "I'm sure I can walk now. It isn't far."

"Far enough. You're blushing again."

"I'm not myself today."

"Who are you?"

"That's a good question, Mr. Thurston."

"Josh."

"Josh," Katie whispered.

It was evening and a fire blazed in the stone hearth. Katie lay on a white linen couch, her sore ankle bandaged and propped upon silken pillows. She was so quiet she hardly seemed to move, to breathe. Firelight reflected on her cheeks, and it seemed a reflection cast on polished ivory.

"A penny for your thoughts." Josh smiled, entering the room. Katie raised her hand toward the wide glass doors. Just beyond, silver-tipped waves lapped the shore and a lone gull swooped low, moonlight dancing on his wings. "The ocean," she replied. "I could watch it forever."

"There's a storm brewing. Listen to the wind."

"Perhaps . . . Perhaps you should be going. Your family will worry."

Josh strode to the fireplace. He took the poker, stirring the flames until they roared and rose up the chimney in a rush of blinding reds and yellows. "I have no family," he said. It was a simple statement, yet is was filled with anguish, the same anguish Katie had once or twice glimpsed in his eyes. "Hobo is my family. . . . He's sleeping off his dinner in your kitchen, by the way. Snug on the hearth rug."

"I wonder what people mean when they talk about a dog's life. Romping on the beach all day. Curling up on the hearth at day's end. What more could anyone ask?"

"That depends. Ordinary country pleasures appeal to city people, in the beginning. They soon tire of them."

"You didn't. You're from the city, Josh. I can tell."

"Can you?"

"I think you probably came here to escape a life you disliked. Sometimes you remember that life and you're sad. I see it in your eyes. You were fortunate to be able to start all over."

Josh did not answer immediately. He turned, stretching his powerful hands to the fire. "What makes you so certain I've started all over?"

"Your tool box. They're carpenter's tools. I don't know what you were in the city, but you're a carpenter now, aren't you?"

"I've always enjoyed building things, even as a boy. My father had other ideas. He was a man of firm convictions."

"I'm sorry. I have no right to pry. I didn't mean to.

I'm ashamed of myself. It's been such a . . . strange day."

"Strange?"

Katie glanced away. Her pulse quickened, for she was remembering Josh's strong arms around her, the touch of his hand when he had bandaged her ankle. She could not know that he, too, was remembering. "You were very kind to stay with me," she said in a small, breathless voice. "I feel much better now."

"Do you?"

"Oh yes, much."

Josh walked to the couch. He dropped to Katie's side, stroking her thick golden hair. "Are you asking me to leave?"

"It's . . . getting late."

Josh's hand moved to Katie's brow, to her cheek, to the smooth, pale curve of her neck. "Are you asking me to leave?"

"We're strangers. We don't—" But Katie said no more, for Josh was kissing her lips. An exquisite thrill ran through her awakened body. "Josh," she whispered. "Josh."

"I'm going to make love to you. You're going to make love to me," Josh murmured, opening the buttons of Katie's blouse. He undressed her, slowly, gently, brushing his mouth against her naked flesh. He took her full breasts in his hands, kissing them again and again until she cried out. "You're so beautiful, Katie. My beautiful, beautiful Katie." He caressed her thighs, the sweet darkness between her long legs. "My beautiful, beautiful Katie," he whispered, sweeping her into his arms.

Josh carried Katie to the bedroom, and there, as

lightning struck the sky, they lay together, seeking, demanding. A clock chimed the hour, and somewhere in the distance a bird called, but the lovers heard only their own cries. They knew only their own great and joyous passion.

A soft, misty rain was falling when Katie awoke the next morning. She smiled, stretching lazily, and then turned on her side. She reached out her arms, but Josh was not there. Atop his pillow sat a little bouquet of wildflowers and a note. *I love you*, read the bold, black scrawl. "He loves me." She sighed, hugging herself.

Katie leapt from the bed. She ran to the window and threw it open, laughing as raindrops sprayed her face. "He loves me," she called to the deserted beach. "Josh Thurston loves me." She was halfway out of the room before she remembered she was naked. "What would Mama think of me now!" she said and laughed again.

The rain did not keep Katie indoors. Wearing a heavy sweater and an old skirt, she strolled her accustomed route along the shore. She stopped often, scanning the horizon for Josh, for the big, floppy-eared dog who had inadvertently brought such happiness to her life. It was late afternoon when Josh appeared, a tall, dark figure at the end of the beach. "Josh," Katie shouted. "Josh." She hurried toward him, running into his arms. "I missed you," she said, ruffling his tousled hair. "So very much."

"I missed you too, my darling. How are you?"

"I'm wonderful!"

"You certainly are." Josh held Katie close. "I do love you. And how wonderful it feels!"

Oblivious to the rain, to the crashing waves, Katie and Josh fell to the sand. Soon their clothes were tossed aside and their bodies pressed together. "My darling," Josh murmured. "My beautiful darling."

"I want to know everything about you," Josh said. "Everything, from the day you were born to the day we met."

"Goodness! All that?"

"All that and more. What's your favorite color?"

"Green."

"Ah, the color of your eyes."

"The color of *your* eyes."

Josh smiled. He stirred the fire and then sat down next to Katie, taking her hand. "What do you do with yourself in the city? Do you work?"

"My husband left me some properties. I manage them." Katie sipped her brandy. She was quiet, considering her answer to Josh's question. It was not a lie, but it was not the whole truth either, and she wondered at her reticence. I'm afraid of scaring him, she thought. He leads a simple life now, and if he knew I owned the St. Clair Hotel . . . I can't tell him. Not yet. "I have a decent income." She shrugged. "I also have three sons."

"Handsome sons. I saw their pictures in the bedroom."

"Those were taken a few years ago. Patrick began college this year."

"College? You must have been ten when you married."

"Fifteen. I was the hired girl at a boardinghouse. Ada McVey's boardinghouse for theatricals. Matt was Ada's nephew. We met there and lived there after we were married."

A deep frown crossed Josh's brow. "My poor darling," he said. "Fifteen? You were only a child."

"No, not a child. I'd already been working for two years." Katie rested her head on Josh's broad shoulder. "We needed the money. Everybody in Hell's Kitchen needed money. I was fortunate to get out. Most of the girls I grew up with are still there, still fighting to put food on the table. I feel guilty sometimes."

"You shouldn't."

"They're still in Hell's Kitchen. Here I am in Southampton. We started out in the same place, but now we're worlds apart. I can't help feeling guilty . . . oh, Josh, life is very complicated."

"It doesn't seem complicated when we're together, holding each other. We must stay together always, my darling. We must find a way."

Katie glanced up. She saw the troubled, faraway look in Josh's eyes. "What's wrong? Are you remembering something sad?"

"Yes, I suppose I am."

"You're not ready to talk about it. You will be, one day. And I'll be here to listen."

I wish I could believe that, thought Josh. I would sell my soul to believe that. "I don't want to lose you, Katie," he said softly. "I waited all my life to find

447

you. All those terrible, empty years."

"You won't lose me. I won't let you. There are so many things I don't know about you, Josh. But there are things you don't know about me. Have you ever heard of Hugh Gallagher?"

"Hugh Gallagher? I've heard of Swag Gallagher, the gangster."

"He's my brother. My other brother is a priest in Buffalo."

"Swag Gallagher is your brother?"

"Yes. Sean is the priest."

"A gangster and a priest?"

"It's true, Josh. Does it . . . make any difference in the way you feel?"

"Darling, I wouldn't care if your brother were Jack the Ripper. I wouldn't care if *you* were Jack the Ripper. I love you."

"Oh," Katie said and released a sigh, relieved. "I was praying you'd say that. You'll never know how worried I was. . . . You deserve a reward." She laughed. "I'm going to fix you a special dinner. Cheese souffle, salad vinaigrette, and brandy pudding."

"Later." Josh slipped his hands beneath Katie's sweater, fondling her bare breasts. "Much later."

During the next week Katie and Josh lived a romantic dream. They made love every night, every day. They took moonlit walks on the beach. They rode a tandem through tiny Southampton village, Hobo trotting happily alongside. They sat by the fire and drank champagne. Lying in each other's arms,

448

they read the sonnets of Shakespeare and Browning. At the end of their first week together, Josh gave Katie a delicate antique locket that had belonged to his grandmother. "For my darling," he said, placing it about her neck.

Now, on a gray and foggy Tuesday morning, Katie sat in the kitchen drinking a cup of tea. She touched her hand to the locket and smiled. She was still smiling when a knock came at the door. She sprang up eagerly, gliding across the tiled floor. "Josh, you're early," she cried, her smile becoming more radiant. "What a wonderful surprise!"

"Good morning, darling."

"What's wrong?" Katie asked, seized by a sudden, nameless fear. She saw that Josh's face was drawn, his gaze dark and despairing. "Are you ill? Come sit down. I have tea ready."

Josh closed the door. He walked to a chair, standing behind it. "I had a telephone call," he said in a ragged voice. "I have to go away for a few days. To Connecticut."

"Is it a carpentry job?"

"It's . . . a personal matter."

"Josh, you're scaring me. What's *wrong*?"

"I'm leaving this morning."

"Please answer me. Tell me what's wrong."

Josh passed his hand over his ashen face. He looked at Katie, at the woman he loved, and the misery in his eyes deepened. "I don't want to lose you," he said, and it was a fervent plea.

"Lose me? You won't lose me. I promise. Whatever it is—"

"You don't understand, Katie. You know me so

well, but there are . . . things . . . you don't know. About my life. My life before I met you. *Existence* is a better word. I didn't really have a life before I met you."

"I know you were unhappy."

"Unhappy!"

Katie heard Josh's bitter laugh. She saw his hands clench, as if in some terrible pain, and she was newly frightened. "The past doesn't matter. It can't hurt us, not any more. Don't you see, Josh? We have each other now. We can start—"

"I'm married, Katie."

"What did you say?"

"I'm married."

"Married?"

"Yes."

Katie fumbled for a chair. She sank into it, sitting very still. "Married," she said dully. "You told me you had no family. You told me . . . oh, my God."

"I told you the truth." Josh bent his head, struggling against the sickness he felt, the torment. "My wife and I have not lived together in many years. It's a marriage on paper only. But there are . . . circumstances which make divorce impossible."

"So you have your little flings instead."

"You mustn't think that. I love you with all my heart and soul." Josh's voice caught. He was silent a moment. "I was afraid of losing you," he said when he was able to speak. "My life is nothing without you. *Nothing*."

All the light had gone from Katie's eyes. Her face was white and stricken. Once or twice she lifted her hand, only to let it fall limply to the table.

Josh knew that Katie's pain was as great as his own. He reached to comfort her but she shrank away, and that single gesture was a knife tearing at his heart. "Please let me explain," he said brokenly. "My marriage—"

"No, I don't want to hear. I can't."

"I can't leave until you understand. I love you, my darling Katie. I won't give you up. I'll never give you up. Never in this world."

"We'll . . . talk about it when you . . . return. I need to be alone now. I need . . . time." But Katie could not resist Josh's outstretched arms. She rose unsteadily, falling into them. "Oh, Josh," she cried. "Josh."

"We'll find a way, my darling. I promise you we'll find a way." They clung together, two tortured people so desperately in love. Moments passed and their arms held fast. "I won't be away long," Josh said. "Three days at most. I'll telephone you every day, every hour if you want."

Katie gazed into the eyes of her beloved, slowly shaking her head. "We'll talk when you return. There's a lot to say, Josh. We can't say it on the telephone."

"Shall I leave Hobo with you?"

"I'd really like to be alone."

Josh kissed Katie's hair, her eyes, her lips. "I can't bear to go. I can't bear to be apart from you. I love you, my darling."

"I love you."

"I wouldn't go if I didn't have to. You must believe me."

"I do." There were tears in Katie's eyes as she

walked Josh to the door. They kissed again, her tears mingling with his. "On your way," she said finally, trying to smile.

"Friday. I'll see you Friday, my darling."

"Yes . . . Friday."

Katie watched Josh disappear into the fog. She watched for a long time and then closed the door, leaning against it. She touched her locket and the tears began again. She sobbed all through the endless morning, stumbling like a sleepwalker from room to room. "*Josh*," she cried. "Oh, Josh."

"New York City?" the conductor asked, taking Katie's bags.

"Yes."

"Lots of seats. You can have your pick."

"Thank you." Katie dropped, exhausted, into the nearest seat. She turned her head to the train window, closing her eyes. I've had a week of perfect happiness, she told herself. I must live on it for the rest of my life.

19

It was a brisk autumn evening in the city. The sky was clear and filled with stars, but Katie did not notice, for her mind and heart were still in Southampton. Even now, as the taxicab neared Murray Hill, she could see ocean and sand and a dark, handsome man running toward her. "Josh," she murmured.

"You say something, lady?"

"What? No, I'm sorry. I was talking to myself." Katie took a square silver compact from her purse. She dabbed a bit of powder on her nose, though she knew cosmetics could do little to help her haggard appearance, her swollen, red-rimmed eyes. Mama will have a hundred questions, she thought. And so will Rory. Tomorrow at the hotel there will be more questions. I can't face it. I just can't. "Driver, I've changed my plans. I want to go to Grand Central Terminal instead."

"You say Grand Central?"

"That's right."

"Okay." The driver shrugged, making an abrupt turn. "You're paying. If you say Grand Central,

Grand Central it is."

Katie sat back. She glanced at her watch and then fished around in her purse until she found her address book. She looked through the listings, pausing when she came to the listing for Jack Snow. Jack's three thousand miles away, she mused. That should be far enough. . . . Dear God, let it be far enough. Let me forget.

"Here you are, lady. Grand Central. I'll get your bags."

Katie gave the driver a five-dollar bill. "Keep the change," she said.

"Hey *thanks*, lady. I hope you have a good trip . . . you didn't change your plans again, did you? I mean, if you did, my cab is your cab."

Katie smiled. She called a redcap over, following him into the cavernous train terminal. "I want to go to California," she said. "Los Angeles."

"Yes, ma'am. The seven-thirty westbound is boarding now on track ten. I'll get you there in time."

"But I haven't a ticket."

"Don't you worry about that, ma'am. You can buy your ticket from the conductor. Lots of folks do, when they're hurrying. Seems like everybody's hurrying these days. Don't you worry, ma'am. I'll get you there. I'm taking a shortcut."

The shortcut led Katie down two flights of stairs, along a darkened platform, and through several gates. Hastily she thrust some bills at the redcap, then jumped aboard the train just as it was pulling out. "I hope this is the right train," she gasped, catching her breath. "California?"

"It's the right train. First stop is Chicago."

454

Katie remained in her compartment all the way to Chicago. The porter brought her meals, meals she scarcely touched. Hour after hour she sat by the window and watched the shifting landscape. Her face was impassive, though tears rolled unchecked down her cheeks. "Josh," she murmured over and over, a litany of despair.

There was a lengthy delay in Chicago, and Katie spent the time making telephone calls. She spoke first to Maeve, hanging up before the inevitable argument could begin. She spoke to her assistant at the St. Clair and to Ben Rossi. She made her last call to Jack Snow. "It took a while," she said, "but I'm accepting your invitation."

Katie's spirits were low as she stepped off the train in Los Angeles. She was tired from her trip, from nights without sleep, and she felt oppressed by the sudden, sultry heat. Her skin was damp, her wool dress sticking to her. Her brow, beneath her wilted hat, ran with perspiration. What have I done, she wondered miserably, shielding her eyes against the bright sun.

"Katie! Here I am, Katie!" Smiling, rotund Jack Snow rushed toward her, waving his arms. "Welcome to California," he cried, embracing his old friend. "I'm delighted to see you. If you aren't a sight for sore eyes!"

"Oh, I'm a sight all right. Hot and wrinkled and dripping wet."

"You won't need that," Jack laughed, plucking the hat from Katie's head. "Nor your gloves. Take 'em off. Relax. You're in California now. We have to get you some California clothes. And some Califor-

455

nia sunshine," he added, peering into her white face. "Are you okay?"

"It was a long trip. But never mind me. You look wonderful, Jack. You haven't changed a bit. No, I'm wrong. You have changed. You look years younger. How do you do it?"

"Well, you know I'm retired. *The Great Bank Caper* was our last picture, Lou's and mine. Let me tell you it's a great life. I play golf every day. I swim in my own pool I play a mean game of poker. The best thing I ever did was come out here. Maybe the best thing you ever did, too. The sun will perk you up in no time."

"There certainly is a lot of it."

"Not like the East. Freezing in winter. Fighting your way through the snow. None of that here. I wear my overcoat five or six times a year, tops. The ladies have their furs, but they're for show. You could wear a bathing suit almost year-round. It's a great life, Katie . . . you'll see. Wait'll you see my place. Mary's so proud. Come, I'll drive you home, and Mary will find you something to wear. Is that all the luggage you brought? Two small suitcases?"

"I really didn't expect to be here, Jack. It was a . . . last minute decision. I guess I needed to see a friendly face."

"Well"—Jack laughed merrily, picking up Katie's bags—"that's me. I made a fortune off this friendly kisser of mine. All those years in vaudeville. It was a living. But a few years in pictures and you live like a king. Want to be a movie star?" he asked with a wink. "I got connections and you got the looks."

"I'll leave it to Rory to be the movie star. He has

show business in his blood, or so he says."

"Still?"

"He's the *star* of his dramatics club at school. I want him to go on to college." Katie sighed. "I doubt he will. He has a mind of his own."

"Like his mother."

"I don't know. I haven't been very wise about my life."

Jack opened the car door, helping Katie inside. "Settle back and relax," he said. "Breathe the fresh air. Fresh air, sunshine, and plenty of good food. That's my prescription."

Katie smiled fondly at Jack. She leaned her head against the cushioned seat, sighing again. I'm here, she thought, but I feel no different. Josh. Oh, Josh.

"Do you want to talk about it, Katie? Who broke your heart?"

"I'm just tired."

"Life goes dark for a time. Then it goes bright again. The trick is to get through the dark part. You got friends to help you through. There's me and my Mary. There's Cornelius. You'll see him next week. We're throwing a big party in your honor. You're not in a party mood now, but that's now. A lot can happen in a week."

Tears stung Katie's eyes. "Yes, a lot can happen." She sniffled, turning her head away.

"Come in, come in." Mary Snow smiled, opening her motherly arms to Katie. "It's grand to see you again."

"And you, Mary. I'll try not to be a bother."

"A bother! You're welcome in our house any time. It's your home now too. I hope you're planning a long, long visit."

"Thank you. You're very kind."

"What's the matter, dear? You look shaky. I suppose my husband drove like a crazy man. He always does. Put him in that car, and he thinks he's in an airplane. See what you've done to the poor girl, Jack. Shame on you."

"None of that. I drove prim and proper, like a little old lady. Like *you* drive." Jack laughed. "Tell her, Katie. She won't believe me."

"It was a lovely drive." Katie nodded. "The palm trees and the . . . I'm sorry." She shrugged. "I'm not making much sense. To tell you the truth, I'm overwhelmed."

"But why, dear?"

"I didn't know you lived in such . . . splendor."

"It's home."

A smile touched Katie's lips, for *home* was a Moorish mansion set upon three acres of manicured lawns and gardens. The reception hall in which she stood was two stories high, with stained glass panels and floors of Spanish tile. Beyond the hall she could see an enormous sunken living room, all curved arches and balconies and wrought-iron chandeliers. "Does everyone in California live this way?" she asked.

"In Beverly Hills," Jack replied. "It's mostly movie people here. There are places bigger than this. Isn't that right, Mary?"

"Yes, that's right. We only have twenty-four rooms." Mary's soft blue eyes twinkled mischievously. "That's small, to some. Of course we have a croquet field out back, so it's all right. We can hold our heads up."

Jack slipped his arm about his wife. "Mary has her fun teasing newcomers," he said. "She loves it here all the same. And she can be as snooty as the rest of them, for all her plain ways."

"Only when somebody snoots me first, Jack Snow . . . but that's enough of that. Katie, I'll show you to your room. You'll want a nap after your long trip. Maxwell will fetch your bags."

"Maxwell?"

"The butler."

Katie laughed, despite herself. "How silly of me to ask."

"When we first moved to this house," Mary said, leading Katie up a winding, wrought-iron staircase, "I tried to do everything myself. Cleaning, cooking, gardening, everything. Well, I caught on soon enough. I telephoned one of them employment agencies and hired a staff. Why not? The money was rolling in. Jack's retired now, but he's got investments. The money's still rolling in."

"Do you ever feel . . . guilty?"

"I'm Irish, aren't I? With all our good luck, I keep waiting for lightning to strike us dead. But I make sure I do my good works. That helps."

"You're a nice woman, Mary. I can't begin to thank you for taking me into your home."

"It's your home now, dear. I want you to rest and get better."

"Oh, I'm fine."

Mary paused, her hand on the doorknob. She

looked at Katie. "You have a sorrow. I don't know what it is. A man, probably. Whatever it is, we're here to help. We've seen more of life than you have. We've had our sorrows. So if you want to talk, don't be shy."

Katie bent, hugging Mary. "You'll have me crying in a minute."

"No, you've done too much crying already." Mary opened the door. "You should be comfortable here," she said. "Let me show you around. This is your sitting room. Through that door is your bedroom, with bath and dressing room, of course."

"Of course." Katie glanced at the rose-sprigged wallpaper, the flounced chairs, gilded mirrors, and thick, creamy carpets. "It's charming."

"It's my granddaughter's suite, when she visits us. And it's a bit fussy. But it has something special. Come, I'll show you." Mary opened the bedroom door, pointing toward a wide, sunny balcony. "I think you'll like the view."

Katie stepped out onto the balcony. She gasped, for below was a magnificent garden massed with many hundreds of red and pink roses. A graveled path led to a gazebo and yet more roses, as far as the eye could see. "My God, how beautiful!" Katie exclaimed, inhaling the perfumed air.

"It's God's work." Mary chuckled. "God and two full-time gardeners. I had an idea you'd be pleased. The guest rooms in the south wing face the pool. This is prettier."

"I don't know what to say."

"Enjoy it, dear. I'll have tea sent up. Then you can nap. You'll find cooler clothes in the big closet there.

My granddaughter's about your size. Tomorrow we'll go shopping."

"Mary—"

"Not another word. You're here to rest and relax. Get started."

Mary left the room. Katie gazed once more at the garden, brushing away a tear. After some moments she came inside and stripped off her sodden wool dress, hurling it to the floor. She took a robe from the closet, running her hand along the rows of dresses and blouses and summery suits.

"Mrs. McVey?"

"Yes? Who's there?"

"It's Maxwell, the butler. I've brought tea, madam. May I enter?"

"Yes, certainly," Katie called, buttoning her robe.

Maxwell wheeled a serving cart into the room. A gleaming silver tea service sat atop the cart; on the lower shelf were Katie's bags. "The maid will be here soon to unpack your things," he said.

"That won't be necessary. I'd rather do it myself."

"As you wish, madam. Will you have your tea on the balcony?"

"Thank you."

Maxwell carried the tea tray outside. Deftly, he arranged little china plates and cups upon a round glass table. "The house telephone is beside your bed, madam, if you need anything."

"Thank you." Katie waited until Maxwell had gone and then sat down. She sipped her tea, nibbling at a chocolate cookie. The garden drew her restless gaze. She stood, walking to the latticed rail. A soft and perfumed breeze touched her bare arm. "*Josh,*" she cried, new tears welling in her eyes.

"Katie's sleeping," Mary said early the next afternoon. "There's no better medicine."

"Maybe." Jack shrugged. "I'm still worried. She didn't come down to dinner last night, or to breakfast this morning. Are you sure she's all right?"

"I looked in on her. She's dead to the world, poor girl. I'll wager this is the first sleep she's had in days. Let her be. Go on to your golf game. I'll see to Katie. Men are no good in these situations anyway, blustering and joking around."

"Who says?"

"I do, Jack Snow. Off with you now. Go play golf. That's what men are good at—games."

"You're in a mood today." Jack laughed, kissing his wife's cheek. "All men aren't scoundrels, you know."

"Not all. I was lucky. But that poor girl upstairs . . . well, what's done is done. We'll see Katie through. She's young. She'll get over it, I hope. Don't drive too fast, Jack."

"Like a little old lady."

Mary was smiling as Jack walked away. She tucked a book under her arm and wandered out to the pool. "Why, Katie," she said, surprised. "I thought you were sleeping. I told the staff to keep clear of your room. They didn't wake you, did they?"

"No. I slept for *twelve* hours. Enough is enough."

"How do you feel?"

"I'm fine, Mary. Really I am. I had a long sleep and

a long bubble bath. Maxwell just brought this wonderful lunch. I'm afraid I'm going to be quite spoiled when I leave here."

"Don't talk about leaving, dear. It's your vacation. Enjoy it. Let me have a look at you," Mary said, walking to Katie's chair. "The dark circles are gone." She nodded. "That's a start . . . but your eyes are so swollen. Did you cry yourself to sleep?"

"I wasn't allowed to cry when I was little," Katie replied with a faint smile. "I'm making up for lost time."

"A likely story."

"Will you join me, Mary? There's chicken and potato salad and strawberry tarts. I'll never be able to finish it all. Please."

"I don't mind if I do. How about some shopping after lunch?"

"I have my checkbook, not much cash."

"Oh, you needn't worry about that. I have charge accounts from one end of the town to the other. Jack says it's my reward for years of sewing my own clothes."

"You're very happy, you and Jack. I'm glad."

Mary took Katie's hand. "You'll be happy too, dear. There's an old Irish expression: The bigger the sorrow, the bigger the happiness to come."

"I love old Irish expressions." Katie sighed. She turned her head, watching the sunlight reflecting on the tiled pool. A soft breeze blew, now and again stirring the clear water. "I could get used to this life, Mary."

"I hope you do. Meanwhile, eat your lunch."

It was an hour later when the two women climbed

into Mary's bright yellow coupe and drove off. They spent the entire afternoon shopping, returning home with a mountain of packages. Katie bought lacy sundresses and off-the-shoulder blouses and a provocative evening gown of clinging black satin beaded at the hem. "I can't wear such a gown in public," Katie protested. But Mary waved her protests aside. "Don't you go to the movies?" she asked. "It's the fashion today. You'll be the star of my party."

Katie tried not to think about the approaching party. During the days she strolled through the vast gardens. She swam and learned to play croquet. In the evenings she dined with Mary and Jack on the patio, diverted by their accounts of the latest Hollywood scandals. She was pampered endlessly, for the servants seemed to anticipate her every wish. "I'm living a movie star's life," she reported in her daily telephone calls home. "It's all terribly glamorous." But as glamorous as life was, it did little to soothe her aching heart. There was no escape from the dark, handsome man who haunted her thoughts, her dreams.

"I'm going home tomorrow, Mary."

"Home! But you've only been here a week."

"A marvelous week. Now it's time to go home. I tried to run away . . . to leave my troubles behind me. I realize I can't. I must manage to live with them somehow. And I must do that at home, in New York. All vacations end, I have responsibilities."

"Katie, you said the hotel was in fine shape."

"I'm not talking about the hotel. I don't care about the hotel. I have two sons at home. I've been away from them long enough. I certainly can't miss

464

Matthew's seventh birthday. It's coming soon. I haven't even bought his presents yet."

"Tell Maeve to put him on the train. He'd love California. That's a *real* present."

Katie smiled. She sat down at her dressing table, brushing her sun-streaked golden hair. "He has school. Besides, if I brought Matthew out, I'd have to bring Rory, too. If I did, I'd never get him back to New York. No, it has to be this way, Mary. I'm so very grateful to you and Jack, but I must go. I'm staying for your party because I know how hard you worked. Tomorrow, I plan to be on the five o'clock train."

"Have you given any thought to moving here? Permanent?"

"Oh yes. I imagine everybody does. California has its charms, but I'm an easterner." Katie shrugged. "I like the change of seasons."

"What can I say to get you to reconsider?"

"Nothing." Katie rose. She went to Mary and kissed her wrinkled brow. "You're the sweetest woman in the world. You make me feel wanted. You make me feel . . . safe. I wish I could stay. I can't. It's impossible."

"I understand."

"Do you?"

"Well, I understand you have to find your own answers. One thing I'll say. You look a hundred times better than when you first came here. Your face isn't so drawn. There's color in your cheeks. I guess we did you some good, eh?"

"You saved my life. I'm serious, Mary. I needed a place to hide, a place where I could pull myself together. Most of all I needed friends."

"You'll always have friends here. Remember that. Now I'll let you get dressed." Mary glanced at the black satin gown lying on the bed. "You'll knock their eyes out," she said, chuckling as she closed the door.

Katie removed her robe and slipped the gown over her head. She blushed to see the deep V of the neckline; futilely tugged it upward. She rouged her lips and swept mascara onto her long, thick lashes. At the last, she brushed her hair in shimmering waves atop her head and secured it with jeweled combs borrowed from Mary.

"Are you decent?" Jack called.

"That's a matter of opinion."

"What?"

"Come in, Jack. I'm dressed. More or less."

"The guests are arriving. I thought I'd escort—Holy smoke! You're gorgeous, Katie! I'm wondering if you'll be safe. Maybe I should put a guard on you. An armed guard."

Katie's face burned. "I didn't want to buy this gown," she said. "Mary insisted."

"Hurray for Mary."

"You're teasing. I don't blame you."

"Teasing? Who's teasing? I meant it. You're *gorgeous*. If I was twenty years younger, and there was no Mary, I'd be after you myself. The way things are, I'll have to be content to escort you downstairs." Smiling, Jack offered his arm. "Ready?"

Katie touched the locket Josh had given her. "Ready."

Hollywood, in later years, would learn to take beauty for granted. Beautiful women from all over

America would flock to the movie colony until those who lived and worked there hardly noticed. But now, in the innocence of 1924, beauty was still given attention. Heads still turned, and certainly they turned as Katie descended the long black staircase. Conversations quieted, then stopped. Several gasps were heard. The startled onlookers did not see that Katie was trembling and unsure. They saw only the radiance of golden hair and ivory skin, the perfect curves of breast and waist and hip so fetchingly arrayed.

"You're a hit, Katie," Jack cried, whooping with laughter. "This is my discovery," he called to the crowd. "Katie McVey."

The guests, hundreds of them it seemed to Katie, surged forward. She was engulfed. Jack began the introductions, but there were too many names, too many faces, and she was silent, holding fast to his arm.

"Give the poor girl air," Mary said, opening a path through the crowd. "My goodness! Such a commotion! It's worse than the crazy fans at the premieres. Katie, come with me. Come, we'll get you some air."

"What was that all about?" Katie asked when they had walked a few steps away. "I was scared to death."

"You should be flattered. Of course you didn't see your entrance. I did. It was something. You took their breath away."

"It's this stupid gown."

"It's what's in the gown, more likely." Mary winked. "You were a vision, dear. And did you hear Jack saying you were his discovery? They believed him. They think you're a new movie star. The new *prize* in town."

"If this is what movie stars have to go through . . ."

"Well, it's not all bad. There are rewards." Mary laughed, glancing around her enormous living room. "And I always said if a person can face this crowd, a person can face anything."

"Yes."

"Come, the rest of the party is outside." Mary led Katie through the tall glass doors to the patio. "What do you think?"

"I'm speechless." Katie gasped, beholding a scene that looked to her like a movie set. There were many people milling about the grounds, the men in elegant evening dress, the women in gowns and furs and glittering jewels. Colored paper lanterns were strung in the trees, their lights reflecting on the pool and on fountains which spouted champagne. A dance floor stretched across the south lawn and at its edge was a twenty-six piece orchestra. There were huge striped tents presided over by armies of uniformed, gloved waiters. There were flowers everywhere and, near the pool, twin ice sculptures of Rayne and Snow in their trademark floppy hats. "I can't believe it, Mary! I simply can't believe it!"

"This is nothing. This is just an ordinary party, by Hollywood standards. See why I keep waiting for lightning to strike us dead? The biggest party I ever had back in Boston was eighteen people. It was family and it was Christmas." Mary shrugged, fingering her long ropes of pearls. "Let me introduce you to our guests. Who do you want to meet? There's Clara Bow over there."

"Clara Bow!" Katie turned, gaping into the

distance at the laughing, flame-haired actress. "Oh, she's lovely! Who's that man? I recognize—My God, it's Ramon Navarro! I saw him in *Scaramouche*!"

"Now you can see him in the flesh. You can meet him."

"No." Katie shook her head. "Give me time to get used to all this. I've known show people most of my life, but *these* people. . . . It's a little disconcerting."

"They're just people, only they're famous and they have lots of money."

"Is Cornelius O'Day here?"

"He's somewhere in the crowd. Let's take a look."

"Mary, I'd really like to wander around by myself. You don't mind, do you? I'd like to get my bearings."

"Sure, go ahead. It's your party. Enjoy yourself, dear."

Katie watched Mary walk away, a small woman in black silk and pearls, a flower in her graying hair. She smiled. After a moment or two she strolled toward the orchestra.

"Hey, beautiful," said a handsome young man. "Dance with me?"

"Later perhaps."

Katie repeated those words often as the evening wore on, for she had no desire to dance. She strolled amongst the guests, staring at faces familiar to her and to millions of moviegoers. She drank champagne. She had her first taste of caviar. She tapped her foot to the strains of "Yes, We Have No Bananas." Cheerfully, she fended off the occasional pinch, the occasional hand brushing her breasts. This is Hollywood, after all, she thought; it's another world.

"Please," a soft voice said, "may I have the honor

of the dance?"

Katie was about to offer her usual reply, when she realized she was gazing into the smoky black eyes of Rudolph Valentino. "Oh, my," she whispered, touching her locket. "Mr. Valentino—"

"Please, it is Rudy. You will dance with me, yes?"

The orchestra leader signaled for a tango and, before Katie could demur, she was swept onto the dance floor by the Great Lover himself. Mama will never believe me, she thought, never in a million years. But photographers routinely attended Hollywood parties and, the next day, Katie's picture would appear in tabloids throughout the country. The caption would read: "The Great Lover and filmdom's newest discovery, Katie McVey."

"Watching you out there with Rudy," Cornelius O'Day was saying, "I couldn't help but remember the scared little girl who came to work at Ada's boardinghouse—a lifetime ago."

"A lifetime," Katie agreed. She sat curled upon a couch in the sprawling living room, her shoes off, a light jacket covering her shoulders. The guests had gone, and now the sun began to rise over the hills. "The future looked pretty bleak in those days."

"Not to Ada. She always had a smile and a joke."

"She must be smiling now. You and Jack were her favorites. You've both had such success."

"And you, Miss Katie. From a boardinghouse to the St. Clair Hotel. . . . I'll be staying there during Christmas. We'll be visiting New York, my whole brood, children, grandchildren. We've reserved five

470

suites. Will you be there?"

"Oh yes. I'm going back to New York tomorrow. I mean today." Katie laughed. "I'll be there to greet you and your brood."

"Good." Cornelius reached for his jacket. He rose, bowing over Katie's hand. "It's been a wonderful reunion," he said. "All of us together again after so many years. Even Herbert and Yvonne. Their bones creak when they walk, but they still dance like a dream."

"It was great fun. I loved it. Shall I see you out, Cornelius?"

"I know my way around. I'm here every Friday night for poker. Jack cheats. You can tell him I said so."

"I will not!"

"Good-bye, Katie. 'Til Christmas."

"Good-bye, Cornelius. Safe home."

Katie stretched her arms high above her head. Through the glass doors she could see the sun growing brighter, sharper, and suddenly she yearned for the sight of clouds, of rain, of anything but the eternal California sunshine. I'm ready to go home, she thought, rising. She put on her shoes and walked across the room. She climbed the stairs, remembering with a smile her triumphant descent down these stairs many hours before.

"I'm glad to see you smiling," Mary said.

"Oh, you startled me. Why aren't you asleep? It's very early."

"I was giving Elizabeth her bottle. She's my only great-granddaughter, and when she's here I like to fuss."

"May I look in on her, Mary? I met your sons and your grandchildren, but I never got a peek at the little one. I'll be quiet. I won't disturb her. Promise."

"Sure, come along. You don't have to ask me twice to show off my Elizabeth." Mary took Katie to a room at the end of the hall. She opened the door, tiptoeing to the ruffled and beribboned bassinet. "Isn't she grand?"

Katie touched the baby's fluff of platinum hair. "She's an angel. Pink and perfect. Such perfect little features. We mustn't wake her."

They tiptoed from the room. "What are your plans for today, Katie? Sleep, I hope."

"First I have to pack. Then I want one last walk in your gardens. Whenever I see roses I'll think of your gardens."

"Stay and enjoy them."

"A tempting idea, but I can't. We've been through this, Mary. My life is in New York. My family is there; my business."

"Your memories?"

"I came here to escape my memories. It didn't work."

"Give it more time."

"I can't."

"Well, I won't argue. I know you're doing what you think best. Do you need help packing, dear?"

"I'll manage." Katie put her arm about Mary's shoulder. "Go back to bed." She smiled. "After that extraordinary party, you've earned your sleep. I intend to sleep all the way to New York. I'll see you and Jack before I leave."

"We're having lunch together, the three of us, a

nice champagne lunch by the pool. If you're determined to leave, at least we can give you a nice send-off."

Katie returned to her silent room. She sighed, for the distractions of the past hours were over now, and she felt a familiar emptiness. She walked out on the balcony, breathing the rose-scented air. She closed her eyes and in that moment, as in so many others, she saw Josh.

Ben Rossi was waiting for Katie when her train pulled into Grand Central. He threaded his way through the knot of passengers and caught her elbow. "Welcome home," he said.

"Ben! What are you doing here?"

"We have a few matters to discuss."

"Are the boys all right?"

"They're fine. Maeve is fine, too, although you won't recognize her. She's bobbed her hair."

"No!"

"Captain Garrity invited her to his retirement party. She went on a shopping spree and had her hair bobbed. It's most becoming." Ben paused, giving instructions to the redcap. He turned back to Katie and took her arm. "Garrity's a widower now, you know."

"What of it? And when did you see Mama? What's going on, Ben?"

"We'll talk in the car." Ben hurried Katie up a flight of stairs into the huge lobby. He stared straight ahead, the shadow of a smile playing about his mouth. "After you," he said, holding the door open.

"Rain. I was beginning to wonder if I'd ever see rain again."

"No rain in California?"

"I believe it's against the law."

"Here's the car." Ben nodded as his chauffeur came to attention. "Be careful. Don't bump your head."

"Are you ready to tell me what's going on?"

"I might ask you the same question, Katie. Running off to California. Refusing my telephone calls."

"It was a vacation. I didn't want to talk business."

"My calls weren't about business."

"*What* then?"

"Josh Thurston."

Katie started. She looked quickly at Ben. "I don't understand."

"You will." Ben pushed a button, closing the partition between front and back seats. "From the little you said before you left, I gathered you had had an unhappy . . . encounter . . . with a local Southampton fellow. A caretaker? A handyman?"

"A carpenter."

"Excuse me. A carpenter." Ben laughed, his dark eyes twinkling with amusement. "A carpenter by the name of Josh Thurston?"

"How do you know his name?"

"Katie, you're wonderful. A true innocent, and in this day and age! Amazing!" Ben laughed again, shaking his head from side to side. "Your *carpenter* is Joshua Reade Thurston, of the Thurston Shipping Lines. He's one of the richest men in America. His personal fortune alone is somewhere around ten million dollars."

"Have you been drinking? Or have you lost your mind? The man I met is a carpenter. His hands are calloused, and he wears shabby old clothes, and he has a big mutt named—"

"Hobo. Hobo III, to be exact."

Katie paled. She grasped Ben's arm. "How do you know that?" she demanded. "You *couldn't* know. You couldn't unless . . . *tell* me how you know."

"I know Josh Thurston. Until a couple of weeks ago, I knew him only as a client of the firm. Now I know him very well indeed. He's been all but camping out in my office."

"Then it's true? Josh is . . . who you say he is?"

"Yes. You read three newspapers a day, Katie. Don't you ever read the society pages?"

"Why would I?"

"Under the circumstances, several reasons occur to me."

"But his hands, his clothes. I don't understand any of this. It doesn't make sense. There must be some mistake."

"There is no mistake. The Thurstons have been clients of Streeter, Carlyle and Hazlet since before the Civil War. Josh Thurston happens to enjoy carpentry. It's his only relaxation from work he despises, from a life he despises. He goes off to Southampton every chance he gets. He builds things and wears old clothes and tries to forget his other life."

"He should have told me."

"I wouldn't be too quick to judge him, if I were you. There are hoards of women just laying in wait for Josh Thurston, not for himself, but for his money and position. After years of that, one grows wary. He confessed he didn't know what to think of you in the beginning. He's accustomed to being recognized, you see. But then, when you so innocently assumed he was poor, a *carpenter*, he was charmed. He would have told you, Katie, given time."

"Josh lied to me."

"While we're on the subject of lies, we might discuss yours. You manage a few properties, do you?" Ben smiled. "You have a *decent* income, do you? A weekly income in four figures is rather more than decent, wouldn't you say?"

"I was afraid I'd scare him with talk of money. I didn't know he was . . . money isn't the only thing he lied about, Ben. He lied about his marriage. He didn't tell me until—"

"I know. That's really what I want to discuss."

"No! Absolutely not! What you've told me is . . . surprising, but it doesn't change anything. Josh *is* married, isn't he?"

"In a manner of speaking."

"Then there's nothing to discuss."

"You're going to listen to me, Katie. You and Matt always had one thing in common, an ability to close your minds to unpleasant facts. Well, not this time. This time you're going to listen."

"I *won't*. I couldn't bear it." Tears burned Katie's eyes, splashing down her cheeks. "I have to forget about Josh. We had a week together. A week," she sobbed. "Now I have to forget."

Ben gave his handkerchief to Katie. He waited until her sobs had quieted, then he reached for her hand. "I'm not trying to hurt you," he said. "But there are some things you must know, in fairness to

476

you and Josh. He loves you, Katie. That's the first thing."

"*Don't.*"

"After I've finished, we need never speak of Josh again. Please let me finish. When Josh returned to find you gone, he immediately telephoned the Winslows. They own the cottage in which you stayed."

"Yes, I know."

"They referred Josh to their attorney, William Streeter. William had been feeling tired, and his wife took him off on a cruise. So the matter fell to me. Josh stormed into my office, demanding to know where you were."

"You didn't tell him, Ben?"

"I pleaded client confidentiality. He threatened to hire private investigators. It was a rough morning. Finally he calmed down long enough to explain his side of the story. I believed it to be an honest explanation. And I agreed to do what I could."

"There's nothing *to* do, Ben. Josh is married."

"Josh and Caroline have not lived as husband and wife for many years. That's no secret. Anyone who reads the society pages knows of their troubles. Their tragedies, really."

"Tragedies?"

"It wasn't a happy marriage from the beginning. Then, ten years ago, Caroline was driving upstate with their children. She lost control of the car somehow and plunged over an embankment. The little girl died instantly. The little boy died the next day. Caroline walked away from the accident unhurt, but soon afterward she suffered a complete mental collapse. She's been in and out of sanatoriums ever since. She's tried to kill herself several times."

New tears filled Katie's eyes. "My God, how awful," she cried. "The poor woman. Poor Josh."

"When he left you, it was in response to a call from Caroline's doctors. She had tried to kill herself again."

"My God."

"A less honorable man would have divorced Caroline by now. Josh feels he has a responsibility to her."

"Of course he does. He's a *good* man, Ben. I just wish he'd told me about . . ."

"It's a painful subject. Beyond that, he was afraid of losing you. Would you have stayed, knowing the circumstances?"

Katie was silent. She turned her head, staring out the car window. Through her tears she saw the blur of traffic, of people rushing to and fro. "No," she said at last. "No, I wouldn't have stayed." She touched her locket. "Oh, Josh," she whispered. "Josh."

"A great many women chase after him because they realize that Caroline will succeed. Sooner of later she will succeed in killing herself."

"What a horrible thing to say!"

"The truth is often horrible."

"I'll write to Josh, if you'll give me his address. I'll explain how . . . I feel. But I won't see him again. I can't."

"Katie—"

"No, Ben . . . I want to run to Josh. I want that more than anything in this world, but I can't. Don't you see? I love him so much. Eventually *I'd* become one of those women you describe. Waiting for his wife to die. Hoping she would. In the end, we'd be destroyed by guilt. Our love would be destroyed. We'd have nothing."

"What do you have now?"

"Memories. I tried to escape my memories. I was wrong. I'll live on them, now and for the rest of my life."

20

Another autumn passed, and another Christmas. Patrick returned home for the holidays, and Katie threw a large party in her Murray Hill apartment. All the twenty-seven visiting O'Days were there and, from Hell's Kitchen, the Muldoons and Dr. Morton and his family. Captain Garrity, retired now, was encouraged to dance a Charleston, and Father Malone was persuaded to dance an Irish jig. Katie watched the festivities, a quiet spectator at her own party. When the last guest had gone, she called Patrick into her study. "We haven't had much chance to talk," she said, sitting down. "I suppose it's now or never. Unless you can stay an extra day or two?"

"Sorry, Ma. I've had a great time, but I have to get back. I have to catch up on my studies." Patrick poured two brandies, giving one to his mother. "You understand."

"Yes. Your father was a dedicated student. You take after him." Katie sipped her brandy, gazing fondly at her son. He was tall and square-jawed and quite blond, with serene blue eyes and a dimpled chin. "What are you going to do when you graduate?

Have you decided yet, Patrick?"

"Well, I'm not going to be a baseball player, except perhaps on weekends, for the fun of it. Actually, I was thinking about joining you in the hotel business. I like people, and I'm taking all those business courses. Any objections?"

"I'm delighted. It's a good business. It can only get better. New York is becoming something of a tourist mecca. You know I bought the hotel with my sons in mind."

"Did you? I doubt we'll be able to convince our Rory to join us. He's pretty determined to be an actor. But there's still Matthew."

"Matthew's in second grade." Katie laughed.

"Kids grow up."

"You'll have kids of your own by the time Matthew's grown up. You'll be an old married man by then. . . . Are you still seeing Marjorie Oaks, or is that prying? I wouldn't want to pry."

"You know very well I'm not. And you know you're glad."

"Marjorie is a bit snooty for my tastes."

"For my tastes too. I've invited Lucy Morton to the spring dance. She's accepted." Patrick loosened his tie. He sat back, clasping his hands behind his head. "You don't have to worry about me." He smiled. "Do I have to worry about you? Grandma says you've been depressed lately."

"Grandma exaggerates."

"There should be more to life than work."

"I'm content with my life, Patrick. I have my family. I have some lovely memories."

"Memories? You're a young woman, Ma, and

482

darned attractive. The fellows at school think you're the cat's meow. Their mothers are sort of dowdy, but you . . . you danced with Valentino, after all."

"My dancing days are over."

"Why? You should be out on the town every night, enjoying yourself. You should be going to parties and speakeasies and—"

"Goodness! I wouldn't get much work done that way."

"Is work really so important to you?"

"It pays the bills."

"I answered your questions, Ma. Won't you answer mine?"

"No, I don't think I will."Katie dropped her glance to the desk. She moved a stack of papers from one side to the other, then rose and went to her son. "I appreciate your concern," she said lightly, "but it's misplaced. I'm fine. Work is a habit with me, Patrick. There are worse habits, you know."

"Is work enough?"

"What a persistent young man!" Katie exclaimed, tousling Patrick's blond hair. "Let's say it's enough for now."

Indeed, work was Katie's refuge. She went to the hotel early and stayed late, losing herself in the daily problems of business. No problem was too small to escape her notice. A broken faucet, a thieving chambermaid, a lost reservation, all these were welcome distractions from the loneliness of her life. She checked the accountant's reports and interviewed personnel and made frequent visits to the kitchens and laundries. She seemed to be everywhere, doing everything; and in such ways did her days pass.

If Katie's life was quiet, the world around her was not. The 1920's roared ahead, giddy times filled with Hollywood scandals and society scandals, all luridly detailed in the tabloid press. There were murders on the streets of Chicago and New York as rival gangsters turned their machine guns on each other. There was jazz and bathtub gin and the bold smile of the flapper. Most of all, there was prosperity.

The coming of 1925 saw the stock market growing richer and richer by the day. Wall Street had once been the province of the mighty, but now clerks and shop girls and taxi drivers rushed to join the game. They had good reason, for everyone had heard of fortunes being made overnight, of modest sums being run into millions. It was Coolidge Prosperity. It was, in the words of a much-quoted General Motors executive, a time when "everybody ought to be rich."

Maeve Gallagher heartily agreed. She had seen her first cautious investments double, then triple, and with each profit her confidence soared. She spent hours at the dining room table, the financial pages spread out before her. She spent hours on the telephone with her broker, buying and selling stocks, considering the latest tips. Rory began calling her the Wizard of Wall Street, and, secretly, she was pleased.

"No, Mama," Katie said one morning in the spring of 1925. She shook her head, waving away the newspaper Maeve held out. "I don't have time for that now. Did you make another *fortune*? I'm glad, but I'm also late." Smiling, she finished her breakfast tea and stood up. "Really, when I think how you used to rail against gambling!"

"Sure and it's not gambling, Katie McVey. It's investing."

"A minor distinction. I'd be careful, Mama. The market is wildly inflated. It's like a great big bubble, and the bubble is going to burst."

"I made two thousand dollars last month. And didn't I take Mrs. Muldoon's ten dollars and turn it into five hundred? Well, didn't I?"

"It can't go on forever."

"Aye, I suppose you're an expert. Sit down, Katie. There's something I have to show you."

Katie glanced at her watch. "Not now," she said. "It's almost eight o'clock. Show me when I get home."

"You're always rushing off. Do you think the hotel will collapse if you're a few minutes late? Do you think someone will steal it?"

"All right, Mama." Katie sighed, sitting down again. "I apologize. What's so important?"

"This."

Katie accepted the newspaper. A feeling of dread gripped her as she saw the headline: "Millionaire's Wife a Suicide." She saw a picture of a pretty, dark-haired woman and then the woman's name, Caroline Selby Thurston. "Oh, my God. Oh, my God."

"Aye, it's terrible. The most terrible sin there is. There's no forgiveness for—"

"Stop it, Mama. The poor woman is dead."

"Aye, by her own hand. Read the story."

"I can't." Katie pushed the newspaper aside. She was trembling, very pale. She felt a chill and she shivered. *Josh*, she cried silently. Oh, Josh.

"It happened in the sanatorium," Maeve said,

sitting next to Katie. "The sanatorium where Caroline Thurston was staying. They took all the dangerous things away, but they didn't know about her handkerchief box. It had a hidden compartment, with a mirror. She smashed the mirror and used the jagged pieces to cut her wrists."

"My God."

"The paper says the Thurston family is in seclusion."

"I don't want to hear any more, Mama." Katie rose, walking aimlessly around the dining room. She touched her locket now and again, the locket she had never once removed. "It's too sad."

"Aye, but it puts a different color on things, doesn't it?"

"What things?"

"You haven't fooled me, Katie. You've been mourning your lost romance for months. I've seen you, and the look in your eyes."

"That's nonsense. There was no romance. I told you I met Josh at the beach, and we spent some pleasant hours together. Period."

"You told me lies. Aye, don't deny it. I wasn't born yesterday, was I? I know when a woman's in love. I know the signs. Sure and I'm not saying you had the right to be in love with him. You didn't. And that's why you lied. That's why Ben lied. He was covering up for you. But I could see between the lines."

"*What* are you talking about, Mama?"

"When Ben came here. You were on your way to California. I thought you'd gone crazy, and that's the truth. Changing your plans all of a sudden; running off clear across the country. Then Ben came here. He said a man named Josh Thurston might be trying to find you. He said it was a business matter. Oh, that Ben is a smooth talker. Smooth or not, I wasn't fooled. I knew there was more to it. Why else would you go running off across the country? Why else would you sound like your heart was breaking? Aye, I figured it out. Maybe I didn't know the details, but I knew it was a romance."

"You're very astute, Mama."

"Don't waste your fancy words on me. I can add two and two, if that's what you mean."

Katie returned to her chair. She sat down, staring at Maeve. "You knew all along, yet you kept silent. Why?"

"What was there to say? You're a grown woman, and not one to share your troubles. Even though you needed comforting, you didn't *want* comforting. So I held my tongue."

"Until today."

"Well, it's different circumstances today."

Katie bent her head. "No, Mama," she replied quietly. "I wrote Josh last fall and told him that what we had was over."

"Aye, it was the right thing to do then. The only thing. He was married then, your Josh. He's not married now."

"Too much time has passed. It's too late for us."

"You're still in love with him."

"It's too late. Besides, I didn't have any idea who he was when we met. I thought he was a carpenter, struggling to earn a living. A carpenter! Joshua Reade Thurston!"

"If that's the way it was, he knows you're not after

his money."

"Mama, you don't understand. You should. Years ago you told me I wasn't good enough for Matt. You said he'd want a *lady*. I was just the hired girl at the boardinghouse. I was reaching above myself—that's what you said. You've certainly changed your tune."

"Years ago was years ago." Maeve shrugged. "I was trying to save you grief. Sure and I'd seen Matt's kind before, the kind with fancy notions and plans. And empty pockets. It always comes to grief in the end, one way or another."

"If it weren't for Matt, we'd be in Hell's Kitchen today."

"Aye, you won't hear me disagreeing. But you had your grief, Katie. That was the price—a high price."

"Everybody has grief. You did."

Maeve shrugged again, twisting her wedding band around. "Whatever you think, I loved your papa. Dear knows I hated the things Joe did, but I loved him. It wasn't the same between you and Matt."

"I loved Matt."

"It was youth. Youth calling to youth. And it was a mistake."

"I don't plan to make a second mistake."

"You're a grown woman now. Josh is a grown man. You've both learned something of life. Aye, hard lessons. He's had his grief too, for all his money. So he's Joshua Reade Thurston. What does it matter? You're the one forever reminding me this isn't the old country. Look at Ben, married into the Streeter family."

"He had to change his religion and his politics to do it. Amy's father even wanted Ben to change his name."

"And what does your Josh want you to change?"

"He's not *my* Josh, Mama."

"I'm thinking that's up to you. I didn't raise you to be a weakling, Katie McVey. I raised you like I was raised, to be strong. Are you listening to me?"

"Yes, Mama."

"Well?"

Katie rose. "It's late," she said. "I'm going to work."

"And then what?"

"And then nothing."

"You could send him your condolences."

"No, I couldn't." Katie took her purse and gloves from the table. "I'd only be opening old wounds."

"You're making excuses."

"Mama, we had a week together, that's all."

"Aye, God created the world in a week."

"I've created my own world. I'm content with it."

"There's plenty of time to be content when you're lying six feet under. You're afraid, aren't you? You're running off again, not to California this time, but to your office. Aye, it's a grand office and it keeps you busy during the days. What about the nights?"

"Mama!"

"Ada used to say there hasn't been a new man since Adam. There hasn't been a new woman either. Sure and women weren't meant to be alone. It's a sin against nature."

"You managed."

"What choice did I have? Tell me that. I had my hands full just keeping a roof over our heads. Do you think I had time to worry about men? About romance? It's not the same, Katie. You have choices. You have money, and that's what money means—choices. In your place, I'd be on the telephone to Josh right now. You wouldn't catch me hemming and hawing and talking about *who* he is. But you"—Maeve sighed—"you were always stubborn."

"Josh knows how I feel. He knows where I am. If he . . . wants to see me, he will."

"Are you expecting him to chase after you? You read too many fairy stories when you were little, and that's the truth. Do you want a man or a knight on a white charger?"

"What do *you* want, Mama? Do you want me to chase after him? I can't. You taught me to know my place, Mama. You taught me well. Despite what you say now, my place *isn't* chasing after a millionaire. If Josh wants to see me, he will."

"Mind your tone."

"Mind your business, Mama."

There was no further discussion of Josh Thurston in the McVey household. Katie went about her life as usual, though she jumped whenever the telephone rang, whenever a knock came at the door. A hundred times she took pen and paper in hand, only to lay them aside. A hundred times she reached for the telephone, only to draw back. She was distracted and occasionally short tempered. She slept poorly and once or twice awoke to feel tears streaming down her face. "For God's sake, *call* him," Ben urged, but she pretended not to hear.

"That's all the correspondence for today," Katie's

secretary said, closing her notebook. "I've moved the staff meeting to eight o'clock tomorrow morning . . . Mrs. McVey? The staff meeting?"

"What? Oh yes, the staff meeting. What about it?"

"Is eight o'clock tomorrow morning all right?"

"Fine."

"Have you decided on the new wallpaper for the suites? If you want the decorating finished by Christmas, we really must get started. It's a big job."

"I don't care, Ellen. The rose stripe is nice, or the beige. I don't care." Katie left her desk. She went to the window, staring out at the bright autumn day. The sun was pale gold. A Southampton sun, she thought, touching her locket. "Choose the wallpaper you like." She sighed. "The samples are on my desk."

"Can I bring you anything, Mrs. McVey? An aspirin?"

"No, thanks. I'm just daydreaming. I've always loved autumn. It's my favorite time of year. Have you ever seen the ocean in autumn? So dark and . . . mysterious." Katie turned. "I'm not much use today, am I?" she asked with a slight smile. "Run along. I know you have work. I won't keep you from it."

"About the flowers, Mrs. McVey? Do you want them in here or shall I leave them outside?"

"There are quite enough flowers in here and outside. Did Porters' deliver extra bouquets this morning?"

"I'm afraid you misunderstood me. These flowers aren't from Porters'. I don't know where they're from. They look a little like wildflowers."

"Wildflowers?" Katie's heart skipped a beat. "Wildflowers!" She rushed past Ellen to the outer

491

office. "They *are* wildflowers," she cried, pressing the blossoms against her cheek. "Southampton wildflowers. Where is the card?"

"I'm sorry, Mrs. McVey. There was no card."

"It must have slipped out. Please find it, Ellen. Hurry."

"But there was no card."

"Your secretary is right, Mrs. McVey. There was no card."

Katie spun around, a vast and radiant smile lighting her face. "*Josh.*"

"Hello, my darling."

"Is it . . . Is it really you?"

Josh laughed. "At long last," he said. "Come here."

Katie ran into the waiting arms of her beloved. She could not speak, for her throat was thick with tears. She felt his lips touch hers, and a great, burning thrill swept her senses. She gazed at him mutely, shaking her head in wonder and joy.

Ellen stood a few steps away, gaping at this intimate scene. She saw a tall, handsome man wearing a custom-tailored suit, an immaculate white shirt, and a necktie of heavy maroon silk. His black hair was meticulously barbered, and his deep sea-green eyes glittered with light. Her lips parted as she realized the man was Joshua Reade Thurston. "Mr. Thurston," she exclaimed, then clapped her hand over her mouth. "Oh, excuse me."

"How do you do?" Josh said, amused. "Ellen, is it? No, you needn't leave." He looked at Katie, touching her cheek. "I thought we'd take a ride to the beach. We have a lot to talk about, my darling."

492

"Yes."

"Come, the car is outside."

"Mrs. McVey . . . the accountants. They're due here any minute."

"Give them my regards." Katie laughed. "I'm going to the beach. Shall we, Mr. Thurston?"

"By all means, Mrs. McVey."

Neither Katie nor Josh noticed the curious stares that followed them across the lobby. They gazed into each other's eyes and smiled foolishly, a man and a woman in love. The murmured to each other, and for the first time in many, many months, they felt complete.

A gleaming silver and gray Rolls Royce was parked at the curb. The chauffeur, clad in the silver and gray livery of the Thurstons, hurried to open the door. "Southampton, sir?" he asked.

"If you please, Thomas." Josh nodded, helping Katie into the car. He arranged a sable lap robe over her legs. "There." He smiled. "I don't want you catching cold."

"You'll keep me warm."

"I certainly plan to."

"Josh," Katie said as the car glided away, "I was so sorry about . . . Caroline."

"She was a fragile woman. Life was too much for her. At least she isn't suffering any more. She suffered a great deal."

"I'm sorry. I wanted to write. I started dozens of letters, but I couldn't find the right words."

"That's in the past now, darling. We have today and tomorrow and all our tomorrows to come. I love you, Katie."

"I love you."

Josh reached into his pocket, removing a small velvet Tiffany box. "In token and pledge of my love," he said.

With trembling fingers, Katie opened the box. She gasped, staring at an immense diamond solitaire. "Josh!"

"Will you marry me, my darling?"

"Oh, Josh."

"Will you marry me? I've waited a year to ask. I can't wait a moment longer."

"I'm still Katie McVey from Hell's Kitchen. My mother was a washerwoman and I was the hired girl. My brother is—" She said no more, for Josh's arms were about her, his lips pressed to hers. "Oh," she murmured. "I love you, I love you."

"Marry me."

"Josh . . . are you sure? What will your family say?"

"My adorable darling. I've already broken the news to my family. That's how sure I am. Mother is very happy. She's a fine old girl. You'll like her. My uncles and cousins and such are mired in gloom. But if they know what's good for them, and they do, they'll keep their gloom to themselves. You'll be properly welcomed into the Thurston family."

"Or else?"

"You might put it that way." Josh shrugged, smiling broadly. "I control the family fortune."

"It was a shock, finding out who you really were."

"Who I really *am* is the man you met on the beach. My hands are calloused because I like to work with my hands. I like long walks and old clothes and mongrel dogs. That's who I am, darling. All the rest is an accident of birth, of circumstance. I don't sneer at money, but I don't revere it either—an attitude my father never understood. The bulk of the family business and the family fortune was to have gone to my brother. . . . Jordan was killed in the war. I returned from France to find myself in the president's office at Thurston Shipping Lines. And there I stayed. I have a duty, and I do it as best I can. Whenever I can, I escape. Southampton is my retreat."

"I didn't mean to pry."

Josh laughed suddenly, kissing Katie's golden hair. "My life is an open book," he said. "The press sees to that. You, my innocent, apparently don't read the tabloids, or the society pages."

"I do now. I've been clipping your pictures and saving them in a book. I have quite a collection."

Josh took Katie's hand, lifting it to his lips. "I love you, my darling. I want you to be my wife. Will you marry me?"

"Yes, I'll marry you."

"Say it again."

"Yes, I'll marry you." Katie smiled, her eyes swimming with tears. "Yes, yes, yes."

Sea gulls circled and soared in the bronze autumn sun of Southampton. A fresh, strong wind blew off the ocean, whipping Katie's skirt about her legs. She laughed, holding on to Josh's arm and breathing in the salt air. "It's wonderful," she called over the roar of the waves. "It's home."

"You're right. Look over there."

Katie turned her head. Beyond the sandy bluffs she saw a rambling white mansion with gabled roofs and wide, gray-shuttered windows. She saw gardens and lawns and winding, terraced paths to the sea. "Oh, how charming! Who lives there, Josh?"

"I do. You do. That *is* home, darling. That's Westerly."

"Westerly?"

"It was called West Point, once upon a time. Until someone remembered the *other* West Point."

"But it's a mansion!"

"Thurstons tend to live in mansions," Josh said, smiling at Katie. "My place in the city is on the small side, but Mother's house is half a block long."

"This is going to take some getting used to. A mansion!"

"Just think of it as a big, friendly old house. It's all those things. I spent summers here when I was a boy. There's a wildflower meadow and a lily pond. Our bedroom opens on the ocean."

"Our bedroom. I like the sound of that."

"I was hoping you would." Josh swept Katie into his arms, carrying her over the bluffs. They came to a flagstone path and he stopped briefly. "You'll have the grand tour later," he said. "But you can see most of Westerly from here. It's yours now, darling."

"Oh, Josh." Katie sighed. "I hope this isn't a dream. I'm not dreaming, am I? If I am, I never want to wake up."

"I love you. I promise we'll live our dream, my darling."

Katie's arms tightened around Josh's neck. "Take

me home," she murmured. "Take me to Westerly."

Westerly was the largest of the great Southampton estates, its grounds encompassing beach and meadowland and rocky cliffs rising above the sea. Various pathways of crushed stone led to guest cottages, to grass tennis courts, to a lovely, old-fashioned pavilion where summer dances had once been held. Marigolds and impatiens and dusty miller filled the gardens. Some distance away, water lilies floated serenely in a clear blue pond.

At the western edge of the estate was the mansion, a white beacon overlooking the shore. Long and deep, it had thirty rooms, many of them grouped into suites. Josh's suite—all warm earth tones and rich woods and shining glass doors—covered half the first floor. His living room opened on the gardens. His study opened on trellised walks. His bedroom, with spectacular views of ocean and sky, opened on the secluded beachfront. "I've never brought anyone here before," he said. "It was my special place. Now it's our special place. Our haven."

Katie gazed out at the pounding surf, at the bronze fire of the sun. She turned to Josh and they embraced. They undressed each other, falling naked upon the bed. The sun moved across the horizon, the sky darkened, and still they clung together, utterly lost in their sweet passion. "I love you, my darling," Josh said again and again, his voice a caress.

It was early evening when Josh reached for the telephone and dialed the garage. He spoke a few words and then walked through the dressing room to the bath. "I told Thomas we'd be ready to leave in an hour. Is that all right?"

Katie lay back in the marble tub. "I'll be ready"—she smiled—"though not necessarily willing. I hate to think of leaving here. Must we?"

Josh poked his head inside. He watched the water lapping Katie's breasts, her long legs. "Well, not this minute," he replied, climbing into the tub.

"You're very naughty, Josh Thurston. Very naughty." Katie sighed rapturously as Josh's mouth once more sought hers.

"You have nice manners," Maeve said, her dark blue eyes fixed on Josh. "Asking me formal for Katie's hand was nice manners. Are you a nice man?"

"I try to be."

"Aye, that's an honest answer. When a man starts bragging about his virtues, I start wondering what he has to hide. But then, maybe you've no need of bragging, being who you are. Growing up in the lap of luxury like you did. Aye, you had things easy. My Katie had things hard."

"I know, Mrs. Gallagher."

"Do you know what it is to go hungry? To go around in rags, winter and summer? Do you know what it is to work from morning 'til night?"

"No, obviously not. I can't change Katie's past life. I *can* give her a new life, a wonderful life. I love your daughter."

"And love solves all the problems, I suppose."

Josh smiled, for Maeve reminded him of his late grandmother, the stern and indomitable Grace Reade. "Don't think I'm a starry-eyed schoolboy," he said. "I know love isn't a magic solution. I realize

Katie and I may have problems adjusting. On the other hand, I'm not easily deterred. Nor is Katie. We've both had some experience with problems, after all. Perhaps we're stronger for them. We've earned our happiness. And Katie *will* be happy, Mrs. Gallagher. You have my promise. I always keep my promises."

"Aye, that's what I wanted to hear. Plain talk. If you'd come in spouting foolishness, spouting moonlight and roses, I'd have washed my hands of you."

"There's a time for moonlight and roses. There's a time for plain talk."

"Do you know Katie has her own money now? Her own business?"

"I've gone to great lengths to know everything about Katie."

"I warn you, she's a stubborn one."

"So am I."

"You're supposed to be, aren't you? You're rich, and a society fella to boot. You're supposed to get your way."

Josh shook his dark head in amusement. "I must remember that," he said, hiding a smile behind his hand. "May I assume Katie and I have your blessing?"

"Aye. To tell the truth of it, I had a long talk with Ben Rossi a few months back. Sure and he had only good things to say about you. Of course, I had to see for myself. I had to see you weren't a fool, like some society fellas I read about. A fool or a weakling."

"I'm glad I passed inspection."

"Do you know about Katie's brother, Hugh?"

"About Hugh and Sean."

"And it makes no difference?"

"None."

Maeve was silent. She stared at Josh. "You'll be married by a priest," she said finally. "You can have any kind of wedding you want, but by a priest."

"We want a very small, private wedding. Katie mentioned a Father Malone. I have no objections."

"Aye, then it's settled."

"What's settled?" Katie asked, walking into the living room. "Is the interview over? Poor man, do you need a drink?"

Josh stood. "I'd rather meet your sons," he said. "You must be Rory." He smiled, holding out his hand. "And you must be Matthew. I'm pleased to meet you both."

Matthew stared up at Josh. "Are you going to be my daddy?" he asked in his piping, young voice. "I never had one before."

"I want very much to be your daddy," Josh replied. On a sudden impulse, he bent and wrapped his strong arms about the child. "I'm very lucky to be getting such a fine son." He thought about his own son, the son so cruelly taken from him, and tears came to his eyes. "We'll have great times together, Matthew. I promise."

"Will we have fun?"

"*Lots* of fun."

"Can I call you Daddy?"

"I wish you would."

"Okay."

"Welcome to the family, sir," Rory said.

"Thank you. You may be too old to want a daddy, but I hope we'll be friends."

500

"I can always use a rich friend," Rory said with a laugh. "You don't have to glare at me, Grandma." He laughed again. "I was just kidding. I'm sorry, sir. I was kidding." He took his mother's hand, holding her huge diamond ring up to the light. "That's not from the five-and-dime." He shrugged. "And it's not every day Ma gets engaged to a Thurston. The Thurstons have a few dollars."

"A few," Josh agreed amiably.

"That's enough, Rory," Katie said. "Josh doesn't understand your *humor* yet. There are times I don't understand it either. My son fancies himself a comedian."

"An actor, Ma. I'm going to be an actor on the stage."

"Right now I'd like you to finish the homework on your desk. Run along. You too, Matthew," Katie said, kissing his reddish head. "It's past your bedtime."

"I'm not tired."

"You will be, come morning. Let's have a hug and then it's off to bed."

Matthew hugged his mother and grandmother. After a moment's hesitation, he hugged Josh. "Good night, Daddy," he said with a grin.

"Good night, son. Sleep well." Josh rose. He stood close to Katie, watching the two boys walk away. He put his arm about her shoulder, stretching his other arm to Maeve. "Well," he said, looking from Maeve to Katie, "we're a family now."

Katie and Josh were married in January of 1926.

The simple ceremony at St. Brendan's was attended only by Katie's family, Josh's mother and uncles, the Rossis, and the Streeters. Katie wore a short, lace-trimmed, ivory silk dress and matching hat. About her neck were the magnificent Thurston pearls clasped with emeralds, a gift from Josh's mother, Sophie. In her hands she carried a bouquet of wildflowers from the Westerly greenhouse. Meg, her lone attendant, was matron of honor. Ben was best man once again, though this time, he noted happily, the groom needed no reassurance.

When the ceremony ended, a small fleet of limousines took the wedding party to a champagne reception aboard the Thurston Lines' *America*. White-gloved stewards served champagne and caviar and delicate sandwiches on silver trays. There was a three-tiered wedding cake decorated with spun sugar doves and flowers. Mementos were distributed to the guests: engraved gold compacts for the women and engraved gold cigar cases for the men.

Katie and Josh bade farewell to their guests at six o'clock. An hour later they stood at the rail holding hands as the *America* began its journey across the Atlantic. "Happy, darling?" Josh asked.

"I keep wondering what I did to deserve such happiness." Katie nestled her head on Josh's shoulder, gazing at the moonlit ocean. "It's so beautiful."

"The best is yet to come. London. Paris. I can hardly wait to show you Europe. In the meantime"—Josh smiled—"I think I'll show you our stateroom."

Their stateroom, the grandest on the ship, had dark wood paneling, crystal lamps, and brocaded chairs. The bed was dressed with silk sheets and comforters, and piled high with ruffled silk pillows. Rose petals had been strewn over the bed, and nearby, a magnum of champagne rested in a polished silver ice bucket.

"I know." Katie nodded, staring at the splendid surroundings. "Thurstons tend to travel in luxury."

"Well, it *is* our ship."

Dimly, Katie remembered another ship, another voyage, thirty years before. She had been only five years old, and her memories were not complete, but still she could recall the terrible stench of hundreds of unwashed bodies pressed together in steerage, the terrible confusion of scared and half-starved immigrants. "Does this ship have a steerage class, Josh?" she asked.

"No. British ships transported the Irish to America, at least for the most part. The Thurstons were never involved in that. I anticipated your question, darling. There's a company history in the dresser. It's an accurate history. I wrote it myself . . . and there are a few other things in the dresser." Josh laughed softly, throwing open the drawers. "Look."

Katie turned, seeing clouds of lingerie, satin nightgowns and teddies, lacy camisoles by the score. "Josh, how lovely. I don't know what to say."

"That's not all."

Katie followed Josh's glance to the closets. Her eyes widened as she saw row upon row of chic dresses and suits and beaded evening gowns. She gasped as she saw coats and capes of mink and sable and silver fox. "My God!"

"That's still not all." Josh bounded across the stateroom and opened a small wall safe. He removed several velvet jewel boxes, spilling their precious contents on the bed. "For you."

Katie stared at the king's ransom of glittering diamonds and emeralds. "I can't," she said after a while. "It's . . . It's too much."

"Are you crying? Darling,"—Josh sighed, taking Katie into his arms—"I just want to make up for all the years you were hungry and cold, all the years you had nothing. I want to spoil you. Is that hard to understand? It shouldn't be. I love you, Mrs. Thurston."

"I love you, Mr. Thurston."

"Let me spoil you. Let me give you the world."

The world Josh offered was luxurious beyond imagination. In London and in Paris they occupied the finest suites in the finest hotels. Limousines whisked them to gala dinners and balls and to romantic picnics in the country. They drank champagne morning, noon, and night, or so it seemed. And when they returned to their rooms in the early hours of dawn, it was to a bed of scented silk sheets and the rapture of their love.

21

It was spring when Katie and Josh returned to New York. Lost in love, in each other, they were unprepared for the throng of newspaper reporters crowding the dock. "I'm sorry, darling," Josh said as cameras clicked. "I should have anticipated this."

"But what do they want?"

"Don't worry, darling. It's all right."

Katie was relieved to see the ship's crew rushing forward, forming a barrier between passengers and press. There were a few scuffles, a few angry curses, but soon a path was opened to the waiting limousine. Josh and Katie hurried away, loud and insistent questions ringing in their ears. "*I* should have anticipated this." Katie sighed, slumping against the upholstered seat. "It's my fault."

"Your fault?"

"Didn't you hear what they were shouting? They know about Hugh. About *Swag* Gallagher, famous gangster. And they know I worked in a boarding-house once. That tall, skinny reporter kept asking—"

"Hush, darling. It's not important. The tall,

skinny one is from the *Bugle*. The *Bugle* is a disgrace. The very *worst* of the tabloids, Katie. I wouldn't wrap fish in the Bugle!"

"Please don't joke. It isn't funny. They're going to drag your name through the papers."

"My name has been dragged through the papers before. I can't even begin to count how many times."

"You'll be embarrassed."

"I? My darling Katie, I stopped being embarrassed years ago, at least by anything the tabloids choose to print." Josh's expression grew serious. He lifted Katie's hand to his lips. "I'm afraid it's going to be unpleasant for you," he said quietly. "I had hoped to spare you the . . . attentions . . . of the press a little while longer. I see now that's impossibe."

"Why don't they just leave people alone?"

"Certain people are news, Katie. Targets, so to speak. The tabloids choose a target and off they go. The best course is to ignore them. Let them have their fun. Let them write what they wish. They will anyway. And then they'll move on to their next target. Three or four unpleasant days and it will be over." Josh gazed into Katie's troubled eyes. "You mustn't worry, darling. Mother calls the tabloids filthy rags. She's right. That's all they are."

"It's a strange feeling . . . knowing your life is going to be in print, for the world to read. How do you stand it?"

Josh smiled, shaking his dark head. "A tough skin," he replied. "A *very* tough skin."

Certainly Katie needed a tough skin in the days that followed. "Millionaire Marries Gangster's Sister," shrieked one headline. "Millionaire Marries

Scullery Maid," announced another. The *Daily Bugle* began referring to her as Boardinghouse Kate, an appellation copied by other tabloids. Nasty insinuations abounded, fueled by a small handful of former Hell's Kitchen neighbors seeking the limelight.

"Who the devil is Lizzie Pierce Murdoch?" Josh asked one afternoon toward the end of the week. "I hope she wasn't a friend, because I intend to sic my lawyers on her."

It was some moments before Katie remembered Lizzie Pierce. She smiled slightly. "Lizzie once told me I was going to go to Hell. I thought it was kind of funny, but Meg was ready to beat her up. Meg was my great protector. . . . Josh, don't tell me the reporters found Lizzie Pierce! It was so long ago."

"They found her. Or perhaps she found them. Either way, she's going to be a very sorry woman when I'm through with her."

"What did she say? Let me see."

"No, darling. I won't have you reading this . . . this libel." Josh slammed the *Bugle* down, his face hard and unsmiling. If he had felt a casual contempt for the tabloid press before, now he felt utter revulsion. "This crosses the line," he said. "It's indecent."

Katie retrieved the newspaper. A photograph showed Lizzie seated on a couch, surrounded by six young children dressed in their Sunday best. The accompanying interview read: "Boardinghouse Kate is the right name for her. Kate Gallagher started working in a boardinghouse when she was thirteen. Oh, it was an awful scandal! There was talk from the

507

beginning, and I always say, 'Where there's smoke, there's fire.' I wasn't allowed to have anything to do with her. None of the nice girls were allowed. Well, she's got herself a millionaire now. How she got him I'm sure I couldn't say. Mr. Murdoch and I are God-fearing people. We wouldn't know about those things. Still, damaged goods is damaged goods."

Katie dropped the paper into the wastebasket. "Lizzie obviously hasn't changed her opinion of my final destination. I can almost see the hellfire."

Josh wrapped his arms around Katie. "The God-fearing Mrs. Murdoch won't get away with this indecency," he said. "My lawyers are going to descend on the Murdochs and destroy them. You won't be hurt again, darling. I promise."

"I admit the idea of revenge is appealing. But it won't accomplish anything. Revenge never does."

"Think of it as justice."

"Josh, we'd only be making a bad situation worse. More headlines, more questions, more reporters. You said yourself the best course was to ignore the stories."

"These stories, these *lies*, go too far. There's a vicious edge to them. I didn't marry you to cause you pain, darling. You can't deny you've been hurt."

"I haven't grown my tough skin yet." Katie smiled. "And it's true I was worried about the boys, but they seem to be coping. Please don't do anything, Josh. Let it be."

"Is that what you really want? Are you certain? If we allow the tabloids to get away with these lies, the next lies will be even more vicious."

"They can't keep writing about me forever."

"Well, perhaps not. Another few days . . ."

The stories continued another two weeks. The Thurston family, whatever they thought privately, in public presented a united front. They followed their usual schedules, betraying not the slightest flicker of concern, referring press inquiries to Streeter, Carlyle, and Hazlet. Josh and Katie had the servants screen all calls coming into their Sixty-Third Street townhouse, but, aside from that, they too went on with their lives.

Josh adopted ten-year-old Matthew in 1927. That same spring Patrick graduated from Yale and began working at the St. Clair Hotel. He married Lucy Morton and, in 1928, gave Katie her first grandchild, a sweet little girl named Ann. It was a happy time, marred only by a sudden burst of headlines trumpeting the latest gang wars.

They were known as the Beer Wars, for much blood was spilled in rival attempts to control the vast wholesale beer trade. On one side were the forces of the "Beer Baron," Dutch Schultz; on the other, the forces of Mad Dog Coll.

Late in 1928 Hugh Gallagher assessed the situation and formed a loose alliance with the Coll mob. "I won't take orders from you," he told the terrible-tempered Vincent Coll, "but me and my men will help you out. Our share is one third." The bargain was struck and now there were armed, bloody raids on Schultz beer drops. Dutch Schultz's closest associates were kidnapped at gunpoint and held for ransom. Some were shot, then dumped unceremoniously in the river or in doorways.

The newspapers spared no details in their reports, for the public was both appalled and fascinated by such mayhem. Each day brought gory new headlines, and it was these headlines that brought Father Sean Gallagher from his Buffalo parish to Manhattan.

"It's my duty to talk to Hugh," he explained, sitting in Katie's spacious living room. "It's something I must do."

"But Hugh won't listen. He's been living this life since he was fifteen. It's too late to change him now."

"I must try. It's my duty."

Katie gazed at her brother. He was twenty-eight years old, though he appeared much younger. His hair was the pale blond of his childhood, his face unmarked by time. She searched his wide blue eyes and saw only innocence. "I'm not sure Hugh will talk to you," she said. "He doesn't have a high opinion of priests."

"Oh, he'll talk to me, Katie. We're family. I must try. For the sake of his immortal soul."

"Have you discussed this with Father Malone?"

Sean smiled, clasping his hands in his lap. "Father Malone thinks I'm on a fool's errand," he replied serenely. "Maybe I am. I won't know until I try. Tell me about you, Katie. I can see it's a grand life," he said, looking around the graceful, antique-filled room. "I hope there's room for God among all your treasures."

"I go to Mass every Sunday."

"And Josh?"

"Josh isn't Catholic. You know that, Sean."

510

"He's a Christian nevertheless. Is he a good Christian?"

"Josh is a good man. He makes my life a joy. Not because he gives me *treasures*." Katie laughed. "Because he gives me love. And he gives Matthew love, a father's love. We're very lucky."

"I'm glad to hear it, Katie. I prayed you'd find happiness. You had a lot on your shoulders. Of course you had success, but success is a poor substitute for love. Now you can be home with your husband and children, where you belong."

"Thanks to Patrick. He's taken over most of my work at the hotel. Doing quite well, too." Katie sat back, a smile lighting her face. "You haven't seen little Ann yet. Shall I call Lucy and ask them to come by? She's the prettiest little girl."

"If there's time, after I've talked to Hugh. I should be on the six o'clock train." Sean rose as Maeve entered the room. "Hello, Mama. I was waiting for you."

"Aye, I just now got home," Maeve replied, kissing her son's smooth cheek. "Veronica said you were here. Why didn't you tell us you were coming, Sean Gallagher?"

"I didn't know myself. I decided yesterday."

"Sure and that was time enough to pick up the telephone."

"We're a poor parish, Mama. I don't like to call long distance."

"Poor, is it? What do you do with all the money Katie sends you? You don't spend it on yourself. Aye, I saw your raggedy coat in the closet. I sent you

511

money to buy a new winter coat. Or did you think I'd forgotten?"

"I use Katie's money and your money for parish needs."

"Parish needs! What about your own needs? A warm coat isn't so much. Did you take a vow against a warm coat?"

"I'm not here to argue, Mama. I had some extra time, and I stopped in to say hello."

Katie explained the purpose of Sean's trip to Manhattan. Maeve listened, shaking her head back and forth. "Are you daft, Sean Gallagher? Do you think a few words from you will change what Hugh is? He's a gangster, in case you don't read the papers. A killer, like all the rest of them. Sure and it's nothing new. *Swag* Gallagher, cock o' the walk. And anybody stepping in his way gets a bullet."

"Mama—"

"It's the truth, Katie. All those devil gangsters with their devil names. Mad Dog and Bugsy and Big Frenchy. *And* Swag."

"I must be going now, Mama."

"You'll see I'm right. It's a waste of time."

Sean kissed his mother then went to Katie, hugging her. "If there's time, I'll stop in later."

"If I know Hugh, there will be plenty of time. Sean?" Katie smiled. "It's a long walk to the Astor Hotel. I have a car and driver waiting for you outside."

"A car and driver? How would that look? A priest with a car and driver?"

"It's a *long* walk."

512

Sean hesitated, considering the wear and tear on his shoe leather. "Well, maybe just this once."

The Astor Hotel was something of a West Side landmark, its French Renaissance façade stretching along Broadway from Forty-Fourth to Forty-Fifth Street. The location was ideal for entertainers and theater people, and for tourists who wanted to be close to the city's nightlife. Hugh and Meg had moved to the Astor several years before, occupying a large penthouse suite. Now Meg opened the door of the suite. "Come in, Sean." She smiled, leading him past the two bodyguards who kept watch in the entry. "What a nice surprise. We don't get many visitors here, not out of the blue, anyhow."

"I'm sorry if it's inconvenient, Meg. I was afraid to call ahead. I thought Hugh might put me off. He couldn't do it so easily with me standing right in the lobby. I decided to chance it."

"I'm glad. We haven't seen you since Katie's wedding. Time sure goes fast. Hugh," Meg called, "here's Father Sean."

Hugh looked up through a cloud of cigar smoke. "Hi, kid," he said. "Still wearing that ratty coat, huh?" He motioned to the two burly men sitting opposite. "Make yourselves useful for a change. Take my brother's hat and coat. And call room service. Let's have some sandwiches. Steak sandwiches with them fried potatoes. That sound okay, kid?"

"You needn't trouble on my account."

"Maybe I want to. Sit down. Go on, sit down. What

513

are you here for, kid? Money?'' Hugh reached into his pocket, removing a huge wad of bills. "How much? Name it and it's yours. I know priests is always doing good deeds. That takes dough."

"I didn't come for money. I came to talk about your life."

"Yeah?" Hugh was quiet, puffing his cigar. He fixed a cold stare on Sean. "What about my life? I'm living in a fancy suite. I'm eating the best food, wearing the best clothes. Meg is wearing diamonds. I got no complaints with my life."

"You hurt people. If even half the newspaper stories are true—"

"I got no complaints with the newspapers neither. They made me famous. I'm a big man in this town. Everybody knows Hugh Gallagher."

"Everybody knows *Swag* Gallagher, the gangster."

"Same thing."

"Is it? Then I'm truly sorry for you."

Hugh's stare was icy now. "I am what I am, kid."

"No, it's never too late to change. God will help you." Sean's voice was earnest, and his manner also. He leaned forward, placing his hand firmly on Hugh's shoulder. "Anything is possible, with God's help. You must pray. Pray for Divine help, for guidance."

Hugh, who had not prayed in twenty-five years, smiled. He shook Sean's hand off, puffing his cigar once again. "What is this?" he asked. "Did you come here to save my soul?"

"To try."

514

Sean's simple and innocent reply touched Hugh. His expression softened, though his eyes remained wary. "Did Ma send you here?"

"It was my own idea. She was against it."

"Yeah? The old lady's getting some sense. . . . So you want to save my soul, huh? You think it's worth saving?"

"There was aways good in you, Hugh. I remember the times when we had nothing to eat but bread, or potato pie. You always gave your share to Francis and Katie and me. You went to bed hungry."

"That was a long time ago, kid. I don't go to bed hungry no more. I want a steak, I pick up the phone and call room service. I want *anything*, I pick up the phone and it's here in a snap. I got money, power."

"How did you get those things, Hugh? With a gun. With killing."

"Well, that's the kind of world it is. That's life."

"That's a life gone wrong. You live in a fancy suite, but it's a fortress. Armed men in the hallway, armed men never far from your side. You can't trust your allies because they may turn on you. You can't trust your friends because they may be your enemies tomorrow."

"Yeah, yeah." Hugh tossed his cigar in an ashtray. He stared at his brother. "I give you credit, kid. You got guts, talking to me like that. You know who you're talking to?"

"I'm talking to Hugh, not Swag. They're not one and the same, despite what you say. I know the difference. Katie knows. And Meg. Have you thought what this life is doing to Meg?"

515

"Meg knew what she was getting into. She knew the score. Of all of you, she was the only one who really knew me. She took me like I was, 'cause that was the deal. I don't hear no complaints. Maybe she wanted a regular home in the beginning. But that was before she had them miscarriages. After that, it was just the two of us, the two of us against the world. It's a lousy world, kid. Priests is always talking pie in the sky. Priests and reformers. So where is it? Where's the pie in the sky? Where was it when we were living on bread and potatoes—when Katie had to go to work in a lousy boardinghouse? That was it for me, kid. The day Katie had to leave her school and go to work, that made up my mind good."

"The boardinghouse was part of God's plan for Katie. Don't you see?" Sean asked, his eyes bright and excited. "Through the boardinghouse she met Matt. Through Matt, she inherited the properties that led to the St. Clair Hotel. Through the St. Clair, she stayed close to Mr. Streeter. And through Mr. Streeter, she met Josh. Don't you see? It was God's plan all along."

Hugh, over the years, had lost his capacity for wonder, but now he stared in amazement at Sean. "You're a pip, kid. A pip! You really believe that stuff? You mean to tell me you really believe it was a . . . a *plan*?"

"God works in mysterious ways."

"Hey, Meg," Hugh called, seeing his wife poised in the doorway. "You should hear this. According to Father Sean, it was God who had Katie on her hands and knees twelve hours a day, scrubbing floors. It was

516

God who sent her to Ada's."

Meg entered the living room. She was smiling, pushing a wheeled cart laden with sandwiches and cakes and pots of tea. "Maybe that's not so funny, sweetheart." She winked. "Katie and I had a long talk on her wedding day. She said the boardinghouse was like a path, and the path brought her finally to Josh."

"There!" Sean cried. "Katie's own words on the subject!"

Hugh grinned, waving his arms in the air. "Okay, okay. So I'm surrounded by crazy people." He reached out and took his wife's hand. "Father Sean came to preach me a sermon. What do you say we give the kid a listen?"

"Fine with me. But first let's have lunch." Meg bustled about the room. At thirty-eight she had a fashionably slim figure and a shining cap of bobbed red hair. Her blue eyes, eyes that had shed oceans of private tears, sparkled now, as they always did when Hugh was home. In the years of their marriage she had had many doubts, many agonies large and small, but these she had been careful to keep to herself. Hugh was her husband, and she loved him above all else—above her family, above her God.

"Dig in, Sean," she said. "It's nice to have a meal together. Like old times."

Old times was the topic of conversation during lunch. It was an easy, lighthearted conversation, for they dwelled on the happy memories, and even Hugh had to admit there were indeed a few happy memories of days past. After lunch, the conversation turned to more serious matters. Sean spoke at length, his soft and earnest voice citing scripture and, once or twice, the troubled lives of the saints. Hugh listened patiently, if without any real interest. "I have to give you credit, kid," he said when Sean had finished. "You preach a good sermon. Father Flynn used to put me to sleep. Not you. You're the McCoy."

"Will you think about what I said, Hugh?"

"Yeah, sure I will. Not this minute. I got business to see to. Some business can't wait. But I'll remember what you said."

"That's all I ask. If you open your mind just a little bit, a crack, light will flood in. The true light."

"Sure, kid. Now how about some money to flood your pockets? Take it," Hugh said, again holding out the huge wad of bills. "Priests always need money."

"You're kind to offer, but I couldn't take it."

"No? Why not?"

"It's blood money."

Hugh's eyes darkened. "You're a lot like Ma," he snapped. "We'd be starving, freezing to death in that lousy flat, and all she'd take was her lousy dollar a week. Well, it's up to you. I don't beg people to take my money."

"Sean, at least take one of Hugh's coats. He has so many."

"There's wear in my coat yet."

"See what I mean?" Hugh asked with a sigh. "You got that streak in you. That streak of *Ma*, the old biddy. Ma or no Ma, I'm paying for your cab to the station."

"But I came in Katie's car. I came in style." Sean

518

laughed. "A car and driver. The driver has the car parked downstairs."

"Yeah? Which car? One of them fancy English jobs?"

"I don't know. It's certainly fancy. And big."

"I'm thinking of getting one of them myself. I'll go downstairs with you and have a look. Want to come, Meg?"

"Sweetheart, we already have four cars."

"So one more makes five. C'mon, Sean. Women don't understand. All our cars is American. I'm ready for a fancy English job." Grinning, Hugh led his brother into the hall. "Well, what are you standing there for, you guys? Get our coats."

"Right, boss."

"Thank you," Sean said as he was helped into his coat. "It's kind of you."

"Yeah, okay. Ain't we going with you, boss?"

"Naw. I'll be back in a minute. C'mon, Sean. I hear the elevator. Hurry up."

The afternoon sun was fading, and a cool, brisk wind blew across Broadway. Sean caught his hat just before it blew away, his eyes scanning the sky. "There's snow coming," he said. "Can you feel it?"

"It's wintertime, kid. Where's the car?"

"Oh, yes. That's it there." Sean smiled, pointing to a stately, gray Rolls Royce. "Is it what you had in mind?"

"It's a beauty. A beauty." Hugh took a step toward the curb. From the corner of his eye he saw another car, long and black and moving very slowly. He saw the open window and then the barrel of a machine gun. "*Sean*," he cried. He lunged at his brother, but too late, for in the next moment a lethal spray of bullets raked the air. "*Sean*."

People were screaming and running, covering their heads with their hands. A woman fainted and was nearly trampled in the terrible chaos. Brakes screeched and horns blared, and it seemed as if the entire avenue had gone mad.

Outside the Astor Hotel, halfway between the entrance and the curb, Hugh and Sean lay dead, their blood spreading in ever-widening circles upon the pavement.

The funeral at St. Brendan's was closed to the public. The doors were barred after the family entered the church, and they remained barred until the service ended. A security force hired by Josh rushed family members to waiting limousines, all the while keeping press and spectators at arm's length. A private burial service had been announced, but there were no doors to bar in the open spaces of the cemetery, and even the security force could not hold back the swarms of press or the gaping onlookers. Father Malone pleaded for dignity, to little avail. The murders of the Gallagher brothers, gangster and priest, were headline news throughout the country. Neither press nor public would be denied.

Katie had been shattered by her brothers' deaths, and now, behind her black veil, she wept bitter tears. Rory wept also, for, of her three sons, he had been the one closest to Hugh. Patrick, his eyes hollow and red, tried to console an inconsolable Meg. She cried. She shrieked. She stretched her arms toward Hugh's casket and, as she did, cameras clicked. Maeve alone seemed calm. She sat stiffly in her chair, looking from Hugh's casket to Sean's. Later, she would get drunk for the first time in her life.

Father Malone finished his prayers. He blessed the corners of the caskets with holy water and then made the sign of the cross. Meg, sobbing and shrieking, broke away from Patrick and flung herself on Hugh's casket. Her hands clawed the heavy bronze. Over and over again she screamed her husband's name.

The press surged forward, cameras held high. They knocked chairs and floral arrangements aside and almost knocked Father Malone off his feet. Hoards of spectators followed, fighting for a closer view of the hysterical widow.

Josh put his body between Katie and the human stampede. He wanted to shield her, to take her away from this nightmare, but all paths were blocked. When he turned around, he was not surprised to see the *Bugle* reporters urging the crowds on. *Bastards*, he thought; dirty, filthy *bastards*.

Six policemen had been assigned to the cemetery, and now they joined the security force to escort the mourners to their limousines. Meg had to be dragged away from the casket, collapsing finally in Patrick's arms. During the ride home she spoke not a word. She spent that night with her mother and then, the next week, she packed her things and boarded a ship for Ireland. "There are too many reminders here, Katie," she explained. "I have to go someplace where there's peace and quiet, where the *Bugle* can't hound me day and night."

Meg's statement needed no clarification, for the *Bugle* was making all their lives miserable. Every day its readers were treated to leering account of the millionaire, the gangster, the priest, and at the center of the stories, Boardinghouse Kate. Never had Josh seen such an outpouring of venom, of naked cruelty. Two weeks later he telephoned Ben Rossi and instructed him to buy the *Bugle*. "I don't care what it costs," he said. "Buy the damned rag. Then fire the so-called reporters, and their bosses. *Do* it, Ben. Do it before I kill them with my bare hands."

The Thurston household moved to Westerly for the Christmas holidays. Still in mourning, Katie canceled the usual festivities, though she was persuaded to have a small tree. Presents began appearing beneath the tree, and by Christmas Eve there was a great mountain of beribboned boxes. Katie protested, but Josh was not deterred. "It's Christmas," he said.

And Maeve agreed with his attitude. "Life goes on," she declared, settling the matter.

Rory found life at Westerly boring. He stayed through Christmas and then returned to New York. "To the bright lights," he said with a smile and a wink. But Matthew, unlike his big brother, loved Westerly. He rode off on his bicycle each morning, his pal Hobo yelping at his side. In the afternoons he and Josh worked on their project, an old sailboat they were restoring. They had long talks while they worked, some of them serious, some of them ending with laughter and good-natured chases along the beach.

The nights belonged to Katie and Josh. They cuddled by the roaring fire, drinking hundred-year-old brandy. They murmured to each other. They made love in the shadow of the moon and again in the first blue rays of dawn. On New Year's Eve they took champagne and glasses to the beach, toasting 1929 as all around them the surf pounded and gulls called.

The new year of 1929 began on a high wave of optimism. Factories were busy, and industry, powered by the booming stock market, reported record profits. It was true that the market suffered occasional setbacks, but these were not considered important. The newly elected President Hoover proclaimed the economy sound, and few voices rose in disagreement. When a small group of economists dared to suggest that trouble lay ahead, the nation and the government yawned.

On a Monday in October of 1929 thirteen million shares of stock were sold, and market losses exceeded ten billion dollars. Even the bankers, with their vast pool of money, were unable to stem the tidal wave of selling. The next day, a day which was forever to be known as Black Tuesday, the market crashed.

There was bedlam on the trading floor as desperate men shouted and screamed and wept. There was bedlam in the streets as desperate crowds gathered to witness the disaster. The toll was stupendous. The selling of twenty-three million shares let loose a panic that would destroy thirty billion dollars in market values. Great corporations were struck a mortal blow, as were the investment trusts. Now the market's big men went down along with the clerks and shopgirls and taxi drivers who had put their last dollars in the golden dreams of Wall Street.

Maeve lost thirty thousand dollars overnight, and for the rest of her life she would insist the market was a "fix." Jack Snow was wiped out, though Mary's various secret hiding places yielded the sum of forty-five thousand dollars, an enormous sum in Depression-era America. They sold their mansion and moved to a bungalow in Palm Springs. The poker games continued as usual until the 1940's, when Jack and Cornelius died within days of each other.

The Thurston family lost a combined total of three million dollars. They would have lost more but for Josh's decision, months earlier, to begin selling off the family holdings. "Are we poor?" Katie asked. "I don't care about the other things, but I hope we can keep Westerly. Can we?"

"Of course. Darling, we're far from poor. The family investment trust is gone. That means some of my cousins will have to go to work. They'll have to earn their living, and it's about time!"

But as the Depression deepened and took hold, there was little work to be found. Fourteen million men were unemployed in 1932, one out of every four American workers. Millions more had only part-time jobs to sustain them and their families. Homes were lost, farmers were forced off their lands, factories were closing by the thousands, and bank failures were rampant. Beggars were seen in the streets. Breadlines and soup kitchens were everywhere, for people were literally starving.

President Hoover continued to proclaim the soundness of the economy. Almost no one believed him. Franklin Roosevelt was elected in a landslide, and, to the strains of "Happy Days are Here Again," a new chapter in American history began.

22

"What did I tell you?" Maeve asked on an autumn afternoon in 1938. "When the world changes, there's a war. Aye, didn't I tell you that? Well, the Depression changed the world, and now there's going to be a war."

Katie looked at the stark black headline: "Hitler Invades Poland." She put the paper down, sighing. "You mustn't say such things, Mama. You mustn't even think them."

"And why not? Hitler's a crazy man. You can see in his eyes he's crazy. Do you suppose he'll be content to stop with Poland? He wants all Europe, Katie Thurston. Aye, maybe all the world. You can see in his eyes—"

"Stop it! I'm tired of hearing about war. War, war, war. Can't people talk about anything else?" Katie stood. She walked slowly, aimlessly, around the living room, pausing to touch the silken chairs, the polished antique cabinets. A crystal bowl filled with wildflowers sat atop one of the tables, and she bent, inhaling their scent. "Matthew was born during a war," she said. "Twenty-one years ago next month.

527

Don't you understand, Mama? If there's war, Matthew will be called. God, I wish sometimes I'd had girls instead of boys."

"Sure and there are worries with girls, just like with boys."

"Not *war* worries. I'm sorry, Mama. I don't mean to snap at you, but I'm frightened. Josh is frightened too, though he pretends otherwise."

"Aye, Josh is a good man. Dear knows he's been a good father to Matthew. You'd think he was his real father."

"He is, in all the ways that are important." Katie crossed the room, looking again at the newspaper. She felt a chill, and she rubbed her hands together. "The Great War was supposed to be the *last* war. People never learn."

"It's a different generation now. A different crazy man."

"Yes, God help us."

"All right, that's enough carrying on. There's no war today, is there? And today's your birthday. Go get dressed, Katie. Josh has a grand evening planned for the both of you. Do you want to keep your husband waiting? Well? Go on. Don't stand there like a goose . . . what are you smiling about?"

"You, Mama. I'm *forty-nine* today, but you're still telling me what to do."

"You're still my daughter, aren't you? Aye, you could be a hundred and you'd still be my daughter. Besides, I need the living room. I'm expecting Captain Garrity."

"When are you going to give in and marry him?"

"Marry him! Are you daft?"

"You've been keeping company for years."

"It's friendship, nothing more. And it's none of your account, Katie Thurston. Marry him! Such foolishness!"

Katie kissed Maeve's brow. She left the room and was on her way to the staircase when the doorbell rang. "I'll get it, Veronica," she called. She opened the door, her eyes brightening. "What a lovely surprise, Rory. Two visits in one week."

"Happy birthday, Ma." Rory took off his hat and coat, throwing them on the hall table. "I meant to come earlier, but I was delayed."

"Your forehead is bruised. What happened?"

"A little accident, Ma. My car had an unfortunate meeting with a lamppost. Don't worry. I'm fine. I wish I could say the same for my car. It's a wreck."

"You're very cheerful, considering it's your third wreck in as many years. Come into the library," Katie said, frowning. "I think it's time we had a talk."

"The library. That means a *serious* talk."

"Sit down, Rory."

"After I give you your present. Here, Ma." Rory grinned, putting a small box in her hand. "Happy birthday."

Katie unwrapped the box. She lifted the velvet lid and saw a dainty butterfly-shaped brooch of pearls and diamonds. "It's beautiful, Rory. And much too extravagant. You shouldn't have."

"I wanted to. What did Patrick give you?"

"Trees."

"Trees?"

"Well, saplings. Josh and I were talking about planting an orchard at Westerly. Patrick sent a dozen saplings. But never mind that." Katie shook her head. "You aren't going to distract me this time. How did you wreck your car? Were you drunk?"

"Not drunk. I'd had a few, but I wasn't drunk. No one was hurt. Of course my car looks like an accordion. It's not worth repairing. The new models are out, and if I could have a modest check—"

"So you came for money. Again."

"That isn't fair, Ma. I came to give you your present, a present I bought weeks ago, by the way. The accident only happened last night." Rory lighted a cigarette. He sat back, shrugging his broad shoulders. "But since I'm here and your checkbook is here . . . I can't manage without a car, Ma. I certainly can't swing the price on my own."

"I'd like to know why not? You have the monthly income from your trust. It's a substantial income, Rory. What do you do with all your money? No, don't even bother to answer. I know what you do with it. You spend it as if you were a royal prince. Custom-made suits by the dozens. Custom-made shirts and shoes. Gold cigarette cases. An apartment large enough for ten people. And let's not forget your nightclubbing. Let's not forget the checks you pick up for everyone, the lavish tips."

"I'm enjoying myself. I admit it."

"What about work? Your acting career got off to such a promising start, Rory. You were eager. You were out there *trying*. Then you came into your trust fund and overnight you were a different person. When is the last time you went to an audition? Can you remember that far back?"

"You know the kind of parts I was being offered,

Ma. They weren't much more than walk-ons."

"But that's how acting careers begin. Did you expect to be a star right away? It's a tough business. It takes years. You grew up around show people, Rory. Were all their struggles lost on you? Were all *my* struggles lost on you? I was bringing home wages when I was half your age. No fancy clothes, no cars. I was grateful to have a warm coat in winter—"

"Not that again, Ma." Rory groaned. "I've heard it a hundred times before. I've heard how you trudged through the snow and the rain. Wasn't there any *good* weather when you were young?"

Katie stared in dismay at her son. She was about to reply when Josh entered the library. "Hello, darling," he said quietly, kissing her cheek. "Why don't you run along and get dressed while I have a word with Rory. I won't be long."

"Rory wants a new car."

"Does he? Run along, darling. I'll see to this."

"It's really between Ma and me, Josh."

"Your mother has other things to do. I'm sure you understand." Josh took Katie's hand and led her to the door. "Don't look so worried." He smiled. "We're just going to have a little talk."

Katie glanced over her shoulder at Rory. She saw the flash of his brilliant blue-green eyes and she sighed. "You won't get very far, I'm afraid. He's in a stubborn mood today. But I wish you'd talk to him about drinking and driving. I didn't even try. We've had that argument too often lately . . . Josh, he had another accident."

"Leave Rory to me. Don't worry about a thing, darling." Josh closed the door. He strode across the room, sitting in a deep leather chair opposite his stepson. "I'll come straight to the point,"he said. "I heard part of your conversation and—"

"Eavesdropping, Josh?" Rory grinned.

"Don't interrupt me again. This isn't a joking matter. Or perhaps it is, to you. Perhaps you find your mother's past struggles amusing. Well, why not? There she was, thirteen years old and scrubbing floors for a living so her family could eat. Surely the stuff of comedy!"

"I'm sorry. I know what Ma went through. Some of it, anyway. But it was a long time ago. It doesn't seem . . . important now."

"Not compared to a new car. I gather you cracked up your old car, which wasn't old at all. You broke your promise, didn't you? You promised you wouldn't drink and drive; then you went ahead and did both."

"It was late. There were no cabs around."

"Where is your driver's license? May I see it?"

"Sure." Rory removed his license from his wallet, handing it to Josh. "It's a regular license." He laughed. "They don't put a black mark on it for— What are you doing?"

"Tearing your license into tiny pieces. You needn't bother to seek a replacement. I intend to make a telephone call, Rory. That call will put your name on a list. Your license will be revoked."

"You *can't.*"

"It's as good as done."

"I can't manage without a car."

"There are cabs, buses, subways. You'll manage. You'll get your license back, Rory, but only when I'm convinced you're responsible enough to have a license."

"You're treating me like some damned *kid*."

"Under the circumstances, that's the treatment you deserve. I gather you squandered your monthly check again. More baubles for more showgirls? Or are you lighting your cigarettes with twenty-dollar bills?"

Rory jumped up. He began to pace, throwing dark looks at Josh. "I'm entitled to something extra," he said finally. "Ma gave the St. Clair to Patrick. She signed a few papers and he's a hotel owner. Matthew will get Thurston Shipping one day. What about me? What do I get?"

"You have your trust fund. You have a very generous trust fund."

"Patrick and Matthew have trust funds too. But Patrick also has the St. Clair, and Matthew will have Thurston Shipping. I've been cut out of the family businesses."

"By your own choice, Rory. Patrick would be glad to take you into the St. Clair, if that's what you want. Is it? I would be glad to take you into Thurston Shipping. There's room for both you and Matthew. You can start tomorrow, *if* that's what you want. Is it?"

"All I'm saying is I'm entitled to my share."

"You're entitled to work for your share. Patrick works. Matthew works. I work. I'm in my office bright and early every morning. I hate it, but I'm there. And you? You party every night. You sleep until noon every day. Then you go off to lunch at one of your theatrical hangouts, and soon, lo and behold, it's time for cocktails. I don't intend to support your playboy ways, Rory."

"It's hard getting started in the theater."

"How would you know? You're too busy partying and sleeping and lunching to get *near* a theater. Ah, there it is." Josh smiled. "The look of wounded innocence. Nice try."

"Do you mind if I have a drink?"

"Help yourself. You're not driving."

"Very funny."

"Very sad. You're wasting your life. Good God, you're almost thirty, and what do you have to show for those years? You're a talented fellow. You're handsome—charming, when you want to be. You have all the attributes an actor needs, yet you waste them."

"It isn't that easy. New York is filled with talented actors looking for the one big break."

"But they *are* looking. They're making rounds, going to auditions. They're learning their craft in regional theater and summer stock. You, on the other hand, seem to favor nightclubs. I'm sorry to say I bear part of the blame. It's true." Josh nodded, his green eyes fast on Rory. "I'll tell you a secret. When I came into my first trust fund, I raised hell for six months. It wasn't the money. I'd been accustomed to money, after all. It was, I think, the sense of power. Whatever the reasons, I became a high-living playboy. An ass, much like you."

"Solid, respectable Josh Thurston?"

"My father let me have my six months, and then he put his foot down, hard. He wasn't often right, where I was concerned, but he was right to do that. That's what I should have done with you. That's what I'm going to do *now*. There will be no money beyond your trust income, Rory. Not a nickel. And if you don't start pulling yourself together, there will be no trust income either."

"Just like that."

"Yes. When my father took action, it was because he wanted me to be an upstanding member of society, a credit to the Thurstons. My own motives are quite different. I want you to be happy, Rory. . . . Are you surprised?"

"A little."

"Well, we were never as close as we should have been. I suppose the timing was wrong. Patrick was grown by the time I came into your lives. Matthew was only a child. But you were somewhere in between, odd man out. I confess I was unsure. I didn't know how to handle the situation. Now I see I handled it badly. I never told you I loved you, son."

"Son?" Rory swallowed, for he felt a sudden lump in his throat. The last traces of anger fled from his eyes. He looked wistful and very young. "Did you call me son?"

Josh rose. He went to Rory, clasping his shoulder. "You *are* my son." He smiled. "My brash, blunt, thoroughly engaging son. It's not too late to be a family, Rory, if you're willing. What do you say? Shall we give it a try? Father and son?"

"Father and son. That . . . means a lot to me. I *was* always odd man out. Patrick was the man of the family and Matthew was the baby. They had their places. I didn't. I didn't fit in. While Patrick was getting straight As at school, I was flunking. While Matthew was being adorable, I was being . . . difficult. I think Ma understood, but she was so busy. She had her work, her problems. Then she married you, and I really felt . . . excluded. I knew I couldn't live up to your standards. I couldn't be serious and good, like Patrick. I couldn't be your son, like Matthew. Odd man out."

"Rory, we should have had this talk a long time ago. Of course you're my son, no less than Matthew. As for being serious and good . . . Patrick is certainly a fine fellow, but you're in *awe* of him. I know because I was in awe of my older brother. Jordan was my idol, until it dawned on me that he didn't want an idolater. All he wanted was a kid brother. That's all Patrick wants. I'm trying to say you must stop making comparisons and start being yourself."

Rory considered Josh's words. He grinned. "To thine own self be true?"

"Mr. Shakespeare was a wise man."

"So are you. I won't let you down again."

"We'll have a pact not to let each other down." Josh was smiling as he walked Rory to the door. He watched him go, then turned and climbed the stairs to the cozy second-floor rooms he shared with Katie. "Darling? Where are you?" he called.

"Here I am." Katie emerged from the dressing room. She wore a long, slim column of black chiffon, its neckline revealing the swell of her breasts. There were diamond clips in her upswept hair and diamonds sparkled at her ears and wrists. "Do you approve?" she asked, spinning around.

"You take my breath away, Katie. You grow more beautiful each year. . . . But do I see worry in your eyes?"

"How is Rory? What happened?"

"He won't be driving for a while. I told him I was going to have his license revoked."

"Oh, Josh, he must be furious."

"He was, at first. He understands now. After I told him to shape up, I told him I loved him. He needed to hear that. He's been feeling excluded, darling. We did those special things for Patrick and Matthew. Rory was lost in the shuffle, or he felt he was. Today we had the talk we should have had long ago."

Katie rushed into Josh's arms. "Thank you," she said. "That's the best birthday present of all. I'm so happy."

"There are some other presents hidden around here."

"Not now." Katie laughed. "If I open them now I'll start to cry and ruin my makeup."

"Makeup? You dare to put makeup on that beautiful face?"

"Surprise, surprise." Katie laughed again. "You're sweet to pretend not to know. Time is catching up with me, Josh."

"Never! You're eternally young, my darling. My beautiful darling."

Katie's birthday was celebrated at her favorite restaurant, a tiny candle-lit cafe near Central Park. She and Josh sat at a secluded rear table, holding hands and murmuring to each other, much as they had on their honeymoon, and much as they would for the rest of their lives. They danced to their favorite songs, and later, in the small, blue-black hours of morning, they took a carriage ride through the park.

It was dawn when Katie and Josh returned home.

There they found a message that William Streeter had died during the night. "He was past eighty." Josh sighed, brushing Katie's tears away. "And he enjoyed every moment of his life."

"Yes. Yes, I know. He was such a *dear* man."

Josh stroked Katie's golden hair. "You mustn't be sad, darling," he said softly. "William wouldn't want you to be sad. . . . Look, there's a bottle of champagne. Shall we have a toast to William?" Josh picked up the bottle. He smiled. "It's from Rory. The card says 'for Ma and Pa.' Well, it took a while, but I'm Rory's pa at last. Shall we have a toast?"

"First to William . . . then to our family." With a chill, Katie remembered the terrible headlines, the terrible talk of war. "Yes," she whispered, choking back her tears, "a toast to family."

There was but one shadow on Katie's family in the years that followed, the long and ominous shadow of war. If war had seemed a distant threat in 1938, it seemed, in the waning months of 1941, an ever more likely possibility. Poland had already fallen to Hitler's armies, as had Holland and Belgium. Britain was under seige, France controlled by the collaborationist government at Vichy.

The war reports were never far from Katie's mind, though she had her distractions—four growing granddaughters and a new daughter-in-law, Rory's wife, Laura. She had Matthew's Sunday night visits. She had, as always, Josh. "Isn't Josh home yet, Mama?" she asked on a quiet Sunday afternoon in December. "Did you look in the library?"

538

"Of course I did. What's the matter with you, Katie? Can't the man go out for an hour without you carrying on? Sure and it's the same when you go out and he's looking for you. You'd think you were still honeymooners."

"We are." Katie walked across the bedroom, throwing open the closet doors. "Besides, we were supposed to go through the closets today. We have a lot of clothing for the War Relief. You said you'd have a few things. Where are they?"

"All packed in my room. Two cartons."

"Good. That's a start."

"At least they'll be able to use my clothes. Sensible clothes, not like your silks and satins. It's no time for fancy dress balls in Europe now."

"We're sending warm coats and suits, Mama."

"Aye, but you'll be needing cartons."

"Patrick brought dozens of cartons from the hotel. All different sizes. I'll get—" Katie stopped, for Josh had entered the room. "There you are." She smiled. "Just in time to do some hard work—What's wrong? Josh, you're white as a sheet. What's wrong?"

"Sit down, darling. Maeve, you too. I'm afraid I have very bad news. The Japanese have bombed our naval bases at Pearl Harbor. The first reports are very bad. It's a disaster."

Maeve's expression did not change, though her hands clenched tightly in her lap. Katie began to cry, and Josh rushed instantly to her side. "This means war," she said through her tears. "Oh, my God. My God."

Josh took Katie and Maeve into the study. There they sat glued to the radio, as did millions of other

Americans across the country. The first reports were worse than bad; they were horrifying. Later reports only confirmed the devastation. They told of bombs raining from the sky, of battleships going down in flames with their crews trapped aboard, of the deaths of more than four thousand men.

Shock gave way to grief and then to rage. "*Damn them,*" Katie cried, not once but over and over again. No reproof came from Maeve, for she too was enraged by the sneak attack. Josh felt a profound sadness, a sadness beyond words. He had fought in the Great War. He had seen death and suffering and unspeakable savagery. Now he knew that Matthew would see those things, and the knowledge was a stone weighing on his heart.

"Katie, where are you going?" Maeve asked.

"I must call Matthew."

"No, darling." Josh rose, leading Katie back to her chair. "You mustn't. He has a great deal to think about. We mustn't interfere."

"He'll be running off to enlist."

"Perhaps. It's Matthew's decision. He'll be here later, I'm sure. When he's ready, he'll tell us what he's decided."

"I'm so frightened."

"I know, darling. These are frightening times."

Matthew arrived at seven o'clock, his usual hour. He joined Katie and Josh in the living room, and for an anxious ten minutes there was no mention of war. Katie sat very close to Josh, but her eyes remained fixed on her son. He was twenty-four years old, tall and solidly built. With his reddish hair and clear blue eyes he was the image of Matt. Katie remembered the day she had seen Matt off to war. She remembered the marching bands and the flags and the laughter. She remembered the telegram: "We regret to inform you . . ." Sighing, she looked away. "We can't keep avoiding the subject," she said quietly. "We all know what happened today. Matthew, what are you going to do?"

"I could wait to be drafted. I thought about it, Mom. I'd rather enlist. It's not that I'm a hero. If you recall my two or three boyhood fights"—Matthew smiled—"you'll recall I'm no hero. Nor am I out for glory. There's no glory in war."

"Then why?"

"America has been attacked. It's our war now, like it or not. I have to do my part. Why wait? A few weeks, a few months, won't make any difference. This thing won't be won overnight. I'll be in the fighting sooner or later. It might as well be sooner. I've decided to join the Navy. Family tradition, eh Dad?"

"The Navy means the Pacific."

"That's fine. I wouldn't mind having a crack at the Japanese."

"A crack at the Japanese?" Katie cried. "It's not a game, Matthew."

"No, it's not. Hirohito didn't send toy planes to Pearl Harbor. Hitler isn't using toy soldiers to gobble up Europe. No, it's not a game." Matthew reached out, taking Katie's hand. "What would you do in my place, Mom?" he asked gently. "Would you wait to be drafted? I don't think so. I think you'd be first in line at the recruiting office."

"It doesn't matter what *I'd* do."

"Mom, you and Dad raised me to be a certain sort of fellow. To respect my elders, to be kind, to work hard, to love my country," Matthew recited, a smile edging his handsome mouth. "Well, my country has been attacked. It's clear what I must do. If I had a wife, children, perhaps I'd wait. I'm not even engaged."

"Whose fault is that?"

Matthew laughed. "Now you sound like Grandma."

"He's right, darling," Josh concurred.

"Yes, I know. And the moment I heard about Pearl Harbor I knew what the result would be. I knew there'd be no stopping our Matthew. It's all those long talks you two had," Katie said, shaking her head at Josh. "Talks about honor and duty."

"You were pretty keen on honor and duty yourself, Mom. You still are. That's why you understand what I'm going to do."

"I understand. I won't pretend I'm happy. No mother is happy sending her son off to war." Katie stood. She went to Matthew and put her arms around him. "My baby a soldier."

"Sailor."

"Excuse me, a sailor . . . I have to admit I'm proud of you, Matthew. I'm scared to death, but I'm proud of you."

Josh watched his wife and son. His eyes were suddenly damp and he blinked. "What about the old man?" he asked. "Doesn't the old man get a hug?"

"Come on, old man." Katie laughed, stretching her arms wide. "The more the merrier."

All over America families were hugging, clinging

together, and the Thurstons were no different. Patrick and Lucy found themselves drawn to the townhouse, as did Rory and Laura. Everyone gathered in front of the roaring fire, talking not of war but of the happy times they had shared. There was laughter and brandy and affectionate teasing as old rivalries were recalled. Rory sang songs from his first Broadway show. Patrick lured Maeve out of her room, and she taught Laura, the newest member of the family, an Irish jig. The impromptu party continued long into the night. It was a party they would remember, for it was to be years before they were together again.

Matthew was assigned to Officer's Training School in 1942, and, ninety days later, he was a Navy ensign on his way to the Pacific. By an odd coincidence, he sailed on a Thurston ship, one of many passenger vessels requisitioned by the government "for the duration." The staterooms had been gutted, and, instead of elegant furnishings and silk sheets, there were narrow cots bolted to the walls and stacked five tiers high. "It's a little like the steerage of old," Matthew wrote in a lighthearted note to Katie and Josh. "But it's okay. It's Navy!"

Rory finished his Broadway run and, to everyone's surprise, joined a USO troupe. He performed at bond rallies and military bases throughout America, singing and dancing and getting young recruits up on the stage to act in skits. Early in 1943 he requested overseas duty, and his request was swiftly granted. "Morale is important too, Ma," he said, kissing Katie good-bye. "Our boys are far from home."

Katie did not have to be reminded that her own

boys were far from home. She and Josh poured over the newspapers, matching every dispatch to the huge map they posted in the library. They arranged their schedules to include the evening news broadcasts on the radio. They learned to content themselves with such rituals, for the letters they received from Matthew and Rory were heavily censored, offering few clues to the whereabouts of their sons.

Like millions of other Americans, Katie and Josh knew moments of great optimism and moments of great despair. They cheered major American victories at Midway and the Coral Sea; they mourned major defeats at Corregidor and Bataan. Casualty lists were long, some of the names known to the Thurstons. One of Josh's cousins was killed at Bataan. Laura's only brother was killed at Guadalcanal in 1943. Ben Rossi's son, just nineteen years old, was killed at Anzio in 1944.

Josh was summoned to Washington in the spring of 1944. When he returned he was very quiet, spending hours locked away in his study. Katie was puzzled at first and then concerned. "What's wrong?" she asked. "You haven't been yourself since you came back from Washington. What is it?"

"This godawful war, that's what it is."

"What happened in Washington, Josh?"

"The President has a spot all picked out for me at the Navy Department. And the President is a hard man to turn down."

"Goodness, did you see the President?"

"Well, we're not exactly strangers. I told you about the parties I went to at Hyde Park and the parties Franklin went to at Westerly. Of course it was years

544

and years ago. Franklin and Eleanor were just starting their family, if my memory is correct. I was still in school." Josh removed his glasses, tossing them on the desk. "Now he's the *President* and he's asked me to join the war effort. He seems to think I can be useful. I don't know much about war, but I know a lot about ships. The President feels that tighter specifications are needed, tighter controls. That's the spot he wants me to fill. It has to be right away. There's a big push coming."

"Josh, you *can't* turn him down."

"No, I can't. It means I'll have to be in Washington five days a week. Six, while the new production schedule is being prepared. Even if you came with me, we wouldn't have any time together." Josh left his desk. He went to Katie, taking her in his arms. "We haven't been apart a single day in eighteen years." He sighed. "Now we'll be lucky to have weekends. I'm sorry, darling. This is a terrible time to leave you, with the boys overseas and—"

"Hush." Katie smiled, her fingers touching Josh's lips. "I understand. I'd be very selfish not to understand. We'll be apart, Josh, but you'll be *safe*. That's all I care about. There are millions of wives who have no idea where their husbands are, much less how they are—Lucy and Laura among them. . . . We *are* lucky, Josh. As long as we have each other, we're the luckiest people in the world."

"My sweet darling. I love you, Katie."

"I love you. Always."

Josh began his Washington assignment in April. Katie kept busy, organizing clothing drives and bond rallies and working with the Red Cross, but still she felt bereft. The nights were the worst times. Unable to sleep, she wandered from room to room, settling finally in the library where she drank tea and played fetch with Hobo IV. "How long do you plan to mope around?" Maeve asked after two weeks had passed. "Are you a child, Katie Thurston? A baby?"

"I miss my husband, Mama."

"Aye, and your husband misses you. But he's doing his job, isn't he? Everybody has to do his job in wartime. I'm at the veterans' hospital every morning. Dear knows it's not much, giving out books and magazines, helping our boys to write letters. But it's my job and I'm glad to do it. At least I'm doing my share."

"So am I."

"Sure and you could be doing *more*, Katie. If you were doing more, you wouldn't have time to mope around. You wouldn't have time to feel sorry for yourself."

"What more can I do?"

"That's for you to figure out. You were smart enough to build a business from nothing. Aye, you're smart enough to figure out something to do to help the war. Think of Rory and Matthew. What would they want you to do?"

The answer came to Katie the next night. The following month, with the cooperation of the veterans' hospitals, and with Josh's approval, she opened Westerly to recuperating servicemen. Chartered buses brought them to Southampton fifty at a time, fifty young soldiers and sailors and marines whose wounds had healed but whose spirits remained low. Each group had ten days of sun and sand and healthy meals prepared around the clock by a willing kitchen staff. In the recreation room, once the main drawing room, they had pool tables and pinball machines and poker games. There was a juke box, and an enormous refrigerator filled top to bottom with beer.

It was a special time for Katie. She watched as color returned to the faces of "her boys," as life once again entered their sad eyes, and she felt her own spirit restored. Now there were not enough hours in the day. There were meals to be served, games and fishing parties and cookouts to be organized, lonely hands to be held. One Sunday late in September, Katie and Josh sat on the beach and counted the names of all the young men who had signed their scrapbook. They counted seven hundred and fifty names. "Mama had asked me what Rory and Matthew would want me to do to help the war," Katie said. "I think they'd be pleased. And perhaps, somewhere, people are opening their homes to them."

In November, bowing to the weather and to the fuel shortage, Katie closed Westerly. In December, Matthew was reported missing in action. After a frantic and despairing few days, the report was amended to "wounded in action." Matthew's wounds kept him in military hospitals for months. He had three different operations in three different hospitals, the last one in California. When finally he was released, he recuperated at Mary Snow's Palm Springs home.

Katie and Josh had planned a gala party for Matthew's return, but on that day President

Roosevelt died, and the Thurstons, along with the rest of the nation, wept. A grieving Josh left immediately for Washington. Katie canceled the party, standing alone at the door when Matthew arrived. "Matthew!" she cried, great tears splashing her face as she embraced her son. "Are you all right? Really all right? Let me look at you." She took a step back and only then did she see the pretty, fair-haired young woman in the doorway. "Hello." She smiled. "Come in, dear. Matthew, introduce me to your girl. Don't be shy."

"I have a surprise for you, Mom. Mrs. Thurston, meet Mrs. Thurston. . . . Yep." Matthew laughed. "I'm married. This is Elizabeth Snow Thurston," he said, draping his arm about his new bride. "Liz and I didn't want any fuss. We eloped."

"Eloped! I hardly know what to say. It's a *wonderful* surprise."

"I'm happy to meet you, Mrs. Thurston. I've heard so much about you from Matthew, and Gran. All good things."

"Welcome to the family, Elizabeth. I'm delighted . . . Elizabeth *Snow*? Are you . . . you couldn't be Mary's great-granddaughter. I don't believe it."

"That's who I am."

"I saw you in your bassinet when you were a tiny baby. My God, it doesn't *seem* that long ago. Look at you now. I can't believe it."

"We called Gran from the station. She wondered if you'd remember. Gran said it was the day after one of their big Hollywood parties. She said you wore a slinky black gown and caused a sensation."

"And danced with Valentino," added Matthew.

"Yes." Katie sighed. "Yes, I remember very well. It *was* that long ago. I'm feeling older by the minute. Come sit down before I begin to shrivel up."

"You look pretty good to me," Matthew said, following Katie into the living room. "Is Josh in Washington?"

"He left as soon as we heard the news. It's a tragedy. I can't imagine this country without President Roosevelt. Poor Mr. Truman. It won't be easy for him. . . . Sit down, Elizabeth. Make yourself comfortable. We had a party planned, but under the circumstances . . . well, we'll have our own little party. Patrick and his family are coming by later. Grandma will be down after her nap. We needn't wait. There's the champagne. Matthew, you do the honors." Katie stepped away, though her gaze remained on her son. She saw a web of small scars on the left side of his face, the result of shell fragments that had almost cost him his sight. She thought of the countless young men who had been blinded and crippled, who had been killed, and fresh tears splashed down her cheeks. "Oh, pay no attention to me," she said. "I'm just so happy to have you home. You and Elizabeth."

"Rory will be home soon too, Mom."

"He's determined to stay with the USO until the war ends. Sometimes . . . Sometimes I think the war will never end."

"To all the men still over there," Matthew said, lifting his glass. "To victory."

The victory so long awaited came in May of 1945, when President Truman announced the unconditional surrender of Germany. Three months later, after the bombing of Hiroshima and Nagasaki, Japan surrendered. The war was over at last.

"How would you like to have a full-time husband?" Josh asked in the winter of 1951. "Could you stand a husband around the house day and night? Or would you shoot him?

"Are you the husband in question?"

"I am."

"Then I certainly wouldn't shoot him." Katie laughed. She looked up from her dressing table, gazing at Josh. There was silver in his black hair now, and his forhead was lined, but he was still the handsomest man she had ever seen. "I would welcome him with open arms. Why do you ask?"

"I've been thinking about retiring, darling. I started thinking about it right after the war ended, but Thurston Lines practically had to be rebuilt. I had to stay on. The last stage of our rebuilding will be completed in another year. I believe Matthew will be ready to take over."

"Josh, it's a tremendous job. Matthew isn't a child, but he's awfully young to have such responsibility."

"I was younger than he when I took over. And youth is on his side. The war changed so many things. Before the war, the only people who traveled to Europe were rich people. They traveled in great luxury, great style. It was a way of life. Those days are gone, Katie. It's a different world. We must reach a newer, younger market. Above all, we must offer cruises that appeal to that market. You understand what I mean, darling."

"Are you really going to retire?"

"Shall we say a year from today?"

"*Really*?"

"Yes." Josh nodded, smiling. "It's time we ran off by ourselves. We can, darling. The children are settled in their careers—Patrick and Matthew in business, Rory in the movies. The grandchildren are fine. Eight of them and not one troublemaker in the bunch. Even the great-grandchildren are fine. . . . It's time for us now."

"I see a very naughty gleam in your eye, Josh Thurston."

"Do you? I wonder why. Perhaps it's because you're so beautiful." Josh bent over Katie, slipping the gown from her shoulders. "My darling," he murmured. "My beautiful darling."

There was to be a New Year's Eve ball at Westerly, and for months painters and carpenters and workmen swarmed through the vast estate, restoring grounds and mansion to their former splendor. Katie planned the ball in honor of Josh's retirement, but Josh had other ideas. "I want it to be Katie's evening," he explained to the family. "A tribute. A *surprise* tribute. We'll each do our part . . . and remember, mum's the word."

Rory and Laura and their two sons came from California. They brought Mary Snow with them, and she, in turn, brought John Costello. Patrick's daughter, Ann, came from Chicago with her husband and children and twin granddaughters. Maeve rounded up scores of Muldoons from all over the country, making their travel arrangements and briskly issuing orders. Meg, plump and rosy cheeked and bursting with excitement, came from Ireland.

Josh spent months locating the servicemen Katie had welcomed to Westerly during the war. Almost a hundred of them, wives and children in tow, arrived in New York and were taken to the St. Clair. Rory was there to meet them. "We're gonna put on a show, kids," he cried happily, "just like Mickey Rooney and Judy Garland." He wrote special lyrics to familiar tunes. He devised simple dance steps. He rehearsed his "chorus line" for three days and three nights. "Knock 'em dead," he said early on New Year's Eve, ushering his charges into the chartered buses.

"Well, darling." Josh smiled. "I hope you're ready for the big night. Are you?"

"I was ready an hour ago. Then you couldn't find your cufflinks." Katie smiled back. "Then you needed a button sewn on. Then you wanted a drink . . . I have a feeling you know something I don't. What do you have up your sleeve?"

"Only my arms."

"Oh, Josh." Katie laughed. "Can we greet our guests now? They must be wondering what happened to us."

"Of course, my darling."

The Westerly ballroom had never looked lovelier. Hundreds of white candles glittered in two magnificent crystal chandeliers. The many tables were dressed with pale blue linen cloths, set with china and silver and masses of wildflowers. The guests, too numerous to count, held glasses of champagne and nibbled on caviar. "They're coming," Matthew called, trying to quiet the crowd. "Mom and Dad."

There were excited murmurings in the room, then silence as all eyes went to the doors. Moments later they opened and Katie entered on Josh's arm. Everyone rose, applauding. "For you, Josh," she said.

"For *you*, Katie. Look again."

"What?" Katie turned her head. Her lips parted and tears rushed to her eyes as she saw the faces of her past—faces from Hell's Kitchen, from Ada's boardhouse, from the war. "Josh . . . I . . . I don't know what to say."

"Enjoy yourself, darling. It's your night."

"It certainly is." Ben Rossi laughed, stepping forward. "And I have the honor of escorting you and Josh to your table."

"Were you in on it too?"

"I was a chief conspirator!"

Katie was beaming as she greeted her guests. She was radiant, a beautiful woman in a long, black velvet sheath, the Thurston pearls clasped about her slender neck. There were pearls at her ears, and more pearls were threaded through her upswept hair. She glided across the room, accepting kisses and hugs, stopping now and then to exchange a few words. Tears came to her eyes, for in the sea of faces she saw the story of her life. A blessed life, she thought, taking her place at the glittering head table.

Father Malone ascended the newly installed stage. "They made me master of ceremonies for the evening," he announced with an exaggerated shrug.

"I always knew my years calling bingo numbers would come to something . . . but I'm not the star of the evening," he added when the laughter had died down. "Katie's the star. To celebrate her, we have another star. The singing and dancing star of MGM movies, Mr. Rory McVey."

Rory bounded onto the stage. He acknowledged the applause, then signaled the musicians to begin. "For you, Ma." He bowed, and for the next hour he sang the songs of Katie's youth. He danced the time step Jack Snow had taught him so many years ago. Tossing his top hat and cane aside, he danced the comic shuffle John Costello had taught him. He finished his performance with a lyrical rendition of "Danny Boy," falling to one knee as the spotlight slowly dimmed. Applause exploded in the ballroom. There were cheers and whistles and it was some time before Father Malone, wiping a tear away, could introduce "Katie's chorus." The former servicemen sang a loud, funny tribute to their wartime stay at Westerly. The reprise, sung over and over again, went: "She gave us sun and sand and surf/She told us not to fear/But most of all/Oh, most of all/She gave us lots of beer."

Maeve took the stage last. She was very frail, clinging to Captain Garrity's arm, but her voice was clear and firm. "Josh asked me to speak a few words about my daughter," she said. "Aye, I'm glad to do it. . . . Katie was just a little girl when I sent her to work at Ada McVey's boardinghouse. It was hard times back then. Most of you here are too young to remember how it was. Poor people worked twelve hours a day and more, but still we went cold and hungry. Potato pie, potato stew—that's what we lived on. If there was ten cents left over for a bit of meat, we gave special thanks to God. Aye, it was hard times . . . so Katie had to leave school and go to work. She didn't complain. Not a peep. She was strong, even in those days. I raised her to be strong, and I'll take my credit for that. But all the rest . . . well, that's her own doing. I was one to see the bad in the world. Katie was one to see the good. Always she followed her heart. Sometimes her heart led her wrong, and she paid the price. Dear knows she had her grief. But in the end, she was right to follow her heart. You're the proof," Maeve said, dabbing a handkerchief to her eyes. "Fine children and grandchildren and great-grandchildren. A fine husband. Fine friends. You're the measure . . . of Katie's life. All through her life, when she did something good, something extra, I told her, 'Keep it up and you'll make me proud." Maeve turned, gazing at her daughter. "Katie, I'm here tonight to say you made me proud. I'm proud of you, and that's the truth . . . I love you, Katie Thurston."

Katie rushed up on stage, taking Maeve in her arms. "Mama," she said through her tears, "I've waited sixty years to hear those words."

"Aye, now you've heard them. Don't let them go to your head."

Katie and Josh strolled hand in hand along the beach. The sky was dark and snow had begun to fall, lacy white flakes skipping over the waves. "Happy, darling?" Josh asked, drawing Katie's sables close about her.

"I'm the happiest woman in the world."

"Really?"

"Really." Katie smiled. "I have my family. I have my Hobo." She laughed suddenly, bending to pet Hobo V. "I have my husband, my wonderful, wonderful husband. I love you, Josh."

"I love you, darling."

Katie lifted her head to the stormy sky. She remembered another stormy sky fifty years in the past, and, still laughing, she tried to catch a snowflake on her tongue.

556

THIS CHERISHED DREAM
by Barbara Harrison

'It was a man's world,' young Mary Kilburne had
been told, 'and a woman could only find a place in
it.' And find a place in it she did! Making her way
to America's golden shores with nothing except a
few pennies and her pride, the ambitious,
chestnut-haired beauty was unwilling to give in to
despair or concede to defeat. She was determined
to work hard, to become rich, to rise above the
Lower East Side squalor – even to give up a once-
in-a-lifetime passion if it meant that she would
succeed.

From the black mists of the moors to the elegance
and grandeur of Sutton Place, from an insecure
scullery maid to a poised, prominent empire
builder, through two world wars and the Great
Depression, Mary Kilburne sacrificed happiness,
betrayed her own heart, but always fought for

0 553 171852   £2.95

SCENTS
by Johanna Kingsley

Once in a great while a novel comes along, so rich in human emotion and glamorous excitement that it remains unforgettable. Scents is such a novel. From '20s Paris to modern New York, from rooming houses to penthouses, Scents sweeps through two generations of dangerous secrets, glamorous desires, boundless ambition.

THEY KNEW THEIR POWER, THEIR MONEY, THEIR MEN. BUT THEY DID NOT KNOW EACH OTHER . . .

They were the fabulous Jolays, half-sisters, bound by blood but not by love. Daughters of an outstanding French perfumer whose world had collapsed, now they are bitter rivals, torn apart by their personal quests for power. Luminous Vie, the ice goddess many men desired but few possessed, the bold genius who parlayed a childhood dream into a fragrance empire. And Marty, dark and sensual, a brilliant rebel who used her body and her mind to achieve the only thing she ever truly desired – recognition.

Through the vital long years of poverty to those of dazzling success, their bitter rivalry grew. It was Vie who created an empire, but it was Marty who was determined to control it. No matter what the cost, she would conquer Vie's glittering world and claim it as her own . . .

0 553 17151 8

£2.95

JEALOUSIES
by Justin Marlowe

Sweeping the globe from Ireland to the fabulous
ranches of the Australian Outback, from the *haut
monde* world of Paris to Maryland's lush horse
country – a tumultuous novel of two sisters, torn
apart by ambition, betrayal, and their consuming
passion for the same man . . .

JEALOUSIES

SHANNON. Her face is her fortune. Her
incandescent and exotic beauty have propelled her
from the dreary life of a ranch hand's daughter to
conquest of the high-fashion world of Paris,
London, and New York – but she would always
be seeking the affections of the one man it seemed
she could never have.

KERRY. She always lived in the shadow of her
older sister Shannon's success – until finally her
own chance comes. A superbly talented
horsewoman, she unscrupulously schemes her way
into one of Maryland's wealthiest horse breeding
families, where she hopes to marry into a new life
of power and privilege. And love doesn't need to
be part of the package.

Shannon and Kerry each had a first love – that
love was the same man. He was a handsome
aristocrat who had eyes only for Shannon – until
Kerry's one, jealous, impulsive act drove him out
of Shannon's life, seemingly forever. Now, the
rebellious, feisty Kerry is forced to turn to her
sister for help – and Shannon is about to learn the
full truth of Kerry's terrible betrayal.

0 553 17205 0   £2.95

A SELECTED LIST OF NOVELS
AVAILABLE FROM BANTAM BOOKS

THE PRICES SHOWN BELOW WERE CORRECT AT THE TIME OF GOING TO PRESS.
HOWEVER BANTAM BOOKS RESERVE THE RIGHT TO SHOW NEW RETAIL PRICES
ON COVERS WHICH MAY DIFFER FROM THOSE PREVIOUSLY ADVERTISED IN THE
TEXT OR ELSEWHERE.

*All these books are available at your book shop or newsagent, or can be ordered direct from the publisher.
Just tick the titles you want and fill in the form below.*

BANTAM BOOKS READERS' SERVICE, 61-63 Uxbridge Road, Ealing, London, W5 5SA.

Please send cheque or postal order, not cash. All cheques and postal orders must be in £ sterling and
made payable to Bantam Books Ltd.

Please allow cost of book(s) plus the following for postage and packing:

U.K./Republic of Ireland Customers:
Orders in excess of £5; no charge
Orders under £5; add 50p

Overseas Customers:
All orders; add £1.50

NAME (Block Letters)..

ADDRESS...

....